PENGU

GR

'Wonderfully freshened vers[illegible] ma[illegible]
Peter Kemp, [illegible] *Times*, Books of the Year

'Infused with the beguiling, dreamlike logic of fairy tales and presented with beautiful simplicity and clarity . . . bewitching'
James Lovegrove, *Financial Times*, Books of the Year

'Beautifully retold' Charlie Higson, *Mail on Sunday*, Books of the Year

'A delightfully wry reworking, by a master storyteller'
Economist, Books of the Year

'All given a wonderfully sharp, vivid Pullman twist'
Kate Saunders, *The Times*, Books of the Year

'Wonderfully lucid, compelling' *Independent*

'There is clarity and energy on almost every page . . . It is Pullman as clear as a bell' *Guardian*

'This wonderful retelling is set to become a classic in its own right' *Sunday Times*

'Beautiful or grotesque, the mad poetry of these tales is often delightfully funny too . . . Pullman's own wry presence is unmistakable' *Economist*

'He has given the tales a new lease of life' *Evening Standard*

ABOUT THE AUTHOR

Philip Pullman was born in Norwich on 19 October 1946. He is the acclaimed author of the *His Dark Materials* trilogy: *Northern Lights, The Subtle Knife* and *The Amber Spyglass*. His other books for children and young adults include *Count Karlstein* and a trilogy of Victorian thrillers featuring Sally Lockhart. *Northern Lights* won the Carnegie Medal and the Guardian Fiction Prize.

Grimm Tales
For Young and Old

In a new English version by

PHILIP PULLMAN

PENGUIN BOOKS

PENGUIN CLASSICS

Published by the Penguin Group
Penguin Books Ltd, 80 Strand, London WC2R ORL, England
Penguin Group (USA) Inc., 375 Hudson Street, New York, New York 10014, USA
Penguin Group (Canada), 90 Eglinton Avenue East, Suite 700, Toronto, Ontario, Canada M4P 2Y3
(a division of Pearson Penguin Canada Inc.)
Penguin Ireland, 25 St Stephen's Green, Dublin 2, Ireland (a division of Penguin Books Ltd)
Penguin Group (Australia), 707 Collins Street, Melbourne, Victoria 3008, Australia
(a division of Pearson Australia Group Pty Ltd)
Penguin Books India Pvt Ltd, 11 Community Centre, Panchsheel Park, New Delhi – 110 017, India
Penguin Group (NZ), 67 Apollo Drive, Rosedale, Auckland 0632, New Zealand
(a division of Pearson New Zealand Ltd)
Penguin Books (South Africa) (Pty) Ltd, Block D, Rosebank Office Park,
181 Jan Smuts Avenue, Parktown North, Gauteng 2193, South Africa

Penguin Books Ltd, Registered Offices: 80 Strand, London WC2R ORL, England

www.penguin.com

First published in Penguin Classics 2012
Published in paperback 2013
001

Set in 10.14/12.98pt Sabon LT Std
Typeset by Jouve (UK), Milton Keynes
Printed in Great Britain by Clays Ltd, St Ives plc

ISBN: 978-0-141-44222-8

www.greenpenguin.co.uk

Penguin Books is committed to a sustainable
future for our business, our readers and our planet.
This book is made from Forest Stewardship
Council™ certified paper.

CONTENTS

GRIMM TALES FOR YOUNG AND OLD

INTRODUCTION

Fed
Up so long and variously by
Our age's fancy narrative concoctions,
I yearned for the kind of unseasoned telling found
In legends, fairy tales, a tone licked clean
Over the centuries by mild old tongues,
Grandam to cub, serene, anonymous.
. . . So my narrative
Wanted to be limpid, unfragmented;
My characters, conventional stock figures
Afflicted to a minimal degree
With personality and past experience –
A witch, a hermit, innocent young lovers,
The kinds of being we recall from Grimm,
Jung, Verdi, and the commedia dell'arte.

So writes the American poet James Merrill at the opening of 'The Book of Ephraim', the first part of his extraordinary long poem *The Changing Light at Sandover* (1982). Discussing the way in which he hopes to tell a story of his own, he singles out two of the most important characteristics of the fairy tale, as he sees it: the 'serene, anonymous' voice in which it's told, and the 'conventional, stock figures' who inhabit it.

When Merrill mentions 'Grimm', he needs to say no more: we all know what he means. For most Western readers and writers in the past two hundred years, the *Kinder- und Hausmärchen* (*Children's and Household Tales*) of the Brothers Grimm has been the fountain and origin of the Western fairy tale, the greatest collection, the most widely distributed in the largest number of languages, the home of all we feel to be unique in that kind of story.

But if the Grimm brothers hadn't collected all those tales, no doubt someone else would have done. Others were already doing something similar, in fact. The early nineteenth century was a time of great intellectual excitement in Germany, a time when scholars of law, of history, of language were examining and arguing about what it meant to be German in the first place, when there was no Germany as such but instead three hundred or so independent states – kingdoms, principalities, grand duchies, duchies, landgraviates, margraviates, electorates, bishoprics and so on, the fragmented detritus of the Holy Roman Empire.

The facts of the Grimm brothers' lives are not remarkable. Jacob (1785–1863) and Wilhelm (1786–1859) were the eldest surviving sons of Philipp Wilhelm Grimm, a prosperous lawyer of Hanau in the principality of Hesse, and his wife Dorothea. They received a classical education and were brought up in the Reformed Calvinist Church. Clever, diligent and serious-minded, they aimed to follow their father into the legal profession, in which they would no doubt have distinguished themselves; but his sudden death in 1796 meant that the family, which now included six children, had to depend on the support of their mother's relatives. Their aunt Henriette Zimmer, a lady-in-waiting at the prince's court in Kassel, helped Jacob and Wilhelm to find places at the *Lyzeum* or high school, where they each graduated at the head of their class. But there was little money, and when they attended the University of Marburg they had to live very frugally.

At Marburg they fell under the influence of Professor Friedrich Carl von Savigny, whose idea that law grew naturally out of the language and history of a people and should not be arbitrarily applied from above turned the Grimms to the study of philology.

Through von Savigny and his wife Kunigunde Brentano, they also made the acquaintance of the circle around her brother Clemens Brentano and Achim von Arnim, who married Brentano's other sister, the writer Bettina. One of the preoccupations of this group was German folklore. Their enthusiasm for this subject resulted in von Arnim and Brentano's *Des Knaben Wunderhorn* (*The Youth's Magic Horn*), a collection of folk songs and folk poetry of all kinds, the first volume of which appeared in 1805 and immediately became popular.

The Grimm brothers were naturally interested in this, but not uncritically: Jacob wrote in a letter to Wilhelm in May 1809 of his disapproval of the way in which Brentano and von Arnim had treated their material, cutting and adding and modernizing and rewriting as they thought fit. Later, the Grimms (and Wilhelm in particular) would be criticized on much the same grounds for the way they treated their source material for the *Kinder- und Hausmärchen*.

At all events, the decision by the Grimm brothers to collect and publish fairy tales was not an isolated phenomenon, but part of a widespread preoccupation of the time.

The sources they depended on were both oral and literary. One thing they did not do was walk the countryside, seeking out peasants in their fields and cottages and taking down their stories word by word. Some of their tales were taken directly from literary sources; two of the finest, 'The Fisherman and His Wife' (p. 93) and 'The Juniper Tree' (p. 187), were sent to them in written form by the painter Philipp Otto Runge, and reproduced by the Grimms in the Low German dialect Runge wrote them in. Much of the rest came in oral form from people at various levels of the middle class, including family friends, one of whom, Dortchen Wild, the daughter of a pharmacist, Wilhelm Grimm eventually married. After two hundred years, it's impossible to say how exact their transcriptions were, but the same is true of any collection of folk tales or songs before the age of tape recording. What matters is the vigour and zest of the versions they published.

The Grimm brothers went on to make great and lasting contributions to philology. Grimm's Law, formulated by Jacob, describes certain sound-changes in the history of Germanic languages; and the brothers together worked on the first great German dictionary. In 1837 came what was probably the most dramatic incident in their lives; together with five other university colleagues, they refused to take an oath of allegiance to the new king of Hanover, Ernst August, because he had illegally dissolved the constitution. As a result they were dismissed from their university posts, and had to take up appointments at the University of Berlin.

But it was the *Kinder- und Hausmärchen* for which their names are mostly remembered. Their first edition was published in 1812, and the collection went through six further editions (Wilhelm, by this stage, doing most of the editorial work) till the seventh and final one of 1857, by which time it was immensely popular. It shares its eminence only with *The Arabian Nights*: the two of them are the most important and influential collections of folk tales ever published. Not only did the collection grow bigger, the tales themselves changed as the nineteenth century went past, becoming in Wilhelm's hands a little longer, in some cases more elaborate, occasionally more prudish, certainly more pious than they were to begin with.

Scholars of literature and folklore, of cultural and political history, theorists of a Freudian, Jungian, Christian, Marxist, structuralist, post-structuralist, feminist, postmodernist and every other kind of tendency have found immense riches for their study in these 210 tales. Some of the books and essays I've found most useful and interesting are listed in the Bibliography, and no doubt they and others have influenced my reading and retelling in ways I'm not conscious of.

But my main interest has always been in how the tales worked *as stories*. All I set out to do in this book was tell the best and most interesting of them, clearing out of the way anything that would prevent them from running freely. I didn't want to put them in modern settings, or produce personal interpretations or compose poetic variations on the originals; I just wanted to produce a version that was as clear as water. My guiding question has been: 'How would I tell this story myself, if I'd heard it told by someone else and wanted to pass it on?' Any changes I've made have been for the purpose of helping the story emerge more naturally in my voice. If, as happened occasionally, I thought an improvement was possible, I've either made a small change or two in the text itself or suggested a larger one in the note that follows the story. (An example of this happens with the story 'Thousandfurs', p. 247, which seems to me only half finished in the original.)

'Conventional stock figures'

There is no psychology in a fairy tale. The characters have little interior life; their motives are clear and obvious. If people are good, they are good, and if bad, they're bad. Even when the princess in 'The Three Snake Leaves' (p. 86) inexplicably and ungratefully turns against her husband, we know about it from the moment it happens. Nothing of that sort is concealed. The tremors and mysteries of human awareness, the whispers of memory, the promptings of half-understood regret or doubt or desire that are so much part of the subject matter of the modern novel are absent entirely. One might almost say that the characters in a fairy tale are not actually conscious.

They seldom have names of their own. More often than not they're known by their occupation or their social position, or by a quirk of their dress: the miller, the princess, the captain,

Bearskin, Little Red Riding Hood. When they do have a name it's usually Hans, just as Jack is the hero of every British fairy tale.

The most fitting pictorial representation of fairy-tale characters seems to me to be found not in any of the beautifully illustrated editions of Grimm that have been published over the years, but in the little cardboard cut-out figures that come with the toy theatre. They are flat, not round. Only one side of them is visible to the audience, but that is the only side we need: the other side is blank. They are depicted in poses of intense activity or passion, so that their part in the drama can be easily read from a distance.

Some of the characters in fairy tales come in sets of multiples. The twelve brothers in the story of that name, the twelve princesses in 'The Shoes that were Danced to Pieces' (p. 344), the seven dwarfs in the story of Snow White (p. 206) – there is little, if anything, to distinguish one from another. James Merrill's reference to the *commedia dell'arte* is apposite here: the *commedia* character Pulcinella was the subject of a famous set of drawings by Giandomenico Tiepolo (1727–1804), depicting him not as a single character but as a swarm of identical nitwits. In one drawing there may be a dozen or more Pulcinellas all trying to make soup at the same time, or gazing in astonishment at an ostrich. Realism cannot cope with the notion of multiples; the twelve princesses who all go out every night and dance their shoes to pieces, the seven dwarfs all asleep in their beds side by side, exist in another realm altogether, between the uncanny and the absurd.

Celerity

Swiftness is a great virtue in the fairy tale. A good tale moves with a dreamlike speed from event to event, pausing only to say as much as is needed and no more. The best tales are perfect examples of what you do need and what you don't: in Rudyard Kipling's image, fires that blaze brightly because all the ashes have been raked out.

The opening of a tale, for example. All we need is the word 'Once . . .' and we're off:

> Once there was a poor man who couldn't support his only son any more. When the son realized this, he said, 'Father, it's no use my staying here. I'm just a burden to you. I'm going to leave home and see if I can earn a living.'
>
> ('The Three Snake Leaves', p. 86)

A few paragraphs later, he's already married a king's daughter. Or this:

> Once there was a farmer who had all the money and land he wanted, but despite his wealth there was one thing missing from his life. He and his wife had never had any children. When he met other farmers in town or at the market, they would often make fun of him and ask why he and his wife had never managed to do what their cattle did regularly. Didn't they know how to do it? In the end he lost his temper, and when he got back home, he swore and said, 'I will have a child, even if it's a hedgehog.'
>
> ('Hans-my-Hedgehog', p. 311)

The speed is exhilarating. You can only go that fast, however, if you're travelling light; so none of the information you'd look for in a modern work of fiction – names, appearances, background, social context, etc. – is present. And that, of course, is part of the explanation for the flatness of the characters. The tale is far more interested in what happens to them, or in what they make happen, than in their individuality.

When composing a tale of this sort, it's not always easy to be sure about which events are necessary and which are superfluous. Anyone who wants to know how to tell a tale could do much worse than study 'The Musicians of Bremen' (p. 143), both a nonsensical little yarn and a masterpiece, in which the narrative carries not one unnecessary ounce. Every paragraph advances the story.

Imagery and description

There is no imagery in fairy tales apart from the most obvious. As white as snow, as red as blood: that's about it. Nor is there any close description of the natural world or of individuals. A forest is deep, the princess is beautiful, her hair is golden; there's no need to say more. When what you want to know is what happens next, beautiful descriptive wordplay can only irritate.

In one story, however, there is a passage that successfully combines beautiful description with the relation of events in such a way that one would not work without the other. The story is 'The Juniper Tree', and the passage I mean comes after the wife has made her wish for a child as red as blood and as white as snow (p. 187). It links her pregnancy with the passing seasons:

> One month went by, and the snow vanished.
>
> Two months went by, and the world turned green.
>
> Three months went by, and flowers bloomed out of the earth.
>
> Four months went by, and all the twigs on all the trees in the forest grew stronger and pressed themselves together, and the birds sang so loud that the woods resounded, and the blossom fell from the trees.
>
> Five months went by, and the woman stood under the juniper tree. It smelled so sweet that her heart leaped in her breast, and she fell to her knees with joy.
>
> Six months went by, and the fruit grew firm and heavy, and the woman fell still.

> When seven months had gone by, she plucked the juniper berries and ate so many that she felt sick and sorrowful.
>
> After the eighth month had gone, she called her husband and said to him, weeping, 'If I die, bury me under the juniper tree.'

This is wonderful, but (as I suggest in my note to the story, p. 198) it's wonderful in a curious way: there's little any teller of this tale can do to improve it. It has to be rendered exactly as it is here, or at least the different months have to be given equally different characteristics, and carefully linked in equally meaningful ways with the growth of the child in his mother's womb, and that growth with the juniper tree that will be instrumental in his later resurrection.

However, that is a great and rare exception. In most of these tales, just as the characters are flat, description is absent. In the later editions, it is true, Wilhelm's telling became a little more florid and inventive, but the real interest of the tale continues to be in what happened, and what happened next. The formulas are so common, the lack of interest in the particularity of things so widespread, that it comes as a real shock to read a sentence like this in 'Jorinda and Joringel' (p. 256):

> It was a lovely evening; the sun shone warmly on the tree trunks against the dark green of the deep woods, and turtledoves cooed mournfully in the old beech trees.

Suddenly that story stops sounding like a fairy tale and begins to sound like something composed in a literary way by a Romantic writer such as Novalis or Jean Paul. The serene, anonymous relation of events has given way, for the space of a sentence, to an individual sensibility: a *single mind* has felt this impression of nature, has seen these details in the mind's eye and written them down. A writer's command of imagery and gift for description is one of the things that make him or her unique, but fairy tales don't come whole and unaltered from the minds of individual writers, after all; uniqueness and originality are of no interest to them.

This is not a text

William Wordsworth's *The Prelude*, or James Joyce's *Ulysses*, or any other literary work, exists as a text first of all. The words on the page are what it is. It's the job of an editor or a literary critic to pay attention to what exactly those words are, and to clarify places where there are divergent readings in different editions, to make sure that the reader can encounter exactly the text that the work consists of.

But a fairy tale is not a text of that sort. It's a transcription made on one or more occasions of the words spoken by one of many people who have told this tale. And all sorts of things, of course, affect the words that are finally written down. A storyteller might tell the tale more richly, more extravagantly, one day than the next, when he's tired or not in the mood. A transcriber might find her own equipment failing: a cold in the head might make hearing more difficult, or cause the writing-down to be interrupted by sneezes or coughs. Another accident might affect it too: a good tale might find itself in the mouth of a less than adequate teller.

That matters a great deal, because tellers vary in their talents, their techniques, their attitudes to the process. The Grimms were highly impressed by the ability of one of their sources, Dorothea Viehmann, to tell a tale a second time in the same words as she'd used before, making it easy to transcribe; and the tales that come from her are typically structured with marvellous care and precision. I was equally impressed when working on her tales for this book.

Similarly, this teller might have a talent for comedy, that one for suspense and drama, another for pathos and sentiment. Naturally they will each choose tales that make the most of their talents. When X the great comedian tells a tale, he will invent ridiculous details or funny episodes that will be remembered and passed on, so the tale will be altered a little by his telling; and when Y the mistress of suspense tells a tale of terror, she will invent in like manner, and her inventions and changes will become part of the tradition of telling that tale, until they're forgotten, or embellished, or improved on in their turn.

The fairy tale is in a perpetual state of becoming and alteration. To keep to one version or one translation alone is to put a robin redbreast in a cage.* If you, the reader, want to tell any of the tales in this book, I hope you will feel free to be no more faithful than you want to be. You are at perfect liberty to invent other details than the ones I've passed on, or invented, here. In fact you're not only at liberty to do so: you have a positive duty to make the story your own.† A fairy tale is not a text.

'A tone licked clean'

Can the writer of any version of a fairy tale ever come near to James Merrill's ideal tone, 'serene, anonymous'? Of course, the writer might not wish to. There have been many, and there will be many more, versions of these tales that are brimful of their author's own dark obsessions, or brilliant personality, or political passions. The tales can stand it. But even if we want to be serene and anonymous, I think it's probably impossible to achieve it

* Which 'puts all Heaven in a Rage' (William Blake, 'Auguries of Innocence', 1803).

† 'The tale is not beautiful if nothing is added to it' – Tuscan proverb quoted by Italo Calvino in his introduction to *Italian Folktales* (London: Penguin Books, 1982).

completely, and that our personal stylistic fingerprints lie impressed on every paragraph without our knowing it.

The only thing to do, it seems to me, is to try for clarity, and stop worrying about it. Telling these stories is a delight it would be a pity to spoil by anxiety. An enormous relief and pleasure, like the mild air that refreshes the young count when he lies down to rest in 'The Goose Girl at the Spring' (p. 389), comes over the writer who realizes that it's not necessary to *invent*: the substance of the tale is there already, just as the sequence of chords in a song is there ready for the jazz musician, and our task is to step from chord to chord, from event to event, with all the lightness and swing we can. Like jazz, storytelling is an art of performance, and writing is performance too.

Finally, I'd say to anyone who wants to tell these tales, don't be afraid to be superstitious. If you have a lucky pen, use it. If you speak with more force and wit when wearing one red sock and one blue one, dress like that. When I'm at work I'm highly superstitious. My own superstition has to do with the voice in which the story comes out. I believe that every story is attended by its own sprite, whose voice we embody when we tell the tale, and that we tell it more successfully if we approach the sprite with a certain degree of respect and courtesy. These sprites are both old and young, male and female, sentimental and cynical, sceptical and credulous, and so on, and what's more, they're completely amoral: like the air-spirits who helped Strong Hans escape from the cave (p. 379), the story-sprites are willing to serve whoever has the ring, whoever is telling the tale. To the accusation that this is nonsense, that all you need to tell a story is a human imagination, I reply, 'Of course, and this is the way my imagination works.'

But we may do our best by these tales, and find that it's still not enough. I suspect that the finest of them have the quality that the great pianist Artur Schnabel attributed to the sonatas of Mozart: they are too easy for children and too difficult for adults.

And these fifty tales are, I think, the cream of the *Kinder- und Hausmärchen*. I have done my best for the sprites who attend each one, as did Dorothea Viehmann, Philipp Otto Runge, Dortchen Wild, and all the other tellers whose work was preserved by the great Brothers Grimm. And I hope we all, tellers and listeners alike, live happily ever after.

Philip Pullman, 2012

BIBLIOGRAPHY

The German edition of Jacob and Wilhelm Grimm's *Kinder- und Hausmärchen* (*Children's and Household Tales*) that I worked from is the most easily available, the seventh edition of 1857. It is published by Wilhelm Goldmann Verlag. The 'tale type' numbers I give in the notes to each story are based on *The Types of International Folktales*, the great index of tale types originally compiled by Antti Aarne and published in 1910, revised by Stith Thompson in 1928 and 1961, and most recently (2004) revised by Hans-Jörg Uther (see full details below) – hence 'ATU' or 'AT' for the earlier edition. This section otherwise includes the works I found most interesting and helpful.

Aesop, *The Complete Fables*, tr. Olivia Temple (London: Penguin Books, 1998)

Afanasyev, Alexander, *Russian Fairy Tales*, tr. Norbert Guterman (New York: Pantheon Books, 1945)

The Arabian Nights: Tales of 1001 Nights, tr. Malcolm C. Lyons with Ursula Lyons, introduced and annotated by Robert Irwin (London: Penguin Books, 2008)

Ashliman, D. L., *A Guide to Folktales in the English Language* (New York: Greenwood Press, 1987)

Bettelheim, Bruno, *The Uses of Enchantment* (London: Peregrine Books, 1978)

Briggs, Katharine M., *A Dictionary of Fairies, Hobgoblins, Brownies, Bogies and Other Supernatural Creatures* (London: Allen Lane, 1976)

—— *Folk Tales of Britain* (London: Folio Society, 2011)

Calvino, Italo, *Italian Folktales*, tr. George Martin (London: Penguin Books, 1982)

Chandler Harris, Joel, *The Complete Tales of Uncle Remus* (New York: Houghton Mifflin, 1955)

Grimm, Jacob and Wilhelm, *Brothers Grimm: Selected Tales*, tr. David Luke, Gilbert McKay and Philip Schofield (London: Penguin Books, 1982)

—— *The Penguin Complete Grimms' Tales for Young and Old*, tr. Ralph Mannheim (London: Penguin Books, 1984)

—— *The Complete Fairy Tales*, tr. Jack Zipes (London: Vintage, 2007)

—— *The Complete Grimm's Fairy Tales*, tr. Margaret Hunt, ed. James Stern, introduced by Padraic Colum and with a commentary by Joseph Campbell (Abingdon: Routledge, 2002)

Lang, Andrew, *Crimson Fairy Book* (New York: Dover Publications, 1967)

—— *Pink Fairy Book* (New York: Dover Publications, 2008)

Perrault, Charles, *Perrault's Complete Fairy Tales*, tr. A. E. Johnson and others (London: Puffin Books, 1999)

Philip, Neil, *The Cinderella Story* (London: Penguin Books, 1989)

Ransome, Arthur, *Old Peter's Russian Tales* (London: Puffin Books, 1974)

Schmiesing Ann, '*Des Knaben Wunderhorn* and the German *Volkslied* in the Eighteenth and Nineteenth Centuries' (http://mahlerfest.org/mfXIV/schmiesing_lecture.html)

Tatar, Maria, *The Hard Facts of the Grimms' Fairy Tales* (Princeton: Princeton University Press, 1987)

Uther, Hans-Jörg, *The Types of International Folktales: A Classification and Bibliography Based on the System of Antti Aarne and Stith Thompson,* vols. 1–3, FF Communications No. 284–86 (Helsinki: Academia Scientiarum Fennica, 2004)

Warner, Marina, *From the Beast to the Blonde: Of Fairy Tales and their Tellers* (London: Vintage, 1995)

—— *No Go the Bogeyman: Scaring, Lulling, and Making Mock* (London: Vintage, 2000)

Zipes, Jack, *The Brothers Grimm: From Enchanted Forests to the Modern World* (New York: Palgrave Macmillan, 2002)

—— *Why Fairy Tales Stick: The Evolution and Relevance of a Genre* (New York: Routledge, 2006)

—— (ed.), *The Great Fairy Tale Tradition: From Straparola and Basile to the Brothers Grimm* (New York: W. W. Norton and Company, 2001)

—— (ed.), *The Oxford Companion to Fairy Tales* (Oxford: Oxford University Press, 2000)

GRIMM TALES

For Young and Old

ONE

THE FROG KING, OR IRON HEINRICH

In the olden days, when wishing still worked, there lived a king whose daughters were all beautiful; but the youngest daughter was so lovely that even the sun, who has seen many things, was struck with wonder every time he shone on her face. Not far away from the king's palace there was a deep dark forest, and under a lime tree in the forest there was a well. In the heat of the day the princess used to go into the forest and sit by the edge of the well, from which a marvellous coolness seemed to flow.

To pass the time she had a golden ball, which she used to throw up in the air and catch. It was her favourite game. Now one day it happened that she threw it a little carelessly, and she couldn't catch it. Instead the ball rolled away from her and towards the well, and then it ran right over the edge and disappeared.

The princess ran after it, and looked down into the water; but it was so deep that she couldn't see the ball. She couldn't even see the bottom of the well.

She began to cry, and she cried louder and louder, inconsolably. But as she wept and sobbed, someone spoke to her. 'What's the matter, princess? You're crying so bitterly, you'd move a stone to pity.'

She looked round to see where the voice was coming from, and saw a frog who'd stuck his big ugly head out of the water.

'Oh, it's you, you old splasher,' she said. 'I'm crying because my golden ball's fallen into the water and it's so deep and I can't see it.'

'Well, you can stop crying now,' said the frog. 'I can help you, but what will you give me if I fetch your ball for you?'

'Whatever you want, frog! Anything! My clothes, my pearls, my jewels, even the golden crown I'm wearing.'

'I don't want your clothes, and your jewels and your golden crown are no good to me, but if you love me and take me as your companion and your playmate, if you let me sit next to you at the table and eat from your dish and drink from your cup and sleep in your bed, then I'll dive down and bring up your golden ball.'

The princess thought, 'What is this stupid frog saying? Whatever he thinks, he'll have to stay in the water where he belongs. Perhaps he can get my ball.' But of course she didn't say that. Instead she said, 'Yes, yes, I'll promise you all of that if you just bring me my ball.'

As soon as the frog heard her say 'Yes', he put his head under the water and dived to the bottom. A moment later he came swimming back up with the ball in his mouth, and he threw it on to the grass.

The princess was so happy to see it that she snatched it up and ran off at once.

'Wait, wait!' called the frog. 'Take me with you! I can't hop as fast as you can run!'

But she took no notice. She hurried home and forgot all about the poor frog, who had to go back down into his well.

Next day the princess was sitting at table with her father the king and all the people of the court, and eating off her golden plate, when something came hopping up the marble steps: *plip plop, plip plop*. When it reached the top, it knocked at the door and called: 'Princess! Youngest princess! Open the door for me!'

She ran to see who it was, and opened the door, and there was the frog.

Frightened, she slammed the door shut at once and ran back to the table.

The king saw that her heart was pounding, and said, 'What are you afraid of, my child? Is there a giant there at the door?'

'Oh, no,' she said, 'it's not a giant, it's a horrible frog.'

'What does the frog want with you?'

'Oh, papa, yesterday when I was playing in the forest near the well, my golden ball fell in the water. And I started to cry and because I was crying so much, the frog got it for me, and because he insisted, I had to promise that he could be my companion. But I didn't think he'd ever leave the water, not really. But there he is outside the door and he wants to come in!'

And then there came a second knock at the door, and a voice called:

'Princess, princess, youngest daughter,
Open up and let me in!
Or else your promise by the water
Isn't worth a rusty pin.
Keep your promise, royal daughter,
Open up and let me in!'

The king said, 'If you make a promise, you have to keep it. Go and let him in.'

She opened the door and the frog hopped in. He hopped all the way to her chair.

'Lift me up,' he said. 'I want to sit next to you.'

She didn't want to, but the king said, 'Go on. Do as he says.'

So she lifted the frog up. Once he was on the chair, he wanted to be on the table, so she had to lift him up there as well, and then he said, 'Push your golden plate a bit closer so I can eat with you.'

She did, but everyone could see that she wasn't enjoying it. The frog was, though; he ate her food with great pleasure, while every mouthful seemed to stick in the princess's throat.

Finally the frog said, 'Well, I've had enough now, thank you, I'd like to go to bed. Carry me up to your room and get your silken bed ready so we can sleep in it.'

The princess began to cry, because the frog's cold skin frightened her. She trembled at the thought of him in her sweet clean bed. But the king frowned and said, 'You shouldn't despise someone who helped you when you were in trouble!'

She picked the frog up between finger and thumb and set him down outside her bedroom door and shut it firmly.

But he kept on knocking and called, 'Let me in! Let me in!'

So she opened the door and said, 'All right! You can come in, but you must sleep on the floor.'

She made him lie down at the foot of her bed. But still he said, 'Let me up! Let me up! I'm just as tired as you.'

'Oh, for goodness' sake!' she said, and picked him up and put him at the far end of her pillow.

'Closer! Closer!' he said.

But that was too much. In a flash of anger she scooped up the frog and threw him against the wall. But when he fell back into the bed, what a surprise! He wasn't a frog any more. In fact he'd become a young man – a prince – with beautiful smiling eyes.

And she loved him and accepted him as her companion, just as the king would have wished. The prince told her that an evil witch had put a spell on him, and that only she, the princess, could have rescued him from the well. What's more, on the following day a carriage would come to take them to the prince's kingdom. Then they fell asleep side by side.

And next morning no sooner had the sun awoken them than a carriage drew up outside the palace, just as the prince had said. It was pulled by eight horses with ostrich plumes nodding on their heads and golden chains shining among their harness. At the back of the coach was Faithful Heinrich. He was the prince's servant, and when he'd learned that his master had been changed into a frog, he was so dismayed that he went straight to the blacksmith and ordered three iron bands to put around his heart to stop it bursting with grief.

Faithful Heinrich helped them into the carriage and took his place at the back. He was overjoyed to see the prince again.

When they'd gone a little way, the prince heard a loud crack from behind. He turned around and called out: 'Heinrich, the coach is breaking!'

'No, no, my lord, it's just my heart. When you were living in the well, when you were a frog, I suffered such great pain that I bound my heart with iron bands to stop it breaking, for iron is stronger than grief. But love is stronger than iron, and now you're human again the iron bands are falling off.'

And twice more they heard the same cracking noise, and each time they thought it was the carriage, but each time they were wrong: it was an iron band breaking away from Faithful Heinrich's heart, because his master was safe again.

* * *

Tale type: ATU 440, 'The Frog King'
Source: a story told to the Grimm brothers by the Wild family
Similar stories: Katharine M. Briggs: 'The Frog', 'The Frog Prince', 'The Frog Sweetheart', 'The Paddo' (*Folk Tales of Britain*)

One of the best-known tales of all. The central notion of the repulsive frog changing into a prince is so appealing and so full of moral implication that it's become a metaphor for a central human experience. The common memory is that the frog becomes a prince when the princess kisses him. Grimm's storyteller knows otherwise, and so do the tellers of the versions in Briggs, where the frog has to be beheaded by the maiden before changing his form. The kiss has a lot to be said for it, however. It is, after all, by now another piece of folklore itself, and what else is the implication of his wishing to share the princess's bed?

There's no doubt that the frog becomes a prince (*ein Königssohn*) although the title of the story calls him a king ('Der Froschkönig'). Perhaps, having once been a frog, he retained the frog association when he inherited his kingdom. It's not the sort of thing that anyone would forget.

The figure of Iron Heinrich appears at the end of the tale out of nowhere, and has so little connection with the rest of it that he is nearly always forgotten, although he must have been thought important enough to share the title. His iron bands are so striking an image that they almost deserve a story to themselves.

TWO

THE CAT AND THE MOUSE SET UP HOUSE

Once there was a cat who struck up a friendship with a mouse. He went on at such length about the warmth of the affection he felt for her, how kind she was, how prudent, how neatly she twirled her tail, and so on, that the mouse finally agreed to set up house with him.

'But we must make provision for the winter,' said the cat. 'If we don't, we'll go hungry just when we need food most of all. And a little mouse like you can't go out foraging in the cold. Even if you didn't die of exposure, you'd be sure to get caught in a trap.'

The mouse thought this advice was excellent, and they put their money together and bought a pot of fat. The next question was where to put it. They discussed the problem at great length, and finally the cat said, 'You know, I don't think there's anywhere safer than the church. No one would dare to steal anything from there. We can put it under the altar, and we won't touch it till we really need it.'

So they hid the pot in the church. But it wasn't long before the cat felt a craving for the delicious fat, so he said to the mouse, 'Oh, by the way, I've been meaning to tell you: my cousin has just given birth to a little boy kitten, white all over with brown spots.'

'Oh, how lovely!' said the mouse.

'Yes, and they've asked me to be godfather. Do you mind if I leave the housekeeping to you for a day and go and hold him at the font?'

'No, of course not,' said the mouse. 'There's sure to be some nice food afterwards. If you get a tasty mouthful, think of me. I'd love to taste that sweet red christening wine.'

Of course, the cat's story was a pack of lies. He had no cousin at all, and no one who knew him would dream of asking him to be a godfather. What he did was to go straight to the church, creep under the altar, open the pot of fat and lick the skin off the top.

Then he strolled out as calm as you please and went up to his usual haunt on the rooftops. There he lay in the sun licking his whiskers and enjoying the memory of the fat. It was evening before he went home.

'Welcome home!' said the mouse. 'Did you have a nice day? What did they call the child?'

'Top Off,' said the cat very coolly, inspecting his claws.

'Top Off? That's a strange thing to call a kitten,' said the mouse. 'Is it an old family name?'

'I can't see anything strange about it,' said the cat. 'It's no odder than Crumb Thief, which is what each of your godchildren is called.'

Not long afterwards the cat felt a yearning for the fat again, and said to the mouse, 'My dear friend, can I ask a favour? I've been asked to be godfather to another kitten, and since he has a white ring around his throat, it would be wrong to refuse. Can you keep house alone once more? I'll be back this evening.'

The good mouse said yes, she didn't mind at all, and wished the kitten well. The cat set off at once, and crept along behind the town wall to the church, where he slunk inside and licked up half the pot of fat.

'Nothing tastes as good as what you eat by yourself,' he thought.

When he got home the mouse said, 'And what did they call the child?'

'Half Gone,' said the cat.

'*Half Gone?* What sort of name is that? I've never heard of such a thing. I'm sure it's not in the almanac of saints.'

The fat had tasted so rich and unctuous that the cat's mouth was soon watering again.

'All good things come in threes,' he said to the mouse. 'What do you think? I've been asked to be godfather yet again. This time the child is totally black – there's not a white hair on his body apart from his paws. That's very rare, you know, it only happens once every few years. You will let me go, won't you?'

'Top Off? Half Gone?' said the mouse. 'Such odd names they have in your family! They make me wonder, they really do.'

'Oh, fiddle-de-dee,' said the cat. 'You sit indoors from morning till night twiddling your tail, and all kinds of nonsense comes into your head. You ought to get out in the fresh air.'

The mouse wasn't sure about that, but while the cat was away she worked hard to clean their house and make everything neat and tidy.

Meanwhile, the cat was in the church, busily licking out the pot of fat. He had to scoop the very last of it out with his paws, and then he sat there admiring his reflection in the bottom of the pot.

'Emptying the pot is such sweet sorrow,' he thought.

It was late at night by the time he waddled home. As soon as he came in, the mouse asked what name had been given the third child.

'I suppose you won't like this one either,' said the cat. 'They called him All Gone.'

'All Gone!' cried the mouse. 'Dear oh dear, I'm worried about that, honestly I am. I've never seen that name in print. What can it mean?'

Then she wrapped her tail around herself and went to sleep.

After that no one asked the cat to be godfather. And when the winter arrived, and there was no food at all to be found outside, the mouse thought of their pot of delicious fat safely hidden under the altar in the church.

She said, 'Come on, Cat, let's go and find that pot of fat we put away. Think how good it'll taste.'

'Yes,' said the cat. 'You'll enjoy it as much as sticking that dainty little tongue of yours out of the window.'

So they set out. And when they got to the church, the pot was still there, to be sure, but of course it was empty.

'Oh! Oh! Oh!' said the mouse. 'I'm beginning to see a pattern here! Now I know what sort of a friend you are. You were no godfather! You came here and guzzled it all up. First top off—'

'Be careful!' said the cat.

'Then half gone—'

'I warn you!'

'Then all—'

'One more word and I'll eat you too!'

'—gone!' said the mouse, but it was too late: the cat sprang on her and gobbled her up in a moment.

Well, what else did you expect? That's just the sort of thing that happens in this world.

* * *

Tale type: ATU 15, 'The Theft of Food by Playing Godfather'
Source: a story told to the Grimm brothers by Gretchen Wild
Similar stories: Italo Calvino: 'Mrs Fox and Mr Wolf' (*Italian Folktales*); Joel Chandler Harris: 'Mr Rabbit Nibbles Up the Butter' (*The Complete Tales of Uncle Remus*)

A simple and very common fable. Several of the variants employ a scatological earthiness: the real culprit smears butter under the sleeping partner's tail to demonstrate the partner's guilt. I borrowed the idea of the reflection in the bottom of the pot from the Uncle Remus tale, which, like this version, ends in a shrug about the world's injustice: 'Tribbalashun seem like she's a waitin' roun' de cornder fer ter ketch one en all un us' (*The Complete Tales of Uncle Remus*, p. 53).

THREE

THE BOY WHO LEFT HOME TO FIND OUT ABOUT THE SHIVERS

Once there was a father who had two sons. The elder one was quick-witted and bright and able to deal with anything, but the younger one was so dim that he understood nothing and learned nothing. Everybody who knew them said, 'His father's going to have trouble with that boy.'

If there was any job that needed doing, it was always the elder son who had to do it. But there was one thing the elder son wouldn't do: if his father asked him to get something as night was falling, or when it was completely dark, and if his way took him through the graveyard or some creepy place like that, he'd say, 'Oh, no, father, I won't go there, it gives me the shivers.'

Or in the evening when people were sitting around the fire telling stories of ghosts or hauntings, the listeners would sometimes say, 'Oh, that gives me the shivers.'

The younger son used to sit in the corner and listen, but he didn't understand what the shivers were. 'Everyone says: "It gives me the shivers, it gives me the shivers!" I don't know what they're talking about. I haven't got any shivers, and I was listening just as hard as they were.'

One day his father said to him: 'Listen, boy, you're getting big and strong. You're growing up, and it's time you began to earn a living. Look at your brother! He's learned to work hard, but you've learned nothing, as far as I can see.'

'Oh, yes, father,' he said. 'I'd like to earn a living, I really would. I'd love to learn how to get the shivers. That's something I don't understand at all.'

His elder brother heard him, and laughed. 'What a blockhead!' he thought. 'He'll never come to any good. You can't make a silk purse out of a sow's ear.'

The father could only sigh. 'Well, it won't do you any harm to find out about the shivers,' he said, 'but you won't get a living by shivering.'

A few days later the sexton dropped in for a chat. The father couldn't help it: he poured out all his worries about the younger son, what a fool he was, how he couldn't learn anything, how he understood nothing at all.

'Take this, for example,' he said. 'When I asked him what he wanted to do for a living, he said he wanted to learn how to get the shivers.'

'If that's what he wants,' said the sexton, 'you send him along to me. I'll give him the shivers all right. It's time he was licked into shape.'

'That's a good idea,' said the father, thinking, 'Maybe it'll come better from someone else. It'll do the boy good, anyway.'

So the sexton took the boy back to his house, and gave him the job of ringing the church bell. Once he'd got the hang of that, the sexton woke him up at midnight one night and told him to go up the church tower and ring the bell.

'Now you'll learn what the shivers are,' he thought, and while the boy was pulling on his clothes, the sexton crept up the tower ahead of him.

The boy reached the belfry, and when he turned around to get hold of the rope, he saw a white figure standing there at the top of the stairs just opposite the sound hole.

'Who's that?' he said.

The figure didn't speak or move.

'You'd better answer me,' shouted the boy. 'You've got no business here in the middle of the night.'

The sexton kept quite still. He was sure the boy would think he was a ghost.

The boy shouted again: 'I warn you. Answer me, or I'll throw you downstairs. Who are you and what do you want?'

The sexton thought, 'He wouldn't throw me downstairs, I'm sure.'

And he stood there like a stone, not making a sound.

So the boy shouted once more, and still getting no answer, he yelled, 'Well, you've asked for it, and here it comes!'

And he rushed at the white figure and shoved him down the stairs. The ghost tumbled all the way down and lay moaning in a heap in the corner. Seeing that there was going to be no more trouble from him, the boy rang the bell as he'd been told and then went back to bed.

The sexton's wife had been waiting all this time, and when her husband didn't come back she started to worry. She went to wake the boy.

'Where's my husband?' she said. 'Did you see him? He climbed the tower before you did.'

'Dunno,' said the boy. 'I never saw him. There was someone in a white sheet standing near the sound hole, and he wouldn't answer and he wouldn't go away, so I thought he was up to no good and I shoved him down the stairs. Go and take a look – he's probably still there. I'd be sorry if it was him. He fell with ever such a thump.'

The wife ran out and found her husband groaning with the pain of a broken leg. She managed to carry him home, and then she ran screaming and yelling to the boy's father.

'Your fool of a son!' she cried. 'D'you know what he's done?

He threw my husband right from the top of the belfry! The poor man's broken his leg and I shouldn't wonder if half the rest of his bones are in pieces as well! Take the good-for-nothing wretch out of our house before he brings it down around our ears. I never want to see him again.'

The father was horrified. He ran to the sexton's house and shook the boy out of his bed.

'What the hell are you playing at?' he said. 'Desecrating the sexton? The Devil must have put you up to it!'

'But father,' said the boy, 'I'm innocent. I had no idea it was the sexton. He was standing there by the sound hole with a white sheet over him. I couldn't tell who it was, and I warned him three times.'

'God in heaven!' said the father. 'You bring me nothing but trouble. Get out of my sight, go on. I don't even want to look at you any more.'

'I'd be glad to,' said the boy. 'Just let me wait till daylight, and I'll go out into the world and leave you alone. I can look for the shivers, and then I'll have a skill and I'll be able to earn a living at last.'

'Shivers, indeed! Do what you like, it's all the same to me. Here you are – here's fifty talers for you. Take them and go out into the wide world, but don't you dare tell anyone where you come from or who your father is. I'd be ashamed.'

'All right, father, yes, I'll do as you wish. If that's all you want me to do, I'll easily remember it.'

And as soon as morning came, the boy put his fifty talers in his pocket and set off, saying to himself all the time, 'I wish I could get the shivers! If only I could get the shivers!'

A man who happened to be going along the same way heard what the boy was saying. They hadn't gone much further when a gallows came in sight.

'Look,' said the man, 'here's a tip for you. See that gallows?

Seven men got married to the rope-maker's daughter there, and now they're learning to fly. If you sit down there beneath it and wait till night comes, then you'll get the shivers all right.'

'Really?' said the boy. 'It's as easy as that? Well, I'll soon learn in that case. If I get the shivers before morning, you can have my fifty talers. Just come back here and see me then.'

He went to the gallows, sat himself down beneath it, and waited for night to fall. He felt cold, so he made himself a fire, but by midnight a wind arose and he couldn't get warm in spite of the blazing logs. The wind pushed the hanged men to and fro so that the bodies jostled against one another, and the boy thought, 'If I'm freezing down here by the fire, those poor fellows up there must be even colder.' He put up a ladder, climbed up and untied them, one after the other, and brought all seven of them down.

Then he put another couple of logs on the fire, and arranged the dead men around it to warm themselves; but all they did was sit there quite still, even when their clothes caught fire.

'Hey, watch out,' he said. 'I'll hang you up again if you're not careful.'

Of course, the dead men took no notice. They just continued to stare at nothing while their clothes blazed up.

This made the boy angry. 'I told you to be careful!' he said. 'I don't want to catch fire just because you're too lazy to pull your legs out of the flames.'

And he hung them all up again in a row, and lay down by his fire and fell asleep.

Next morning, he woke up to find the man demanding his fifty talers.

'You got the shivers last night all right, didn't you?' he said.

'No,' said the boy. 'How could I learn anything from those stupid fellows? They didn't say a word, and they just sat there quite still while their trousers caught fire.'

The man saw there was no chance of getting his fifty talers, so he threw his hands in the air and left. 'What a fool!' he said to himself. 'I've never met such a dimwit in all my life.'

The boy went on his way, still muttering to himself, 'If only I could get the shivers! If only I could get the shivers!'

A carter was walking along behind him, and hearing what he said, caught up with him and asked: 'Who are you?'

'Dunno,' said the boy.

'Where d'you come from, eh?'

'Dunno.'

'Who's your father, then?'

'I'm not allowed to say.'

'And what are you muttering to yourself all the time?'

'Oh,' said the boy, 'I want to get the shivers, but no one can teach me how.'

'You're a poor simpleton,' said the carter. 'Step along with me and I'll see that you find a place to stay, at least.'

The boy went along with him, and that evening they came to an inn where they decided to stay the night. As they went into the parlour the boy said again, 'If only I could get the shivers! Oh, if only I could get the shivers!'

The innkeeper heard what he said, and laughed, saying, 'If that's what you want, you're in luck. There's a chance for you very close to here.'

'Sshh,' said the innkeeper's wife, 'don't talk about that. Think of all those poor fellows who lost their lives. It would be such a pity if this young man's lovely eyes never saw the light of day again!'

'But I want to get the shivers,' said the boy. 'That's why I left home. What did you mean? What's the chance you talked about? Where is it?'

He wouldn't stop pestering till the innkeeper told him that there was a haunted castle nearby, where anyone who wanted to learn about the shivers could do so easily if only he managed to keep watch there for three nights.

'The king promised that whoever does that can have his daughter in marriage,' he said, 'and I swear the princess is the most beautiful girl who ever lived. What's more there are great heaps of treasure in the castle, guarded by evil spirits. You can have the treasure too, if you stay there for three nights – there's enough to make anyone rich. Plenty of young men have gone up there and tried, but no one's come out again.'

Next morning the boy went to the king and said, 'If you let me, I'll stay three nights in the haunted castle.'

The king eyed him, and liked the look of him. So he said, 'I'll let you take three things into the castle with you, but they must be things that aren't alive.'

The boy said, 'In that case, I'd like things to make a fire with, a lathe and a woodcarver's bench with a knife.'

The king ordered that all these things should be taken to the castle during daylight. When night fell the boy went inside and lit a bright fire in one of the rooms, dragged the woodcarver's bench and knife beside it, and sat down at the lathe.

'Oh, if only I could get the shivers!' he said. 'But this place doesn't look very promising either.'

When it was nearly midnight he stirred the fire up. He was just blowing on it when he heard voices from a corner of the room.

'*Miaow, miaow!* We're so cold!' they said.

'What are you yelling about?' he said over his shoulder. 'If you're cold, come and sit down by the fire.'

Next moment two huge black cats leaped out of the shadows and sat on either side of him, staring at him with their coal-red eyes.

'Fancy a game of cards?' they said.

'Why not?' he replied. 'But let me see your claws first.'

So they stretched out their paws.

'Good God,' he said, 'what long nails you've got. I'll have to trim them before we start to play.'

And he seized the cats by their necks, lifted them up to the woodcarver's bench, and tightened the vice around their paws.

'I don't like the look of these at all,' he said. 'They've put me right off the idea of playing cards.'

And he struck them both dead, and threw them into the moat.

He had just sat down again when from every corner of the room there came black cats and black dogs, each of them wearing a red-hot collar with a red-hot chain. They piled in from every direction until he couldn't move. They howled, they barked, they shrieked horribly, they jumped into the fire and scattered the burning logs in all directions.

He watched curiously for a minute or two, but finally he lost patience. Seizing his knife, he cried, 'Out with you, you scoundrels!'

And he hacked away merrily. Some of them he killed, and the others ran away. When all the live ones had fled, he threw the dead ones into the moat, and came back inside to warm up.

But his eyes wouldn't stay open, so he went to the large bed in the corner of the room.

'This looks comfortable,' he thought. 'Just the job!'

But as soon as he lay down, the bed began to move. It trundled to the door, which flew open, and then rolled all the way through the castle, gathering speed as it went.

'Not bad,' he said, 'but let's go faster still.'

And on it rolled as though drawn by six fine horses, along the corridors, up the stairs and down again, until suddenly – hop! It turned upside down, trapping him underneath. It lay on him like a mountain.

But he threw off the blankets and the pillows and clambered out.

'I've finished with the bed now,' he called out. 'If anyone else wants it, they can have it.'

And he lay down by his fire, and went peacefully to sleep.

When the king came in the morning he found him lying there, and said, 'Oh, that's a pity. The ghosts have killed him. Such a handsome young man, too!'

The boy heard him, and got up at once. 'They haven't killed me yet, your majesty,' he said.

'Oh! You're alive!' said the king. 'Well, I'm glad to see you. How did you get on?'

'Very well, thanks,' said the boy. 'One night down, two more to go.'

He went back to the inn. The innkeeper was astonished.

'You're alive! I never thought I'd see you again. Did you get the shivers?'

'No, not once. I hope someone can give me the shivers tonight.'

The second night he went up to the castle, lit his fire, and sat down again.

'Oh!' he said. 'I wish someone could give me the shivers.'

As midnight approached he heard a commotion up in the chimney. Banging and shouting, scuffling, screaming, and finally, with a loud yell, the lower half of a man fell down into the fireplace.

'What are you doing?' said the boy. 'Where's your other half?'

But the half-man, not having eyes or ears, couldn't hear him or see where anything was, and it ran around the room knocking into things and falling over and scrambling up again.

Then there was more noise from the chimney, and in a cloud of soot the missing top half fell down, and scrambled away from the fire.

'Not hot enough for you?' said the boy.

'Legs! Legs! This way! Over here!' called the top half, but the bottom half couldn't hear and kept on blundering around till the boy grabbed him around the knees and hung on. The top half leaped on board, and they became one man again at once. He was hideous. He sat down on the boy's bench next to the fire, and wouldn't give way, so the boy knocked him off and sat down himself.

Then there was yet more commotion, and half a dozen dead men fell down the chimney, one after the other. They had nine thigh-bones and two skulls with them, and set them up to play skittles.

'Can I play too?' asked the boy.

'Well, have you got any money?'

'Plenty,' he said. 'But your bowling balls aren't round enough.'

He took the skulls, put them on the lathe, and turned them till they were round.

'That's better,' he said. 'Now they'll roll properly. This will be fun!'

He played with the dead men for a while and lost some of his money. Finally, at midnight, the clock struck twelve and they all vanished, every one of them. The boy lay down peacefully and went to sleep.

Next morning the king came in again to see how he'd got on.

'How did you do this time?' he said.

'I had a game of skittles,' said the boy. 'I lost some money, too.'

'And did you get the shivers?'

'Not a bit of it,' he replied. 'I enjoyed the game, but that was it. If only I could get the shivers!'

On the third night he sat down again on his bench by the fire and sighed. 'Only one night left,' he said. 'I hope this is the night I'll get the shivers.'

When it was nearly midnight, he heard a heavy tread coming slowly towards the room, and in came six huge men carrying a coffin.

'Oh, so someone's dead?' the boy said. 'I expect it's my cousin. He died a few days ago.'

He whistled and beckoned, saying, 'Come on out, cousin! Come and say hello!'

The six men put the coffin down and walked out. The boy opened the lid and looked at the dead man lying inside. He felt the dead face, but of course it was as cold as ice.

'Never mind,' he said, 'I'll warm you up.'

He warmed his hands by the fire and held them to the dead man's cheeks, but the face stayed cold.

Then he took the body out, laid it by the fire with the dead man's head on his lap, and rubbed his arms to get the circulation going. That didn't work either.

'I know!' he said. 'When two people lie together, they warm each other up. I'll take you to bed with me, that's what I'll do.'

So he put the dead man in his bed and got in beside him, pulling the covers over them both. After a few minutes the dead man began to move.

'That's it!' said the boy, to encourage him. 'Come on, cousin! You're nearly alive again.'

But the dead man suddenly sat up and roared out, 'Who are you? Eh? I'll strangle you, you dirty devil!'

And he reached for the boy's neck, but the boy was too quick for him, and after a struggle he soon had him back in his coffin.

'Fine thanks I get from you,' he said, banging in the nails to keep the lid down.

As soon as the lid was fixed, the six men appeared again. They picked up the coffin and carried it slowly out.

'Oh, it's no good,' said the boy, in despair. 'I'm never going to learn about the shivers here.'

As he said that, an old man stepped out of the darkness in the corner of the room. He was even bigger than the men who carried the coffin, and he had a long white beard and eyes that glowed with evil.

'You miserable worm,' he said. 'You shall soon learn what the shivers are. Tonight you're going to die.'

'You think so? You'll have to catch me first,' said the boy.

'You won't get away from me, no matter how fast you run!'

'I'm as strong as you are, and probably stronger,' said the boy.

'We'll see about that,' said the old man. 'If you turn out to be stronger than me, I'll let you go. But you won't. Now come along this way.'

The old man led the boy through the castle, along dark corridors and down dark stairways, till they came to a smithy deep in the bowels of the earth.

'Now let's see who's stronger,' he said, and he took an axe and with one blow drove an anvil into the ground.

'I can do better than that,' said the boy. He took the axe and struck the other anvil in such a way that it split wide open for a moment, and in that moment the boy seized the old man's beard and wedged it in the anvil. The anvil closed up, and there was the old man, caught.

'I've got you,' said the boy. 'Now you'll see who's going to die.'

And he took an iron bar and beat the old man mercilessly, raining blows on him till he whimpered and moaned and cried, 'All right! Stop! I give in!'

And he promised to give the boy great riches if only he'd let him go. The boy twisted the axe in the crack and released his beard, and the old man led him to another cellar deep under the castle, and showed him three chests full of gold.

'One of these is for the poor,' he explained, 'one is for the king, and the third is yours.'

At that moment midnight struck, and the old man disappeared, leaving the boy in the dark.

'Well, so much for that,' he said. 'I can find my own way back.'

Groping along the walls, he made his way back to the bedroom and fell asleep by the fire.

In the morning the king came in.

'You must have learned how to shudder by now,' he said.

'No,' said the boy. 'I wonder what they can be, these shivers? I lay down with my dead cousin, and then an old man with a long beard came and showed me some treasure, but no one showed me how to shiver.'

They brought the gold up and shared it out, and then the boy and the princess were married. In due course he inherited the kingdom. But no matter how much he loved his wife, or how happy he was, the young king kept on saying, 'If only I could get the shivers! If only I knew what it meant to get the shivers!'

In the end it got on the young queen's nerves. She told her chambermaid, who said, 'Leave it to me, your majesty. I'll give him the shivers all right.'

The maid went down to the brook and caught a bucketful of minnows. That night when the young king was sleeping, the maid told the queen to pull the covers off and pour the bucket over him.

So that was what she did. The young king felt first the cold water and then the little fish wriggling and flipping about all over him.

'Oh, oh, oh!' he cried. 'Ooh! What's making me shiver? Ooh! Ow! Yes, I'm shivering! I've got the shivers at last! Bless you, dear wife! You did what no one else could do. I've got the shivers!'

* * *

Tale type: ATU 326, 'The Youth Who Wanted to Learn What Fear Is'
Source: A shorter version of this was published in the Grimms' first edition of 1812, but the story as it is here was published in their second edition of 1819, following a written version sent to them by Ferdinand Siebert of Treysa, near Kassel.

Similar stories: Alexander Afanasyev: 'The Man Who Did Not Know Fear' (*Russian Fairy Tales*); Katharine M. Briggs: 'The Boy Who Feared Nothing', 'The Dauntless Girl', 'A Wager Won' (*Folk Tales of Britain*); Italo Calvino: 'Dauntless Little John', 'The Dead Man's Arm', 'Fearless Simpleton', 'The Queen of the Three Mountains of Gold' (*Italian Folktales*)

A widespread tale, another version of which was included in the Grimms' volume of annotations to the *Children's and Household Tales* that they published in 1856. Calvino's 'The Dead Man's Arm' is the most lively and amusing of his four versions, but as its hero does not specifically set out to learn fear, he doesn't need the final lesson from the bucket of minnows. Neither does the heroine of Briggs's 'The Dauntless Girl', a fine story from Norfolk, which does share with this one the unfortunate fate of the sexton and the ghost's revealing of the treasure in the cellar. I think the Grimms' version is the best of all.

High spirits colour most of the variants of this tale; the ghosts and dead men are comic rather than terrifying. Marina Warner, in *From the Beast to the Blonde*, suggests a sexual interpretation of the bucket of minnows.

FOUR

FAITHFUL JOHANNES

Once upon a time there was an old king who fell ill, and as he was lying in pain he thought, 'This bed I'm lying on will be my deathbed.' And he said, 'Send for Faithful Johannes – I want to speak to him.'

Faithful Johannes was his favourite servant. He had that name because he'd been true and loyal to the king all his life long. When he came into the king's bedroom the king beckoned him close to the bed, and said, 'My good and faithful Johannes, I'm not long for this world. The only thing that troubles me is my son. He's a good lad, but he's young, and he doesn't always know what's best for him. I won't be able to close my eyes in peace unless you promise to be like a foster father to him, and teach him all he ought to know.'

Faithful Johannes said, 'I'll do that gladly. I won't forsake him, and I'll serve him faithfully even if it costs me my life.'

'That's a comfort to me,' said the king. 'I can die peacefully now. When I've gone, this is what you must do: show him over the whole castle, all the vaults, the chambers, the halls, and all the treasure they contain. But keep him away from the last room in the long gallery. There's a portrait of the Princess of the Golden Roof in there, and if he sees that picture, he'll fall in love with her. You'll know if that's happened, because he'll fall down unconscious. And then he'll put himself into all kinds of dangers for her sake. Keep him away from all that, Johannes: that's the last thing I ask of you.'

Faithful Johannes gave his promise, and the old king lay back on his pillow and died.

After the funeral, Faithful Johannes said to the young king, 'It's time you saw all your possessions, your majesty. Your father asked me to show you over the castle. It belongs to you now, and you need to know about all the treasures it holds.'

Johannes took him everywhere, upstairs and downstairs, up in the attics and way below ground in the cellars. All the magnificent rooms were open to him – all but one, that is, because Faithful Johannes kept the young king away from the last room in the long gallery, where the portrait of the Princess of the Golden Roof was hung. The picture was displayed in such a way that anyone entering the room would see it at once, and it was painted so well and so vividly that the princess seemed to live and breathe. No one could imagine anything in the world more beautiful.

The king noticed that Faithful Johannes always ushered him past that door, or tried to distract him when they were near it, and said, 'Come on, Johannes, I can see you're trying to stop me going in there. Why do you never open this door?'

'There's something horrifying in there, your majesty. You don't want to see it.'

'I certainly do! I've seen the whole castle now, and this is the last room. I want to know what's in it!'

And he tried to open the door by force, but Faithful Johannes held him back. 'I promised the king your father that I wouldn't let you see inside this room,' he said. 'It will bring nothing but bad luck for both of us.'

'Well, you're wrong about that,' said the young king. 'I'm so curious to see what's inside, it'll be bad luck if I can't. I shall have no peace, day or night, till I know what's in there. Johannes, open the door!'

Faithful Johannes saw that he had no choice. With a heavy heart and sighing deeply, he took the key from the ring and opened the door. He went in first, thinking that he might block the portrait from the young king's eyes, but that didn't work: the king stood on tiptoes and looked over his shoulder. And it happened just as the old king had said it would: the young man saw the portrait, and at once he fell unconscious to the floor.

Faithful Johannes picked him up and carried him to his room. 'Oh, Lord,' he thought, 'this is a bad start to his reign. What bad luck will come to us now?'

The king soon came back to his senses, however, and said, 'What a beautiful picture! What a beautiful girl! Who is she?'

'She's the Princess of the Golden Roof,' said Faithful Johannes.

'Oh, I'm in love, Johannes! I love her so much that if all the leaves on all the trees were tongues, they couldn't express it. I'd risk my life to win her love. Johannes, my faithful servant, you must help me! How can we reach her?'

Faithful Johannes thought hard about this. It was well known that the princess was a reclusive character. However, he soon thought of a plan, and went to tell the king.

'Everything she has around her is gold,' he explained, 'tables, chairs, dishes, sofas, knives and forks, all solid gold. Now among your treasures, your majesty, as you'll no doubt remember, are five tons of gold. What I suggest is to get the royal goldsmiths to take, say, a ton of it and make all manner of pretty things, birds and beasts and strange animals and the like. They might take her fancy, and we could try our luck.'

The king summoned all the goldsmiths and told them what he wanted. They worked night and day and produced a large number of pieces so beautiful that the young king was sure the princess would never have seen the like.

They loaded everything on board a ship, and Faithful Johannes and the king disguised themselves as merchants so that they were quite unrecognizable. Then they weighed anchor, and they sailed across the sea until they came to the city of the Princess of the Golden Roof.

Faithful Johannes said to the king, 'I think you should wait on the ship, your majesty. I'll go ashore and see if I can interest the princess in our gold. What you'd best do is set some things out for her to look at. Decorate the ship a bit.'

The king set to eagerly, and Faithful Johannes went ashore with some of the smaller gold objects in his apron, and went straight to the palace. In the courtyard he found a beautiful girl drawing water from two wells with two golden buckets, one for plain water and one for sparkling. She was about to turn and go in when she saw Faithful Johannes and asked who he was.

'I'm a merchant,' he said. 'I've come from a far land to see if anyone's interested in our gold.'

He opened his apron to show her.

'Oh, what lovely things!' she said, putting the buckets down and taking up the gold pieces one after the other. 'I must tell the princess about them. She loves gold, you know, and I'm sure she'd buy everything you've got.'

She took Faithful Johannes by the hand, and led him upstairs, for she was the princess's own chambermaid. When the princess saw the golden objects she was delighted.

'I've never seen such beautifully made things,' she said. 'I can't resist them. Name your price! I'll buy them all.'

Faithful Johannes said, 'Well, your royal highness, I'm only the servant really. My master is the merchant – he usually deals with that side of things. And these little samples of mine aren't to be compared with what he's got on the ship. They're the most beautiful things that have ever been made in gold.'

'Bring them all here!' she said.

'Ah, well, I'd like to oblige you, but there's so many of them. It would take days to bring them all up here, and besides, it would need so much space to set all the pieces out that I don't think your palace has got enough rooms, big and splendid though it is.' He thought that would make her curious, and he was right, because she said, 'Then I'll come to your ship. Take me there now, and I'll look at all your master's treasures.'

Faithful Johannes led her to the ship, feeling very pleased. When the young king saw the princess on the quayside, he realized that she was even more beautiful than her portrait, and his heart nearly burst. But he escorted her on board and led her below, while Faithful Johannes remained on deck. 'Cast off and set all the sail you have,' he told the bosun. 'Fly like a bird in the air.'

Meanwhile below decks the king was showing the princess the golden vessels and all the other beautiful objects, the birds, the animals, the trees and flowers, both realistic and fantastical. Hours went by, and she didn't notice that they were sailing. When she'd seen everything she gave a little sigh of contentment.

'Thank you, sir,' she said. 'What a beautiful collection! I've never seen anything like it. Truly exquisite! But it's time I went home.'

And then she looked through the porthole, and saw that they were on the high seas.

'What are you doing?' she cried. 'Where are we? I've been betrayed! To fall into the hands of a merchant – but you can't be a merchant! You must be a pirate! Have you kidnapped me? Oh, I'd rather die!'

The king took her hand and said, 'I'm not a merchant. I'm a king, just as well born as you are. If I tricked you into coming on board, it's only because I was overpowered by love. When I saw your portrait in my palace, I fell to the ground unconscious.'

The Princess of the Golden Roof was reassured by his gentle manner, and presently her heart was moved, and she agreed to become his wife.

Now as the ship sailed onwards, Faithful Johannes happened to be sitting in the bows, playing the fiddle. While he was doing that, three ravens flew around the ship and settled on the bowsprit, and he stopped playing and listened to what they were saying, for he knew the language of the birds.

The first said, '*Kraak!* Look! That's the Princess of the Golden Roof! He's taking her home with him!'

The second one said, 'Yes, but he hasn't got her yet.'

The third one said, 'Yes, he has! *Kraak!* There she is, sitting next to him on the deck.'

'That won't do him any good,' said the first one. 'As soon as they step ashore, a chestnut horse will run up to greet them, and the prince will try and mount it. *Kraak!* But if he does, the horse will leap into the air and carry him away, and he'll never see her again.'

'*Kraak!*' said the second. 'Isn't there any way of preventing that?'

'Yes, of course there is, but they don't know it. If someone else jumps in the saddle, takes the pistol from the holster and shoots the horse dead, the king will be safe. *Kraak!* But whoever does that must never tell the king why he did it, because if he does, he'll be turned to stone up to his knees.'

'I know more than that,' said the second raven. 'Even if the horse is killed, the king isn't safe. When they go into the palace, they'll find a beautiful wedding robe laid out for him on a golden tray. It'll seem to be made of gold and silver, but really it's made of sulphur and pitch, and if he puts it on it'll burn his flesh away right down to the marrow. *Kraak!*'

'Surely they won't be able to save him from that,' said the third.

'Oh, yes, it's easy, but they don't know how. Someone wearing gloves will have to take the robe and throw it on the fire, and then it'll burn up safely and the king won't be harmed. *Kraak!*

But if he tells the king why he did it, he'll be turned to stone from his knees to his heart.'

'What a fate!' said the third. 'And the dangers don't end there, either. Even if the robe burns up, I don't think this king is destined to have his bride. After the ceremony, when the dancing begins, the young queen will suddenly turn pale and fall down as though dead.'

'And can she be saved?' said the first.

'With the greatest of ease, if anyone knew. All they have to do is lift her up, bite her right breast, draw three drops of blood from it and spit them out. Then she'll come to life again. But if they tell the king why they've done it, their entire body will turn to stone, from the crown of their head to the soles of their feet. *Kraak!*'

And then the ravens flew away. Faithful Johannes had understood every word, and from then on he grew silent and sorrowful. If he didn't do what the ravens had said, his master would die, and yet if he explained to the king why he'd done these strange things, he would be turned to stone.

But finally he said to himself, 'Well, he's my master, and I'll save his life even if I have to give up my life in doing so.'

When they landed, it happened exactly as the raven had said it would. A magnificent chestnut horse came galloping up, saddled and bridled in gold.

'A good omen!' said the king. 'He can carry me to the palace.'

And he was about to climb into the saddle when Faithful Johannes pushed him aside and leaped up himself. A moment later he'd pulled out the pistol from the saddle holster and shot the horse dead.

The king's other servants didn't care much for Johannes, and they said, 'What a shame to kill such a beautiful horse! And to shove the king aside like that, what's more, just as it was going to carry him to the palace.'

'Hold your tongues,' said the king. 'This is Faithful Johannes you're talking about. I'm sure he had a good reason for it.'

They went into the palace, and there in the hall was a beautiful robe laid out on a golden tray, just as the raven had said. Faithful Johannes was watching closely, and as soon as the king moved to pick it up, Johannes pulled his gloves on, snatched the robe away, and threw it on the fire. It blazed up fiercely.

The other servants whispered together again: 'See that? See what he did? He burned the king's wedding robe!'

But the young king said, 'Enough of that! I'm sure Johannes had a good reason. Leave him alone.'

Then the wedding took place. After the service the dancing began, and Faithful Johannes stood at the edge of the ballroom, never taking his eyes off the queen. Suddenly she turned pale and fell to the floor. At once Johannes ran to her, picked her up, and carried her to the royal bedchamber. He laid her down, and then knelt and first bit her right breast and then sucked out three drops of blood, and spat them out. Instantly she opened her eyes and looked around, and then sat up, breathing easily, perfectly well again.

The king had seen everything, and not understanding why Johannes had behaved like that, became angry and ordered the guards to take him to prison at once.

Next morning Faithful Johannes was condemned to death and led to the gallows. As he stood on the scaffold with the noose around his neck he said, 'Everyone condemned to die is allowed to say one last thing. Do I also have the right?'

'Yes,' said the king. 'You have that right.'

'I've been unjustly condemned,' said Faithful Johannes. 'I've always been loyal to you, your majesty, just as I was to your father.' And he told all about the conversation between the ravens on the bowsprit, and how he had to do these strange things in order to save the king and queen from death.

Hearing that, the king cried out, 'Oh, my Faithful Johannes! A pardon! A pardon for you! Bring him down at once!'

But something strange was happening to Johannes: as he spoke the very last word, his feet and then his legs and then his trunk and his arms and finally his head changed into stone.

The king and the queen were grief-stricken.

'Oh, what a terrible reward for his loyalty to us!' the king said, and he ordered the stone figure to be carried to his bedchamber and placed next to his bed. Every time he looked at it, the tears flowed down his cheeks, and he'd say, 'Oh, if only I could bring you back to life, my dear, most faithful Johannes!'

Time went by, and the queen gave birth to twin boys, who were healthy and happy and became her greatest delight. One day when the queen was at church, the two boys were playing in their father's bedroom, and their father the king looked at the stone figure and said, as he always did, 'Oh, my dear faithful Johannes, if only I could bring you back to life!'

And then to his astonishment the stone began to speak and said, 'You can bring me back to life, if you sacrifice what you love most.'

The king said, 'For you I'll give up everything I have!'

The stone went on, 'If you cut off your children's heads with your own hand and sprinkle their blood on me, I shall come back to life.'

The king was horrified. To kill his own beloved children! What a terrible price to pay! But he remembered how Faithful Johannes had been ready to give his own life for those he served, and he steeled himself, drew his sword, and lopped off his two children's heads in a moment. And when he had sprinkled the stone figure with their blood, the stone changed into flesh again, starting at the head and going all the way down to the toes, and there was Faithful Johannes, healthy and well.

He said to the king, 'You were faithful to me, your majesty, and you won't go unrewarded.'

And Johannes took the children's heads and put them on again, rubbing their necks with their own blood, and they sat up and blinked and came alive once more, and went on jumping around and playing as if nothing had happened.

The king was overjoyed. And then he heard the queen coming back from church, and he made Johannes and the children hide in the wardrobe. When she came in, he said, 'My dear, have you been praying?'

'Yes,' she said, 'but my mind was always on Faithful Johannes and what a dreadful thing happened to him because of us.'

'Well,' said the king, 'we can bring him back to life, but it'll be at a heavy cost. We shall have to sacrifice our two little boys.'

The queen turned pale, and horror nearly stopped her heart. But she said, 'We owe him that much, for his great loyalty.'

The king rejoiced to hear that her response was the same as his, and he opened the wardrobe and out came Faithful Johannes and the two little boys.

'God be praised!' said the king. 'Faithful Johannes has been saved, and our two sons are alive as well!'

He told the queen how everything had come about. And after that they lived together happily till the end of their lives.

* * *

Tale type: ATU 516, 'Faithful John'
Source: a story told to the Grimm brothers by Dorothea Viehmann
Similar stories: Alexander Afanasyev: 'Koshchey the Deathless' (*Russian Fairy Tales*)

There are several intriguing motifs in this story: the portrait that must be hidden, the fatal knowledge acquired by overhearing what the birds say, the dreadful fate of poor Johannes and the appalling dilemma faced by the king.

The story in Afanasyev is not as tight and well contructed as the Grimms' version, which moves with great swiftness and skill from event to event. As elsewhere in their tales, we can see the organizing hand of Dorothea Viehmann (see the note to 'The Riddle', p. 132).

FIVE

THE TWELVE BROTHERS

Once there were a king and queen who lived together happily and ruled their kingdom well. They had twelve children, and every single one was a boy.

One day the king said to his wife, 'You're carrying our thirteenth child in your womb. If she turns out to be a girl, then the other twelve must die. I want her to inherit the kingdom and all my wealth.'

And to show her that he meant it, he had twelve coffins made. Each one was filled with wood shavings, and at the head of each one there was a feather pillow and a folded shroud. He had them put in a locked room and gave the key to the queen.

'Tell no one about this,' he said.

The mother sat weeping all day long, until her youngest son, who was called Benjamin after the boy in the Bible, asked, 'Mother, why are you so sad?'

'My dear child,' she said, 'I can't tell you.'

But he wasn't satisfied with that answer. He gave her no peace until she unlocked the room and showed him the twelve coffins all in a row, with the wood shavings and the pillows and the folded shrouds.

Weeping as she spoke, she said, 'My sweet Benjamin, these coffins are for you and your brothers. If this child I'm expecting is a girl, you will all be killed and buried in them.'

Benjamin embraced her and said, 'Don't cry, mother. We'll run away and look after ourselves.'

'Yes!' she said. 'That's a good idea. Go out into the forest, and find the highest tree you can. Keep watch on the castle tower. If I give birth to a little boy I'll raise a white flag, but if it's a girl I'll raise a red one, and then you should escape as fast as you can. May God protect you! I'll get up every night and pray for you all. In winter I'll pray that you'll always have a fire to warm yourselves at, and in summer I'll pray that you won't be oppressed by the heat.'

When she had given them her blessing, the twelve brothers went out into the forest. They took turns to keep watch from a lofty oak tree, and after eleven days had passed and it was Benjamin's turn, he saw the flutter of a flag being raised; but it wasn't a white flag, it was a red one.

He scrambled down the tree and told his brothers. They were furious.

'Why should we suffer for the sake of a girl?' they said. 'We must take revenge for this! Any girl who crosses our path will regret it. Her red blood will flow!'

They set off deeper into the forest, and in the deepest, darkest heart of it, they found a little cottage. Sitting outside it, with her suitcase packed, was an old woman.

'Here you are at last!' she said. 'I've kept the cottage clean and warm for you. And I've planted twelve lilies here outside the window. As long as those lilies bloom, you will be safe. Now I must be going.'

And she picked up her suitcase and disappeared down a dark path before they could say a word.

'Well, let's live here,' they said. 'It looks comfortable enough, and she did say it was intended for us. Benjamin, you're the youngest and weakest, so you can stay at home and keep house. The rest of us will hunt for food.'

So the older brothers went out into the forest every day and shot rabbits, deer, birds, whatever they could eat. They took it home to Benjamin, who cooked it and laid it on the table for them. They spent ten years in the little cottage, where they were safe, and the time passed quickly.

Meanwhile the little daughter was growing. She turned out to have a kindly heart, a beautiful face, and a golden star on her forehead. One day when all the laundry had been done at the palace, she saw twelve linen shirts on the line, each one slightly smaller than the next, and said to her mother, 'Whose are those shirts, mother? They are too small for father.'

The queen answered with a heavy heart: 'They belong to your twelve brothers, my dear.'

'I didn't know I had twelve brothers!' said the girl. 'Where are they?'

'Only God knows. They went into the forest, and they might be anywhere now. Come with me, my dear, and I'll tell you all about it.'

And she took the girl to the locked room and showed her the twelve coffins with the wood shavings, and the pillows, and the shrouds.

'These coffins were made for your brothers,' she explained, 'but they ran away before you were born.' And she told her how everything had happened.

The girl said, 'Don't cry, mother! I'll go and look for my brothers. I'm sure I can find them.'

And she ironed the twelve shirts and packed them neatly, and went out into the forest. She walked all day, and in the evening she came to the little cottage.

She went inside and found a young boy. He said, 'Who are you? Where have you come from?'

He knew she was a princess, because of her fine dress, but he was astonished at how beautiful she was, and at the golden star on her forehead.

'I am a princess,' she said, 'and I'm looking for my twelve brothers. I've vowed to walk on as far as the sky is blue till I've found them.'

And she showed him the twelve shirts, each one slightly smaller than the next. Benjamin saw at once that this girl was his sister, and said, 'You've found us! I'm your youngest brother, and my name is Benjamin.'

She wept for joy, and so did he. They kissed and embraced lovingly.

But then he remembered what his brothers had vowed, and said, 'Sister dear, I have to warn you: my brothers have sworn that every girl they meet must die, since it was because of a girl that we had to leave our kingdom.'

She said, 'I'll willingly give up my life, if I can free my brothers from their exile.'

'No,' he said, 'you shan't die. I won't let it happen. Sit under this tub till our brothers come home, and I'll make it all right.'

So she did. When they came home from hunting at nightfall, they sat down to eat and said to Benjamin, 'Any news?'

'Don't you know?' he said.

'Know what?'

'You've been in the forest all day long, and I've been here at home, and yet I know more than you do.'

'Know what? Tell us!'

'I'll tell you,' he said, 'as long as you promise that the next girl you meet shall not be killed.'

By this time they were so curious that they all cried, 'Yes! We promise! We'll be merciful! Just tell us!'

Then he said, 'Here is our sister,' and lifted up the tub.

The princess came out in her royal clothes, looking so lovely, with the golden star on her forehead, and everything about her was delicate, and fine, and perfect.

They all wept with joy, and embraced her and kissed her, and they loved her at once.

From then on she stayed at home with Benjamin and helped with the housework. The eleven older brothers went out into the forest every day and shot game, deer and pigeons and wild boar, and the sister and Benjamin prepared it all for the table. They gathered wood for the fire and herbs for the pot so that supper was always ready as soon as the others came home, they kept the house in order and swept the floors and made the beds, and the sister always did the washing and hung up their shirts, each one slightly smaller than the next, to dry in the sunshine.

One day they had prepared a fine meal, and they were all sitting down to eat when the sister thought that some parsley would taste very good sprinkled over the stew. So she went outside and gathered a bunch from their little herb garden, and then she saw twelve fine lilies growing by the window, and thought she would please the brothers by bringing them in to decorate the table.

But the moment she cut the lilies the cottage disappeared, and the twelve brothers were changed into twelve ravens that flew away over the trees with a dismal cry and vanished. The poor girl was left standing in the little forest clearing all on her own.

She looked around in dismay, and saw an old woman standing close by.

'My child, what have you done?' said the old woman. 'Now your brothers have been changed into twelve ravens, and there's no way of changing them back.'

'No way at all?' said the girl, trembling.

'Well, there is one way,' said the old woman, 'but it's so difficult that no one could ever do it.'

'Tell me! Tell me, please!' said the girl.

'You must remain silent for seven whole years, neither speaking nor laughing. If you speak a single word, even if it's in the very last minute of the very last day of the very last year, it will all be for nothing, for your brothers will all be killed by that single word.'

And the old woman hurried off down a dark path before the girl could say another word.

But she said in her heart: 'I *can* do it! I *know* I can do it! I'll redeem my brothers, see if I don't.'

She chose a tall tree and climbed up high among the branches, where she sat spinning some thread, and thinking: 'Don't speak! Don't laugh!'

Now it happened that sometimes a king came hunting in that part of the forest. This king had a favourite greyhound, and as they were making their way along a path the hound suddenly ran to a tree and started barking and jumping up at it. The king followed, and when he saw the princess with the gold star on her forehead, he was so struck by her beauty that he fell in love at once. He called up and asked if she would be his wife.

She didn't say a word, but she nodded, and he knew she'd understood. He climbed up the tree to help her down, put her on his horse, and they went home together.

The wedding was celebrated with great joy and festivity, but people remarked on the bride's strange silence. Not only did she not speak, she didn't laugh either.

However, the marriage was a happy one. But after they had spent some years together, the king's mother began to speak evil of the young queen. She would say to the king, 'That wretch you brought home with you – she's no better than a common beggar. Who can tell what wicked things she's thinking of? And she might be a mute, but any decent person can laugh from time to time. Anyone who doesn't laugh has something on their conscience, you can be sure of that.'

At first the king didn't want to listen to that sort of talk, but as time went by the old woman kept on and on, inventing all kinds of evil things to accuse the young queen of, and the king finally began to believe she must be right. The young queen was arraigned before a court packed with the old woman's favourites, and they didn't hesitate to sentence her to death.

A great fire was built in the courtyard where she was to be burned to death. The king watched from an upstairs window, tears flowing down his cheeks, for he still loved her dearly. She was tied to the stake, and the red fire was already rising higher and licking at her dress, when the last moment of the seven years passed.

And then twelve ravens flew down, the sound of their wing-beats filling the courtyard. As soon as their feet touched the ground they became her brothers again, and they rushed to the fire, kicking the burning logs this way and that, and untied their sister's bonds and brushed off the sparks that were beginning to set her dress alight. They kissed and embraced her, carrying her away from the stake.

And as for the young queen, she was laughing and talking as well as ever. The king was amazed. Now that she could speak, she told him why she had been silent so long. He rejoiced to hear she was innocent of all the terrible things his mother had accused her of.

But then it was the old woman's turn to be accused, and the court had no difficulty in finding her guilty. She was put into a barrel filled with poisonous snakes and boiling oil, and she didn't last long after that.

* * *

Tale type: ATU 451, 'The Maiden Who Seeks Her Brothers'
Source: a story told to the Grimm brothers by Julia and Charlotte Ramus
Similar stories: Alexander Afanasyev: 'The Magic Swan Geese' (*Russian Fairy Tales*); Katharine M. Briggs: 'The Seven

Brothers' (*Folk Tales of Britain*); Italo Calvino: 'The Calf with the Golden Horns', 'The Twelve Oxen' (*Italian Folktales*); Jacob and Wilhelm Grimm: 'The Seven Ravens' (*Children's and Household Tales*)

This tale has many cousins and it's easy to see why. The charm of the chorus of nearly identical brothers, who are turned into birds; of the sister who unwittingly causes the transformation, and who is placed under a nearly impossible prohibition; of her fidelity and courage, and the terrible fate that seems about to engulf her, and the perfect timing of the brothers' return and the sound of their wingbeats – it all makes a very pretty story.

The version in Grimm deals clumsily with the matter of the magic cottage and the lilies. I introduce the old woman earlier than she appears in the original, for the sake of timing.

One interesting detail is that the king's mother is first called *Mutter* and then, a few sentences later, *Stiefmutter*, as if correcting an earlier slip of the tongue. Which is she, mother or stepmother? This is not the only time this question will come up. The storyteller has to decide; no one else can.

SIX

LITTLE BROTHER AND LITTLE SISTER

Little Brother took Little Sister by the hand.

'Listen,' he whispered, 'since our mother died we haven't been happy for a single hour. The stepmother beats us every day, and her one-eyed daughter kicks us away whenever we try to go near her. What's more, stale bread crusts are all we get to eat. The dog under the table eats better than we do; he often gets a tasty bit of meat. God knows, if our mother could see how we have to live! Let's go away together into the wide world. We couldn't live any worse if we were tramps.'

Little Sister nodded, because every word her brother said was true.

They waited till their stepmother was having a nap, and then they left the house, closing the door very quietly behind them, and they walked the whole day over meadows and fields, over pasture land and stony land. It began to rain, and Little Sister said, 'God's crying now, and our hearts are crying with him.'

In the evening they came to the forest. They were so exhausted, so hungry and sorrowful, and so frightened of the dark that was gathering around them, that all they could do was climb into a hollow tree and fall asleep.

When they awoke in the morning, the sun was already shining down into their tree.

Little Brother said, 'Sister, wake up! It's warm and sunny and I'm thirsty. I think I can hear a spring – come and let's drink!'

Little Sister woke up too, and hand in hand they went to search for the spring they could hear among the trees.

Now the trouble was that their stepmother was a witch. She could see through her eyelids, and she was watching the children all the time as they tiptoed out of the house. She crept after them, as witches do, flattening herself close to the ground, and she put a spell on all the springs in the forest before creeping back to the house.

Soon Little Brother and Little Sister found the spring they'd heard, and saw the fresh cold water glistening as it ran over the stones. It looked so inviting that they both knelt down to drink.

But Little Sister had learned how to listen to what running water was saying, and she could hear the spring talking. Just as little brother was raising his cupped hands to his dry mouth she cried out, 'Don't drink! The spring is bewitched. Anyone who drinks from it will become a tiger. Put it down, put it down! You'll tear me to pieces!'

Little Brother did as she said, thirsty as he was. They walked on and soon found another spring. This time she knelt first and put her head close to the water.

'No, not this one either!' she said. 'It says, "Whoever drinks from me will become a wolf." I think the stepmother must have put a spell on it.'

'But I'm so thirsty!' he said.

'If you become a wolf, you'll eat me up at once.'

'I promise I won't!'

'Wolves don't remember promises. There must be a spring she hasn't bewitched. Let's keep looking.'

It wasn't long before they found a third spring. This time Little

Sister bent over and listened carefully and heard the water say, 'Whoever drinks me will be turned into a deer. Whoever drinks me will be turned into a deer.'

She turned to tell her brother – but it was too late. He was so thirsty that he'd thrown himself full length and plunged his face into the water. And at once his face changed, and lengthened, and became covered in fine hairs, and his limbs changed into a deer's legs and he stood up, tottering uncertainly – and there he was, a young deer, a fawn.

Little Sister saw him looking around nervously, about to flee, and she flung her arms around his neck.

'Brother, it's me! Your sister! Don't flee away, or we'll both be lost for ever! Oh, what have you done, my poor brother? What have you done?'

She wept, and the fawn wept too. Finally Little Sister gathered herself and said, 'Stop crying, my sweet little deer. I'll never leave you, never. Come on, let's make the best of this.'

She took off the golden garter that she wore and put it around the fawn's neck, and then she wove some rushes into a cord and tied it to the garter. Leading him along with this, she walked onwards, further and deeper into the forest.

After they'd walked a long way they came to a clearing, and in the clearing there was a little house.

Little Sister stopped and looked all around. It was very quiet. The garden was neatly kept, and the door of the house was open.

'Is anyone at home?' she called.

There was no reply. She and the fawn went inside, and found the neatest and cleanest little home they'd ever seen. Their stepmother the witch didn't care for housekeeping, and her house was always cold and dirty. But this one was delightful.

'What we'll do,' she said to the fawn, 'is we'll look after this house really well and keep it nice and clean for whoever it belongs to. Then they won't mind us staying here.'

She spoke to the fawn all the time. He understood her well enough, and obeyed her when she said, 'Don't eat the plants in the garden, and when you want to do pee-pee or the other thing, you go outside.'

She made him a bed on the hearth from soft moss and leaves. Every morning she went out and gathered food for herself: wild berries, or nuts, or sweet-tasting roots. There were carrots and beans and cabbages in the vegetable garden, and she always gathered plenty of fresh sweet grass for the deer, who ate it from her hand. He was happy to play around her, and in the evening, when Little Sister had washed and said her prayers, she lay down with her head on the deer's back for a pillow. If only Little Brother had still been human, their life would have been perfect.

They lived like that for some time. But one day it happened that the king held a great hunt in the forest. The trees resounded with the notes of the horn, the barking of the hounds, the joyful shouts of the huntsmen. The fawn pricked up his ears and longed to be outside with the hunt.

'Let me go with them, Sister!' he begged. 'I'd give anything to join them in the hunt!'

He pleaded so passionately that she gave in.

'But,' she said as she opened the door, 'make sure you come back by evening. I'm going to lock the door in case the wild huntsmen come by, so to let me know it's you, knock and say, "Sister dear, your brother's here." If you don't say that, I shan't open the door.'

The young deer was out through the door in a flash, bounding away into the trees. He had never felt so good, so happy, or so free as when the huntsmen saw him and started after him, and failed to catch him; whenever they came near and thought they'd surely caught him this time, he leaped away into the bushes and disappeared.

When it was getting dark he ran to the little house and knocked on the door.

'Sister dear, your brother's here!'

Little Sister opened the door, and he trotted in happily and told her all about the hunt. He slept deeply all night.

When morning came and he heard the distant music of the horn and the hounds once more, he couldn't resist.

'Sister, please! Open the door, I beg you! I must go and join in, or I'll die of longing!'

Unhappily Little Sister opened the door, and said, 'Don't forget the password when you come back.'

He didn't reply, but bounded away towards the hunt. When the king and his huntsmen saw the deer with the golden collar, they gave chase at once. Through brakes and briars, through thickets and across clearings the little deer ran all day long, and he led the hunt on a wild chase. Several times they nearly caught him, and when the sun was setting, a shot from a gun wounded him in the leg. He couldn't run fast any more, and one of the huntsmen managed to follow him home, and saw him knock, and heard the words, 'Sister dear, your brother's here!'

And the huntsman saw the door open, and the girl let in the deer and shut the door again. He went and told the king.

'Is that so?' said the king. 'Well, we shall hunt him all the harder tomorrow.'

Little Sister was frightened when she saw that her deer was wounded. She washed the blood off his leg, and bound a poultice of herbs there to help it heal. In fact the wound wasn't a serious one, and when he woke up in the morning the little deer had forgotten all about it. He begged to go out for a third time.

'Sister, I can't tell you the passion in my breast for the hunt! I must go and join in, or I shall go mad!'

Little Sister began to weep. 'Yesterday they wounded you,' she sobbed, 'and today they'll kill you. And I'll be left alone in the wild woods – think of that! I'll have no one left! I can't let you out, I can't!'

'Then I'll die here in front of you. When I hear the notes of the horn, I feel every atom of my body leaping with joy. My longing is too much for me, Sister! I beg you, let me go!'

She couldn't resist his pleas, and with a heavy heart she unlocked the door. Without a backward glance the deer leaped out and bounded away into the forest.

The king had given orders to his huntsmen that they should do the deer with the golden collar no harm. 'If you see him, put your guns up, and hold the hounds back. Ten golden talers to the man who sees him first!'

They hunted the deer through every part of the forest all day long, and finally as the sun was setting the king called the huntsman to him.

'Show me where that cottage is. If we can't catch him one way, we'll trap him another. What was the little rhyme he said?'

The huntsman repeated it for him. When they reached the cottage, the king knocked on the door and said: 'Sister dear, your brother's here!'

The door opened at once. The king walked in, and found standing there a girl more beautiful than any he had seen. She was frightened to see a man and not her little deer, but the man was wearing a golden crown, and he smiled kindly. He reached out his hand and took hers.

'Will you come to my palace with me,' he said, 'and be my wife?'

'Why, yes,' said Little Sister. 'But my little deer must come too. I won't go without him.'

'He can come by all means,' said the king. 'He shall live as long as you do, and he shall want for nothing.'

And as he said that, the deer himself came bounding in. Little Sister caught his golden collar and tied the cord of rushes to it.

The king lifted the girl on to his horse, and they went home to the palace, the deer trotting proudly behind his sister and the king.

Soon afterwards the wedding was celebrated, and Little Sister became the queen. As for Little Brother the deer, he had the whole palace garden to play in, and a team of servants to look after him: the Groom of the Grass, the Valet of the Horns and the Hooves, and the Maid of the Golden Curry Comb, whose job it was to groom him thoroughly every day before he went to bed and deal with any ticks or fleas or lice he might have picked up. So they were all very happy.

Now all this time the wicked stepmother had thought that the brother and sister must have been torn to pieces by wild animals. But when she read in the paper that Little Sister had become a queen, and that her constant companion was a deer, it didn't take her long to work out what had happened.

'That wretched boy must have drunk from the stream I put the deer-magic on!' she said to her daughter.

'It's not fair,' the daughter whined. 'I ought to be a queen, not her.'

'Shut your moaning,' said the old woman. 'When the time comes you'll get what you deserve.'

Time went past, and the queen gave birth to a child, a handsome little boy. The king was out hunting at the time. The witch and her daughter went to the palace disguised as chambermaids, and managed to find their way to the queen's bedchamber.

'Come now, your majesty,' the witch said to the queen, who was lying weak and exhausted in her bed. 'Your bath is ready. It'll make you feel so much better. Come with us!'

They carried her to the bathroom and put her in the tub. Then they lit a fire underneath it, such a great fire that the queen suffocated from the smoke. To hide their crime they closed the wall up by magic where the door had been, and hung a tapestry over it.

'Now you get into the bed,' the witch said to her daughter, and when the girl had clambered in, the old woman put a spell on her so that she looked exactly like the queen. The one thing she couldn't do anything about was the missing eye.

'Lie with that side of your head on the pillow,' she said, 'and if anyone speaks to you, just mumble.'

When the king came home that evening and heard that he had a little son, he was delighted. He went to his dear wife's bedchamber and was about to open the curtains to see how she was, but the false chambermaid said, 'Don't, your majesty! Don't open the curtains on any account! She needs rest, and she mustn't be disturbed.'

The king tiptoed away, and he didn't discover that a false queen was lying there in the bed.

That night the deer wouldn't sleep in his stable. He climbed the stairs to the nursery where the baby lay, and refused to leave it. He had to do so without explaining, for since the death of the queen he had lost the power to speak, so he lay down beside the cradle and went to sleep.

At midnight the nurse who slept there awoke suddenly to see the queen coming into the nursery, and she seemed to be wet from head to foot, as if she'd just come from the bath. She bent over the cradle and kissed the baby, and then she stroked the deer and said:

'How is my child? How is my deer?
I'll come here twice more, then I must disappear.'

And then she went out without another word.

The nurse was too frightened to tell anyone. She had thought the queen was still lying in bed recovering from childbirth.

But next night the same thing happened again, except that this time the queen seemed to be covered in little flames, and she said:

'How is my child? How is my deer?
I'll come here once more, then I must disappear.'

The nurse thought she should tell the king. So next night he waited in the nursery with her, and when midnight struck, once again the queen came into the room. This time she was wreathed in thick black smoke.

The king cried, 'Dear God, what's this?'

The queen ignored him, but went to the child and the deer as she'd done before, and said:

'How is my child? How is my deer?
I've come for the last time – I must disappear . . .'

The king tried to embrace her, but she faded into smoke and drifted out of his arms and mingled with the air.

The deer tugged the king's sleeve, and pulled him to the place where the tapestry hung. Then he tugged the tapestry down and butted the wall with his little horns. The king understood, and ordered his servants to knock the wall down. In all the disturbance the false queen got out of bed without anyone noticing and tiptoed away. When the wall was down they discovered the bathroom all blackened with soot, and the queen's body lying clean and pale and fresh in the bath.

The king cried, 'My wife! My dear wife!'

He bent to embrace her body, and by the grace of God she came alive again. She told him about the dreadful crime that had been committed, and the king sent his swiftest messenger to the palace gates, just in time to tell the watchmen to arrest the witch and her daughter as they tried to creep out.

The two of them were brought before the court. Judgement was pronounced: the daughter was to be led into the woods where the wild beasts would eat her, and the witch was to be burned. As soon as the old woman was reduced to ashes, her spell lost its power over the deer and he was transformed into Little Brother, human again. And he and Little Sister lived happily together for the rest of their lives.

* * *

Tale type: ATU 450, 'Little Brother and Little Sister'
Source: a story told to the Grimm brothers by the Hassenpflug family
Similar stories: Alexander Afanasyev: 'Sister Alionushka, Brother Ivanushka' (*Russian Fairy Tales*); Giambattista Basile: 'Ninnillo and Nennella' (*The Great Fairy Tale Tradition*, ed. Jack Zipes); Jacob and Wilhelm Grimm: 'The Little Lamb and the Little Fish', 'The Three Little Men in the Woods' (*Children's and Household Tales*); Arthur Ransome: 'Alenoushka and Her Brother' (*Old Peter's Russian Tales*)

One of the few ghost stories in the collection, and similar in that way to 'The Three Little Men in the Woods' (p. 65).

According to David Luke, in his introduction to *Brothers Grimm: Selected Tales*, the first transcription of the story in 1812 only had one bewitched stream, so that the brother was changed into a deer at once, but Wilhelm Grimm in a later edition added the other two for the sake of the fairy-tale three-ness.

The tale as the Grimms have it begins well and tails off limply. The final section has several unhelpful gaps and transitions which leave this reader at least puzzling: if the witch and her daughter murdered Little Sister in the queen's bathroom, what happened to the body? Why didn't the deer speak up when he saw her ghost? In fact, why hasn't the deer got anything to do at all? Why did the nurse not say anything about the apparition of the queen until 'many nights' had passed? Did the witch's daughter remain in bed all that time?

These are not just the sort of thing that fairy tales don't bother with, and to which it's silly to expect answers; they are more than that: they are clumsy storytelling. I thought it was possible to deal with them and improve the story.

SEVEN

RAPUNZEL

There once lived a husband and wife who longed to have a child, but they longed in vain for quite some time. At last, however, the wife noticed unmistakable signs that God had granted their wish.

Now in the wall of their house there was a little window that overlooked a magnificent garden full of every kind of fruit and vegetable. There was a high wall around that garden, and no one dared go into it, because it was the property of a very powerful witch who was feared by everyone. One day the woman was standing at that window, and she saw a bed of lamb's lettuce, or rapunzel. It looked so fresh and so green that she longed to taste some, and this longing grew stronger every day, so that eventually she became really ill.

Her husband was alarmed at her condition, and said, 'My dear wife, what is the matter?'

'Oh,' she said, 'if I can't have any of that rapunzel in the garden behind our house, I'll die.'

The man loved his wife dearly, and he thought, 'Rather than let her die, I must get her some of that rapunzel. I don't care what it costs.'

So as night was falling he climbed over the high wall and got into the witch's garden, where he pulled up a handful of rapunzel.

He scrambled back hastily and took it to his wife, who made it into a salad at once, and ate it hungrily.

It tasted good. In fact it tasted so good that her desire for it grew stronger and stronger, and she begged her husband to go and get some more. So once again, just as it was getting dark, he set off and climbed the wall. But when he set foot on the ground and turned to go to the bed of rapunzel, he had a shock, for there was the witch standing in front of him.

'So you're the wretch who's been stealing my rapunzel!' she said, glaring at him. 'You'll pay for this, let me tell you.'

'That's fair,' said the man. 'I can't argue with that, but let me plead for mercy. I had to do this. My wife saw your rapunzel from our window up there, and she felt a craving – you know how it is; it was so strong she thought she might die if she couldn't have some. So I had no choice.'

The witch understood the reason. The anger went out of her expression, and she nodded.

'I see,' she said. 'Well, if that's the case, you can have as much rapunzel as you want. But there's a condition: the child your wife is bearing shall belong to me. It will be perfectly safe; I shall look after it like a mother.'

In his fear the man agreed to this, and hurried back home with the rapunzel. And when in due course the wife gave birth, the witch appeared by her bed and took up the little girl in her arms.

'I name this child Rapunzel,' she said, and vanished with her.

Rapunzel grew up to become the most beautiful child the sun had ever shone on. When she was twelve years old, the witch took her into the depths of the forest and shut her in a tower that had no door, no stairs and no windows except one very small one in a room right at the top. When the witch wanted to go in she would call:

'Rapunzel, Rapunzel,
Let down your hair.'

Rapunzel had beautiful hair, as fine as spun gold, and of the same lustrous colour. When she heard the witch calling, she untied her hair and fastened it around the window hook before letting down its full length all the way to the ground, twenty yards down, whereupon the witch climbed up it to her little room.

After she had been in the tower for some years, it happened that the king's son was riding through the forest. As he came near the tower he heard a song so lovely that he had to stop and listen to it. Of course it was the lonely Rapunzel, singing to pass the time, and she had a sweet voice, too.

The prince wanted to go up to her, but there was no door to be found. He was baffled, and he rode home determined to come again and see if there was another way to get up the tower.

Next day he came back, but with no more success. Such a beautiful song, and no singer to be seen! But while he was pondering, he heard someone coming and hid behind a tree. It was the witch. When she was at the base of the tower, the prince heard her call out:

'Rapunzel, Rapunzel,
Let down your hair.'

To his astonishment, down from the window tumbled a length of golden hair. The witch seized hold and climbed all the way up, and clambered in through the window.

'Well,' thought the prince, 'if that's the way up, I'll try my luck with it.'

So the following day, as darkness was falling, he went to the tower and called out:

'Rapunzel, Rapunzel,
Let down your hair.'

Down came the hair, and the prince took its fragrant thickness into his hands and climbed up and jumped in through the window.

At first Rapunzel was terrified. She had never seen a man before. He was nothing like the witch, so he was strange and unfamiliar to her, but he was so handsome that she was confused and didn't know what to say. However, a prince is never lost for words, and he begged her not to be frightened. He explained how he'd heard her lovely voice singing from the tower, and how he couldn't rest until he found the singer; and how, now that he'd seen her, he found her face even more beautiful than her voice.

Rapunzel was charmed by this, and soon lost her fear. Instead she felt delight in the young prince's company, and eagerly agreed to let him visit her again. Before many days had gone by their friendship had developed into love, and when the prince asked her to marry him, Rapunzel consented at once.

As for the witch, she suspected nothing at first. But one day Rapunzel said to her, 'You know, it's funny, but my clothes no longer fit me. Every dress I have is too tight.'

The witch knew at once what that meant.

'You wicked girl!' she said. 'You've deceived me! All this time you've been entertaining a lover, and now we see the consequences! Well, I shall put an end to that.'

She took Rapunzel's beautiful hair in her left hand and snatched up some scissors with her right, and *snip-snap!* and down fell the lustrous strands up which the prince had climbed.

The witch then transported Rapunzel by magic to a wild place far away. There the poor young woman suffered greatly and, after a few months, gave birth to twins, a boy and a girl. They lived like tramps: they had no money, no home, and only what they could beg from passers-by who heard Rapunzel sing. They were often hungry: in the winter they nearly perished of the cold, and in the summer they were scorched by the burning sun.

But back to the tower.

On the evening of the day when Rapunzel's hair was cut off, the prince came to the tower as usual and called:

'Rapunzel, Rapunzel,
Let down your hair.'

The witch was lying in wait. She had tied Rapunzel's hair to the window hook, and when she heard him call, she threw it down as the girl had done. The prince climbed up, but instead of his beloved Rapunzel, at the window he found an ugly old woman, demented with anger, whose eyes flashed with fury as she railed at him:

'You're her fancy-boy, are you? You worm your way into the tower, you worm your way into her affections, you worm your way into her bed, you rogue, you leech, you lounge-lizard, you high-born mongrel! Well, the bird's not in her nest any more! The cat got her. What d'you think of that, eh? And the cat'll scratch your pretty eyes out too before she's finished. Rapunzel's gone, you understand? You'll never see her again!'

And the witch forced the prince backwards and backwards until he fell out of the window. A thorn bush broke his fall, but at the terrible cost of piercing his eyes. Blinded in body and broken in spirit, the prince wandered away.

He lived as a beggar for some time, not knowing which country he was in. But one day he heard a familiar voice, a voice that he loved, and stumbled towards it. And as he did so he heard two more voices joining in, the voices of children – and suddenly they stopped singing, for their mother Rapunzel had recognized the prince and was running towards him.

They embraced, both of them crying with joy; and then two of Rapunzel's tears fell into the prince's eyes, and his vision became clear once more. He saw his dear Rapunzel, and he saw his two children for the first time.

So, reunited, they travelled back to the prince's kingdom, where they were welcomed; and there they lived for the rest of their long and happy lives.

* * *

Tale type: ATU 310, 'The Maiden in the Tower'
Source: a story told to the Grimm brothers by Friedrich Schultz, based on Charlotte-Rose de Caumont de La Force's 'Persinette' from *Les Contes des contes* (*Tales of Tales*; 1698)
Similar stories: Giambattista Basile: 'Petrosinella' (*The Great Fairy Tale Tradition*, ed. Jack Zipes); Italo Calvino: 'Prezzemolina' (*Italian Folktales*)

Like 'The Frog King' (p. 3), 'Rapunzel' survives in the popular mind as a single event rather than a connected narrative. The image of the yards of hair tumbling down from the window in the tower is unforgettable. But what happens before and after the hair episode is often forgotten. What about her poor parents, for example? They long for years to have a child, and then she's born, and the witch takes her away, and then we hear no more about them. This is one way, of course, in which fairy tales are different from novels.

In later versions of the Grimm brothers' tales, Wilhelm Grimm bowdlerized the exchange between Rapunzel and the witch that had existed in all previous versions, and indeed in the Grimms' own first edition of 1812. Instead of revealing her pregnancy by saying that her clothes no longer fit, Rapunzel asks the witch why she is so much harder to pull up than the young prince. This is not an improvement: it makes her stupid instead of innocent. Besides, the story is preoccupied with pregnancy: according to Marina Warner, in

From the Beast to the Blonde, the particular plant longed for by the wife, which was originally parsley, was a well-known abortifacient. What's more, 'Persinette', the title of the de La Force story on which 'Rapunzel' is based, means 'Little Parsley'.

EIGHT

THE THREE LITTLE MEN IN THE WOODS

Once there was a man whose wife died, and a woman whose husband died; and the man had a daughter, and so did the woman. The girls knew each other, and one day they went for a walk together, and they came to the woman's house.

The woman took the man's daughter aside, and when her own daughter wasn't listening, she said, 'You know, I'd like to marry your father. Tell him that, and see what he says. If he says yes, I promise you'll have milk to wash your face in every day, it's very good for your complexion, and wine to drink. And my daughter will only have water. That's how much I'd like to marry him.'

The girl went home and told her father what the woman had said.

The man said, 'Marry her? Oh, good grief. What shall I do? Marriage is delightful, but it can be a torment as well, you know.'

He couldn't make up his mind. Finally, he pulled off his boot and said to his daughter, 'Here, take this boot. It's got a hole in the sole. Hang it up in the attic, and then fill it up with water. If it holds the water, I'll take a wife, but if the water runs away then I won't.'

The girl did as she was told. The water made the leather swell and squeeze the hole shut, so that when she filled up the boot, all the water stayed in it. The girl told her father, and he went up to the attic to see.

'Well, fancy that! I shall have to marry her, then,' he said. 'You can't go back once you've made a vow.'

He put his best suit on and went to woo the widow, and presently they were married.

Next morning when the two girls got up, the man's daughter found there was milk for her to wash her face in and wine for her to drink. The woman's daughter only had water.

On the second morning, both girls had water for washing and water to drink.

On the third morning, the man's daughter had water, but the woman's daughter had milk to wash in and wine to drink, and so it was on every morning after that.

The fact was that the woman hated her stepdaughter, and every day she thought of new ways to torment her. At the root of her hatred was bitter envy, because her stepdaughter was beautiful and sweet-tempered, whereas her own daughter was ugly and selfish, and not even full-cream milk made her complexion any nicer.

One winter's day, when everything was frozen hard, the woman made a dress out of paper. She called her stepdaughter and said, 'Here, put this on. Then go into the woods and gather some strawberries for me. I want some, and nothing else will do.'

'But strawberries don't grow in the winter,' said the girl. 'Everything's covered in snow, and the ground's as hard as iron. And why must I wear this dress made of paper? The wind will blow through it, and the brambles will tear it to pieces.'

'Don't you dare argue with me!' said the stepmother. 'Be on your way, and don't come back till you've filled the basket with strawberries.' Then she gave the girl a piece of bread as hard as wood. 'Here's your food,' she said. 'You'll have to make it last all day, we're not made of money.'

Secretly she thought, 'If the cold doesn't kill her, the hunger will, and I'll never have to see her again.'

The girl did as she was told. She put on the flimsy paper dress and went out with the basket. Of course there was snow everywhere, with not a green leaf to be seen, far less a strawberry. She didn't know where to look, so she went into the woods along a path she didn't know, and soon she came to a little house that was about as high as her head. Sitting on a bench outside it smoking their pipes were three little men, each about as tall as her knee, as she saw when they all got up and bowed.

'Good morning,' she said.

'What a nice girl!' one of them said.

'Well mannered,' said a second.

'Ask her in,' said the third. 'It's cold.'

'She's wearing paper,' said the first.

'Fashionable, I expect,' said the second.

'Chilly, though,' said the third.

'Would you like to come inside, miss?' they all said together.

'How kind of you,' she said. 'Yes, I would.'

They knocked out their pipes before opening the door.

'Mustn't smoke near paper,' said one.

'Catch fire in a moment,' said the second.

'Terrible danger,' said the third.

They gave her a little chair to sit on, and all three of them sat on a bench next to the fire. She felt hungry, so she took out her piece of bread.

'Do you mind if I eat my breakfast?' she said.

'What is it?'

'Just a piece of bread.'

'Can we have a bit?'

'Of course,' she said, and broke it in two. It was so hard she had to knock it on the edge of the little table. She gave the little men the bigger bit, and started to gnaw the smaller one.

'What are you doing out here in the wild woods?' they said.

'I'm supposed to gather strawberries,' she said. 'I don't know where I'm going to find any, but I'm not allowed to go home till I've filled my basket.'

The first little man whispered something to the second, and the second whispered to the third, and then the third whispered to the first. Then they all looked at her.

'Will you sweep the path for us?' they said. 'There's a broom in the corner. Just clear the path a bit next to the back door.'

'Yes, I'd be glad to,' she said, and she took the broom and went out.

When she'd gone they said, 'What shall we give her? Such a polite girl. Shared her bread with us, and it was all she had! Gave us the biggest bit! Kindly as well as polite. What shall we give her?'

And the first one said, 'I'll make sure she grows more and more beautiful each day.'

The second one said, 'I'll make sure that every time she speaks, a gold piece will fall from her mouth.'

The third one said, 'I'll make sure that a king will come along and marry her.'

Meanwhile, the girl was brushing away the snow from the path, and what did she find there but strawberries, dozens of them, as red and ripe as if it were summer. She looked back at the house, and she saw the three little men all looking from the back window. Yes, they nodded, go ahead, pick as many as you want.

She filled the basket, and went to thank the little men. They all lined up to bow and shake her hand.

'Goodbye! Goodbye! Goodbye!'

She went home and gave the basket to her stepmother.

'Where did you get these?' the woman snapped.

'I found a little house—' she began, but a gold piece fell out of her mouth. As she continued to speak, more and more gold pieces fell to the floor, till they were heaped around her ankles.

'Look at her showing off!' said her stepsister. 'I could do that if I wanted. It's not that clever.'

Of course, the stepsister was really wild with envy, and as soon as they were alone she said to her mother: 'Let me go to the woods and pick strawberries! I want to! I really want to!'

'No, darling,' said her mother, 'it's too cold. You could freeze to death.'

'Oh, go on! Please! I'll give you half the gold coins that fall out of my mouth! Go *on*!'

Finally the mother gave in. She took her best fur coat and altered it so it fitted the girl, and gave her chicken-liver pâté sandwiches and a big piece of chocolate cake for the journey.

The stepsister went into the woods and found the little house. The three little men were inside, looking through the window, but she didn't see them, and she opened the door and went straight in.

'Move out the way,' she said. 'I want to sit next to the fire.'

The three little men sat on their bench and watched as she took out her chicken-liver pâté sandwiches.

'What's that?' they said.

'My lunch,' she said with her mouth full.

'Can we have some?'

'Certainly not.'

'What about that cake? It's a big piece. Do you want all of it?'

'There's hardly enough for me. Get your own cake.'

When she'd finished eating they said, 'You can sweep the path now.'

'I'm not sweeping any path,' she said. 'D'you think I'm your servant? What a nerve.'

They just smoked their pipes and looked at her, and since they obviously weren't going to give her anything, she left and looked around for strawberries.

'What a rude girl!' said the first little man.

'Selfish, too,' said the second.

'Not as good as the last one, by a long way,' said the third. 'What shall we give her?'

'I'll make sure that she gets uglier every day.'

'I'll make sure that every time she speaks, a toad jumps out of her mouth.'

'I'll make sure she dies an uncomfortable death.'

The girl couldn't find any strawberries, so she went home to complain. Every time she opened her mouth a toad jumped out, and soon the floor was covered in the crawling, squatting, flopping things, and even her mother found her repellent.

After that the stepmother became obsessed. It was as if she had a worm gnawing in her brain. The only thing she thought about was how to make her stepdaughter's life a misery, and to add to her torment, the girl was growing more and more beautiful each day.

Finally the woman boiled a skein of yarn and hung it over the girl's shoulder.

'Here,' she said, 'take the axe and go and chop a hole in the ice on the river. Rinse this yarn, and don't take all day about it.'

She hoped the girl would fall in and drown, of course.

Her stepdaughter did what she was told. She took the axe and the yarn to the river, and she was just about to step on to the ice when a passing carriage drew to a halt. In the carriage there happened to be a king.

'Stop! What are you doing?' he called. 'That ice isn't safe!'

'I've got to rinse this yarn,' the girl explained.

The king saw how beautiful she was, and opened the carriage door.

'Would you like to come with me?' he said.

'Yes, I would,' she said, 'gladly,' because she was happy to get away from the woman and her daughter.

So she got in and the carriage drove away.

'Now I happen to be looking for a wife,' the king said. 'My advisers have told me it's time I got married. You're not married, are you?'

'No,' said the girl, and neatly dropped the gold piece into her pocket.

The king was fascinated.

'What a clever trick!' he said. 'Will you marry me?'

She agreed, and their wedding was celebrated as soon as possible. So it all came about as the little men had promised.

A year later the young queen gave birth to a baby boy. The whole country rejoiced, and it was reported in all the newspapers. The stepmother heard about it, and she and her daughter went to the palace, pretending to pay the queen a friendly visit. The king happened to be out, and when no one else was around, the woman and her daughter got hold of the queen and threw her out of the window into the stream running below, where she drowned at once. Her body sank to the bottom and was hidden by the water-weeds.

'Now you lie down in her bed,' the woman said to her daughter. 'Don't say anything, whatever you do.'

'Why not?'

'Toads,' said the woman, picking up the one that had just jumped out, and throwing it out of the window after the queen. 'Now just lie there. Do as I say.'

The woman covered her daughter's head, because quite apart from the toads she had indeed grown even uglier every day. When the king came back, the woman explained that the queen had a fever. 'She must be quiet,' she said. 'No conversation. Mustn't speak at all. You must let her rest.'

The king murmured some tender words to the daughter under the blankets, and left. Next morning he came to see her again, and before the woman could stop her, the daughter answered him when he spoke. Out jumped a toad.

'Good Lord,' he said, 'what's that?'

'I can't help it,' said the daughter, as another toad came out, 'it's not *my* fault,' and another.

'What's going on?' said the king. 'Whatever's the matter?'

'She's got toad flu,' said the woman. 'It's very infectious. But she'll soon get over it, as long as she's not disturbed.'

'I do hope so,' said the king.

That night, the kitchen boy was wiping the last of the pots and pans when he saw a white duck swimming up the drain that led out of the scullery into the stream.

The duck said:

'The king's asleep, and I must weep.'

The kitchen boy didn't know what to say. Then the duck spoke again:

'And what of my guests?'

'They're taking their rest,' said the kitchen boy.

'And my sweet little baby?'

'He's sleeping too,' said the boy, 'maybe.'

Then the duck shimmered and her form changed into that of the queen. She went upstairs to the baby's cradle, and took him out and nursed him, and then she laid him down tenderly and tucked him in and kissed him. Finally she floated back to the kitchen, changed back into the form of the duck, and swam down the gutter and back to the stream.

The kitchen boy had followed her, and seen everything.

Next night she came again, and the same thing happened. On the third night, the ghost said to the boy: 'Go and tell the king what you've seen. Tell him to bring his sword and pass it over my head three times, and then cut my head off.'

The kitchen boy ran to the king and told him everything. The king was horrified. He tiptoed into the queen's bedchamber, lifted the blankets from her head, and gasped at the sight of the ugly daughter lying there snoring, with a toad for company.

'Take me to the ghost!' he said, strapping on his sword.

When they got to the kitchen the queen's ghost stood in front of him, and the king waved his sword three times over her head. At once her form shimmered and changed into that of the white duck, and immediately the king swung his sword and cut her head off. A moment later the duck vanished, and in her place stood the real queen, alive again.

They greeted each other joyfully. But the king had a plan, and the queen agreed to hide in a different bedchamber till the following Sunday, when the baby was going to be baptized. At the baptism the false queen stood there heavily veiled, with her mother close, both pretending that she was too ill to speak.

The king said, 'What punishment should someone receive who drags an innocent victim out of bed and throws her into the river to drown?'

The stepmother said at once, 'That's a dreadful crime. The murderer should be put into a barrel studded with nails, and rolled downhill into the water.'

'Then that is what we shall do,' said the king.

He ordered such a barrel made, and as soon as it was ready, the woman and her daughter were put inside and the top was nailed down. The barrel was rolled downhill till it fell into the river, and that was the end of them.

* * *

Tale type: ATU 403, 'The Black and the White Bride'
Source: a story told to the Grimm brothers by Dortchen Wild
Similar stories: Italo Calvino: 'Belmiele and Belsole', 'The King of the Peacocks' (*Italian Folktales*); Jacob and Wilhelm Grimm: 'Little Brother and Little Sister', 'The White Bride and the Black Bride' (*Children's and Household Tales*)

The second part of this story is similar to 'Little Brother and Little Sister' (p. 47), but the first half, with the comedy of the three little men, has a quite different tone. I gave the three dwarfs a little more to say than the Grimms do.

NINE

HANSEL AND GRETEL

At the edge of a great forest lived a poor woodcutter with his wife and his two children, a boy called Hansel and a girl called Gretel. The family had little to eat at the best of times, and what's more there was a famine in the land, and often the father couldn't even provide their daily bread.

One night as he lay in bed worrying about their poverty, he sighed and said to his wife, 'What's going to become of us? How can we keep the children fed when we haven't any food for ourselves?'

'I tell you what,' she said. 'This is what we'll do. Early tomorrow morning we'll take them into the thickest part of the forest, make them comfortable, light a fire to keep them warm, give them a little bit of bread, and then leave them there by themselves. They won't find their way home, and we'll be rid of them.'

'No, no, no,' said the husband, 'I won't do that. Abandon my own children in the forest? Never! Wild animals would tear them to pieces.'

'You're a fool,' said his wife. 'If we don't get rid of them, all four of us will starve. You may as well start planing the wood for our coffins.'

She gave him no peace until he gave in.

'But I don't like it,' he said. 'I can't help feeling sorry for them . . .'

In the next room, the children were awake. They couldn't sleep because they were so hungry, and they heard every word their stepmother said.

Gretel wept bitterly and whispered, 'Oh, Hansel, it's the end for us!'

'Hush,' said Hansel. 'Stop worrying. I know what we can do.'

As soon as the grown-ups had fallen asleep, Hansel got out of bed, put on his old jacket, opened the lower half of the door and crept outside. The moon was shining brightly, and the white pebbles in front of the house glittered like silver coins. Hansel crouched down and filled his pockets with as many as he could cram in.

Then he went back inside and got into bed and whispered, 'Don't worry, Gretel. Go to sleep now. God will look after us. Anyway, I've got a plan.'

At daybreak, even before the sun had risen, the woman came in and pulled the covers off their bed.

'Get up, you layabouts!' she said. 'We're going into the forest to get some wood.'

She gave them each a slice of dry bread.

'That's your lunch,' she said, 'and don't gobble it up too soon, because there's nothing else.'

Gretel put the bread in her apron, because Hansel's pockets were full of pebbles. They all set off together into the forest. From time to time Hansel would stop and look back at the house, until finally his father said, 'What are you doing, boy? Keep up. Use your legs.'

'I'm looking at my white kitten,' Hansel said. 'He's sitting on the roof. He wants to say goodbye to me.'

'Stupid boy,' said the woman. 'That's not your kitten, it's the sun shining on the chimney.'

In fact, Hansel had been dropping the pebbles one by one on the path behind them. He was looking back because he wanted to make sure they could be seen.

When they got to the middle of the forest their father said, 'Go and fetch some kindling. I'll make a fire so you won't freeze.'

The children gathered some small twigs, a whole pile of them, and their father set them alight. When the fire was burning well the woman said, 'Make yourselves comfortable, my dears. Lie down by the fire and snuggle up warm. We'll go off and cut some wood now, and when we've finished we'll come and get you.'

Hansel and Gretel sat down by the fire. When they felt it must be midday they ate their bread. They could hear the sound of an axe not far away, so they thought their father was nearby; but it wasn't an axe, it was a branch that he'd tied to a dead tree. The wind swung it back and forth, so it knocked on the wood.

The children sat there for a long time, and gradually their eyelids began to feel heavy. As the afternoon went past and the light faded, they leaned closer together and fell sound asleep.

They awoke to find themselves in darkness. Gretel began to cry. 'How can we ever find our way out?' she sobbed.

'Wait till the moon comes up,' said Hansel. 'Then you'll see how my plan will work.'

When the moon did come up it was full and brilliant, and the white stones Hansel had dropped shone like newly minted coins. Hand in hand, the two children followed the trail all through the night, and just as dawn was breaking, they arrived at their father's house.

The door was locked, so they knocked loudly. When the woman opened it her eyes opened too, in shock. 'You wretched children! You made us so worried!' And she hugged them so tightly they couldn't breathe. 'Why did you sleep so long? We thought you didn't want to come back!'

And she pinched their cheeks as if she were really glad to see them. When their father came down a moment later, the relief and joy in his face was real, because he hadn't wanted to leave them at all.

So that time they were safe. But not long afterwards, food was short again, and many people went hungry. One night the children heard the woman say to their father, 'It's no good. We've only got half a loaf left, and then we'll all starve. We must get rid of the children, and do it properly this time. They must have had some trick before, but if we take them deep enough into the woods they'll never find their way out.'

'Oh, I don't like it,' said the father. 'There's not just wild animals in the forest, you know. There are goblins and witches and the Lord knows what. Wouldn't it be better to share the loaf with the children?'

'Don't be stupid,' said the woman. 'Where's the sense in that? You're soft, that's the trouble with you. Soft and stupid.'

She tore him to shreds with her criticism, and he had no defence; if you've given in once, you have to give in ever after.

The children were awake, and they had heard the conversation. When the adults were asleep, Hansel got up and tried to go outside again, but the woman had locked the door and hidden the key. Nevertheless, he comforted his sister when he got back into bed, and said, 'Don't worry, Gretel. Go to sleep now. God will protect us.'

Early next morning the woman came and woke the children as she'd done before, and gave them each a piece of bread, though it was even smaller this time. As they went into the forest, Hansel crumbled his bread up and dropped the crumbs on the path, stopping every so often to make sure he could see them.

'Hansel, keep going,' said his father. 'Stop looking back all the time.'

'I was looking at my pigeon sitting on the roof,' said Hansel. 'She wants to say goodbye to me.'

'That's not your pigeon, you fool,' said the woman, 'it's the sun shining on the chimney. Stop dawdling.'

Hansel didn't look back again, but he kept crumbling up the

bread in his pocket and dropping it on the path. The woman made them all walk fast, and they went deeper into the forest than they'd ever gone in all their lives.

Finally she said, 'This'll do,' and once again they made a fire for the children to sit by.

'Now don't you move,' the woman told them. 'Sit here and don't budge till we come and get you. We've got enough to worry about without you wandering off. We'll be back in the evening.'

The children sat there until they felt it must be midday, and then they shared Gretel's little piece of bread, because Hansel had used all his up. Then they fell asleep, and the whole day went by, but no one came for them.

It was dark when they woke up. 'Hush, don't cry,' Hansel said to Gretel. 'When the moon comes up, we'll see the crumbs and find our way home.'

The moon came up, and they began to look for the crumbs, but they couldn't find any. The thousands of birds that fly about in the woods and the fields had pecked them all up.

'We'll find our way,' said Hansel.

But no matter which way they went, they couldn't find the way home. They walked all through the night and then all through the following day, and still they were lost. They were hungry, too, terribly hungry, because all they'd had to eat was a few berries that they'd found. They were so tired by this time that they lay down under a tree and fell asleep at once. And when they awoke on the third morning, and struggled to their feet, they were still lost, and with every step they seemed to be going deeper and deeper into the forest. If they didn't find help soon, they'd die.

But at midday, they saw a little snow-white bird sitting on a branch nearby. It sang so beautifully that they stopped to listen, and when it stretched its wings and flew a little way ahead, they followed it. It perched and sang again, and again flew a little way ahead, moving no faster than they could walk, so that it really seemed to be guiding them.

And all of a sudden they found themselves in front of a little house. The bird perched on the roof, and there was something strange about the look of that roof. In fact—

'It's made of cake!' said Hansel.

And as for the walls—

'They're made of bread!' said Gretel.

And as for the windows, they were made of sugar.

The poor children were so hungry that they didn't even think of knocking at the door and asking permission. Hansel broke off a piece of roof, and Gretel knocked through a window, and they sat down right where they were and started to eat at once.

After a good few mouthfuls, they heard a soft voice from inside:

'Nibble, nibble, little mouse,
Who's that nibbling at my house?'

The children answered:

'The wind so wild,
The Heavenly Child.'

And then they went on eating, they were so ravenous. Hansel liked the taste of the roof so much that he pulled off a piece as long as his arm, and Gretel carefully pushed out another windowpane and started crunching her way through it.

Suddenly the door opened and an old, old woman came hobbling out. Hansel and Gretel were so surprised that they stopped eating and stared at her with their mouths full.

But the old woman shook her head said, 'Don't be frightened, my little dears! Who brought you here? Just come inside, my darlings, come and rest your poor selves in my little box of treats. It's as safe as houses!'

She pinched their cheeks fondly, and took each of them by the hand and led them into the cottage. As if she'd known they were coming, there was a table laid with two places, and she served them a delicious meal of milk and pancakes with sugar and spices, and apples and nuts.

After that she showed them into a little bedroom where two beds were made up ready, with snow-white sheets. Hansel and Gretel went to bed, thinking they were in heaven, and fell asleep at once.

But the old woman had only pretended to be friendly. In fact she was a wicked witch, and she had built her delicious house in order to lure children to her. Once she'd captured a child, whether a boy or a girl, she killed them, cooked them, and ate them. It was a feast day for her when that happened. Like other witches, she had red eyes and couldn't see very far, but she had a keen sense of smell, and she knew at once when humans were nearby. Once Hansel and Gretel were tucked up in bed, she laughed and rubbed her knobbly hands together.

'I've got 'em now!' she cackled. 'They won't get away from me!'

Early next morning she got up and went to their room, and looked at the two of them lying there asleep. She could barely keep her hands from their full red cheeks.

'Nice mouthfuls!' she thought.

Then she seized Hansel and before he could utter a cry she dragged him out of the cottage and into a little shed, where she shut him in a cage. He cried then all right, but there was no one to hear.

Then the witch shook Gretel awake saying, 'Get up, you lump! Go and fetch some water from the well and cook something for your brother. He's in the shed, and I want him fattened up. When he's fat enough, I'm going to eat him.'

Gretel began to cry, but it was no good: she had to do everything the witch ordered. Hansel was given delicious food every day, while she had to live on crayfish shells.

Every morning the witch limped down to the shed, leaning on her stick, and said to Hansel: 'Boy! Stick your finger out! I want to see if you're fat yet.'

But Hansel was too clever for that: he stuck a little bone through the bars, and the witch, peering through her red eyes, thought it was his finger. She couldn't understand why he wasn't fat.

Four weeks went by, and she thought Hansel was still thin. But then she thought of his nice red cheeks, and she shouted to Gretel: 'Hey! Girl! Go and fetch lots of water. Fill the cauldron and set it on to boil. Fat or thin, skinny or plump, I'm going to slaughter that brother of yours tomorrow and boil him up for a stew.'

Poor Gretel! She wept and wept, but she had to fetch the water as the witch ordered. 'Please, God, help us!' she sobbed. 'If only the wolves had eaten us in the forest, at least we'd have died together.'

'Stop your snivelling,' said the witch. 'It won't do you any good.'

In the morning Gretel had to light a fire under the oven.

'We'll do the baking first,' said the witch. 'I've kneaded the dough already. Is that fire hot enough yet?'

She dragged Gretel to the oven door. Flames were spitting and flaring under the iron floor.

'Climb in and see if it's hot enough,' said the witch. 'Go on, in you go.'

Of course, the witch intended to shut the door when Gretel was inside, and cook her as well. But Gretel saw what she was up to, so she said, 'I don't quite understand. You want me to get inside? How can I do that?'

'Stupid goose,' said the witch. 'Get out of the way, I'll show you. It's easy enough.'

And she bent down and put her head inside the oven. As soon as she did, Gretel shoved her so hard that she overbalanced and fell in. Gretel closed the door at once and secured it with an iron bar. Horrible shrieks and screams and howls came from the oven, but Gretel closed her ears and ran outside. The witch burned to death.

Gretel ran straight to the shed and cried: 'Hansel, we're safe! The old witch is dead!'

Hansel leaped out, as joyful as a bird that finds its cage open. They were so happy! They threw their arms around each other's necks, they hugged, they jumped for joy, they kissed each other's cheeks. There was nothing to fear any more, so they ran into the cottage and looked around. In every corner there were trunks and chests full of precious stones.

'These are better than pebbles!' said Hansel, dropping some in his pocket.

'I'll take some too,' said Gretel, and filled her apron with them.

'And now let's go,' said Hansel. 'Let's leave these witchy woods behind.'

After walking a few hours, they came to a lake.

'It's going to be difficult to get across,' said Hansel. 'I can't see a bridge anywhere.'

'There aren't any boats either. But look,' said Gretel, 'there's a white duck. I'll see if she can help us get across.'

She called out:

'Little duckling, little duck,
Be kind enough to bring us luck!
The water's deep and cold and wide,
And we must reach the other side.'

The little duck swam up to them, and Hansel climbed on her back.

'Come on, Gretel!' he said. 'Climb on with me!'

'No,' said Gretel, 'that would be too much of a cargo. We should go one at a time.'

So the good little bird took them one after the other. When they were safely ashore again they walked on further, and soon the forest began to grow more familiar. At last they saw their own home in the distance, and they ran up and rushed inside and threw themselves into their father's arms.

The man hadn't had one happy moment since he'd left his children in the forest. Not long after that, his wife had died, and he was all alone, and poorer than ever. But now Gretel unfolded her little apron and shook out all the jewels so that they bounced and scattered all over the room, and Hansel threw handful after handful after them.

So all their troubles were over, and they lived happily ever after.

The mouse has run,
My tale is done –
And if you catch it, you can make yourself a great big furry hat.

* * *

Tale type: ATU 327, 'Hansel and Gretel'
Source: story told to the Grimm brothers by the Wild family
Similar stories: Alexander Afanasyev: 'Baba Yaga and the Brave Youth' (*Russian Fairy Tales*); Giambattista Basile: 'Ninnillo and Nennella' (*The Great Fairy Tale Tradition*, ed. Jack Zipes); Italo Calvino: 'Chick', 'The Garden Witch' (*Italian Folktales*); Charles Perrault: 'Little Thumbling' (*Perrault's Complete Fairy Tales*)

The best-known tales, of which this is certainly one, have lived on in countless anthologies and picture-books and theatrical adaptations (and, in this case, opera) until familiarity threatens to dull their fine qualities. But this is a great and ferocious classic. The wonderful invention of the edible house, together with the implacable cruelty of the witch and the wit and bravery of Gretel in dealing with her so neatly, make it unforgettable.

Mother, or stepmother? In the Grimms' first edition, of 1812, the woman is simply 'the mother'. By the time of the seventh edition of 1857 she had become a stepmother, and so she remains. Marina Warner, in *From the Beast to the Blonde*, is very interesting on the Grimms' reasons for this (the only way they could preserve an ideal vision of the Mother was to banish and replace her) and also on Bruno Bettelheim's Freudian interpretation (the mother/stepmother split allows the listening children to deal guiltlessly with their anger at their own mother's threatening side). From the storytelling point of view, I go for simplicity.

Jack Zipes, in *Why Fairy Tales Stick*, points out that underlying this tale, which to many seems a matter of pure fancy, is the unhappy reality of rural poverty and the prospect of real starvation for many families. Desperate times, desperate remedies, no doubt, but shouldn't the story condemn the father a little more? And the death of the stepmother is very convenient, especially given the association of stepmother and witch that many modern storytellers have built on (including myself). It would have been a sorry ending for the children to come home and find her still ruling the roost. Perhaps the father killed her. If I were writing this tale as a novel, he would have done.

The episode of the duck is a curious little intervention in the story from the Grimms' final edition. It didn't exist before that, at least in print, but I think it works, so I've included it too. The lake is an impassable barrier between the threatening forest and the safety of home, and a barrier is a desirable thing to have unless you're on the wrong side of it; but it can be crossed with a combination of the benevolence of nature and human ingenuity.

TEN

THE THREE SNAKE LEAVES

Once there was a poor man who couldn't support his only son any more. When the son realized this, he said, 'Father, it's no use my staying here. I'm just a burden to you. I'm going to leave home and see if I can earn a living.'

The father gave him his blessing, and they parted sorrowfully.

The king of a nearby country was a powerful ruler, and at that time he was waging war. The young man enlisted in his army and soon found himself at the front where a great battle was being fought. The bullets flew like hail, the danger was hideous, and his comrades were falling dead all around. When the general himself fell dead, the last of the troops were going to flee, but the young man took his place and yelled: 'We won't be defeated! Follow me, and God save the king!'

The men followed him as he led the charge, and they soon had the enemy on the run. When the king heard of the young man's part in the victory, he promoted him to field marshal, gave him gold and treasure, and bestowed on him the highest honours in the kingdom.

Now the king had a daughter who was very beautiful, but she had one strange obsession. She had sworn an oath not to marry any man unless he promised to let himself be buried alive with her if she died first. 'After all, if he really loves me,' she said, 'why would he want to go on living?' And she said that she would do the same and be buried with him if he was the first to die.

This grim condition had put off many young men who would otherwise have begged to marry her, but the soldier was so struck by her beauty that nothing would discourage him. So he asked the king for her hand.

'Do you know what you must promise?' said the king.

'If she dies before me, I must go to the grave with her,' said the soldier. 'But I love her so much that I'm willing to risk that.'

The king consented, and the wedding was celebrated with great splendour.

For a while they lived together happily, but one day the princess fell ill. Doctors came from all over the kingdom, but none of them could help her, and presently she died. And then the young soldier remembered the promise he'd had to make, and shuddered. There was no way of getting out of it, even if he'd wanted to break the promise, because the king was going to put sentries at the grave itself and all around the cemetery in case he tried to escape. When the day came for the princess to be buried, they carried her body to the royal vault, made sure the young man was inside, and the king personally locked and bolted the door.

They had put some provisions in there: on a table there were four candles, four loaves of bread and four bottles of wine. The soldier sat there beside the princess's body day after day, taking only a mouthful of bread and a sip of wine, making them last as long as possible. When he'd taken the last sip but one and eaten the last mouthful but one, and when the last candle was down to its last inch, he knew that his time had nearly come.

But as he sat there in despair, he saw a snake crawl out of a corner of the vault and move towards the body. Thinking it intended to eat her, the young man drew his sword. 'While I live, you shan't touch her!' he said, and struck the snake three times, cutting it to pieces.

Shortly afterwards, a second snake came crawling out of the corner. It came to the body of the first snake, and looked at it, piece by piece, and then crawled away again. Soon it came back, and this time it had three green leaves in its mouth. Carefully moving the first snake's body together again, it laid a leaf on each of the wounds, and in a moment the dead snake stirred into life, the wounds closed up, and it was whole again. The two snakes hurried away together.

But the leaves were still lying where they'd left them, and the young man thought that if their miraculous power had brought the snake back to life, it might do the same for a human being. So he picked up the leaves and laid them on the dead princess's white face, one on her mouth and the other two on her eyes.

And as soon as he did this, her blood began to stir. A healthy pink came into her cheeks, and she drew a breath and opened her eyes.

'God in heaven!' she said. 'Where am I?'

'You're with me, my dear wife,' said the soldier, and told her all that had happened. He gave her the very last mouthful of bread and the very last sip of wine, and then they banged on the door and shouted so loudly that the sentries outside heard them and went running to the king.

The king came to the graveyard himself and personally unlocked and unbolted the door of the vault. The princess tumbled into his arms, he shook the young man's hand, and everyone rejoiced at the miracle that had brought her back to life.

As for the snake leaves, the soldier was a careful man, and he told no one about how the princess had been revived. But he had an honest and reliable servant, so he gave this servant the three snake leaves to look after. 'Take good care of them,' he said, 'and make sure you keep them with you wherever we go. You never know when we might need them again.'

Now after she was brought back to life, a change came over the princess. All the love she had for her husband drained away from her heart. She still pretended to love him, however, and when he suggested making a sea voyage to visit his old father, she agreed at once. 'What a pleasure it'll be to meet the noble father of my dearest husband!' she said.

But once at sea she forgot the great devotion the young man had shown her, because she felt a lust growing in her for the captain of the ship. Nothing would satisfy her but to sleep with him, and soon they were lovers. One night in his arms she whispered, 'Oh, if only my husband were dead! What a marriage we two would make!'

'That is easily arranged,' said the captain.

He took a length of cord and, with the princess at his side, crept into the cabin where the young man was sleeping. The princess held one end of the cord and the captain wound the other around her husband's neck, and then they pulled so hard that, struggle as he might, he couldn't fight them off, and soon they had strangled him.

The princess took her dead husband by the head and the captain took him by the feet, and they threw him over the ship's rail. 'Let's go home now,' said the princess. 'I'll tell my father that he died at sea, and I'll sing your praises, and he'll let us be married and you can inherit the kingdom.'

But the faithful servant had seen everything they'd done, and as soon as their backs were turned he untied a boat from the ship and rowed back in search of his master's body. He soon found it, and after hauling it into the boat he untied the cord from around the young man's neck and put the three snake leaves on his eyes and mouth, and he came back to life at once.

Then the two of them rowed with all their might. Day and night they rowed, stopping for nothing, and their boat flew over the waves so fast that they reached the shore a day before the ship, and went straight to the palace. The king was amazed to see them.

'What's happened?' he said. 'Where's my daughter?'

They told him everything, and he was shocked to hear of his daughter's treachery.

'I can't believe she'd do such a terrible thing!' he said. 'But the truth will soon come to light.'

And so it did. Very soon the ship arrived at the port, and on hearing of this the king made the young man and his servant wait in a hidden room, where they could listen to everything that was said.

The princess, dressed all in black, came sobbing to her father.

'Why have you come back alone?' he said. 'Where's your husband? And why are you wearing mourning?'

'Oh, father dear,' she said, 'I'm inconsolable! My husband took ill with the yellow fever and died. The captain and I had to bury him at sea. If he hadn't helped me, I don't know what I would have done. But the captain's such a good man – he looked after my dear husband when the fever was at its height, no matter what the danger. He can tell you all about it.'

'Oh, your husband's dead, is he?' said the king. 'Let's see if I can bring him back to life.'

And he opened the door and invited the other two to come out.

When the princess saw the young man, she fell to the ground as if she'd been struck by lightning. She tried to say that her husband must have been hallucinating in his fever, that he must have fallen into a coma so deep they mistook it for death; but the servant produced the cord, and in the face of that evidence she had to admit her guilt.

'Yes, we did it,' she sobbed, 'but please, father – show some mercy!'

'Don't speak to me of mercy,' said the king. 'Your husband was ready to die in the grave with you, and he gave you back your life, but you killed him in his sleep. You'll get the punishment you deserve.'

And she and the captain were put on board a ship with holes drilled in the hull, and sent out over the stormy sea. Soon they sank with the ship, and were never seen again.

* * *

Tale type: ATU 612, 'The Three Snake Leaves'
Source: stories told to the Grimm brothers by Johann Friedrich Krause and the von Haxthausen family
Similar stories: Italo Calvino: 'The Captain and the General', 'The Lion's Grass' (*Italian Folktales*)

A vivid and intriguing tale, which falls into two halves, the first half being magic and the second romantic/realistic. The version in Grimm ties both halves together skilfully by means of the leaves in the title. I haven't altered it apart from the business of the young man's murder. In the original he's just thrown over the side of the ship, but in the two similar tales in Calvino the hero is executed, by firing squad in the first case and on the gallows in the second, and is thus incontrovertibly dead before being brought back to life by means of the magic leaves. I thought that the young man in this story ought to be unmistakably and dramatically killed too, hence the strangling, which also allows the servant to prove the wife's guilt by producing the cord.

But into how many pieces is the snake cut? This vital question seems to have foxed everyone, including the Grimms themselves. The text has unequivocally '*und hieb sie in drei Stücke*' – 'and cut it into three pieces' – and David Luke, Ralph Mannheim and Jack Zipes all leave that as it is in their translations of the story. Yet to do that would only take two blows of the young man's sword, and consequently there would be only two places to put the leaves, not three. We need to look at what's essential, and what's essential is the number three (the three leaves, the princess's eyes and mouth, the classic fairy-tale 'three'), so there need to be three places for the second snake to put the leaves, hence there need to be three blows of the sword, which would cut the snake not into three but into four. But to say that introduces the idea of *four* unhelpfully into the reader's or listener's mind. I think the best solution is what I've done above.

ELEVEN

THE FISHERMAN AND HIS WIFE

Once upon a time there were a fisherman and his wife who lived together in a shack that was so filthy it might as well have been a pisspot. Every day the fisherman went out to fish, and he fished and he fished. One day he sat there looking down into the clear water, and he sat, and he sat, and his line went all the way down to the bottom of the sea. And when he pulled it out, there was a great big flounder on the hook.

The flounder said, 'Now look, fisherman – what about letting me live, eh? I'm no ordinary flounder. I'm an enchanted prince. What good would it do you to kill me? I wouldn't taste nice at all. Put me back in the water, there's a good fellow.'

'Fair enough,' said the fisherman. 'Say no more. The word of a talking fish is good enough for me.'

And he put the flounder back in the water, and down it swam to the bottom, leaving a long trail of blood behind it.

Then the fisherman went back to his wife in their filthy shack.

'Didn't you catch anything today?' she said.

'Oh, yes,' he said. 'I caught a flounder. A great big 'un. But he told me he was an enchanted prince, so I let him go.'

'Typical!' said the wife. 'Why didn't you ask him for something?'

'I dunno,' said the fisherman. 'What should I have asked for?'

'Those enchanted princes can do anything,' said the wife. 'And look at this shack. It stinks, the rain comes in, the shelves keep falling off the walls; it's a terrible place to live. Go back and call that flounder up and tell him we want a nice cottage, all clean and neat. Go on.'

The fisherman didn't really feel like doing that, but on the other hand he knew what would happen if he didn't do what his wife wanted, so back he went to the seashore. When he got there the water wasn't clear any more, but dark green and murky yellow.

He stood on the shore and said:

'Flounder, flounder, in the sea,
Listen up and come to me.
My wife, the lovely Ilsebill,
Has sent me here to do her will.'

The flounder came up and said, 'Well, what does she want?'

'Oh, there you are. Well, it's not my idea, you understand, but what she says is I should have asked you to grant a wish. And she told me what to wish for. She says she's tired of living in a shack like a pisspot, and she wants to live in a cottage.'

'Go home,' said the flounder. 'She's got her wish already.'

The fisherman went home, and there was his wife standing in front of a neat little cottage.

'There!' she said. 'Isn't that better?'

There was a little garden at the front, and a pretty little parlour, and a bedroom with a proper feather bed, and a kitchen, and a pantry. All the rooms were furnished beautifully and the tin bowls and the copper saucepans were polished so bright they sparkled. Outside at the back there was a little yard and a pond with chickens and ducks, and a garden with vegetables and fruit trees.

'Well, what did I tell you?' said the wife.

'Oh, yes,' said the fisherman. 'This is very nice. We can live here all right.'

'We'll see,' said his wife.

Then they had supper and went to bed.

Everything was fine for a week or two. Then the wife said, 'Listen to me. This cottage is too small. I can barely turn around in the kitchen, and as for the garden, half a dozen steps and you've reached the other side. It's not good enough. That flounder could have given us a bigger place if he'd wanted to, it's all the same to him. I want to live in a palace all made of marble. Go back and ask him for a palace.'

'Oh, wife,' said the man, 'this is good enough for us. We don't want a palace. What would we do in a palace?'

'Plenty of things,' said his wife. 'You're a defeatist, that's what you are. Go on, go and ask for a palace.'

'Oh, dear, I don't know . . . He's just given us the cottage. I don't want to bother him again. He might get angry with me.'

'Don't be so feeble. He can do it. He won't mind a bit. Go on.'

The fisherman felt bad about it. He didn't want to go at all. 'It's not right,' he said to himself, but he went anyway.

When he got to the shore the water had changed colour again. Now it was dark blue and purple and grey. He stood at the water's edge and said:

'Flounder, flounder, in the sea,
Listen up and come to me.
My wife, the gracious Ilsebill,
Has sent me here to do her will.'

'What does she want this time?' said the flounder.

'Well, you see, she says the cottage is a bit small. She'd like to live in a palace.'

'Go home. She's already standing in front of the door.'

The fisherman set off home, and when he arrived, there was no cottage any more but a great palace all made of marble. His wife was standing at the top of the steps, about to open the door.

'Come on!' she said. 'Don't drag your feet! Come and have a look!'

He went in with her. The first room was a great hall with a black-and-white stone floor. There were large doors in every wall, and beside each door was a servant who bowed and flung it open. They could see rooms in every direction, and all the walls were painted white and covered with beautiful tapestries. The chairs and tables in every room were made of pure gold, and a crystal chandelier hung from every ceiling with a thousand diamonds twinkling in each one. The carpets were so deep the fishermen and his wife found their feet sinking to the ankles, and in the dining room was spread a feast so enormous that the tables had had to be reinforced with oak struts to stop them collapsing. Outside the palace there was a large courtyard covered in pure white gravel, each stone individually polished, and there stood a row of scarlet carriages of every size with white horses to pull each one, and as the fisherman and his wife came out, all the horses bowed their heads and dropped a curtsey. Beyond the courtyard was a garden of indescribable loveliness, with flowers whose scent perfumed the air for miles around, and fruit trees laden with apples and pears and oranges and lemons, and beyond the garden was a park half a mile long at least, with elk and deer and hares and every kind of decorative wild beast.

'Isn't this nice?' said the wife.

'Oh, yes,' said the fisherman. 'This is plenty good enough for me. We can live here and want for nothing.'

'We'll see,' said the wife. 'Let's sleep on it and see how we feel in the morning.'

Next morning the wife woke up first. The sun was just rising, and as she sat up in bed she could see the garden and the parkland and the mountains beyond. Her husband was snoring happily beside her, but she poked him in the ribs and said, 'Husband! Get up. Come on, I want you to look out of the window.'

He yawned and stretched and dragged himself to the window. 'What is it?' he said.

'Well, we have the garden. That's all very well. And we have the parkland. That's very fine and large. But look beyond! Mountains! I want to be king, so we can have the mountains as well.'

'Oh, wife,' said the fisherman, 'I don't want to be king. Why would we want to be king? We haven't seen all the rooms of this palace yet.'

'That's your trouble,' she told him, 'no ambition. Even if *you* don't want to be king, *I* want to be king.'

'Oh, wife, I can't ask him that. He's been so generous already. I can't tell him you want to be king.'

'Yes, you can. Be off with you.'

'*Ohhh*,' sighed the fisherman. Off he went, heavy-hearted. The fish won't like it, he thought, but he went anyway.

When he got to the shore the water was dark grey, and waves were heaving themselves up from the depths with a horrible smell.

The fisherman said:

'Flounder, flounder, in the sea,
Listen up and come to me.
My wife, the gentle Ilsebill,
Has sent me here to do her will.'

'Well?' said the flounder.

'I'm sorry, but she wants to be king.'

'Go home. She's king already.'

So back he went. When he arrived at the palace it had become twice as large as before, and a tall tower stood over the entrance with a scarlet flag flying from the top. Sentries stood guarding the doors, and when the fisherman cautiously walked up to it they saluted him with such a crash of rifles he nearly jumped out of his shoes. Drummers beat their drums and trumpeters blew a fanfare and the great doors flew open.

He tiptoed inside and found that everything had been gilded, and was twice as big as before. Every cushion was covered in crimson velvet with gold embroidery. Golden tassels hung on everything that had a handle, every wall was hung with gold-framed portraits of the fisherman and his wife dressed as Roman emperors or kings and queens or gods and goddesses, and all the clocks chimed in welcome as he passed. Then a huge pair of doors flew open, and there was the whole court waiting to receive him.

A major-domo bellowed: 'His Majesty the Fisherman!'

He went in, and hundreds of lords and ladies bowed low, and parted to let him walk up to the throne. And sitting on the throne, there was his wife wearing a robe of silk all covered in pearls and sapphires and emeralds. She had a golden crown on her head, and she was holding a sceptre made of gold and studded with rubies each at least the size of the fisherman's big toe. On either side of the throne stood a line of ladies-in-waiting, each one a head shorter than the next, who all curtseyed as he approached.

'Well, wife,' said the fisherman, 'are you king now?'

'Yes, I'm king now,' she said.

'I'm glad to hear it,' he said. 'That's very nice. Now we don't have to do any more wishing.'

'H'mm,' she said, tapping her fingers on the arm of the throne. 'I'm not sure about that. I've been king so long I'm getting bored. Go back to the flounder and tell him that I want to be emperor.'

'Oh, wife, think about it,' said the fisherman. 'He can't make you emperor. There's already an emperor, and there can only be one at a time.'

'Don't you dare speak to me like that! I'm the king, don't you forget! You do as you're told and go and talk to that flounder. If he can make me king, he can make me emperor. It's all the same to him. Go on, go!'

So off he went, but he was very uneasy. This isn't going to end well, he thought; the flounder will get fed up with all this wishing.

When he arrived at the seashore the water was black and dense and boiling up from the depths. A strong wind whipped the waves into foam. The fishermen stood there and said:

'Flounder, flounder, in the sea,
Listen up and come to me.
My wife, the dainty Ilsebill,
Has sent me here to do her will.'

'Well, tell me,' said the flounder.

'She wants to be emperor.'

'Go home. She's already emperor.'

So he went home again, and this time he found that the palace was even higher than before, with turrets at every corner, a row of cannons in front of it, and an entire regiment of soldiers marching up and down in scarlet uniforms. As soon as they saw him they stood to attention and saluted, and the cannons fired a volley that made his ears ache. The gate flew open and in he went, to discover that the entire inside of the building had been gilded, and that alabaster statues of himself and his wife in heroic postures stood along the walls. Everywhere he went, dukes or princes hastened to hold open the doors and bow low. In the throne room he found his wife sitting on a throne made of one piece of solid gold two miles high, and he could only see her because she was wearing a crown that was three yards high and two yards across. That was solid gold as well, set with carbuncles and emeralds. In one hand she held a sceptre and in the other, the imperial orb. Two rows of soldiers formed her personal guard, each one smaller than the next, ranging from giants as tall as the throne to little men no bigger than my finger, and all bristling with weapons. Princes, dukes, counts and earls and barons all waited in attendance.

The fishermen went to the foot of the throne and called up: 'Wife, are you emperor now?'

'What does it look like?'

'Very impressive. I expect you'll stop wishing at last.'

'That's you all over. Poverty of aspiration. This isn't good enough, let me tell you.'

'Oh, wife, not again!'

'Go back to the flounder. Tell him I want to be pope.'

'But you can't be pope! There's only one pope in the whole of Christendom!'

'I'm the emperor,' she shrieked, 'and I'm telling you: go back to the flounder and order him to make me pope.'

'No, no, that's too much. Come on. I can't do that.'

'Nonsense! I order you to go to the flounder! Now go!'

The fisherman was frightened now. He felt sick, and his knees were trembling, and the wind was blowing wildly and tearing leaves from the trees. Darkness was falling. When he got to the shore, the waves were roaring and crashing on to the rocks with explosions like cannon fire. Out at sea he could see ships firing distress rockets as they tossed and weltered in the waves. There was one little bit of blue left in the sky, but it was surrounded by blood-red clouds and flashes of lightning.

In despair the fisherman cried:

'Flounder, flounder, in the sea,
Listen up and come to me.
My wife, the tender Ilsebill,
Has sent me here to do her will.'

'Well, what does she want?'

'She wants to be pope.'

'Go home. She's pope already.'

When he got home he found an immense church where the castle used to be. It was surrounded by palaces of every size and shape, but the church spire was higher than any of them. A vast crowd of people surged around trying to get in through the doors, but the crowd inside was even thicker, so the fisherman had to push and shove and struggle to get through. The church was illuminated by thousands and thousands of candles, and in every niche stood a box where a priest was busy hearing confessions. In the very centre was a vast golden throne, on which sat his wife, with three crowns on her head, one on top of another, and scarlet slippers on her feet. A row of bishops waited in line to crawl along the floor and kiss her right slipper, and an equally long line of abbots waited to crawl along and kiss the left. On her right hand she had a ring as big as a cockerel, and on her left a ring as big as a goose, and a long line of cardinals waited to kiss the right ring and a long line of archbishops to kiss the left.

The fisherman called up: 'Wife, are you pope now?'

'What does it look like?'

'I've never seen a pope. I don't know. Are you happy at last?'

She sat completely still and said nothing. All the kisses being showered on her hands and feet sounded like a lot of sparrows pecking at the dirt. The fisherman thought she hadn't heard him, so he shouted up again: 'Wife, are you happy yet?'

'I don't know. I'm not sure. I'll have to think about it.'

They both went to bed, and the fisherman slept well, because he'd had a busy day. But his wife tossed and turned all night. She couldn't decide if she was satisfied or not, and she couldn't think what else to be after pope, so she had a poor night of it.

Finally the sun rose, and when she saw the light she sat up in bed at once.

'I've got it!' she said. 'Husband, wake up. Come on! Wake up!'

She dug him in the ribs till he groaned and opened his eyes.

'What is it? What do you want?'

'Go back to the flounder at once. I want to be God!'

That made him sit up. 'What?'

'I want to be God. I want to cause the sun and the moon to rise. I can't bear it when I see them rising and I haven't had anything to do with it. But if I were God, I could make it all happen. I could make them go backwards if I wanted. So go and tell the flounder I want to be God.'

He rubbed his eyes and looked at her, but she looked so crazy that he was scared, and got out of bed quickly.

'Now!' she screamed. 'Go!'

'Oh, please, wife,' begged the poor man, falling to his knees, 'think again, my love, think again. The flounder made you emperor and he made you pope, but he can't make you God. That's really impossible.'

She flew out of bed and hit him, her hair sticking out wildly from her head, her eyes rolling. She tore off her nightdress and screamed and stamped, shouting, 'I can't bear it to wait so long! You're driving me insane! Go and do as I tell you right now!'

The fisherman tugged on his trousers, hopping out of the bedroom, and ran to the seashore. There was such a storm raging that he could hardly stand up against it. Rain lashed his face, trees were being torn up from the ground, houses were tumbled in every direction as great boulders came flying through the air, torn off the cliffs. The thunder crashed and the lightning flared, and the waves on the sea were as high as churches and castles and mountains, with sheets of foam flying from their crests.

'Flounder, flounder, in the sea,
Listen up and come to me.
My wife, the modest Ilsebill,
Has sent me here to do her will.'

'What does she want?'

'Well, you see, she wants to be God.'

'Go home. She's back in the pisspot.'

And so she was, and there they are to this day.

Tale type: ATU 555, 'The Fisherman and His Wife'
Source: a story written by Philipp Otto Runge
Similar stories: Alexander Afanasyev: 'The Goldfish' (*Russian Fairy Tales*); Italo Calvino: 'The Dragon with Seven Heads' (*Italian Folktales*); Jacob and Wilhelm Grimm: 'The Golden Children' (*Children's and Household Tales*)

A popular and widespread tale. The Calvino story, 'The Dragon with Seven Heads', shows how a very different story can be unfolded from a very similar beginning.

This version is full of energy and inventive detail. Like 'The Juniper Tree' (p. 187), it comes from the pen of the Romantic painter Philipp Otto Runge (1777–1810), and was written in Plattdeutsch, or Low German, the dialect of his native Pomerania:

> Dar wöör maal eens en Fischer un syne Fru, de waanden tosamen in'n Pißputt, dicht an der See . . .

It came to the Grimms with the help of Clemens Brentano and Achim von Arnim, writers who shared their growing interest in folk tales. On the evidence of these two stories, Runge was at least as gifted with the pen as with the brush. The climax builds with brilliant speed and effect, the gathering storm functioning as a celestial comment on the wife's growing obsession.

Most translators have rendered *Pißputt* as 'pigsty' or some other such term. I couldn't find anything better than 'pisspot'.

TWELVE

THE BRAVE LITTLE TAILOR

One sunny morning a little tailor was sitting cross-legged on his table, as usual, next to the window on the top floor overlooking the street. He was in high spirits, sewing away with all his might, when along the street came an old woman selling jam.

'Fine jam for sale! Buy my sweet jam!'

The little tailor liked the sound of that, so he called down: 'Bring it up here, love! Let's have a look!'

The old woman lugged her basket all the way up three flights of stairs. When she got there the tailor made her unpack every single jar, and examined each one closely, weighing it in his hand, holding it up to the light, sniffing the jam, and so forth. Finally he said, 'This looks like a good 'un, this jar of strawberry. Weigh me out three ounces of that, my good woman, and if it comes to a quarter of a pound, so much the better.'

'Don't you want the whole pot?'

'Good Lord, no. I can only afford a small amount.'

She weighed it out, grumbling, and went her way.

'Well, God bless this jam, and may it give health and strength to all who eat it!' said the tailor, and fetched a loaf of bread and a knife. He cut himself a hearty slice and spread it with jam.

'That'll taste good,' he said, 'but I'll finish this jacket before I tuck in.'

He sprang on to the table again and took up the needle, sewing faster and faster. Meanwhile the sweet scent of the jam rose in the air, and floated round the room, and drifted out of the window. A squadron of flies who had been feasting on the corpse of a dog in the street outside caught the scent, and rose at once and flew up to look for it. They came in through the window and settled on the bread.

'Hey! Who invited you?' said the little tailor, and flapped his hand to drive them away. But they didn't understand a word, and besides they were already busy with the jam, and they took no notice.

Finally the tailor lost his temper. 'All right, you've asked for it now!' he said, and he snatched up a piece of cloth and set about them furiously. When he drew breath and stood back, there were no fewer than seven of them lying dead with their legs in the air.

'Well, what a hero I am!' he said. 'I'd better let the town know about this right away.'

He seized his scissors and quickly cut out a sash of crimson silk, and sewed on it in big letters of gold: 'SEVEN WITH ONE BLOW!'

He put it on and looked in the mirror.

'The town?' he thought. 'The whole world must know about this!'

And his heart skipped for joy like a lamb's tail wagging. Before he set off to show the world, he looked around for something to take with him, but he could find only a bowl of cream cheese. He scooped that up and put it in his pocket, and ran downstairs and off through the streets. Outside the town gate he found a bird caught in a bush, and he put that in his pocket too. Then off he marched to see the world.

He was light and agile, so he didn't tire easily. He followed the road all the way to the top of a mountain, and there he found a giant sitting on a rock taking his ease and admiring the view.

The little tailor marched up to him and said, 'Good morning, friend! Are you out to see the world? That's what I'm up to. How about joining forces and going along together?'

The giant looked at the little fellow with deep scorn. 'You, you pipsqueak! You, you runt! Join forces with an insect like you?'

'Oh, is that what you think?' said the tailor, and unbuttoned his coat to show his sash. 'This'll show you the kind of man I am.'

The giant carefully spelt it out letter by letter: 'SEVEN WITH ONE BLOW!' And then his eyes opened wide.

'Respect!' he said. But he felt he still ought to test this fellow, so he went on: 'You may have killed seven men with one blow, but that's no great feat, if they were all little mice like you. Let's see how strong you are. Can you do this?'

And he picked up a stone and squeezed it until his hand was trembling and his face was bright red and the veins were standing out on his head. He squeezed the stone so hard that he even managed to squeeze a few drops of water out of it.

'Let's see you do that, if you have the strength!' he said.

'Is that all?' said the little tailor. 'Nothing to it. Watch this.'

And he took the cream cheese out of his pocket and squeezed that. Of course the cheese was full of whey, and it was soon dripping down all over the tailor's hand and on to the ground.

'That was better than your effort,' he said.

The giant scratched his head. 'Well,' he said. 'Umm. All right then. Try this.'

He picked up another stone and threw it as high as he could. The stone went so high that it almost disappeared.

'Not bad,' said the little tailor, 'but look, here it comes down again. I can do better than that.'

He took the bird out of his pocket and threw it up into the air, and as soon as the bird felt its freedom, it flew upwards and vanished.

'When I throw something into the air, it never comes down,' he said. 'What d'you think of that, my extra-large friend?'

'Umm,' said the giant. 'Well, you can squeeze and you can throw. But here comes the real test: let's see what you can carry.'

He led the little tailor to the edge of the forest, where a great oak tree had just been cut down.

'Help me carry this,' the giant said.

'With pleasure. You take the trunk and I'll carry the leaves and the twigs, which are heavier anyway, as everyone knows.'

The giant bent down and held his breath and then hoisted the trunk on to his shoulder. Seeing that the giant couldn't look behind, the little tailor jumped up and sat himself comfortably among the leaves, whistling 'Three Tailors Bold Rode Out One Day', while the giant staggered along the path carrying the whole weight of the tree on his shoulder.

The giant couldn't go very far, because it was a huge tree, and pretty soon he came to a stop.

'Hey, listen! I can't go any further,' he called out, and the tailor jumped down quickly before he could turn round, and took hold of a bunch of leaves and twigs with both arms, as if he'd just been carrying them.

'A big fellow like you,' he said, 'and you can't even manage half a tree? Dear oh dear, you need some exercise.'

They walked on a little way until they came to a cherry tree. The giant took hold of the topmost branches and pulled them down low, showing the tailor the ripest fruit.

'Just hold on to this for a moment while I take a stone out of my shoe,' he said, and the tailor took hold of the branch. When the giant let go, the branch shot back up, and the tailor, not being heavy enough to hold it down, was whisked up into the air.

But he was agile, and he was lucky enough to fall on a grassy bank where he could tumble down without hurting himself. He even managed to turn a neat somersault and end up on his feet.

'Not strong enough to hold it down!' said the giant. 'Ha!'

'Not at all,' said the tailor. 'A man who's killed seven with one blow can hold any number of trees down. The fact is that those hunters over there were about to shoot into the thicket, and I thought I'd better get out of the way. I bet you can't jump as high as I did. Have a try, go on.'

The giant took a run-up and tried, but he had a lot of weight to get off the ground, and he crashed into the top of the cherry tree and ended up tangled in the branches. So the little tailor won that contest too.

'Well,' said the giant, when he had clambered down to the ground again, 'if you think you're such a hero, come and spend the night in our cave. I live with a couple of other giants, and we're not easily impressed, I can tell you.'

The tailor agreed with pleasure, and they set off for the cave. It was dark when they got there, and the two other giants were sitting next to a blazing fire. Each of them had a whole roast sheep in his hands, and was gnawing at it vigorously, with horrible grinding sucking noises.

The little tailor looked around. 'It's a lot bigger than my workshop,' he said. 'Where am I going to sleep?'

His giant showed him a gigantic bed. The tailor climbed up and lay down, but he couldn't get comfortable, so while the giants were mumbling together by the fire he climbed down and tucked himself up in a corner of the cave.

At midnight the first giant, thinking that the little tailor was asleep, took a massive club and with one blow smashed the bed in half.

'That'll squash that grasshopper,' he thought.

Early next morning the giants woke up and lumbered off into the woods. They'd completely forgotten about the little tailor. But he'd woken up bright and cheerful, and he came skipping after them, whistling and singing, and when they saw him they were struck with terror.

'He's alive!'

'Help!'

'Run for your life!'

And off they ran.

'Well, so much for giants,' said the tailor to himself. 'Let's go and look for another adventure.'

Following his nose, he wandered here and there for several days, until he came to a splendid palace. Flags were flying, soldiers were changing guard, and the tailor sat down on a grassy bank to admire it all. Feeling sleepy, he lay down and closed his eyes, and in a moment he was fast asleep.

While he slept, several passers-by caught sight of his crimson sash with the gold letters saying: 'SEVEN WITH ONE BLOW!' And they started talking:

'He must be a great hero!'

'But what's he doing here?'

'This is a time of peace, after all.'

'I'm sure he's a duke or something. Look at the nobility in his face.'

'No, I reckon he's a man of the people, but he's certainly seen combat. You can see his proud military bearing, even in his sleep.'

'*Seven with one blow* – imagine!'

'We'd better tell the king.'

'That's a good idea. Let's go right away!'

A group of them immediately sought an audience with the king, who listened with close attention. If the worst should happen and war were to break out, they said, at all costs they should try and obtain the services of this hero.

'You're absolutely right,' said the king, and called for the chief of the defence staff. 'Go and wait till that gentleman wakes up,' the king told him, 'and offer him the post of field marshal. We can't afford to let any other kingdom get his services.'

The chief of the defence staff went and waited by the little tailor until he woke up.

'His majesty would like to offer you the post of field marshal,' he said, 'with immediate command over the whole army.'

'That's exactly why I'm here!' said the little tailor. 'I'm ready and willing to enter the service of the king, and all my valour is at his disposal.'

A guard of honour was formed, and the little tailor was received with great ceremonial, and given his own apartment in the palace. He was also allowed to design his own uniform.

However, the soldiers he was going to command were very doubtful about the whole thing.

'Suppose he takes a dislike to us?'

'Or suppose he gives us commands we don't like, and we try and argue with him?'

'Yes! He can kill seven of us with one blow. We're just ordinary soldiers. We can't fight against someone like that.'

They talked about it in the barracks, and sent a delegation to the king.

'Your majesty, we ask to be released from your service! We can't stand up to a man who can kill seven of us with one blow. He's a weapon of mass destruction!'

'Let me think about it,' said the king.

He was dismayed by the situation. To lose all his faithful soldiers just because of one man! But if he tried to get rid of the little tailor, who knew what would happen? The tailor might kill him and all the army, and then set himself up on the throne.

He thought long and hard about it, and finally had an idea. He sent for the little tailor and said: 'Field marshal, I have a task that only you can perform. A great hero like you won't refuse, I'm sure. In one of my forests there's a pair of giants who are running riot through all the countryside, robbing, murdering, plundering, burning houses, and I don't know what else. No one dares go near them for fear of their life. Now if you can get rid of these giants, I'll give you my daughter in marriage, and half the kingdom besides for a dowry. And you can have a hundred horsemen to back you up.'

'That's the sort of offer I've been waiting for,' thought the little tailor. 'Your majesty, I accept the task with pleasure!' he said. 'I know how to deal with giants. But I don't need the horsemen. Anyone who has killed seven with one blow doesn't need to be afraid of two.'

So he set off, and he let the hundred horsemen come too, just for the sake of display. When they came to the edge of the forest, he said to them, 'You wait here. I'll deal with the giants, and when it's safe to come in, I'll call you.'

The little tailor marched boldly into the forest, looking this way and that. He soon found the giants. They were both asleep under an oak tree, snoring so hard that they blew the branches up and down. The tailor didn't waste a moment. He filled his pockets with stones, climbed the tree and clambered out on to a branch till he was directly above the giants.

Then he dropped one stone after another on to the chest of one of the sleepers. The giant didn't feel anything at first, but at last he woke up and clouted his companion.

'What d'you think you're doing, throwing stones at me?'

'I'm not throwing stones!' said the other giant. 'You're dreaming.'

They fell asleep again, and the tailor started throwing stones at the second giant, who woke up and thumped the first one.

'Oy! Stop doing that!'

'I'm not doing anything! What are you talking about?'

They grumbled a bit, but they were tired after all their plundering and pillaging, and they soon fell asleep again. So the little tailor chose his largest stone, and took careful aim, and hit the first giant right on the nose.

He woke with a roar. 'That's too much!' he shouted. 'I'm not putting up with this a moment longer!'

And he shoved the other giant so hard against the tree that it shook. The little tailor clung on tight so as not to fall off, and then he watched as the two giants set about each other in earnest. They thumped and bashed and kicked and walloped, and finally they were so angry that they both pulled up trees and hit each other with them so hard that they both fell dead at the same moment.

The little tailor jumped down. 'Good thing they didn't pull this tree up,' he thought. 'I'd have had to skip out like a squirrel. But my family have always been light on their feet.'

He drew his sword and gave each giant a good few slices around the chest, and then he went back to the horsemen waiting outside.

'It's all done,' he said. 'I finished them both off. It was hot work for a minute or so, because they pulled up trees to try and defend themselves, but it didn't do them any good. I can kill seven with one blow.'

'You're not hurt?'

'No, not a scratch. Well, my jacket's a bit torn – see that. Go and have a look at the giants' bodies if you don't believe me.'

The horsemen rode in, and found the two giants just as he'd said, lying in their own blood with uprooted trees all around them.

So the little tailor went back to the king, expecting the reward. But the king had had time to think about it, and he regretted promising his daughter to this man, who might be dangerous, after all.

'Before I give you my daughter and half my kingdom,' he said, 'there's another task that calls for a hero. In the woods there's a frightful rhinoceros that's causing all sorts of damage, and I want you to capture it.'

'Nothing to it, your majesty,' said the little tailor. 'One rhinoceros is even less trouble than two giants.'

He took an axe and a coil of rope, and marched off to the woods, once again telling the regiment that had come with him to wait behind. It didn't take him long to find the rhinoceros. It came charging towards him with its horn out in front as if it wanted to spear him through, but he just stood quite still until the beast was only a yard or so away, and then he skipped aside. Right behind him was a tree. The rhinoceros ran straight into it, and its horn stuck fast.

'Well, my pretty little beast,' said the tailor, 'you're caught now, aren't you?'

He tied the rope around its neck and then chopped away at the tree with the axe until the horn came free again. The rhinoceros was quite docile by this time, and it let him lead it tamely out of the woods.

He took it into the palace and presented it to the king.

'Ah,' said the king. 'Well. H'mm. There is just one more thing. Before you marry my daughter I'd like you to capture a wild boar that's digging up a lot of orchards and farms and things. I'll send the huntsmen along to help.'

'Oh, I won't need any huntsmen,' said the little tailor, which pleased the huntsmen, because they'd come across the boar a good few times and had no wish to do so again. They came with him, however, for the sake of show, and stayed outside the woods playing dice until he was ready to lead them back again.

There was a little chapel in the woods. The tailor went there and waited till the boar came near, knowing it would catch his scent and charge. Soon the great beast came smashing its way through the undergrowth and charged right at him, foaming at the mouth and gnashing its razor-sharp tusks. As soon as he saw it, the tailor ran into the chapel, and of course the boar charged in after him.

But the tailor jumped out of the window and ran round to shut the door before the boar could work out where he'd gone. And there it was, caught. The huntsmen gave him a round of applause and blew their horns as they accompanied him back to the palace.

The hero went and told the king, who had to keep his promise at last, whether he wanted to or not. So the wedding was arranged with great splendour but little joy, and the tailor became a king.

A little while later the young queen heard her husband call out in the night: 'Boy! Hurry up with that jacket, and patch the trousers, or I'll clout you round the ears with a yardstick.'

Next morning she went to her father. 'Daddy,' she said, 'I think my husband's nothing but a common tailor,' and she told him what she'd heard the tailor call out in his dream.

'D'you know, I suspected something of the sort,' said the king. 'This is what we'll do. Leave your bedroom door unlocked tonight, and my servants will wait outside. As soon as he falls asleep, you tiptoe out and tell them, and they'll come in and tie him up and put him on a ship that'll take him all the way to China.'

That sounded like a good plan to the young queen. However, the king's little sword-bearer, who greatly admired the tailor, had heard everything, and he ran to tell the tailor the whole plot.

'I'll deal with that,' said the tailor. 'You leave it to me.'

That night he went to bed at the usual time, and when his wife thought he was asleep, she tiptoed to the door. But the tailor, who was only pretending to be asleep, called out in a loud voice: 'Boy! Make that jacket, and hurry up and patch the trousers, or I'll crack the yardstick around your ears! I've slaughtered seven with one blow, killed two giants, tamed a wild rhinoceros, and captured the wild boar, and I'm supposed to be afraid of a few quivering servants standing outside the bedroom!'

When the servants heard that, they were so terrified that they turned and ran as if the Wild Hunt was after them. None of them ever dared to go near him again.

So the little tailor was a king, and he stayed a king for the rest of his days.

* * *

Tale type: ATU 1640, 'The Brave Little Tailor'
Source: a story in Martinus Montanus's *Wegkürtzer* (*c.*1557)
Similar stories: Alexander Afanasyev: 'Foma Berennikov', 'Ivan the Simpleton' (*Russian Fairy Tales*); Katharine M. Briggs: 'John Glaick, the Brave Tailor' (*Folk Tales of Britain*); Italo Calvino: 'Jack Strong, Slayer of Five Hundred', 'John Balento' (*Italian Folktales*)

A popular story, with cousins in many languages. The small, nimble, quick-witted character is always the audience's favourite when pitted against the big blundering giant: David and Goliath are the best-known example. This version of the Grimms' is one of the liveliest.

'Nine tailors make a man', says the proverb, but it's not easy to see why.

THIRTEEN

CINDERELLA

There was once a rich man whose wife became ill. When she felt she was near to death, she called her only daughter to her bedside.

'My dear child,' she said, 'be as good as gold and as meek as a lamb, and then the blessed Lord will always protect you. What's more I shall look down from heaven myself and be close to you.'

When she had said these words, she closed her eyes and died.

Every day the girl went to her mother's grave near the dovecote and wept, and she was as good as gold and as meek as a lamb. When winter came the snow lay like a white cloth over the grave; and when the spring sun came and took the snow away, the man married another wife.

His new wife had two daughters. They were beautiful, but they had hard, selfish, arrogant hearts. After the wedding all three moved into the house, and then things began to go badly for the poor stepdaughter.

'Why should that stupid goose sit in the parlour with us?' the sisters would say. 'If she wants to eat bread, she must earn it. The kitchen's the place for her.'

They took away the beautiful clothes her mother had made for her and gave her a shabby grey dress and wooden shoes.

'Look at Princess Perfect now! Dressed to kill!' they jeered as they led her to the kitchen.

She was made to work like a slave from morning till night. She had to get up at daybreak, carry water from the well, clean the fireplaces and make the fires, cook all the food and wash all the dishes. But that wasn't all, because the sisters did everything they could to make things worse for the poor girl. They mocked her, they made fun of her to their silly friends, and they had a special torment that never failed to amuse them: they would scatter dried peas or lentils in among the ashes, so she had to sit on the floor and pick them all out again. And when she was worn out at the end of the day, could she look forward to a comfortable bed? Not a bit of it. She had to sleep on the hearth, in among the ashes and the cinders. And she never had a chance to wash and clean herself, so she always looked dusty and grubby.

Because of that, they found a special name for her.

'What shall we call her – Ashy-face?'

'Sootybottom?'

'Cinderina?'

'Cinderella – that's it!'

One day their father had to go to the town on business, and he asked his stepdaughters what they'd like him to bring back for them.

'Clothes!' said one. 'Lots of lovely dresses.'

'Jewels for me,' said the other. 'Pearls and rubies and things.'

'And what about you, Cinderella?' he said.

'Father, just bring me back the first branch that brushes against your hat on the way home.'

So he came back from town with beautiful dresses for the one, and costly jewels for the other. And he'd ridden through a thicket on the way home, and a hazel branch had brushed his hat, so he'd broken it off the tree and brought it home for Cinderella.

She thanked him and planted it at once on her mother's grave. Her tears watered it, and it grew into a lovely tree. She tended it three times a day, and it was a favourite of the birds, too, for doves and pigeons used to perch in it.

One day an invitation came from the royal palace. The king was holding a great festival that was to last for three days, and all the young ladies in the kingdom were invited, so that the prince could choose a bride. When the two stepsisters heard about it, they were thrilled, and started getting ready at once.

'Cinderella! Come here. Hurry up, girl! Brush my hair. Don't *pull*! Be *careful*! Now polish the buckles on our shoes. Let my dress out under the arms. Give me that necklace of your mother's. Put my hair up like the girl's in this picture. No, not that tight, you fool,' and so on, and so on.

Cinderella did everything they asked, but she wept, because she would have liked to go to the ball as well. She pleaded with her stepmother.

'*You*? Go to the ball? Who do you think you are? You're a dirty little slattern, that's all you are. And how do you think you're going to manage at a high society ball, with no charm, no looks and no conversation to speak of? Back to the kitchen, child.'

But Cinderella persisted, and her stepmother finally lost her patience, and threw a bowl of lentils into the ashes.

'Pick those out in two hours,' she said, 'and sort them out, good from bad, and you can come to the ball.'

Cinderella went out through the back door and into the garden. She stood under the hazel tree and said:

'Turtledoves and little pigeons,
All the birds beneath the sky,
Help me pick the lentils out
From the ashes where they lie!
All the good ones in the pot,
All the others in your crop.'

Two turtledoves flew down through the door and into the kitchen, and started to pick at the lentils in the ashes. They nodded their heads and went *pick, pick, pick, pick*. And then some wood pigeons came, and laughing doves and collared doves and stock doves and rock doves, and joined them in the ashes, going *pick, pick, pick, pick*. In less than an hour they were finished, and they all flew out of the door and away.

The girl took the bowl to her stepmother, thinking that now she'd be allowed to come to the ball.

'That's no good,' said the woman. 'You've got nothing to wear, and you don't know how to dance. Do you want them all to laugh at you?' And she threw two bowls of lentils into the ashes, and said, 'Sort those out, go on. If you can do it in under an hour you can go to the ball.'

And she thought, 'She'll never manage to do that.'

Cinderella went out through the back door again. She stood under the hazel tree and said:

'Birds of the air, whatever you be,
Come to the shade of the hazel tree!
And in the ashes peck about,
And help me sort the lentils out.
All the good ones in the pot,
All the others in your crop.'

So down flew two white doves, and they flew straight into the kitchen and started, *pick, pick, pick, pick*. Then came a pair of robins, and then a pair of blackbirds, and then a pair of wagtails, and then a pair of song thrushes, and then a pair of mistle thrushes, and then a pair of wrens, and they all went *pick, pick, pick, pick*.

Before half an hour had passed, Cinderella took the bowls to her stepmother. The poor girl was innocent enough to think that this time the woman would say yes.

'It's no use,' her stepmother said. 'You haven't got any shoes worth being seen in. Do you think you can come to a ball wearing a pair of wooden clogs? What sort of a simpleton will people think you are? We'd be ashamed to be seen in your company.'

And off she went with her two daughters, leaving Cinderella on her own.

First she washed herself from head to toe and brushed her hair till not a speck of ash and soot remained. Then she went out of the back door and whispered to the hazel tree:

'Hazel tree, be kind to me!
Shake your leaves and set me free!
I'm very poor, and I confess
I'd love to wear a pretty dress.'

'What colour?' whispered the leaves.

'Oh! I'd like a dress the colour of starlight.'

There was a little shake among the leaves, and there hanging on the lowest branch, just beside her, was a beautiful ball gown the colour of starlight, together with a pair of silken slippers.

'Thank you!' Cinderella said, and ran inside to put them on.

They fitted perfectly. She had no mirror, so she couldn't see how lovely she looked, and when she arrived at the ball she was surprised to find how well she was treated, how everyone made way for her, how the ladies invited her to sit and take tea with them, how the lords asked her to dance. Not many people had ever been nice to her, and she was a stranger to the feeling of being popular and sought after.

She wouldn't dance with any of the lords, though, young or old, rich or handsome. Only when the prince himself bowed and asked her did she stand up and take to the dance floor. She danced so lightly and so gracefully that everyone else had to stop and look at her, even her two sisters. They didn't recognize her at all, thinking that Cinderella was at home among the ashes, and this lovely stranger was a princess from a foreign land. In fact her beauty had a strange effect on them, for it banished all the envy from their hard little hearts for a time, and made them honestly admire her.

But Cinderella didn't stay long. Once she'd danced with the prince, and he'd got her to promise to dance with no one but him, she took advantage of an interval in the music to slip outside and run back home.

The prince followed her, but she ran so fast he couldn't keep up, and when they reached home, she'd vanished. The prince waited, and her father appeared.

'Have you seen the mysterious princess?' the prince asked him. 'I think she went into your dovecote.'

Her father thought, 'Could that be my Cinderella?' and he went and fetched the key of the dovecote, and opened it up. There was no sign of her. The prince had to go back to the ball alone.

Cinderella had slipped out of the back of the dovecote and taken off the starlight-coloured dress and the silken slippers, and put them on their hanger and hung it on the hazel tree. There was a sort of shiver, and they disappeared. Then she lay down in her old clothes by the cold fireplace. When her stepmother and sisters came home, they woke her up to help them out of their corsets, because they could hardly breathe.

'Ooof! That's better,' said one.

'Oh, Cinderella, you should have been there,' said the other.

'What a sensation!' they went on. 'There was a princess from a foreign land, no one knows her name, and the prince wouldn't dance with anyone else. She was so lovely you wouldn't believe it. I can see her still! She had the loveliest dress on, just the colour of starlight. I can't imagine where you could get such a dress! There's no one in this country who could make one like it. Why, Cinderella, you wouldn't believe it, but she made everyone else – even us! – look just a little dowdy.'

Next day they spent even longer getting ready. Cinderella had to brush their wiry hair with a hundred strokes, and lace their corsets even tighter, and polish their shoes till they could see their faces in them.

As soon as they'd gone, she ran outside to the hazel tree and whispered:

'Hazel tree, oh, hazel tree,
Shake your leaves again for me!
Help me out in my distress,
And let me have another dress!'

'What colour?' said the leaves.

'I'd like a dress the colour of moonlight,' she said.

There was a rustle, and there it was on a hanger right next to her, a dress the soft silver colour of moonlight, and a pair of silver slippers.

'Thank you!' she whispered, and ran to put them on, and hastened to the ball.

This time the prince had been waiting for her, and as soon as she appeared he hurried to her side and asked her to dance. When anyone else asked her, he said, 'This lady is my partner in every dance.'

So the evening passed like the one before, except that there was even more excitement and speculation among the lords and ladies. Who could this lovely stranger be? She must be a princess from a great and wealthy kingdom. But no one knew, and no one noticed when she slipped away, except the prince himself. He ran after her through the dark, and followed her as far as her house. In the garden there was a beautiful pear tree, covered in heavy fruit. Cinderella climbed up nimbly and hid among the branches, and the prince had no idea where she'd gone.

When Cinderella's father came home, he found the prince still there.

'I think she climbed that tree,' he said.

The father thought, 'Surely that couldn't be Cinderella?'

He brought an axe and cut down the tree, but there was no one there among the branches. Cinderella had slipped down the other side, taken the moonlight-coloured dress back to the hazel tree, and gone inside to curl up in the ashes as usual.

On the third night everything happened as before. The stepmother and sisters went off to the ball, and Cinderella whispered to the hazel tree:

'Hazel tree, oh, hazel tree,
Send another dress for me!
This is the last night of the ball,
So let it be the best of all!'

'What colour?' rustled the leaves.

'This time I'd like a dress the colour of sunlight,' she said.

And once more the tree shivered, and down fell a dress so lovely that Cinderella hardly dared to touch it. It was pure gold, and it shone and gleamed like the morning sun. And there was a pair of golden slippers to wear with it.

'Thank you!' said Cinderella

At the ball, the prince had eyes for no one else. They danced all evening, and he wouldn't leave her side. When she said it was time to go, he wanted to come with her, but she slipped away before he could stop her. This time, though, he'd laid a trap. He'd told his servants to spread pitch on the stairs, and as she ran down, one of her slippers got stuck and she had to leave it behind.

The prince picked it up and wouldn't let anyone else touch it. He cleaned off the pitch and found that it was pure gold.

In the morning there was a proclamation made throughout the whole kingdom: 'Whoever lost her slipper at the prince's ball may come and claim it from the palace. And the prince will marry whoever it fits!'

Noble ladies and servant girls, peasants and princesses came from all over that kingdom and from many kingdoms besides, but not one of them could put her foot in the slipper. Finally the choice came down to Cinderella's stepsisters. As it happens, their feet were their best feature, being shapely and well formed, and each of them thought she could wear the slipper. But just in case, the mother took the first sister aside and whispered to her: 'If it doesn't fit, take this knife and cut a bit off your heel. It'll only hurt for a bit, and you'll be queen.'

The first sister went into her bedroom to try. She couldn't get her foot in, so she did as her mother said and sliced off a bit of her heel. She jammed her foot in the slipper and limped out, trying to smile.

The prince had to do as he'd said, and he accepted her as his bride and helped her up on to his horse. But as he was riding away, the doves called from the hazel tree:

'Roocoo-coo, roocoo-coo,
There's blood in the shoe!
Her foot's too wide,
This isn't the bride!'

The prince looked down and saw that they were right. Blood was dripping from the slipper. He turned the horse around and went back.

The mother said to the second sister: 'If it doesn't fit, cut off your big toe. It won't hurt much – just a twinge – and you'll marry the prince.'

The second sister did as her mother had said, and the prince set her on his horse and began to ride away. But the doves called again from the hazel tree:

'Roocoo-coo, roocoo-coo,
There's blood in the shoe!
Her foot's too long,
The girl is wrong!'

The prince took her back and said to the father, 'I'm sure

I followed the mystery princess to this house. Haven't you got another daughter?'

'Well, there's only Cinderella,' said her father, 'but surely it can't be her.'

'It can't possibly be her!' said the stepmother. 'We can't let her out, your royal highness. She's much too dirty to be seen.'

'If you have another daughter, I insist on seeing her,' said the prince. 'Bring her out at once.'

So they had to fetch Cinderella from the kitchen. She wouldn't come till she'd washed, and of course they had to rinse out the golden slipper, so the prince had to wait. But finally Cinderella came in and curtseyed, and his heart beat hard in his chest at the sight of her; and she sat down, and he fitted the slipper on her foot, and it slipped on and fitted her perfectly, just like that.

'This is my bride!' he said, and took her in his arms.

The stepmother and sisters turned ghastly pale, and nearly bit their own fingers off with rage and mortification.

The prince set Cinderella on his horse and rode away, and the doves in the hazel tree called:

> *'Roocoo-coo, roocoo-coo,*
> *No blood in the shoe!*
> *It's not too tight,*
> *This bride is right!'*

Then they flew down and landed on Cinderella's shoulders, one on each side, and there they stayed.

At the wedding the two stepsisters were keen to toady to the royal couple, hoping to share in Cinderella's good luck. When the prince and his bride walked into the church, the older sister walked on their right and the younger sister on their left, and the doves flew down and pecked out one eye from each of them. After the ceremony, when they came out of the church, the older one was on the left and the younger on the right, and the doves flew down and pecked out their other eyes.

So for their wickedness and falsity, they were punished with blindness to the end of their days.

* * *

Tale type: ATU 510A, 'Cinderella'
Source: an anonymous storyteller from the Elizabeth Hospital in Marburg, with additional material by Dorothea Viehmann
Similar stories: Giambattista Basile: 'The Cat Cinderella' (*The Great Fairy Tale Tradition*, ed. Jack Zipes); Katharine M. Briggs: 'Ashpitel', 'The Little Cinder-Girl', 'Mossycoat', 'Rashin Coatie' (*Folk Tales of Britain*); Italo Calvino: 'Gràttula-Bedàttulla' (*Italian Folktales*); Charles Perrault: 'Cinderella' (*Perrault's Complete Fairy Tales*); Neil Philip: *The Cinderella Story* (containing twenty-four different versions of the story, with an excellent commentary)

The story of Cinderella must be one of the most closely studied stories in the entire corpus of folk tale. Entire books have been written about it and its variants. It is the most popular pantomime of all. But more importantly, it always seems to work.

Much of its popularity must be due to Charles Perrault, whose inventiveness and charm delighted readers from the moment his *Histoires ou contes du temps passé* (*Stories or Fairy Tales from Past Times*, more famously known by its subtitle, *Tales of Mother Goose*) was published in 1697. The one thing that everyone knows about Perrault is that he mistook *vair*, fur, for *verre*, glass, but I don't believe it. Perrault was quite inventive enough to have thought of a glass slipper, which is absurd, impossible, magical, and infinitely more memorable than fur. It was Perrault, too, who turned the helping principle in the story (which is always a surrogate mother, whether a hazel tree growing from the real mother's grave, or a goat, or a cow, or a dove) into a godmother, whose function is immediately easy to understand.

One popular misapprehension is that the story is simply a rags-to-riches tale. There are rags and there are riches, but according to Bruno Bettelheim, in *The Uses of Enchantment*, the most important theme is sibling rivalry, compounded by the girl's arriving at sexual maturity, symbolized by the marriage. This is why the function embodied by the fairy godmother is so important: she represents the mother by doing what a good mother should do, and helping the girl appear as beautiful on the outside as she is on the inside.

For this version I borrowed the idea that her dresses are of different colours from the British 'Mossycoat', which to my mind is the best Cinderella of all.

In the first version the Grimms published, in 1812, there is no punishment for the stepsisters. The story ends with the doves calling out that this bride is the right one. The punishment of blinding was added in their version of 1819, and kept in all later versions. Blinding is all very well in a story, but it would be hard to take on the stage. This is not *King Lear*. No ugly sisters are blinded in pantomime, and neither are they in opera: Massenet's *Cendrillon* (1899) and Rossini's *La Cenerentola* (1817) both end with happiness all round. In Perrault, where sweetness reigns, the sisters are actually married off to lords of the court.

She has many names. The Grimms call her Aschenputtel, but she is firmly Cinderella in English. In our centrally heated homes today, when few children have ever seen a cinder or know what one is, Cinderella just sounds like a pretty name, but I thought it needed a little context.

FOURTEEN

THE RIDDLE

Once there was a prince who took it into his head to travel about the world, taking no one with him but a faithful servant. One day they came to a great forest, and when evening came they could find no place to shelter. They didn't know where they could spend the night.

But then the prince saw a little house, and walking towards the house there was a girl, and as they came closer they saw that she was young and beautiful.

He caught up with her and said, 'Tell me, miss, can my servant and I find shelter for the night in that little house?'

'Yes,' she said sadly, 'you can, but I don't think it's a good idea. I wouldn't go in if I were you.'

'Why ever not?' asked the prince.

The girl sighed. 'My stepmother lives there,' she said, 'and she practises the evil arts. What's more, she doesn't like strangers. But if you must go in, don't eat or drink anything she offers you.'

The prince realized that this was the house of a witch. But it was dark and they couldn't go any further, and besides, he was afraid of nothing, so he knocked and went in.

The old woman was sitting in an armchair by the fire, and when she looked at the prince, her eyes glowed like the coals.

'Good evening, young sirs,' she said in her friendliest voice. 'Sit down and rest yourselves.'

She blew on the fire and stirred something in a little pot. Because of the girl's warning, the prince and his servant didn't eat or drink anything; they wrapped themselves up and slept soundly till morning.

When morning came they got ready to leave. The prince was already mounted on his horse when the old woman came out and said, 'Wait a minute. Just let me give you a little drink to see you on your way.'

While she went back into the house the prince rode away, but the servant had to tighten the girth of his saddle, and he was still there when the witch came out with the drink.

'Here you are,' she said. 'Take this to your master.'

But he had no time to do that, because as soon as he took it from her hand, the glass burst and the drink splashed on to his horse. It was poison, of course, and it was so strong that the poor animal fell dead at once. The servant ran after the prince and told him what had happened, and he'd have left with the prince right there and then except that he didn't want to abandon his saddle; so he went back to get it. When he reached the dead horse, he found a raven already perching on its head and pecking out its eyes.

'Who knows? We might find nothing better to eat today,' he thought, so he killed the raven and took it with him.

They wandered in the woods all day long, but they couldn't find their way out. As night fell they came to an inn, and the servant gave the raven to the innkeeper and told him to prepare it for their supper.

Now what they didn't know was that they'd fallen into a den of brigands – murderers, in fact. And just as the prince and his servant were sitting down, twelve of these rascals turned up, meaning to do away with them, but seeing the supper arrive, the murderers thought they might as well eat first. It was the last meal they ever had, for they hadn't swallowed more than a mouthful of the raven stew when they all fell dead. The poison in the horse had been so strong that it had passed on to the raven, and that had been enough to kill every one of them.

The innkeeper had fled, seeing what had happened, and there was no one left in the house but the innkeeper's daughter. She was a good girl and had had nothing to do with the murderers and their wickedness. She unlocked a hidden door and showed the prince all the treasure they'd stolen: piles of gold and silver, and mounds of jewels. The prince said she should keep it for herself: he wanted nothing to do with it.

And once again he and his servant rode on their way.

They travelled about for a long time, and one day they came to a town where there was a princess who was both very beautiful and very proud. She had announced that she would marry any man who asked her a riddle that she couldn't solve. However, if she managed to solve it to the satisfaction of twelve wise riddle-masters, his head would be cut off. She would have three days to think about it, but she was so clever that she always solved it long before that time was up. Already nine men had tried to beat her, but each of them had lost his head.

However, that didn't worry the prince; he was so dazzled by her great beauty that he was willing to risk his life. He went to the palace and asked his riddle.

'One killed none,' he said, 'but still killed twelve. What is it?'

She had no idea what it could be. She thought and thought, but nothing came to mind. She consulted all her riddle books, but there had been nothing like it in all the history of riddles. It seemed as if she'd met her match at last.

However, she wasn't willing to give up, so that night she sent her chambermaid to creep quietly into the prince's bedroom. There she had to listen carefully to anything he said in his sleep, in case he revealed the answer to the riddle in his dreams. But that came to nothing, because the prince's servant had taken his place, and when the maid came in he snatched away the robe she'd covered herself with, and chased her away with a stick. So that didn't work.

On the second night she sent another maid, to see if she'd be any more successful. His servant took her robe as well, and chased her away with an even bigger stick. So that didn't work either.

On the third night the prince decided to wait and watch himself. This time the princess came herself. She was wearing a beautiful mist-grey robe, and she sat down softly on the bed next to him and waited till she was sure he was asleep.

But he was still awake, and when she whispered, 'One killed none. What is that?' he answered, 'A raven ate the flesh of a horse that was poisoned, and died itself.'

Then she said, 'But still killed twelve. What does that mean?'

He answered, 'Twelve murderers ate a stew made from the raven, and died of it.'

She was sure she had the answer now, and she tried to tiptoe away, but the prince caught hold of her robe and held it so tight that she had to leave it behind.

Next morning the princess announced that she had solved the riddle. She sent for the twelve riddle-masters and told them what it meant. It looked as if the prince was doomed, but he asked to be heard.

'The princess came into my room when she thought I was asleep,' he said, 'and asked me what the answer was. She would never have guessed it otherwise.'

The riddle-masters conferred together and said, 'Have you any proof?'

Then the prince's servant brought in the three robes. When the riddle-masters saw the mist-grey one which no one but the princess ever wore, they said, 'Have this robe embroidered with gold and silver, your highness, for it will be your wedding gown. The young man has won!'

Tale type: ATU 851, 'The Princess Who Cannot Solve the Riddle'
Source: a story told to the Grimm brothers by Dorothea Viehmann
Similar stories: Alexander Afanasyev: 'The Princess Who Wanted to Solve Riddles' (*Russian Fairy Tales*); Katharine M. Briggs: 'The Young Prince' (*Folk Tales of Britain*); Italo Calvino: 'The Son of the Merchant from Milan' (*Italian Folktales*)

This is a widely distributed tale type, a variation of it turning up, for example, in Puccini's opera *Turandot* of 1926. The Grimms' version is much better than most, not least for its neatness and the clarity of the three-part structure. Neatness and clarity are great virtues when you're telling a story. The Grimms' source for this story was Dorothea Viehmann, a fruit-seller from Zwehrn, not far from Kassel where the Grimm brothers lived. She provided several tales for them, a number of which appear in this collection, and had the unusual ability not only to tell a story vividly and fluently, but then to go back and repeat it phrase by phrase so they could take it down accurately. The brothers paid tribute to her in the preface to their first edition:

> Those who believe that oral narratives are routinely falsified, that they are not carefully preserved, and that long recitations are, as a rule, impossible, should have the chance to hear how precisely she stays with each story and how keen she is to narrate correctly; when she retells something, she never changes its substance and corrects an error as soon as she notices it, even if it means interrupting herself.
>
> (Quoted in translation by Maria Tatar in *The Hard Facts of the Grimms' Fairy Tales*)

FIFTEEN

THE MOUSE, THE BIRD AND THE SAUSAGE

A mouse, a bird and a sausage decided to set up home together. For a long time they carried on happily, living within their means and even managing to save a little. The bird's job was to go into the forest every day and bring back wood for the fire, the mouse had to get water from the well, make the fire and lay the table, and the sausage did the cooking.

But we're never content with living well if we think we can live better. One day, as the bird was in the forest, he met another bird and boasted about his pleasant way of life. The other bird only called him a poor dupe.

'What d'you mean?'

'Well, who's doing the lion's share of the work? You are. You have to fly back and forth carrying heavy bits of wood, while the other two take it easy. They're taking advantage of you, make no mistake about it.'

The bird thought about it. It was true that after the mouse had lit the fire and carried the water in, she usually went to her little room and had a snooze before getting up in time to lay the table. The sausage stayed by the pot most of the time, keeping an eye on the vegetables, and from time to time he'd slither through the water to give it a bit of flavouring. If it needed seasoning, he'd swim more slowly. That was more or less all he did. When the bird came home with the wood, they'd stack it neatly by the fire, sit down to eat, and then sleep soundly till the next day. That was how they lived, and a fine way of life it was.

However, the bird couldn't help thinking about what the other bird had said, and next day he refused to go and gather wood.

'I've been your slave long enough,' he declared. 'You must have taken me for a fool. It's high time we tried a better arrangement.'

'But this works so well!' said the mouse.

'You would say that, wouldn't you?'

'Besides,' said the sausage, 'this suits our different talents.'

'Only because we've never tried to do it any other way.'

The mouse and the sausage argued, but the bird wouldn't be denied. Finally they gave in and drew lots, and the job of gathering wood fell to the sausage, of cooking to the mouse, and of fetching water and making the fire to the bird.

What happened?

After the sausage went out to gather some wood, the bird lit the fire and the mouse put the saucepan on the stove. Then they waited for the sausage to come back with the first load of wood, but he was gone so long that they began to worry about him, so the bird went out to see if he was all right.

Not far from the house he came across a dog licking his lips.

'You haven't seen a sausage, have you?'

'Yeah, I just ate him. Delicious.'

'What d'you mean? You can't do that! That's appalling! I'll have you up before the law!'

'He was fair game. There's no sausage season that I know of.'

'He certainly was not fair game! He was innocently going about his business! This is outright murder!'

'Well, that's just where you're wrong, chum. He was carrying forged papers, and that's a capital crime.'

'Forged papers – I've never heard such nonsense. Where are they? Where's your proof?'

'I ate them too.'

There was nothing the bird could do. In a fight between a dog and a bird, there's only one winner, and it isn't the bird. He turned back home and told the mouse what had happened.

'Eaten?' she said. 'Oh, that's dreadful! I shall miss him terribly.'

'It's very sad. We'll just have to do the best we can without him,' said the bird.

The bird laid the table while the mouse put the finishing touches to the stew. She remembered how easily the sausage had managed to swim round and round to season it, and thought she could do the same, so she clambered on to the saucepan handle and launched herself in; but either it was too hot and she suffocated, or else she couldn't swim at all and she drowned, but at all events she never came out.

When the bird saw the vegetable stew coming to the boil with a dead mouse in it, he panicked. He was making up the fire at the time, and in his shock and alarm he scattered the burning logs all over the place and set fire to the house. He raced to the well to get some water to put it out, but got his foot caught in the rope; and when the bucket plunged down the well, down he went with it. So he was drowned, and that was the end of them all.

* * *

Tale type: ATU 85, 'The Mouse, the Bird and the Sausage'
Source: a story in Hans Michael Moscherosch's *Wunderliche und Wahrhafftige Gesichte Philanders von Sittewald* (*The Wonderful True Story of Philander von Sittewald*; 1650)

Unlike the cat and the mouse (p. 9) these housemates are not fundamentally ill-matched. They could have lived happily together for a long time, if the bird's satisfaction had not been fatally undermined. That's the only moral of this story, but it is a sort of fable, like the tale of the cat and the mouse, so a moral is only to be expected.

Some enquiring readers might like to know what sort of sausage it was. After all, according to the internet, Germany has over 1,500 kinds of sausage: from which could we expect this sort of selfless domesticity? Well, it – I mean he – was a bratwurst. But somehow the word 'bratwurst' isn't as funny as the word 'sausage'. According to a famous comedian whose name has slipped my mind, 'sausage' is the funniest word in the English language. This story would certainly have a different kind of poignancy if it had been about a mouse, a bird and a lamb chop.

SIXTEEN

LITTLE RED RIDING HOOD

Once upon a time there was a little girl who was so sweet and kind that everyone loved her. Her grandmother, who loved her more than anyone, gave her a little cap made of red velvet, which suited her so well that she wanted to wear it all the time. Because of that everyone took to calling her Little Red Riding Hood.

One day her mother said to her: 'Little Red Riding Hood, I've got a job for you. Your grandmother isn't very well, and I want you to take her this cake and a bottle of wine. They'll make her feel a lot better. You be polite when you go into her house, and give her a kiss from me. Be careful on the way there, and don't step off the path or you might trip over and break the bottle and drop the cake, and then there'd be nothing for her. When you go into her parlour don't forget to say, "Good morning, Granny," and don't go peering in all the corners.'

'I'll do everything right, don't worry,' said Little Red Riding Hood, and kissed her mother goodbye.

Her grandmother lived in the woods, about half an hour's walk away. When Little Red Riding Hood had only been walking a few minutes, a wolf came up to her. She didn't know what a wicked animal he was, so she wasn't afraid of him.

'Good morning, Little Red Riding Hood!' said the wolf.

'Thank you, wolf, and good morning to you.'

'Where are you going so early this morning?'

'To Granny's house.'

'And what's in that basket of yours?'

'Granny's not very well, so I'm taking her some cake and some wine. We baked the cake yesterday, and it's full of good things like flour and eggs, and it'll be good for her and make her feel better.'

'Where does your granny live, Little Red Riding Hood?'

'Well, I have to walk along this path till I come to three big oak trees, and there's her house, behind a hedge of hazel bushes. It's not very far away, about fifteen minutes' walk, I suppose. You must know the place,' said Little Red Riding Hood.

The wolf thought, 'Now, this dainty young thing looks a very tasty mouthful. She'll taste even better than the old woman, but if I'm careful I'll be able to eat them both.'

So he walked along a while with Little Red Riding Hood, and then he said, 'Look at those flowers, Little Red Riding Hood! Aren't they lovely? The ones under the trees over there. Why don't you go closer so you can see them properly? And you seem as though you're walking to school, all serious and determined. You'll never hear the birds if you go along like that. It's so lovely in the woods – it's a shame not to enjoy it.'

Little Red Riding Hood looked where he was pointing, and when she saw the sunbeams dancing here and there between the trees, and how the beautiful flowers grew everywhere, she thought, 'I could gather some flowers to take to Granny! She'll be very pleased with those. And it's still early – I've got time to do that and still be home on time.'

So she stepped off the path, and ran into the trees to pick some flowers; but each time she picked one she saw an even prettier one a bit further away, so she ran to get that as well. And all the time she went further and further into the wood.

But while she was doing that, the wolf ran straight to the grandmother's house and knocked on the door.

'Who's there?'

'Little Red Riding Hood,' said the wolf. 'I've got some cake and wine for you. Open the door!'

'Just lift the latch,' said the grandmother. 'I'm feeling too weak to get out of bed.'

The wolf lifted the latch and the door opened. He went inside, looked around to see where she was, and then leaped on the grandmother's bed and ate her all up in one big gulp. Then he put on her clothes and put her nightcap on his head, and pulled the curtains tight shut, and got into bed.

All that time, Little Red Riding Hood had been wandering about picking flowers. Once she had gathered so many that she couldn't hold any more, she remembered what she was supposed to be doing, and set off along the path to her grandmother's house. She had a surprise when she got there, because the door was open and the room was dark.

'My goodness,' she thought, 'I don't like this. I feel afraid and I usually like it at Granny's house.'

She called out, 'Good morning, Granny!' but there was no answer.

She went to the bed and pulled open the curtains. There was her grandmother, lying with her cap pulled down and looking very strange.

'Oh, Granny, what big ears you've got!'

'All the better to hear you with.'

'Granny, what big eyes you've got!'

'All the better to see you with.'

'And Granny, what big hands you've got!'

'All the better to hold you with.'

'And oh, Granny, what a great grim ghastly mouth you've got—'

'All the better to eat you with!'

And as soon as the wolf said that, he leaped out of bed and

gobbled up Little Red Riding Hood. Once he'd swallowed her he felt full and satisfied, and since the bed was so nice and soft, he climbed back in, fell deeply asleep, and began to snore very loudly indeed.

Just then a huntsman was passing by.

'The old woman's making such a noise,' he thought, 'I'd better go and see if she's all right.'

He went into the parlour, and when he came near the bed he stopped in astonishment.

'You old sinner!' he thought. 'I've been looking for you for a long time. Found you at last!'

He raised his rifle to his shoulder, but then he put it down again, because it occurred to him that the wolf might have eaten the old lady, and he might be able to rescue her. So he put down the rifle and took a pair of scissors, and began to snip open the wolf's bulging belly. After only a couple of snips he saw the red velvet cap, and a few snips later the girl jumped out.

'Oh, that was horrible!' she said. 'I was so frightened! It was so dark in the wolf's belly!'

And then the grandmother began to clamber out, a bit out of breath but not much the worse for her experience. While the hunter helped her to a chair, Little Red Riding Hood ran outside to fetch some heavy stones. They filled the wolf's body with them, and then Little Red Riding Hood sewed him up very neatly, and then they woke him up.

Seeing the hunter there with his gun, the wolf panicked and ran outside, but he didn't get very far. The stones were so heavy that soon he fell down dead.

All three of them were very happy. The hunter skinned the wolf and went home with the pelt, Granny ate the cake and drank the wine, and Little Red Riding Hood thought, 'What a narrow escape! As long as I live, I'll never do that again. If mother tells me to stay on the path, that's exactly what I'll do.'

Tale type: ATU 333, 'Little Red Riding Hood'
Source: a story told to the Grimm brothers by Jeanette and Marie Hassenpflug
Similar stories: Italo Calvino: 'The False Grandmother', 'The Wolf and the Three Girls' (*Italian Folktales*); Charles Perrault: 'Little Red Riding Hood' (*Perrault's Complete Fairy Tales*)

I suppose that this and 'Cinderella' (p. 116) are the two best-known fairy tales (in Britain, at any rate), and they both owe a great deal of their popularity to Charles Perrault (see the note to 'Cinderella', p. 126). His version differs from Grimm mainly in that it ends with the wolf eating Little Red Riding Hood. There is no rescue by a brave huntsman; instead, a moralistic verse warns that not all wolves are wild – some of them are smooth-talking seducers.

The huntsman is an interesting detail. The German forests were not just wildernesses, belonging to no one: their owners were often of princely rank, and after the great demand for ship-building timber and the destruction of the forests to make way for crops and cattle to feed the armies of the Thirty Years War, what they wanted most from their woods was pleasure and recreation: hunting, in a word. As John Eliot Gardiner says in his forthcoming work on J. S. Bach: 'In terms of influencing the way their [i.e. the princely owners'] woods were managed, the huntsman eclipsed the trained forester (just as the pheasant and the gamekeeper today so often has more sway than the woodman).'

Perhaps a forester, being less confident with wild animals than a huntsman, and less likely to carry a gun, too, would have tiptoed away carefully from the sleeping wolf and left Little Red Riding Hood and her grandmother to be digested.

Whatever the likelihood of that, both Perrault and Grimm reinforce the moral of bourgeois respectability. Little Red Riding Hood, in the Grimms' version, has no need of a moralistic reminder not to leave the path – she's learned her lesson. (During the panic about paedophilia, it was common to hear this story used to remind children of 'stranger danger'.) She'll never leave the path again.

Gustave Doré's famous engraving, published in 1863 to illustrate an edition of Perrault's version, showing Little Red Riding Hood actually in bed with the wolf reminds us of part of this story's power: wolves *are* sexy. And so are foxes, as Beatrix Potter knew when creating and drawing the suave 'gentleman with the sandy-coloured whiskers' in *The Tale of Jemima Puddle-Duck* (1908), her own variation on the Little Red Riding Hood story. Perrault would have recognized him at once.

Perhaps Charles Dickens's comment sums up the attraction of the heroine most vividly. 'Little Red Riding Hood was my first love,' Bruno Bettelheim quotes him as saying. 'I felt that if I could have married Little Red Riding Hood, I should have known perfect bliss' (*The Uses of Enchantment*, p. 23).

SEVENTEEN

THE MUSICIANS OF BREMEN

Once there was a man who had a donkey, and for years this donkey had carried sacks of grain to the mill without a word of complaint; but now his strength was running out, so he couldn't work as hard as he used to, and his master thought it was time to stop feeding him. The donkey noticed this, and didn't like it a bit, so he ran away and looked for the road to Bremen. His plan was to become a town musician.

When he'd gone a little way he came across a hunting hound lying in the road. The dog was panting as if he'd just run for miles.

'What are you panting for, Grabber?' said the donkey.

'Well, I'm getting old, you see,' explained the hound, 'and I can't run as far as I used to. My master reckons I'm no good any more, and he wanted to kill me, so I ran away; but I don't know how to earn my living in any other way, and I'm getting hungry.'

'Well, I tell you what,' said the donkey, 'I'm in more or less the same position, but I've got a plan. I'm going to Bremen, because they pay their town musicians a decent wage there. Come with me and take up music. I'm going to play the lute – it doesn't look very difficult – and you can play the drums.'

'That's a very good idea,' said the dog, and joined up with the donkey.

They walked on a little way, and then they saw a cat sitting at the roadside who looked as if he'd lost a pound and found a penny.

'What's the trouble, old Whisker Wiper?' said the donkey.

'Dear oh dear,' said the cat, 'I'm in a dreadful pickle. I'm getting on a bit – I don't expect you noticed, but I'm not as young as I was, and my teeth are getting blunt. I used to catch mice, rats, any sort of vermin, you name it, but I'd rather sit by the stove and snooze these days. My mistress was going to drown me, but I ran away. I haven't a clue what to do now. You got any ideas?'

'Come with us to Bremen,' said the donkey. 'We're going to join the town musicians. You know how to sing – I've heard your sort singing very sweetly at night – come along with us.'

The cat thought this was a very good idea, and they all went along together. Presently they came to a farmyard. Standing on the roof was a cockerel, crowing with all his might.

'What are you crowing for?' said the donkey. 'It's long past daybreak.'

'I'm forecasting the weather,' said the cockerel. 'It's Our Lady's Day, when she washes the Christ Child's shirts and hangs them out to dry. I'm telling the family it's going to be dry and sunny, and you'd think they'd be grateful, but not a bit of it. They've got guests coming tomorrow, and they want to eat me, so the farmer's wife has told the cook that this evening she's going to chop my head off. I'm going to crow and crow while I've still got some breath in my lungs.'

'Well, that's a poor show,' said the donkey. 'Why don't you come with us to Bremen? We're going to be musicians. You've got a lovely voice, and when we all make music together, we'll be irresistible.'

The cockerel agreed. Off they went, but they couldn't reach the city of Bremen in one day, and in the evening they decided to look for shelter in the forest where they happened to find themselves. The donkey and the dog lay down under a big tree, the cat took to the branches, and the cockerel flew right to the top. Presently he came all the way down again with some news. Before falling asleep he'd looked all around, north, south, east, and west, and he thought there must be a house not far away, because he'd seen a light shining.

'Well, let's go there,' said the donkey. 'It can't be worse than this.'

'And if there's a house,' said the dog, 'there might be a few bones with a bit of meat on them.'

So they set off in the direction of the light, and soon they saw it glowing through the trees. It became larger and larger, and then they were right in front of it. The donkey, being the tallest of them, went up to the window and looked in.

'What can you see, Grey Face?' asked the cockerel.

'I can see a table covered with good things to eat and drink, but . . .'

'But what?'

'Sitting around the table are a dozen robbers, all tucking in as hard as they can.'

'If only that were us!' said the cockerel.

They discussed how they could drive the robbers away, and finally they agreed on a plan: the donkey would stand with his front feet on the windowsill, the dog would stand on his back, the cat would stand on the dog, and the cockerel would perch on the cat, and then they'd make some music. So they got themselves ready, and after the donkey had counted them in, they all started singing together as loud as they could: the donkey brayed, the dog barked, the cat miaowed and the cockerel crowed. When they'd finished they all jumped through the window, shattering the glass and making a terrible noise.

The robbers all leaped up at once, thinking it was the Devil, or at least a ghost, and fled into the woods in terrible fear. The four musicians sat themselves down and ate freely of the food that was left, guzzling as if they might not get any more food for a month.

When they'd finished they felt tired, because they'd had a long day, so they lay down to sleep, each finding the place he liked best: the donkey lay by the dung heap outside, the dog curled up behind the door, the cat stretched out on the hearth next to the fire, and the cockerel perched on the roof-beam.

At midnight the robbers, who were watching from some way off, saw that the light had gone out.

'We shouldn't have let ourselves be chased away like that,' said the chief. 'That's not very brave, is it? Here, Lefty, go back and have a look. See what's going on.'

Lefty crept back to the house. He could hear nothing, so he tiptoed into the kitchen and looked around. There was nothing to see but the cat's fiery eyes. Lefty thought these were live coals, so he struck a match to make them blaze up again, and touched it to the cat's nose.

Naturally, the cat didn't like that. He leaped up, spitting and shrieking, and clawed at the robber's face.

'Eeeek!' yelled Lefty, and ran towards the door. He stumbled over the dog, who bit him hard in the leg.

'Yeowh!' cried Lefty, and ran out into the yard. The donkey woke up and kicked him hard on the backside.

'Aaagghh!' shrieked Lefty, and that woke up the cockerel, who crowed, '*Cock-a-doodle-doo!*'

'Nohhh!' bellowed Lefty, and ran for the woods in terror of his life.

'What is it? What is it?' said the robber chief.

'We can't go back there!' said Lefty. 'There's a horrible witch in the kitchen, and she scratched me with her nails. And there's a man with a knife behind the door, and he stabbed me in the leg. And there's a brute with a club outside, and he whacked me so hard I think he broke my fundament. And the judge is sitting on the roof, and he called out, "Bring the prisoner here!" So I ran and ran and ran.'

From then on, the robbers didn't dare go back to the house. The four musicians of Bremen, on the other hand, liked it so much that they never left. They're living there still, and as for the last person who told this story, his lips are still moving.

* * *

Tale type: ATU 130, 'The Animals in Night Quarters'
Source: stories told to the Grimm brothers by the von Haxthausen family and Dorothea Viehmann
Similar stories: Katharine M. Briggs: 'The Bull, the Tup, the Cock and the Steg', 'How Jack Went to Seek His Fortune' (*Folk Tales of Britain*)

The poor old superannuated animals, with their fond ideas of playing music in the city of Bremen, come out on top in the end, and a good thing too. I'm fond of this tale because of the simplicity and power of its form. When a tale is shaped so well that the line of the narrative seems to have been able to take no other path, and to have touched every important event in making for its end, one can only bow with respect for the teller.

EIGHTEEN

THE SINGING BONE

In a certain country at one time, many people were concerned about a wild boar that was churning up the farmers' fields, killing the cattle, and ripping the life out of people with its tusks. The king proclaimed that whoever could rid the land of this brute would receive a great reward, but the animal was so huge and strong that no one dared go near the forest where it lived. In the end the king announced that anyone who could kill or capture it should have his only daughter for wife.

Now in that country there were two brothers, the sons of a poor man, and they declared that they would take on this fearful task. The older brother, who was cunning and clever, did so out of arrogance, but the younger, who was simple and innocent, was moved only by the goodness of his heart.

The king said, 'If you want to be sure of finding the beast, you should go into the forest from opposite sides.'

Taking his advice, the older brother entered the forest from the west, and his younger brother from the east.

The younger had not walked for very long when a little man appeared on the path, carrying a black spear. He said, 'I'm going to give you this spear because you've got an innocent heart. You can use it to kill the wild boar, and you can be sure it'll work. It won't do any harm to you.'

The younger brother thanked the little man and walked further into the forest, carrying the spear on his shoulder. And quite soon he came across the great beast itself. It charged at him, but he held the spear firmly, and in its blind rage the boar ran right on to the spear with such force that the spear-point cut its heart in two.

The young man hauled the monster up on to his back and set off, intending to take it to the king; but when he reached the edge of the forest, he came to a tavern where people were having a good time drinking and dancing. Among them was his elder brother. That scoundrel hadn't been brave enough to go into the forest, and reckoning that the boar wasn't going anywhere else in a hurry, he'd decided to drink some wine to give himself a bit of courage. When he saw his younger brother coming out of the trees with the boar over his shoulder, his wicked envious heart began to tempt him.

He called out: 'Brother! What a great deed you've done! Congratulations! Now come in and sit down, and let's drink to your victory.'

The young man, in his simplicity, suspected nothing. He told his elder brother about the little man and the black spear with which he'd killed the boar.

They stayed there till evening came, and then they set off together. When it was dark they came to a bridge over a stream.

'You go first,' said the elder.

The younger brother went ahead. When he had reached the middle of the bridge, the elder struck him so hard on the head that he fell dead on the spot. The murderer buried him on the bank beneath the bridge, lifted the boar up on his own shoulders, and took it to the king.

'I killed it,' he said, 'but I haven't seen my poor brother. I hope he's safe.'

The king kept his word, and the elder brother married the princess. After a little time had gone by and his brother still hadn't returned, he said, 'I'm afraid the boar must have ripped him apart. Oh, my poor brother!'

Everyone believed him, and they thought that was the end of the matter.

But nothing is hidden from the eye of God. After many years, a shepherd was driving his sheep across the bridge when he saw something glinting white down on the bank below. He thought he might be able to do something with it, and he went down to pick it up, finding a snow-white bone, which he took home and carved into a mouthpiece for his horn.

But to his amazement, when he blew into it the bone began to sing by itself:

'Shepherd, blow your horn and play me,
Let my voice be heard once more,
Since my brother chose to slay me,
Bury me and steal the boar.
He did this vile and cruel thing
To wed the daughter of the king.'

'What a wonderful mouthpiece!' said the shepherd. 'It makes my horn sing all by itself. I must take it to the king.'

When he brought it to the king the horn began to sing again, just as before. The king was no fool: he understood at once what must have happened, and he had the earth beneath the bridge dug up. The whole skeleton of the dead man was lying there, all but one bone.

The wicked brother couldn't deny it. By order of the king, he was sewn into a sack and drowned in the same stream beside which his brother's body had been lying. As for the younger brother, his bones were laid to rest in a beautiful grave in the churchyard.

Tale type: ATU 780, 'The Singing Bone'
Source: a story told to the Grimm brothers by Dortchen Wild
Similar stories: Alexander Afanasyev: 'The Miraculous Pipe' (*Russian Fairy Tales*); Katharine M. Briggs: 'Binnorie' (*Folk Tales of Britain*); Italo Calvino: 'The Peacock Feather' (*Italian Folktales*)

Take out the story's only supernatural elements, the little man who gives the younger brother the boar-killing spear and the bone that sings, and this could easily be one of the homely tales in Johann Peter Hebel's enormously popular anthology *Schatzkästlein des Rheinischen Hausfreundes* (*The Treasure Chest*), published in 1811, a year before the Grimms' first edition. Hebel's speciality was tales of everyday life with an amusing or sensational or moral character, and the murder that comes to light by chance figures in more than one of his anecdotes.

But the supernatural character of this tale is important, and widespread. Sometimes the magic instrument that sings the truth is made from a bone, sometimes from a reed, and sometimes it's a harp made from the victim's breastbone and hair, as in the British 'Binnorie'; but the truth always comes out.

NINETEEN

THE DEVIL WITH THE THREE GOLDEN HAIRS

There was once a poor woman who bore a son, and the baby had a caul on his head. That's a sign of good luck, and when the village fortune-teller heard about it, she prophesied that when he was fourteen years old the boy would marry the king's daughter.

A few days later the king himself came to the village. He was travelling incognito, so no one recognized him, and when he asked what had been happening, was there any news, what were people talking about in the village, and so on, they told him that a child had been born with a caul. Apparently, they said, that meant he was going to be lucky, and marry the king's daughter when he was fourteen.

Now the king was a wicked man, and this prophecy didn't please him at all. He went to the parents and said, 'My friends, you've got a lucky boy there, and I'm a rich man. Here's the first sign of his luck: entrust your child to me, and I'll take good care of him.'

At first they refused, but when the stranger offered them a good deal of gold they saw the merit of his proposition, and said, 'Well, he's a lucky child, after all, and things are bound to turn out all right for him'; so in the end they agreed, and gave him the child.

The king put the baby in a box and rode away until he came to a deep river. He threw the box in the water, and thought: 'That's a good day's work done. I've saved my daughter from an unwelcome suitor.'

Then he rode off home. If he'd stayed to watch he'd have seen that the box didn't sink, as he'd hoped, but floated like a little boat, and not a drop of water got inside. It floated down the river to within two miles of the capital city, to a spot where there happened to be a mill, and there it got caught in the weir. The miller's apprentice was fishing there at the time, and he pulled it out with a boathook, thinking that he'd found a great treasure. When he opened the box, though, he was astonished to find a little baby, fresh and rosy-cheeked. Having no use for a baby himself, he took it to the miller and his wife. They were delighted with this little child, because they had no children of their own. 'God must have given him to us,' they said.

So they took him in and looked after him. They brought the luck-child up well, and taught him to mind his manners and always be good and honest.

Time went by, and some years later the king happened to be caught in a thunderstorm when he was out hunting, and he sought shelter in that same mill. He asked the miller and his wife if the fine young man he saw was their son.

'No,' they said. 'He's a foundling. Fourteen years ago he floated to the weir in a box, and our apprentice fished him out.'

The king realized that the boy was none other than the luck-child that he himself had thrown into the water, and he said, 'My good people, would you let the young fellow take a letter to the queen? I'll pay him two gold pieces.'

The couple agreed, and told the boy to get ready. Meanwhile

the king took some paper and wrote to the queen: 'As soon as the boy who bears this letter arrives, he must be put to death and buried. This must be done before I come home.'

The boy took the letter and set off, but he soon got lost, and by evening he was wandering in a great forest. In the gathering darkness he saw a single glowing light between the trees. It was the only light to be seen, so he made for it, and before long he found himself outside a little cottage. Inside there was an old woman dozing in front of the fire. She started when she saw him, and said, 'Where have you sprung from? And where are you going?'

'I've come from the mill,' he said, 'and I'm taking a letter to the queen. But I got lost in the forest, and now I'd like to spend the night here, please.'

'You poor young man,' said the old woman, 'you've wandered into a robbers' hideout. They're out at the moment doing a job, but when they come back they'll kill you, as sure as eggs.'

'Let them come,' said the luck-child, 'I'm not afraid of robbers. But I've got to lie down and sleep, because I'm worn out.'

And he lay down on the bench and fell asleep at once. Soon afterwards the robbers came in, and asked angrily: 'Who's this kid lying here?'

'He's just an innocent boy,' said the old woman. 'He got lost in the woods and I let him lie down because he was so tired. He's carrying a letter to the queen.'

'Is he?' said the robber chief. 'Let's have a look at it.'

They took the letter from his pocket and opened it, and carefully spelled out what it said: that the boy should be killed as soon as he delivered the letter.

'Oh, that's not right,' said the chief. 'That's a dirty trick.'

Even the robbers, hard-hearted as they were, were moved to pity. The chief took another piece of paper and wrote a new letter, saying that the boy should be married to the king's daughter as soon as he arrived. They let him stay asleep on the bench till the morning, and when he woke up they gave him the letter and showed him the way to the palace.

And when he arrived there and gave the letter to the queen, sure enough she ordered a magnificent wedding, and the boy was married to the princess. Because he was good-looking and kindly and polite to everyone, she was happy enough about it.

Eventually the king came back, and discovered that the village prophecy had held true, and despite everything the boy was married to his daughter.

'How can that have happened?' he said to the queen. 'Didn't you get my letter? I said nothing about marriage.'

The queen showed him the letter. The king read it, and saw what had happened. He sent for the boy and said, 'What d'you mean by this? I didn't give you this letter. I gave you quite a different one. What's your explanation, eh?'

'I'm afraid I can't explain it,' the boy replied. 'I spent the night in the forest, and someone must have changed it when I was asleep.'

'Well, you needn't think you're going to get away with it,' snarled the king. 'Whoever marries my daughter will have to travel all the way to hell and bring back the three golden hairs from the head of the Devil.'

'Oh, I can do that,' said the boy. 'I'll bring back the golden hairs for you; I'm not afraid of the Devil.'

With that he made his farewell and set off. The first place he came to was a big city with a porter at the gate.

'What's your trade? And what do you know?'

'I know everything,' said the boy, 'and what I don't know, I can find out.'

'Well, you can do us a favour, then. There's a fountain in the market square that used to gush with wine, and now it doesn't even give any water. What's the matter with it?'

'I'll find out, I guarantee,' said the boy. 'I'll tell you on my way back.'

He went on and soon came to a town where the watchman asked him the same question: 'What trade do you follow? And what do you know?'

'I know everything,' said the boy, 'and what I don't know, I can find out.'

'Tell me this, then: there's a tree in the park that used to bear golden apples. But something's gone wrong and now it won't even bear any leaves.'

'Leave it to me,' said the boy. 'I'll tell you on the way back.'

He went on a little further and came to a river where a ferryman was waiting to carry people back and forth.

'What's your trade? And what do you know?'

'I know everything,' said the boy, 'and what I don't know, I can find out.'

'Well, here's a question for you. Why do I have to keep on crossing the river without anyone coming to relieve me?'

'Don't worry,' said the boy, 'I'll find the answer, sure enough.'

Not long after crossing the river, the boy found the entrance to hell. It was dark and smoky and abominable. The Devil wasn't at home just then, but sitting in a big armchair reading the paper was the Devil's grandmother.

'What do you want?' she said.

She didn't look all that evil, so the boy told her what he'd come for.

'The king said that if I don't get the three golden hairs from the Devil's head,' he said, 'I won't be able to stay married to my wife.'

'That won't be very easy,' said the grandmother. 'If he finds out you're here, he'll probably eat you. But you're a good-looking boy, and I feel sorry for you, so I'll do my best. First I'll change you into an ant.'

She did that, and picked him up on her fingertip to make sure he could hear her.

'Hide in my skirts,' she said, 'and I'll pluck the hairs for you.'

'There's another thing,' said the ant. 'I need to know the answer to some questions. Why does the fountain in the market square no longer even give water, when it used to flow with wine? Why does the tree in the park that used to give golden apples no longer even produce leaves? And why does the ferryman have to keep on carrying people over the river?'

'That's not so easy,' she said. 'I can't promise anything. But keep quiet, and listen very carefully to what he says.'

The ant nodded his tiny head, and she tucked him under her skirts. It was just in time, too, because the Devil came home at that very moment, and started roaring.

'What is it?' said his grandmother.

'Human! I can smell it! Who's been here? Eh?'

He prowled around the room, lifting up chairs, looking in every corner.

'For evil's sake!' she said. 'I've just tidied the place, can't you see? You'll make it all messy again. Sit down and have your supper, and stop making a fuss about nothing.'

'I can, though,' the Devil muttered. 'I can smell it.'

But he sat at the table and gobbled up his supper, and then he lay down and put his head in his grandmother's lap.

'Pick the lice out of my hair, Granny,' he said.

She started to pick through his hair, and presently he fell asleep and started snoring. As soon as she heard that, the old woman got hold of one of the golden hairs, and tweaked it out.

'*Oww!*' yelled the Devil, waking up at once. 'What are you doing?'

'I had a dream,' said his granny, carefully putting the golden hair down beside her where he couldn't see.

'What dream? What was it about?'

'A fountain,' she said. 'It was in the market square. Years ago it ran with wine, and everyone could help themselves, but now it won't even give water.'

'Stupid people,' muttered the Devil, settling his head on her lap again. 'All they have to do is dig out the toad under the stone in the fountain. If they kill that, the wine will flow again.'

The grandmother went back to picking out the lice, and once again he began to snore. Searching through his tangled hairs, she found another golden one, and pulled it out.

'*Ow!* Why d'you keep doing that?'

'Sorry, sweetie,' she said. 'I had another dream, and I didn't know what I was doing.'

'Another dream, eh? What was it about this time?'

'There was a tree in the park, and it didn't even produce leaves any more. Years ago it used to give golden apples.'

'They don't know anything in that town. They should dig around the roots, and they'll find a mouse gnawing at them. Kill the mouse and they'll get their golden apples again.'

'There, there,' she said. 'If only I was as clever as you, I wouldn't wake you up. Go back to sleep now, my pet.'

The Devil shifted about and put his head back in her lap. Presently the snoring began again. She waited a little longer this time, and then nipped out the third golden hair, putting it with the others.

'*Yeow!* You're doing it again! What's the matter with you, you stupid old woman?'

'There, there,' she said. 'It was that cheese I had for supper. It's making me dream again.'

'You and your dreams. If you do that again I'll thump you. What did you dream?'

'I dreamed about a ferryman. He's been ferrying people back and forth for years and years, and no one will relieve him.'

'Huh. Do they know nothing, these people? All he has to do is hand his pole to the next person who wants to cross, and that person will have to take over.'

'There, there,' she said, 'you go back to sleep, my pretty one. I won't have any more dreams.'

Since she let him be for the rest of the night, the Devil slept well. When he woke up and went out to work the next morning, his grandmother waited till she was sure he was gone and then took out the ant from her skirts and turned him back into the boy.

'Did you hear all that?' she said.

'Yes, every word,' he said. 'And did you manage to get the three hairs?'

'Here you are,' she said, and handed them over.

Being a polite young man he thanked her very much and went on his way, happy that he'd got everything he needed.

When he came to the river the ferryman said, 'Well? Did you find out?'

'Take me across first,' replied the boy, and when they were at the other side he said, 'All you have to do is put the pole into the hands of the next person who wants to cross, and you'll be free.'

He walked on till he came to the city with the barren tree. The porter at the gate was expecting his answer too.

'Kill the mouse that's been chewing away at the roots, and it'll bear golden apples again,' the boy told him.

The mayor and corporation were so relieved that they rewarded him with two donkeys laden with gold. Leading his donkeys homewards, he stopped at the other city where the fountain had dried up.

'Dig up the stone that's in the fountain and kill the toad hiding beneath it,' he told them.

They did so at once and sure enough the fountain began flowing with wine. They drank to the boy's health, and rewarded him with another two donkeys laden with gold.

Leading his four donkeys, he travelled home. Everyone was very happy to see him again, especially his wife, and when the king saw the donkeys and their cargo he was delighted.

'My dear boy!' he said. 'How wonderful to see you! And these hairs from the Devil's head – splendid – put them on the sideboard. But where did you get all this gold?'

'A ferryman took me across a river. Instead of sand, the bank on the other side is covered in gold – you can just pick up as much as you want. I should take several sacks if I were you.'

The king was intensely greedy, so he set off at once. He hurried all day till he came to the river, and then he beckoned the ferryman impatiently.

'Steady now,' said the ferryman as the king stepped on board. 'Don't rock the boat. Would you mind just holding this pole for me?'

Of course the king did so, and the ferryman jumped out at once. He laughed and sang and jumped for joy and ran away, and the king was compelled to stay in the boat for ever, ferrying people back and forth as a punishment for his sins.

* * *

Tale type: ATU 930, 'The Prophecy', continuing as ATU 461, 'Three Hairs from the Devil's Beard'

Source: a story told to the Grimm brothers by Dorothea Viehmann

Similar stories: Alexander Afanasyev: 'Marco the Rich and Vassily the Luckless' (*Russian Fairy Tales*); Katharine M. Briggs: 'Fairest of All Others', 'The Fish and the Ring', 'The Stepney Lady' (*Folk Tales of Britain*); Italo Calvino: 'The Feathered Ogre', 'The Ismailian Merchant', 'Mandorlinfiore' (*Italian Folktales*); Jacob and Wilhelm Grimm: 'The Griffin' (*Children's and Household Tales*)

Like 'The Three Snake Leaves' (p. 86), this story falls into two halves. In some of the related tales, the prophecy about the child (usually a girl) born to marry a rich man is followed by a test of a different sort: instead of acquiring three hairs from the Devil (or feathers from the ogre, or whatever), she has to find a ring that the unwilling bridegroom throws into the sea, and the wedding can't take place till it turns up, which it duly does, in the stomach of a fish. I like the version here because the reward is for courage, not just for luck.

TWENTY

THE GIRL WITH NO HANDS

There was once a miller who sank little by little into poverty, until all he had left was his mill and a fine apple tree standing behind it. One day he'd just set off into the forest to gather some wood when an old man he'd never seen before appeared in front of him.

'Why are you wearing yourself out chopping wood?' said the old man. 'Just promise to give me whatever's standing behind your mill, and I'll make you rich.'

'What's behind the mill?' thought the miller. 'It can only be the apple tree.'

'All right,' he said, 'I'll do it.'

The old man wrote out a contract, and the miller signed it. The old man took it with a strange kind of laugh.

'I'll come back for it,' he said, 'in three years. Don't you forget now.'

The miller hurried home, and his wife came out to meet him.

'Oh, husband,' she said, 'you'll never guess what's happened! Boxes and chests of treasure all over the house – all at once – full to the brim – gold coins, all sorts of money and jewels and so forth – where can it have come from? Is the good Lord blessing us at last?'

'He's kept his side of the bargain then,' said the miller, and he told his wife about the old man in the forest. 'All I had to do was sign over whatever is standing behind the mill. This treasure's worth an apple tree, isn't it?'

'Oh, husband! You don't know what you've done! That must have been the Devil! He didn't mean the apple tree. He meant our daughter! She was out there sweeping the path!'

The miller's daughter, who was a lovely girl, lived the next three years worshipping God piously. When the time was up for the Evil One to come and get her, she washed herself from top to toe, put on her white dress, and drew a chalk circle around herself on the floor. The Devil turned up first thing in the morning, and found that he couldn't get near her.

He said to the miller, 'What did you let her wash herself for, you old fool? Don't let her have any water, not a drop, or else I won't be able to touch her.'

The miller was terrified. He did as the Devil told him, and didn't let his daughter have a drop of water, no matter how thirsty she was. Next morning the Devil came back.

'Look! Her hands are clean! Why did you let her wash her hands?'

It turned out that she'd wept all night, and her tears had washed her hands clean. The Devil was furious, because he still couldn't touch her.

'Right,' he said, 'now you'll have to chop her hands off.'

The miller was horrified. 'I can't do that!' he cried. 'My own child – I can't do that to her!'

'Well, if you don't,' said the Devil, 'I'll just have to take you instead.'

That was too much for the miller. He went to the girl and said, 'My dear daughter, I've got to chop your hands off or the Devil will have me, and I'm so afraid. Forgive me, my child! Help me with this, and forgive me!'

The girl said, 'Father dear, I'm your daughter. You can do

whatever you like to me.' And she stretched out her hands and let her father chop them off.

The Devil came back once more, but the poor girl had wept again and covered her stumps with tears, so that they were perfectly clean. He had to give up then, because he'd tried three times, and that was the limit.

The miller said, 'My dear, it's all because of you that we're as rich as we are. You won't want for a thing – I'll make sure you live in luxury all your life long.'

But she said, 'I can't live here any more. I'm going to go away. The kindness of strangers will provide everything I need.'

She asked them to tie her maimed arms to her back and off she went. She walked all day, and she didn't stop till it was dark. The moon was shining, and by its light she saw across a river into a royal garden where the trees were covered with beautiful fruit. She longed for something to eat, but she couldn't get there, because of the water.

She hadn't had a bite to eat all day, and she was suffering badly from hunger. She thought, 'Oh, if only I were in the garden! I could eat the fruit straight off the tree. If I can't do that, I'll perish.'

She knelt down and prayed. And straight away an angel appeared. He went to the river and closed a sluice gate, and the stream dried up, so that she could walk across.

She went into the garden, with the angel following. She saw a tree covered in beautiful ripe pears, which had all been numbered so that none could be stolen, but she couldn't help that: she stepped up to the tree and ate from it, just one pear, enough to satisfy her hunger, but no more. After she'd eaten it she went to lie down in the bushes.

The gardener was watching, but he saw the angel with her and thought the girl was a spirit, too. He didn't dare make a noise.

Next morning the king came and looked around. He saw at

once that one of the pears had been eaten, and summoned the gardener.

'Oh, your majesty! Last night a spirit came and walked across the stream and ate the pear right off the tree! It had no hands, your majesty!'

'How did it walk across the stream?'

'An angel came down and closed the sluice gate for it, and let the stream dry up. I was afraid, your majesty, so I didn't call out and stop it. After the spirit had eaten the pear, it went away somewhere.'

'That doesn't sound very likely,' said the king. 'I'd better keep watch with you tonight in case it happens again.'

Next night the king came quietly to the garden, accompanied by a priest who was going to talk to the spirit if it appeared again. They sat down nearby and waited, and sure enough, at midnight the girl came out from hiding, stepped up to the tree, and ate a pear just with her mouth. Next to her an angel dressed in white was standing guard.

The priest went up to them and said, 'Where do you come from, my child? From God, or from the world? Are you a spirit or a human being?'

'I'm not a spirit,' she said, 'I'm a poor woman who's been forsaken by everyone except God.'

The king heard what she said, and replied, 'Even if the whole world has forsaken you, I shall not.'

He took her back to his castle. She was so beautiful and good that he fell in love with her, and took her as his wife, and had silver hands made for her. And they lived in happiness.

After a year, the king had to go to war. He left his young queen in the care of his mother. 'If she has a baby,' he said, 'look after mother and child well, and write and tell me the news at once.'

A little later she gave birth to a beautiful son. The king's mother wrote as he'd told her, telling him the joyful news.

But on his way to the king, the messenger stopped at a brook to rest. All this time the Devil had been watching over the girl, determined to destroy her happiness, and now he took the letter away and substituted one that said the queen had given birth to a monster.

When the king read this he was horrified and saddened, but he wrote back to say they should take good care of her till he came back. Once again the messenger lay down to sleep, and once again the Devil came and put a letter of his own in place of the one the messenger was carrying. This one said that they should kill the queen and her child.

The queen mother was shocked and frightened when she read this letter. She wrote to her son again, but got the same answer, because the Devil was watching and kept switching the letters around. The last letter even said that they should keep the queen's eyes and tongue as proof. When the old queen read this, she wept bitterly at the shedding of such innocent blood, but then she had an idea, and had a doe slaughtered, and cut out it eyes and its tongue and kept them safe.

'My dear,' she said to the queen, 'you can't stay here. I don't know why the king has sent this terrible command, but here it is, in his writing, and the only thing for you to do is to go away with the child out into the wide world, and never come back.'

The queen mother tied the baby on to his mother's back, and the poor woman went away once more, weeping. She walked and walked till she came to a deep, dark forest, and there she knelt down to pray.

And an angel appeared to her, just as he had before, and this time he led her to a little house. A sign above the door said: 'Here anyone is welcome, and all live free.'

Out of the house came a maiden as snow-white as the angel, and said, 'Your majesty, come inside.'

She untied the little baby from her back and held him to the queen's breast so she could suckle him, and then showed them a beautifully made bed.

'How do you know that I'm a queen?'

'I'm an angel, sent by heaven to take care of you. You needn't worry about a thing.'

And for seven years she lived in the little house, and she and her son were looked after very well. And during that time, through the grace of heaven and because of her own piety, her hands grew back.

Finally the king came home from the war, and the first thing he wanted to do was to greet his dear wife and their child.

His old mother began to weep. 'You wicked man! How can you say that, when you wanted them killed?'

The king was astonished, but she showed him the letters the Devil had forged. 'And I did what you told me to!' she said. 'Here's the proof: her eyes and her tongue.'

The king began to weep even more bitterly than his mother. Finally the old woman had mercy on him, and said, 'Something wicked has been happening here. But there's no need to weep, because your wife is still alive. These are the eyes and tongue of a doe. I tied the baby on his mother's back and told her to go out into the world, and promise never to come back here, because you were so angry with her.'

'You're right,' said the king. 'This is the work of the Devil. But I'll go out and look for her, and I'll neither eat nor drink, nor sleep in a bed till I've found my dear wife and my child.'

The king travelled all over the world for nearly seven years, searching in every cave and hovel, every town and village, and found no sign of her, so he began to think that perhaps she had perished. As he had vowed, he ate and drank nothing all that time, but the favour of heaven kept him alive. Finally he came to a great forest, where he found a little house with a sign over the door saying: 'Here anyone is welcome, and all live free.'

The snow-white angel came out and took him by the hand.

'Welcome, your majesty! Where have you come from?'

'I've been travelling about the world for nearly seven years,' he said. 'I've been looking for my wife and my child, but I can't find them anywhere.'

The angel offered him some food and drink, but he refused, saying that all he wanted was to rest a little. He lay down and covered his face with a handkerchief.

The angel went into the next room, where the queen was sitting with her son, whom she had come to call Sorrowful.

The angel said, 'Go into the parlour, and take your son. Your husband has come looking for you.'

She hurried to where he was lying, and the handkerchief fell from his face.

'Pick up the cloth, Sorrowful,' she said, 'and put it back over your father's face.'

The little boy picked it up and put it back over the king's face. The king heard this in his sleep, and deliberately let the cloth fall once more.

Then the child grew impatient and said, 'But mama, how can I cover my father's face? You've told me I had no father in this world, only a father in heaven, the one I pray to when I say, "Our father, which art in heaven". How can this wild man be my father?'

Hearing this, the king sat up and asked the woman who she was.

'I'm your wife,' she said, 'and this is your son, Sorrowful.'

But he looked at her hands, and saw they were real living hands.

'My wife had silver hands,' he said.

She replied, 'In his mercy, the dear Lord caused my hands to grow back.'

The angel brought the silver hands from the other room, and

that convinced him. This was his beloved wife and his child, there was no doubt about it, and he kissed them and embraced them and said joyfully, 'A heavy stone has fallen from my heart!'

The angel gave them all something to eat, and they went back home to his good old mother. When the news was heard throughout the kingdom, everyone was joyful. The king and queen celebrated their wedding once again, and they lived happily ever afterwards.

* * *

Tale type: ATU 706, 'The Maiden Without Hands'
Source: stories told to the Grimm brothers by Marie Hassenpflug, Dorothea Viehmann and Johann H. B. Bauer
Similar stories: Alexander Afanasyev: 'The Armless Maiden' (*Russian Fairy Tales*); Katharine M. Briggs: 'The Cruel Stepmother', 'Daughter Doris' (*Folk Tales of Britain*); Italo Calvino: 'Olive', 'The Turkey Hen' (*Italian Folktales*)

This is a widely dispersed story type. The elements are vivid and gruesome and the outcome satisfying, with the royal family restored, hands included. And the picture we're given of the beautiful handless girl, dressed all in white and accompanied by an angel, nibbling her way through a pear in the moonlit garden, is very affecting and strange.

However, the tale itself is disgusting. The most repellent aspect is the cowardice of the miller, which goes quite unpunished. The tone of never-shaken piety is nauseating, and the restoration of the poor woman's hands simply preposterous.

'But aren't fairy tales supposed to be full of preposterous things?'

No. The resurrection of the little boy in 'The Juniper Tree', for example (p. 187), feels truthful and right. This feels merely silly: instead of being struck by wonder, here we laugh. It's ridiculous. This tale and others like it must have spoken very deeply to many audiences, though, for it to spread so widely, or perhaps a great many people like stories of maiming, cruelty and sentimental piety.

TWENTY-ONE

THE ELVES

First Story

There was once a shoemaker who had become so poor (through no fault of his own) that he had hardly any leather left – only enough to make one pair of shoes, in fact. He cut them out in the evening, intending to start work on them in the morning, and then went to bed. He had a clear conscience, so he said his prayers and then slept peacefully.

Next morning he woke up, had a bite of dry bread, and sat down at his bench, only to find the shoes completed already. He was astonished. He picked them up and looked at them closely from all angles. Every stitch was neat and tight; nothing was out of place. He couldn't have done better himself.

A customer soon came in, looking for shoes of just that size, and liked them so much he bought them at once for a good price.

That gave the shoemaker enough money to buy leather for two pairs of shoes. So he did that, and as before he cut them out in the evening, meaning to carry on in the morning in good heart. But he had no need to: when he got up, the shoes were already made, just as before, stitched as if by a master craftsman. He soon found customers for them, and that left him enough profit to buy leather for four pairs; and next morning they were finished, and he sold them, and so it went on. Each evening he cut the shoes out, next morning they were finished, so that pretty soon he was making a good income, and not much later he was a wealthy man.

One evening not long before Christmas, he cut out a number of shoes as usual, and then said to his wife just as they were going to bed: 'Why don't we stay up a bit tonight and see if we can find out who's been helping us?'

His wife thought that was a good idea, and they lit the lamp and hid behind a rail of clothes hanging up in the corner of the workroom.

At midnight two little naked men squeezed in under the door and jumped up to the workbench, where they set to work at once, sewing together the cut-out shoes at a speed the shoemaker could hardly believe. They worked until they'd finished every one, and then they put the shoes on the bench and went out under the door.

In the morning the shoemaker's wife said, 'I think we should do something in return for those two little men. After all, they've made us rich, and there they are, running about in the cold with nothing on. I'm going to sew them some shirts and jackets, and some underwear and some trousers, and knit a pair of stockings for each of them as well. And you can make them each a little pair of shoes.'

'That's a good idea,' said the shoemaker, and they set to work.

That evening they set the clothes out on the bench instead of the cut-out shoes, and hid again to see what the little men would do. At midnight they came in and leaped up to the bench as before, intending to start work, and then they stopped, looking at the clothes and scratching their heads in puzzlement. Then they realized what they were for, and jumped for joy, put them on at once, and preened themselves, singing:

'We're finer than we were before –
We shan't be cobblers any more!'

They leaped about like a pair of kittens, on the chairs, the bench, the hearth, the windowsill, and finally they darted under the door and were gone.

They never came back, but the shoemaker prospered. All his work went well from then on, and he and his wife lived happy and wealthy till the end of their days.

Second Story

Once there was a poor servant girl who always worked hard and was diligent and neat in all she did. Every day she would sweep out the house and pile the rubbish outside the back door.

One morning, just as she was about to start work, she saw a letter in among the rubbish. Since she couldn't read, she stood her broom in the corner and took the letter to her mistress. It turned out to be an invitation from the elves, inviting the girl to stand as godmother at the forthcoming baptism of an elf-child.

'I don't know what to do, ma'am!' she said.

'No, it's difficult, Gretchen,' said her mistress. 'But I've heard that it's not right to turn down an invitation from the elves. I think you should accept.'

'Well, if you say so, ma'am,' said Gretchen.

The mistress helped her write a letter accepting the invitation. She left it where she'd found the other one, and when her back was turned, it vanished; and shortly afterwards three elves turned up and led her to a hollow mountain. She had to bend her head a little to go in, but once she was inside she was amazed at the beauty of everything she saw, which was delicate and precious beyond description.

The new mother was lying on a bed of the blackest ebony inset with pearly shells. The counterpane was embroidered with gold thread, the cradle was of ivory, and the little bathtub of solid gold. The baby was no bigger than her little fingernail.

The girl stood in as godmother, and then she asked to go back home, because she was needed to work the next day; but the elves pleaded with her to stay with them, just for three days. They were so persuasive and so friendly that she gave in, and had a fine time; they did everything they could to make her happy.

When three days had gone by she told them that she really must return home. They filled her pockets with gold and led her outside. She set off homewards, and reached the house late in the morning, finding her broom still in the corner where she'd left it. She picked it up and started sweeping as usual, but was astonished when some strangers came out of the house and asked her what she was doing. It turned out that her old employer had died, and she hadn't spent three days in the mountain, as she'd thought, but seven years.

Third Story

A mother had her baby stolen from his cradle by the elves, and in his place they laid a changeling, a little monster with a great thick head and staring eyes who did nothing but eat and drink.

In distress she went to a neighbour and asked her advice. The neighbour told her to take the changeling into the kitchen, lay him on the hearth, and make a fire. Then she should take two eggshells and boil some water in them. That would make the changeling laugh, and as soon as he laughed, it would be all up with him.

The woman did everything just as her neighbour said. And when she put the eggshells on the fire to boil, the blockhead sang out:

'I'm as old
As the Westerwald,
But I've never seen anyone try to boil water in an eggshell!'

And he roared with laughter. As soon as he did that, a crowd of little elves appeared, carrying the rightful child. They set him on the hearth and took the changeling away, and the woman never saw them again.

* * *

Tale type: First story: ATU 503, 'The Gifts of the Little People'; second story: ATU 476, 'Midwife in the Underworld'; third story: AT 504, 'The Changeling'
Source: all three tales told to the Grimm brothers by Dortchen Wild
Similar stories: Katharine M. Briggs: 'Food and Fire and Company', 'Goblin Combe', 'That's Enough to Go On With', 'The Two Humphs' (*Folk Tales of Britain*); Italo Calvino: 'The Two Hunchbacks' (*Italian Folktales*)

This is a group of the very few fairy tales in Grimm that actually feature fairies. Whatever we call this sort of supernatural being, elves, fairies or (the usual name for them in Britain) brownies, there are definite points of etiquette to bear in mind when dealing with them. Katharine M. Briggs, the great authority on British folk tales, says, 'Any offer of reward for its services drove the brownie away; it seemed to be an absolute taboo' (*A Dictionary of Fairies*, p. 46). However, that seems to be contradicted by her story 'That's Enough to Go On With', in which the polite children are rewarded and the rude farmer punished. Perhaps you just have to be lucky as well as careful.

The second and third tales here are little more than anecdotes, as we have them, though of course they could be elaborated. The first is the most familiar: some readers might recognize a shadowy resemblance to Beatrix Potter's *The Tailor of Gloucester* (1902).

TWENTY-TWO

THE ROBBER BRIDEGROOM

There was once a miller who had a beautiful daughter. When she came of age to be married, he thought he should look out for a suitable husband for her. 'If anyone respectable comes along,' he said to himself, 'I'll give her to him.'

Word got around, and before long a gentleman appeared to ask about this beautiful daughter. The miller interviewed him, found no fault with him, and promised that he could marry her.

However, the daughter didn't take to him at all. There was something about him she didn't trust, and what's more, whenever she thought about him or heard his name mentioned, she felt her heart contract with horror.

One day the prospective bridegroom said to her, 'You know, my dear, we're engaged to be married, but you've never paid me a visit. Why not come to my house? After all, it will soon be your own home.'

'I don't know where your house is,' the girl said.

'It's out in the forest,' he told her. 'A beautiful situation, you'll see.'

'I don't think I'll ever be able to find my way there,' she said.

'No, no, you must come on Sunday. I've already invited some guests – they're looking forward to meeting you. I'll make a trail of ashes, so you can follow it through the trees.'

On Sunday the girl felt an awful foreboding; she'd rather do anything than set off through the woods to the bridegroom's house. She filled her pockets with peas, to mark the trail in case anything happened. At the edge of the forest she found the trail of ashes, and after every step she threw a couple of peas to left and right. She walked almost the whole day till she came to a part of the forest where the trees grew so thick and high that it was dark underneath them, and there, right in the heart of the woods, she found the bridegroom's house. It was dark and silent and seemed to be deserted; there was no one inside but a bird in a cage, and he was no comfort either, because all he could sing was:

'Turn back! Get out! Go home! Take care!
This is a murderer's house! Beware!'

She looked up at the bird and said, 'Can't you tell me any more than that, little bird?'

The bird sang again:

'Turn back! Get out! Go home! Take care!
This is a murderer's house! Beware!'

The bride wandered from one room to another, but she didn't see anyone till she went down to the cellar. There she found a very old woman sitting by the light of a fire, shaking her head.

'Please can you tell me if my bridegroom lives here?' said the girl.

'Oh, you poor child,' replied the old woman, 'why ever did you come to this house? It's a den of murderers. You talk of a bridegroom – the only bridegroom you'll be marrying is Death. See this big pot of water on the fire? They made me set it there to boil. When they turn up, they're going to chop you in pieces and throw you in the pot, cook you till you're tender, and eat you all up. They're a pack of cannibals. Now I've taken pity on you, because you're a poor innocent thing, and besides, you've got a pretty face. Come over here.'

The old woman led her behind a large barrel, where she was out of sight from the rest of the cellar.

'Stay there and don't make a sound,' she said. 'If they hear you, that's the end of you. When they're asleep later on, we'll escape.'

No sooner had she said this than the band of murderers came home, dragging with them another girl whom they'd captured. She screamed and sobbed, but they were drunk and took no notice of her pleas for mercy. They forced her to drink a glass of red wine, then one of white, and then one of yellow, and the third one was too much for her; her heart burst apart.

Then they tore off her fine clothes and laid her on the table before chopping her in pieces and sprinkling her with salt. The poor bride-to-be behind the barrel trembled in every limb, seeing what fate the murderers had in mind for her.

Then one of them saw a gold ring on the dead girl's finger. He took an axe and chopped the finger off, but it flew in the air and right over the barrel and into the bride's lap. He couldn't see where it had gone, so he took a light and looked for it.

Another murderer said, 'Look behind the big barrel – I think it went over there.'

But the old woman called out, 'Come and eat your supper. The finger won't run away – you can find it in the morning.'

'She's right,' said the others, and they pulled up chairs and sat down to eat. The old woman poured a sleeping-draught in their wine, so that before they'd even finished eating they all slumped to the floor and fell asleep.

When the bride heard them snoring, she crept out from behind the barrel. She had to step over the sleeping murderers where they all lay on the cellar floor. She was terribly afraid she'd step on one and wake him up.

'Dear God, help me!' she whispered, and she got to the cellar steps safely, where the old woman was waiting. They crept upstairs, opened the door, and hurried out as fast as they could.

It was as well that the girl had brought peas to throw on the ground, because the ashes that showed the path had all blown away. The peas had sprouted, though, and in the moonlight they could see them, and followed the trail all the way to the mill, where they arrived just as the sun was rising. The girl told her father everything that had happened, from beginning to end, and the old woman confirmed it.

When the wedding day arrived, the bridegroom appeared, smiling all round and being pleasant to everyone. The miller had invited all his relations and all his friends, and they were impressed by this handsome friendly man. As they sat down to eat, each guest was asked to tell a story. The bride said nothing at all as they listened to the stories going round the table, and finally the bridegroom said, 'Come on, my darling, haven't you got a story to tell? Just tell us something.'

So she said, 'All right. I'll tell you about a dream I had. I was walking in the forest, when I came to a dark house. There wasn't a soul in sight – there was only a little bird in a cage that said, "Turn back! Get out! Go home! Take care! This is a murderer's house! Beware!"

'It said that twice, but my dear heart, it was only a dream. I went through all the rooms, and although there was no one there, something was uncanny about the place. Finally I went down to the cellar, where I found an old woman shaking her head. I said to her, "Does my bridegroom live in this house?"

'She said, "Alas, poor child, you're in the house of a murderer. Your bridegroom does live here, but he's going to chop you into pieces and cook you and eat you."'

'That isn't so!' said the bridegroom.

'Dear heart, don't worry – it was only a dream. The old woman hid me behind a great big barrel, and as soon as I was there the robbers came back, dragging a poor girl with them screaming and pleading for mercy. They forced her to drink three glasses of wine, one red, one white and one yellow, and that made her heart burst apart so she died.'

'That isn't so, and it wasn't so!' cried the bridegroom.

'Dear heart, sit still – it was only a dream. They took off her fine clothes, laid her on the table, and chopped her to pieces and sprinkled salt on them.'

'That isn't so, and it wasn't so, and God forbid it should be so!' shouted the bridegroom.

'Dear heart, stay where you are – it was only a dream. Then one of the robbers saw a gold ring on the poor girl's finger. He took an axe and chopped it off, and the finger flew through the air and landed in my lap. And here is that finger, with the ring.'

With those words she held up the finger and the ring so that everyone could see.

The bridegroom, who had become as white as chalk, leaped up and tried to escape, but the guests seized him and held him tight and then marched him to the court. Soldiers were sent out to capture the rest of the band, and they were all put to death for their wicked deeds.

* * *

Tale type: ATU 955, 'The Robber Bridegroom'
Source: a story told to the Grimm brothers by Marie Hassenpflug
Similar stories: Katharine M. Briggs: 'The Cellar of Blood', 'Dr Forster', 'Mr Fox' (*Folk Tales of Britain*); Italo Calvino: 'The Marriage of a Queen and a Bandit' (*Italian Folktales*)

There's nothing in the least supernatural in this tale: it's a good gory shocker, and firmly enough set in our own world for it not to be entirely surprising that in one of the variants, Katherine M. Briggs's 'The Cellar of Blood', the brave girl's parents phone Scotland Yard and ask them to send some detectives to the storytelling party.

Britain is particularly rich in variants of this story, for some reason. I borrowed the robber bridegroom's interjections to the bride's tale of her dream from another of them, 'Mr Fox'. Shakespeare borrowed them too:

> BENEDICK: Like the old tale, my lord: 'it is not so, nor 'twas not so, but, indeed, God forbid it should be so.'
>
> (*Much Ado About Nothing*, Act I, Scene 1)

TWENTY-THREE

GODFATHER DEATH

A poor man had twelve children, and had to work day and night just to get them a little food to eat. So when his wife gave birth to a thirteenth, he didn't know what to do, and he ran out into the road, thinking he might as well ask the first person he met to stand godfather.

The first person who came along was God himself. Since he knew everything, he didn't have to ask what was in the man's mind.

'My poor man,' he said, 'I'm sorry for you. I'd be glad to hold your child at his baptism. I'll look after him, don't you worry about that.'

'Who are you?' said the man.

'I am God.'

'Well, be on your way. I don't want you for a godfather. You give to the rich who don't need it, and you let the poor starve.'

Of course, he only said that because he didn't know God's purpose in being so kind to the rich and so cruel to the poor.

He went on his way, and the next person he met was a gentleman dressed in the finest clothes.

'I'd be glad to help,' he said. 'Make me your child's godfather and I'll give him all the riches of the world, and I'll make sure he has a good time, too.'

'And who are you?'

'I'm the Devil.'

'What! I don't want you for a godfather. You deceive people and lead them into sin – I've heard all about you.'

So he went on, and the next person he met was an old man tottering towards him on withered legs.

'Take me as your child's godfather,' the old man said.

'Who are you?'

'I'm Death, and I make everyone equal.'

'Then you're the one,' said the poor man. 'You take away the poor, and you take away the rich. You shall be godfather to my child.'

'That's a wise decision,' said Death. 'I'll make your child rich and famous. Anyone who has me for a friend can't fail.'

'Next Sunday, then,' said the man. 'Make sure you turn up on time.'

Death appeared at the baptism just as he'd promised, and swore all the vows, and behaved with perfect propriety.

So the boy grew up, and when he became of age his godfather came to the house and said, 'Come with me, young man.'

The boy followed his godfather out into the forest, where the old man showed him a particular herb.

'This is a present from your godfather,' he said. 'I'm going to make you a famous physician. Whenever you're called to the bed of a sick person, just look around and you'll see me. If I'm standing by the patient's head, you can tell his family that all will be well. Then give him a little of this herb, any way you like – give him a leaf to chew, make some tea from the flowers, grind the roots up into a paste and make pills, doesn't make any difference: in a day or so he'll be perfectly well again. But if I'm standing at the foot of the bed, he belongs to me, remember? You have to say there's no help for him, no doctor in the world could save him. Now this will always work, but watch out: if you give the herb to anyone who belongs to me, something very bad will happen to you.'

The young man did as his godfather said, and it wasn't long before he was the most famous doctor in the world. People were amazed by his ability to know at once whether the patient would live or die, and they came from every country in the world to consult him, and gave him so much money that he soon became a very wealthy man.

Now it so happened that the king of that country fell ill. The famous physician was sent for, and the courtiers asked him to say whether the royal patient was likely to survive. However, when the young man entered the bedroom, he saw his godfather standing at the foot of the bed. The king was doomed. That wasn't what the king's family wanted to hear, of course.

'If only I could contradict my godfather, just once!' thought the physician. 'He'll be angry, no doubt, but I am his godson, after all. Maybe he'll overlook it. I'll risk it, anyway.'

So he turned the patient round so that Death was standing at his head, and gave him a decoction of the leaves to drink, and pretty soon the king was sitting up and feeling much better.

However, immediately the young man was alone Death came to him, frowning darkly and shaking his finger.

'You tricked me!' he said. 'I take a very dim view of that. I'll overlook it this time because you're my godson, but try it just once again and you'll be sorry, because I'll take *you* away with me when I go.'

Not long afterwards the king's daughter fell gravely ill. She was his only child, and the king wept day and night until his eyes were so swollen he could barely see. He announced far and wide that whoever could cure her would marry her and inherit the kingdom.

Naturally, the young man was among those who came to try. And once again, when he entered the sick room, there was Death standing at the patient's feet. This time, though, the young man hardly saw his godfather, because after one look at the princess's face he was lost: she was so beautiful that he could think of nothing else. Death was frowning and snarling and shaking his fist, and the young man hardly noticed: he turned the princess round, gave her two pills, and presently she was sitting up with the colour returning to her cheeks.

But Death, having been cheated for a second time, was in no mood to wait. He seized the physician with his bony hand and said, 'Right, my boy, you're done for now.'

And he pulled him away from the princess's bedside, and away from the palace, and away from the town, and his ice-cold grasp was so firm that the young man couldn't pull free, no matter how hard he tried. Death led him to a great cavern under the mountains, where thousands and thousands of candles were burning, some of them tall, some of them medium-sized, and others so short they were on the point of going out. In fact at every moment some candles did go out, and others elsewhere suddenly came alight, so that the little flames seemed to be leaping about from one spot to another in constant movement.

'See these candles?' said godfather Death. 'Everyone alive on earth has a candle burning down here. The tall ones belong to children, the middle-sized ones to married people in the prime of life, and the little ones to old people. Mostly, that is. Some people who are only young have a very short candle.'

'Which is mine?' said the young man, thinking that his candle was bound to have a long way to burn down yet.

Death pointed to a little stump where the flame was already guttering. The young man was horrified.

'Oh, godfather, dear godfather, light another one for me, I beg you! I long to marry the princess – you know why I had to turn her round – I fell in love with her at once – I couldn't help it! Please, dear godfather, let me live my life!'

'That's impossible,' said Death. 'I can't light another one without letting the first go out.'

'Oh, I beg you – please – put this one on top of a new one so it can carry on burning when the first one's finished!'

Death pretended that he was going to do that, and he took a new long candle and set it upright before taking the little stump that was nearly out; but he was determined to have his revenge, and in tipping it over to light the new one, he let the old flame go out. The physician fell to the ground at once, for he was equal to everyone else: he had fallen into the hands of Death.

* * *

Tale type: ATU 332, 'Godfather Death'
Source: a story told to the Grimm brothers by Marie Elisabeth Wild
Similar stories: Italo Calvino: 'The Land Where No One Ever Dies' (*Italian Folktales*); Jacob and Wilhelm Grimm: 'The Godfather', 'The Messengers of Death' (*Children's and Household Tales*)

The other Grimm tale of this type, 'The Godfather', is short and facetious, with little of this story's power. The story in Calvino is similar only in its conclusion – that no one can escape falling into the hands of death. Of course, there are innumerable variations on that idea, Geoffrey Chaucer's 'The Pardoner's Tale' being one of the best known.

TWENTY-FOUR

THE JUNIPER TREE

Two thousand years ago, or a very long time anyway, there lived a rich man and his good and beautiful wife. They loved each other dearly. There was only one thing needed to complete their happiness, and that was children, but as much as they longed for a child, and as much as the woman prayed both day and night, no child came, and no child came.

Now in front of their house was a courtyard, where there grew a juniper tree. One winter's day the woman stood under the tree peeling an apple, and as she did so she cut her finger, and a drop of blood fell into the snow.

'Oh,' she sighed, 'if only I had a child as red as blood and as white as snow!'

As she said that her heart lifted, and she felt happy. She went back into the house, feeling sure everything would end well.

One month went by, and the snow vanished.

Two months went by, and the world turned green.

Three months went by, and flowers bloomed out of the earth.

Four months went by, and all the twigs on all the trees in the forest grew stronger and pressed themselves together, and the birds sang so loud that the woods resounded, and the blossom fell from the trees.

Five months went by, and the woman stood under the juniper

tree. It smelled so sweet that her heart leaped in her breast, and she fell to her knees with joy.

Six months went by, and the fruit grew firm and heavy, and the woman fell still.

When seven months had gone by, she plucked the juniper berries and ate so many that she felt sick and sorrowful.

After the eighth month had gone, she called her husband and said to him, weeping, 'If I die, bury me under the juniper tree.'

She felt comforted by his promise, and then one more month went by, and she had a child as red as blood and as white as snow; when she saw the baby her heart could not contain her joy, and she died.

Her husband buried her under the juniper tree, weeping bitterly. After a little time his first anguish ebbed away, and although he still wept, it was less bitterly than before. And after a little more time had gone by, he took a second wife.

He had a daughter by the second wife, but his first wife's child, as red as blood and as white as snow, was a son. The second wife loved her daughter, but whenever she looked at the little boy she felt her heart twist with hatred, because she knew he would inherit her husband's wealth, and she feared her daughter would get nothing. Seeing this, the Devil got into her and let her think of nothing else, and from then on she never left the little boy alone: she slapped him and cuffed him, she shouted at him and made him stand in the corner, until the poor child was so afraid he hardly dared come home from school, for there was nowhere he could find any peace.

One day the woman had gone into the pantry when her little daughter Marleenken came in after her and said, 'Mama, can I have an apple?'

'Of course, my dear,' said the woman, and gave her a fine red apple from the chest. This chest had a heavy lid with a sharp iron lock.

'Mama, can my brother have one too?' said Marleenken.

Mention of the little boy made the woman angry, but she contained herself and said, 'Yes, of course, when he comes home from school.'

Just then she happened to look out of the window and saw the little boy coming home. And it was as if the Devil himself entered her head, because she seized the apple from the girl and said, 'You're not going to have one before your brother.' She threw the apple into the chest and shut it, and Marleenken went up to her room.

Then the little boy came in, and the Devil made the woman say sweetly, 'My son, would you like an apple?'

But her eyes were fierce.

'Mama,' said the little boy, 'you look so angry! Yes, I'd like an apple.'

She couldn't stop. She had to go on.

'Come with me,' she said, opening the lid of the chest. 'Choose an apple for yourself. Lean right in – that's it – the best ones are at the back . . .'

And while the little boy was leaning in, the Evil One nudged her, and bam! She slammed down the lid, and his head fell off and rolled in among the red apples.

Then she felt horribly afraid, and she thought, 'What can I do? But maybe there's a way . . .' And she ran upstairs to her chest of drawers and took a white scarf, and then she sat the little boy in a chair by the kitchen door and set his head on his neck again, and tied the scarf around it so nothing could be seen. Then she put an apple in his hand, and went into the kitchen to put some water on the stove to boil.

And Marleenken came into the kitchen and said, 'Mama, brother is sitting by the door, and he's got an apple in his hand, and his face is so white! I asked him to give me the apple, but he didn't answer me, and I was frightened.'

'Well, you go back out there and speak to him again,' said the mother, 'and if he won't answer you this time, smack his face.'

So Marleenken went to the little boy and said, 'Brother, give me the apple.'

But he sat still and said nothing, so she smacked his face, and his head fell off. Poor Marleenken was terrified. She screamed and ran to her mother and cried, 'Oh mother, mother, I've knocked my brother's head off!' She sobbed and cried and nothing would comfort her.

'Oh, Marleenken, you bad girl,' said her mother, 'what have you done? But be quiet, hush, don't say a word about it. It can't be helped. We won't tell anyone. We'll put him in the stew.'

So she took the little boy and chopped him into pieces and put them in the pot. Marleenken couldn't stop crying; in fact so many tears fell in the water that there was no need for salt.

Presently the father came home and sat down at the table. He looked around and said, 'Where's my little boy?'

The woman put a large dish of stew on the table. Marleenken was crying and crying helplessly.

The father said again, 'Where's my son? Why isn't he here at the table?'

'Oh,' the woman said, 'he's gone away to visit his mother's great-uncle's family. He's going to stay with them for a while.'

'But why? He didn't even say goodbye.'

'He wanted to go. He said he was going to stay for six weeks. Don't worry, they'll look after him.'

'Well, I'm upset about that,' said the father. 'He shouldn't have gone like that without asking me. I'm sorry he's not here. He should have said goodbye.' And he began to eat, and he said, 'Marleenken dear, why are you crying? Your brother will come back, don't worry.'

And he ate some more stew, and then he said, 'Wife, this is the best stew I've ever tasted. It's delicious! Give me some more. You two aren't having any. I've got a feeling that this is all for me.' And he ate the whole dish, every scrap, and threw the bones under the table.

Marleenken went to her chest of drawers and took out her best silk scarf. Then she gathered up all the bones from under the table, tied them up in the scarf, and took them outside. Her poor eyes had wept so much they had no tears left, and she could only cry blood.

She laid the bones down on the green grass under the juniper tree, and as she did so she felt her heart lighten, and she stopped crying.

And the juniper tree began to move. First the branches moved apart, and then they moved together again, like someone clapping their hands. As that happened a golden mist gathered among the branches and then rose up like a flame, and at the heart of the flame there was a beautiful bird that flew high into the air singing and chirping merrily. And when the bird was gone, the juniper tree was just as it had been before, but the scarf and the bones had vanished. Marleenken felt happy again, just as happy as if her brother was still alive, and she ran into the house and sat down to eat her supper.

Meanwhile the bird was flying far away. He flew to a town and settled on the roof of a goldsmith's house and began to sing:

'My mother cut my head off,
My father swallowed me,
My sister buried all my bones
Under the juniper tree.
Keewitt! Keewitt! You'll never find
A prettier bird than me!'

Inside his workshop the goldsmith was making a golden chain. He heard the bird singing overhead and thought how lovely it sounded, so he stood up to run outside and see what sort of bird it could be. He left the house in such a hurry one of his slippers fell off on the way, and he stood in the middle of the street in his leather apron and one slipper, with his pincers in one hand and the golden chain in the other, and he looked up to see the bird and shaded his eyes from the bright sun and called out: 'Hey, bird! That's a lovely song you're singing! Sing it again for me!'

'Oh, no,' said the bird, 'I don't sing twice for nothing. Give me that golden chain and I'll sing it again for you.'

'Here you are, and welcome,' said the goldsmith. 'Come and take it, but do sing that song again!'

The bird flew down and took the golden chain in his right claw, and perched on the garden fence and sang:

'My mother cut my head off,
My father swallowed me,
My sister buried all my bones
Under the juniper tree.
Keewitt! Keewitt! You'll never find
A prettier bird than me!'

Then the bird flew away and found a shoemaker's house, and he perched on the roof and sang:

'My mother cut my head off,
My father swallowed me,
My sister buried all my bones
Under the juniper tree.
Keewitt! Keewitt! You'll never find
A prettier bird than me!'

The shoemaker was tapping away at his last, but his hammer fell still as he heard the song, and he ran out of doors and looked up at the roof. He had to shade his eyes because the sun was so bright.

'Bird,' he called out, 'you're a wonderful singer! I've never heard a song like it!' He ran back inside and called, 'Wife, come out and listen to this bird! He's a marvel!'

He called his daughter and her children, and his apprentices, and the maid, and they all came out into the street and gazed up in amazement. The bird's red and green feathers were shining, and the golden feathers of his neck were dazzling in the sunlight, and his eyes sparkled like stars.

'Bird,' the shoemaker called up, 'sing that song again!'

'Oh, no,' said the bird, 'I don't sing twice for nothing. Give me those red slippers I can see on your bench.'

The wife ran into the shop and brought out the slippers, and the bird flew down and seized them in his left claw. Then he flew around their heads, singing:

'My mother cut my head off,
My father swallowed me,
My sister buried all my bones
Under the juniper tree.
Keewitt! Keewitt! You'll never find
A prettier bird than me!'

Then he flew away, out of the town and along the river, and in his right claw he had the golden chain and in his left he had the slippers. He flew and he flew till he came to a mill, and the mill wheel was going *clippety-clap, clippety-clap, clippety-clap*. Outside the mill twenty apprentices were sitting down chiselling a new millstone, *hick-hack, hick-hack, hick-hack,* and the mill went *clippety-clap, clippety-clap, clippety-clap.*

The bird flew round and perched on a linden tree that stood in front of the mill, and began to sing:

'My mother cut my head off—'

And one of the apprentices stopped working and looked up.

'My father swallowed me—'

Two more stopped working and listened.

'My sister buried all my bones—'

Four of them stopped.

'Under the juniper tree—'

And eight put their chisels down.

'Keewitt! Keewitt! You'll never find—'

And now four more looked all around.

'A prettier bird than me!'

Finally the last apprentice heard, and dropped his chisel, and then all twenty burst into cheers and clapped and threw their hats in the air.

'Bird,' cried the last apprentice, 'that's the best song I've ever heard! But I only heard the last line. Sing it again for me!'

'Oh, no,' said the bird, 'I don't sing twice for nothing. Give me that millstone you're all working on, and I'll sing you the song again.'

'If it only belonged to me, you could have it like a shot!' he said. 'But . . .'

'Oh, come on,' said the others. 'If he sings again, he can have it and welcome.'

So the twenty apprentices took a long beam and laid the end under the edge of the millstone and heaved it up: Heave-*hup*! Heave-*hup*! Heave-*hup*!

The bird flew down and put his head through the hole in the middle, and wearing it like a collar he flew back up to the tree and sang again:

'My mother cut my head off,
My father swallowed me,
My sister buried all my bones
Under the juniper tree.
Keewitt! Keewitt! You'll never find
A prettier bird than me!'

When he'd finished the song he spread his wings and flew up in the air. In his right claw he had the golden chain, in his left claw he had the shoes, and around his neck was the millstone. He flew and he flew all the way back to his father's house.

Inside the house, father and mother and Marleenken were sitting at the table.

Father said, 'You know, I feel happy for some reason. I feel better than I've done for days.'

'It's all very well for you,' said the wife. 'I don't feel well at all. I feel as if a bad storm were coming.'

As for Marleenken, she just sat and wept.

At that moment, the bird arrived. He flew around the house and settled on the roof, and as he did that, father said, 'No, I don't think I've ever felt so well. The sun's shining outside, and I feel as if I'm going to see an old friend.'

'Well, I feel terrible!' said the woman. 'I don't know what's the matter with me. I feel cold and hot all over. My teeth are chattering and my veins are filled with fire.'

She tore open her bodice with trembling hands. Marleenken sat in the corner, weeping and weeping so much that her handkerchief was soaked right through.

Then the bird left the roof and flew to the juniper tree, where they could all see him, and he sang:

'My mother cut my head off—'

The mother pressed her hands over her ears and squeezed her

eyes tight shut. There was a roaring in her head, and behind her eyelids lightning burned and flashed.

'My father swallowed me—'

'Wife, look at this!' cried the man. 'You've never seen such a lovely bird! He's singing like an angel, and the sun's shining so warmly, and the air smells like cinnamon!'

'My sister buried all my bones—'

Marleenken laid her head on her knees sobbing and crying, but the father said, 'I'm going out. I've got to see this bird close to!'

'No! Don't go!' cried the wife. 'I feel as if the whole house is shaking and burning!'

But the father ran out into the sunshine and gazed up at the bird as he sang:

'Under the juniper tree.
Keewitt! Keewitt! You'll never find
A prettier bird than me!'

As he sang the last note he dropped the golden chain, and it fell around the father's neck and fitted him as if it had been made for him. The father ran in at once, and said, 'What a beautiful bird! And see what he's given me – look!'

The woman was too terrified to look. She fell down on the floor, and her cap fell off her head and rolled away into the corner.

Then the bird sang once more:

'My mother cut my head off—'

'No! I can't bear it! I wish I were a thousand feet under the ground, so I wouldn't have to hear that song!'

'My father swallowed me—'

And the wife fell down again as if she'd been stunned, and her fingernails were scratching at the floor.

'My sister buried all my bones—'

And Marleenken wiped her eyes and got up. 'I'll go and see if the bird will give me something,' she said, and ran outside.

'Under the juniper tree—'

As he said that, the bird threw down the little red shoes.

'Keewitt! Keewitt! You'll never find
A prettier bird than me!'

Marleenken put on the shoes, and found they fitted her perfectly. She was delighted, and she danced and skipped into the house and said, 'Oh, what a beautiful bird! I was so sad when I went out, and see what he's given me! Mama, look at these lovely shoes!'

'No! No!' cried the woman. She jumped to her feet, and her hair stood out all round her head like flames of fire. 'I can't stand any more! I feel as if the world were coming to an end! I can't stand it!'

And she ran out of the door and out on to the grass, and – *bam!* The bird dropped the millstone on her head, and she was crushed to death.

The father and Marleenken heard the crash and ran out. Smoke and flames and fire were rising from the spot, and then came a breath of wind and cleared them all away; and when they were gone, there was little brother standing there.

And he took his father by one hand and Marleenken by the other, and all three of them were very happy; and so they went inside their house and sat down at the table and ate their supper.

* * *

Tale type: ATU 720, 'The Juniper Tree'
Source: a story written by Philipp Otto Runge
Similar stories: Katharine M. Briggs: 'The Little Bird', 'The Milk-White Doo', 'Orange and Lemon', 'The Rose Tree' (*Folk Tales of Britain*)

For beauty, for horror, for perfection of form, this story has no equal. Like 'The Fisherman and His Wife' (p. 93), it is the work of the painter Philipp Otto Runge, and came to the Grimms in manuscript form and in the Pomeranian dialect of Plattdeutsch or Low German.

A comparison with the several versions of the story in Katharine M. Briggs's *Folk Tales of Britain* will show how much Runge improved the basic thread of the narrative. Her versions are thin and insubstantial: this is a masterpiece.

The prelude, with its lovely evocation of the seasons changing as the wife's pregnancy develops, associates the child in her womb with the regenerative powers of nature, and especially with the juniper tree itself. After the mother's death comes the first part of the story proper, the gruesome tale of the stepmother and the little boy up to the appearance of the bird, which would be simple Grand Guignol were it not for the unusual depths of malice shown in the character of the mother. The parallels with Greek drama (Atreus feeding Thyestes his own sons) and Shakespeare (Titus Andronicus feeding Tamora hers) are interesting too. The father's eating the son is capable of many interpretations: a student of mine once suggested that the father is unconsciously aware of the threat posed to his son by the stepmother, and is putting him in a place where he'll be perfectly safe. I thought that was ingenious.

After the horror of the first part of the story proper, everything is sunshine and light. At first we can't understand what the bird is doing, but the golden chain and the red slippers are pretty, and the comedy of the goldsmith running out of the house and losing his own slipper is diverting. Finally we come to the mill, and the second part of the story ends with the bird improbably but convincingly flying away with the millstone as well as the slippers and the chain. Then we begin to understand.

The final part of the story is reminiscent of the climax of 'The Fisherman and His Wife', with the storm paralleling the climax of guilt and madness felt by the wife. This time, the storm is internal: the father and Marleenken feel nothing but delight and pleasure as the little boy is returned to them, while the mother is demented with terror.

There is an interesting point connected with the actual telling of this story, which bears out its literary nature. It matters a great deal to remember exactly the sequence of events as the woman's pregnancy develops, and the number of apprentices who stop chipping at the millstone with each line of the verse, and the precise way the mother's terror is interlined with the bird's singing and the gifts of the chain and the slippers. The precision of Runge's narration deserves – and rewards – complete faithfulness.

What a privilege it is to tell this story.

TWENTY-FIVE

BRIAR ROSE

Once there were a king and queen who said to each other every day, 'Wouldn't it be good to have a child?' But for all their wishing, all their praying, all their expensive medicine and special diets, no child came.

Then one day, when the queen was bathing, a frog crept out of the water and sat on the bank and said to her, 'Your wish will be granted. Before a year has passed, you'll bring a daughter into the world.'

The frog's words came true. After a year the queen gave birth to a baby girl who was so beautiful that the king couldn't contain his joy, and he ordered a great celebration to which he invited not only his royal relatives from every nearby country, but also friends and distinguished people of every kind. Among those were the thirteen Wise Women. The king wanted them there so that they'd be well disposed towards his daughter, but the trouble was that he only had twelve gold plates for them to eat off. One of the Wise Women would have to stay at home.

The feasting and celebrating went on for some time, and it ended with the Wise Women presenting the new princess with special gifts. This one gave her virtue, that one gave her beauty, a third gave her wealth, and so on; everything anyone could wish for was hers.

The eleventh one had just given her gift (patience) when there was a disturbance at the door. The guards were trying to keep someone out, but she swept them aside and came in anyway. It was the thirteenth Wise Woman.

'So you didn't think me worth inviting?' she said to the king. 'What a mistake that was! Here's my answer to that insult: in her fifteenth year, the princess will prick her finger on a spindle and fall down dead.'

And she turned on her heel and swept out.

Everyone was shocked. But the twelfth Wise Woman, who hadn't given her gift yet, stepped forward and said: 'I can't completely undo that evil wish, but I can soften it. The princess will not die, but fall asleep for a hundred years.'

The king, wanting to protect his daughter, issued a command that every spindle in the land should be burned. As the princess grew up it was clear that all the Wise Women's gifts were there in full abundance: never had anyone known a girl kinder, more beautiful, more clever or more sweet-tempered. She was loved by everyone who knew her.

Now on the day when the princess turned fifteen, it happened that the king and the queen were away, and the girl was alone in the castle. She wandered about from one place to the next, looking into this room or that, into the cellar, up on the rooftop, going wherever she wanted; and at last she came to an old tower where she'd never been before. She climbed up the dusty spiral staircase and found a small door at the top with a rusty key in the lock.

Curious, the princess turned the key and at once the door sprang open. In the little room sat an old woman with a spindle, busily spinning flax.

'Good morning, old lady,' said the princess. 'What's that you're doing?'

'I'm spinning,' said the old woman.

Of course, the princess had never seen anyone spinning before.

'What's that little thing bouncing around at the end of the thread?' she said.

The old woman offered to show her how to do it. The princess took hold of the spindle, and a second later she felt a prick in her finger – and down she fell on the bed that lay ready, fast asleep.

The sleep was so deep that it spread through all the castle. The king and queen had just returned, and as soon as they walked into the hall they fell down where they stood. Their servants and attendants fell down too, like dominoes in a line, and so did the horses in the stables and the grooms looking after them, and the pigeons on the roof and the dogs in the courtyard. One dog was scratching himself: he fell asleep just like that, with his back paw behind his ear. The flies on the wall fell asleep. Down in the kitchen the very flames under the roasting ox fell asleep. A drop of fat that was about to fall from the sizzling carcass stayed where it was and didn't move. The cook had been about to clout the kitchen boy; her hand fell still six inches from his ear, and his face remained screwed up waiting for the blow. Outside the wind stopped blowing; not a leaf stirred; the very ripples on the lake stayed as they were, as if made of glass.

In all the castle and its grounds the only thing that moved was a thorny hedge. Every year it grew a little more, and it slowly grew and grew till it reached the castle walls, and then it climbed and climbed year by year till it covered the entire castle. Nothing of the building could be seen, not even the flag on the roof.

Of course people wondered why this was happening, and where the king and queen and their beautiful daughter were. But there were a few people who'd been guests at the celebration of the princess's birth, and who remembered the Wise Women and their gifts, and the curse of the one who'd been left out.

'It's all because the beautiful princess fell asleep,' they said. 'She must be in there still. Anyone who makes his way in and rescues her will marry her, you'll see.'

Naturally, as time passed, various young men came – princes, soldiers, farmers' sons, beggars – all kinds of them, trying to cut their way in through the hedge and find the door of the castle. They were sure that once they were inside they'd find the princess and wake her up with a kiss and break the spell.

But none of them managed it. The hedge was immensely thick, and the thorns so long and sharp that they dug into the clothes and the flesh of anyone trying to force his way through. All the young men got stuck. The more they struggled the deeper the thorns stabbed them, and they couldn't go on and they couldn't turn back and they couldn't get free, and they all died helplessly in the hedge.

Many, many years later, after the story of the sleeping princess had been almost forgotten, a young prince came to that country. He was travelling incognito, and when he stayed at a humble inn not far from the castle, nobody knew who he was. One night he listened to an old man telling a story by the fire. It was a story about the great thorn hedge: inside the hedge there was a castle, and inside the castle was a tower, and inside the tower was a room where a lovely princess lay asleep.

'And there's many a brave young man has tried to get through the hedge,' he said, 'and not one of 'em made it. If you go up close you can see their skeletons, or bits of 'em that's close enough to see. But no one's seen the princess, and she's lying there asleep to this day.'

'I'll try!' said the young man. 'My sword's sharp enough to deal with thorns.'

'Don't do it, son!' said the old man. 'Once you get in that hedge, no power on earth will get you out. You'll blunt your sword on a hundred thorns before you've gone a yard.'

'No,' declared the prince. 'I'm going to do it, and that's that. I'll start in the morning.'

As it happened, the very next day was the day when the hundred years were up. Of course the prince didn't know about that, but he set off with a heart full of courage. He came to the great thorn hedge and found it not at all as the old man had said, because as well as thorns the hedge was bearing pretty pink flowers, thousands upon thousands of them. For all that, though, he could see the skeletons of many other young men tangled deep in the briars. A sweet fragrance like apples filled the air, and as the prince came close to the hedge, the branches pulled apart by themselves to let him through, closing up behind him afterwards.

He came to the courtyard and saw the pigeons asleep, the dog still with its paw behind its neck, the flies asleep on the wall; he went down into the kitchen and saw the kitchen boy's face still screwed up waiting for the clout from the cook's hand, the flames standing quite still in the hearth, the drop of fat still about to drop from the roasting ox; he wandered through the rooms upstairs and saw servant after servant asleep in the middle of whatever they'd been doing, and the king and the queen asleep on the floor of the hall, exactly where they'd fallen.

Then he came to the tower. He climbed the dusty spiral staircase, he found the little door, he turned the rusty handle. The door opened at once. There on the bed lay the most beautiful princess the young man had ever seen, or could ever imagine.

He bent over her and kissed her lips, and Briar Rose opened her eyes and gave a little sigh of surprise and smiled at the young man, who fell in love with her at once.

They went downstairs together, watching everyone wake up all around them. The king and the queen woke up, and stared all around wide-eyed, because of the great hedge that had grown all over the castle. The horses woke up and shook themselves and neighed; the pigeons on the roof woke up, the dog in the courtyard carried on scratching, the cook boxed the kitchen boy's ears so hard that he yelled, the drop of fat fell into the fire with a sizzle.

And in due course the prince was married to Briar Rose. The wedding was celebrated with great splendour, and they lived happily together to the end of their lives.

Tale type: ATU 410, 'Sleeping Beauty'
Source: a story told to the Grimm brothers by Marie Hassenpflug
Similar stories: Giambattista Basile: 'Sun, Moon and Talia' (*The Great Fairy Tale Tradition*, ed. Jack Zipes); Italo Calvino: 'The Neapolitan Soldier' (*Italian Folktales*); Jacob and Wilhelm Grimm: 'The Glass Coffin' (*Children's and Household Tales*); Charles Perrault: 'The Sleeping Beauty in the Wood' (*Perrault's Complete Fairy Tales*)

Bruno Bettelheim, as might be expected, takes a thoroughly Freudian view of this tale. According to him, the sleep of a hundred years that follows the unexpected loss of blood 'is nothing but a time of quiet growth and preparation, from which the person will awake mature, ready for sexual union' (*The Uses of Enchantment*, p. 232).

Furthermore, it's no use trying to forestall what is bound to happen to a growing child. The king tries to destroy all the spindles in the kingdom 'to prevent the princess's fateful bleeding once she reaches puberty, at fifteen, as the evil fairy predicted. Whatever precautions a father takes, when the daughter is ripe for it, puberty will set in.'

Bettelheim's interpretation is persuasive. But whether it's the underlying symbolism that is responsible for the enduring popularity of this story or the wealth of delightful detail (the poor little kitchen boy, doomed to wait a hundred years for the clout the cook is lining up), it remains one of the most well loved of all the Grimms' tales.

And the princess needs her hundred years and her hedge of thorns. At fifteen, she's not grown up yet; or as Louis Jordan used to sing: 'That chick's too young to fry.'

TWENTY-SIX

SNOW WHITE

One winter's day, when the snowflakes were falling like feathers, a queen sat sewing at her window, which had a frame of the blackest ebony. She opened the window to look up at the sky, and as she did so she pricked her finger, and three drops of blood fell into the snow on the windowsill. The red and the white looked so beautiful together that she said to herself, 'I wish I had a child as white as snow, as red as blood, and as black as the wood in the window frame.'

And soon afterwards she had a little daughter, and she was as white as snow and as red as blood and as black as ebony, so they called her Little Snow White. As soon as the baby was born, the queen died.

A year later, the king married another wife. She was a beautiful woman, but she was proud and arrogant, and she couldn't bear to think that anyone was more beautiful than she was. She had a magic mirror, and every morning she used to stand in front of it and gaze at her reflection and say:

'Mirror, mirror on the wall,
Who in this land is the fairest of all?'

And the mirror would reply:

'Your majesty, you are the fairest of all.'

She was satisfied then, because she knew that the mirror could only tell the truth.

But meanwhile, Snow White was growing up. When she was seven years old she was as lovely as a spring day, and even more beautiful, in fact, than the queen.

So one day when the queen asked her mirror:

'Mirror, mirror on the wall,
Who in this land is the fairest of all?'

the mirror answered:

'Your majesty, you are still lovely, it's true,
But Snow White is a thousand times fairer than you.'

Immediately the queen took fright. Envy churned in her bowels, and her flawless complexion took on a sickly yellow-green. From that moment on, she only had to look at Snow White to feel her heart tightening with malice. Her envy and pride grew strong like a weed in her soul, and she felt no peace by day or by night.

Finally she called one of the king's huntsmen and said to him, 'Take that child deep into the woods. I never want to set eyes on her again. Make sure she's dead, and bring me her lungs and liver as proof.'

The huntsman did as she ordered. When he had taken Snow White far into the heart of the forest, he took out his knife, and was about to thrust it into her innocent heart when she began to cry, 'Oh please, dear huntsman, spare my life! I'll run away into the wild woods and never come home again, I promise!'

She was so beautiful that the huntsman took pity on her and said, 'You poor child, go on then – run away.'

'The wild beasts will eat her soon in any case,' he thought, but knowing that he wouldn't have to kill her was like feeling a heavy weight lift from his heart.

Just then a young boar came running through the bushes. The huntsman killed it and cut out its lungs and liver, and took them back to the queen as proof of Snow White's death. The cook was ordered to season them well, dredge them in flour and fry them, and the wicked queen ate them all up. And that, she thought, was the end of Snow White.

But meanwhile, Snow White was alone in the great forest with no idea what to do or where to go. She looked all around, but nothing she could see among the leaves and the bushes was any help. She was frightened, and she began to run, ignoring the sharp stones and the brambles and the small animals that leaped at her. She ran and she ran, and just as the light was fading and the evening was near, she saw a little cottage. She knocked, but there was no one at home, so she went inside hoping to rest.

Everything in the house was small, but very neat and clean. There was a pot of stew beside the fire, and a little table covered with a snowy-white tablecloth, on which stood seven little bowls, with a slice of bread beside each one, and seven little knives and forks and spoons and seven little mugs. Upstairs there were seven little beds, all standing in a row, all neatly made with snowy-white linen, and a little table beside each bed with a little glass and a little toothbrush.

Snow White was very hungry and thirsty, so she ate some stew from the pot and took a bite of each slice of bread and a sip of wine from each mug. And then she realized how tired she was, so she lay down on one of the beds, but it was too big; and she tried another, but it was too short; but the seventh one was just right. So she said her prayers, and lay down and closed her eyes and was asleep in a moment.

Presently, when it was dark, the owners of the cottage came home. They were seven dwarfs, and they earned their living by mining for precious ore under the mountains. They came in and lit their lanterns, and then they saw that things were not as they had left them.

'Someone's been sitting in my chair!'

'Someone's been eating from my bowl!'

'There's a bite out of my bread – look!'

'The ladle's been used – someone's eaten some stew!'

'And they've used my knife—'

'And they've used my fork—'

'And they've drunk from my mug!'

They looked at each other with wide eyes. Then they all looked up at the ceiling, and they all tiptoed up the stairs, and they all looked at their beds, and whispered:

'Someone's tried my bed!'

'And mine—'

'And mine—'

'And mine—'

'And mine—'

'And mine—'

'Oh, *look*!'

The seventh dwarf had found Snow White asleep. They all tiptoed up and looked at her in wonder. The lantern light shone over her face on the snowy-white pillow.

'Good heavens! What a beautiful child!'

'Who can she be?'

'We can't wake her up! She's fast asleep . . .'

'What a lovely face!'

'I wonder where she came from?'

'It's a mystery, brothers! A deep mystery!'

'Come back downstairs. We must discuss what to do . . .'

They tiptoed back downstairs and sat around the table.

'She looks exhausted, poor little thing.'

'Better not wake her up.'

'The morning'll be soon enough for that.'

'Maybe she's escaping from a witch . . .'

'Fool! There's no such things as witches.'

'I think she's a angel.'

'And so she might be, but she's in my bed, and where am *I* going to sleep?'

The other six agreed to let the seventh one share their beds, an hour each throughout the night. And so they went to sleep.

When Snow White woke up in the morning and found the seven dwarfs all looking at her (they'd woken up and got dressed already), she was alarmed.

'Don't be frightened, miss!'

'We're friendly enough!'

'Not pretty, maybe—'

'But we won't do you no harm.'

'That's a promise!'

'You're safe here.'

'What's your name, my dear?'

'I'm called Snow White,' she said.

They asked where she came from, how she'd found her way to their cottage, and so on, and she told them how her stepmother had tried to kill her, and how the huntsman had spared her life, and how she'd run in a panic through the bushes and the brambles till she found their cottage.

The dwarfs withdrew to the corner of the room and whispered together, and then came back and said:

'If you'll keep house for us—'

'Sweep and clean, you know, all that—'

'And cook! Don't forget cooking!'

'Yes, and cook, and make the beds—'

'And wash the linen—'

'And sew and knit and darn our socks—'

'Then you can stay with us, my dear, and you shall have everything you want.'

'Oh, I'll do that with all my heart!' said Snow White.

So they agreed on that, and Snow White began to keep house for them. Every morning they tramped off to the mountain to dig for gold and copper and silver, and when they came back in the evening their dinner was ready for them, and the cottage was neat and clean and everything was in order.

During the day, of course, Snow White was all alone, and the dwarfs warned her: 'Be careful. That stepmother of yours will be looking for you once she finds out you're alive. Don't let anyone in!'

Once the queen had eaten the liver and lungs that she thought were Snow White's, she wasn't afraid to look in her magic mirror again and say:

'Mirror, mirror on the wall,
Who in this land is the fairest of all?'

But she got a terrible shock when the mirror answered:

'Your majesty, you are still lovely, it's true,
But far, far away in the forest so deep
Where she lives with the dwarfs since they found her asleep,
Snow White is a thousand times fairer than you.'

The queen recoiled with horror, for she knew the mirror couldn't lie, and she realized that the huntsman must have deceived her. Snow White was still alive! All her thoughts circled around one question: how could she kill Snow White? If she, the queen, wasn't the most beautiful woman in the whole country, she knew her envy would torment her day and night.

At last she thought of a plan. She made up her face carefully and disguised herself as an old pedlar, so skilfully that she knew no one would recognize her. She made her way to the house of the seven dwarfs, and when they were at work down under the mountain, she knocked on the door.

Snow White was making the beds. She heard the knock and opened an upstairs window.

'Good day,' she called down. 'What are you selling?'

'Fine laces and pretty ribbons,' the queen called up. 'Would you like to see what I have, my dear? Here's a lovely one, look!'

She pulled out a lace made of braided silk. Snow White thought it was very pretty indeed, and surely this old woman had an honest face. It must be safe to let her in.

She ran down and unbolted the door and looked at the lace.

'Would you like to try it?' said the pedlar-woman. 'Dear me, child, you need looking after. Come here, sweetie, let me do up your bodice with this pretty lace.'

Snow White stood there not suspecting a thing while the old woman threaded the lace through and through her bodice, and then pulled and pulled and pulled so tight that Snow White couldn't breathe. The poor girl's eyes fluttered and her lips moved and then she fell down senseless.

'You're not so beautiful now you're dead,' muttered the old woman, and hurried away.

Soon afterwards the dwarfs came home, because the day was ending. When they saw Snow White lying there not breathing, they were terrified. They picked her up and then realized what was causing the trouble, and quickly they cut through the lace so she could breathe. Little by little she came back to life and told them what had happened.

'Well, you know who that pedlar-woman was, don't you?'

'It was the wicked queen!'

'Couldn't have been anyone else.'

'Don't let her in again, whatever you do!'

'Take care, Snow White! Oh, do take care.'

'Remember now – be on your guard!'

'Don't let *anyone* in.'

Meanwhile the queen was hurrying home. As soon as she was safe in her boudoir, she asked the mirror:

'Mirror, mirror on the wall,
Who in this land is the fairest of all?'

And the mirror answered:

'Your majesty, you are still lovely, it's true,
But they cut through the lace with a sharp little knife
And they brought their Snow White back to life –
And she's still a thousand times lovelier than you.'

When the queen heard that, her heart gave a sickening lurch and squeezed her blood so hard she thought her eyes would burst.

'Still alive! Still alive! We'll see about that!' she said. 'She won't be alive for long, I promise.'

The queen understood the art of witchcraft, and she crushed some rare herbs while saying a spell, and then dipped a pretty comb in the herb-juice. It was deadly poison. With the aid of a little more magic, she changed her appearance entirely so she didn't look at all like the previous old woman, and set off for the dwarfs' cottage.

She knocked on the door and called out, 'Pretty knick-knacks for sale! Combs and pins and mirrors! Pretty trinkets for pretty girls!'

Snow White looked out of the upstairs window and answered, 'I can't let you in. I'm not allowed. You'd better go away.'

'That's all right, sweetheart,' said the old woman, 'I won't step over the threshold. I'm sure no one would mind if you took a look, though. What about this lovely comb here, look!'

It *was* very pretty, and Snow White thought it would do no harm just to look. She ran down and opened the door.

'Oh, such lovely hair!' said the old woman. 'So black and so rich and shiny! But oh, a terrible tangle – when did you last brush it properly, sweetheart? Don't they look after you here?'

She was running her fingers through Snow White's hair as she spoke.

'Let me just tease out a tangle or two with this pretty comb – you like it, don't you? I can see – come here, darling . . .'

Snow White obediently bent her head, and the old woman dug the comb into her scalp so viciously the poor girl fell straight down without even a cry.

'That's done for you, missy! Let's see how lovely you are when you start to rot!' said the queen, and she hurried away before the dwarfs came home.

Luckily it was almost evening, and not long after the wicked queen left Snow White lying there, the dwarfs came home and found her.

'Snow White! What's happened?'

'Is she breathing?'

'That wicked queen again—'

'What's that stuck in her hair?'

'Pull it out, quick!'

'Mind – it'll be poisoned!'

'Careful . . . careful . . .'

They wrapped a handkerchief around the comb and pulled it delicately out, and almost at once Snow White sighed and opened her eyes.

'Oh, dwarfs, I'm so stupid! She didn't look at all like she did before, and I thought it would be all right . . .'

They told her it would only be all right if she kept her wits about her and did as they told her. She mustn't open the door for *anyone*.

The queen hurried back and threw off her disguise before standing in front of the magic mirror. She said:

'Mirror, mirror on the wall,
Who in this land is the fairest of all?'

And the mirror answered:

'Your majesty, you are still lovely, it's true,
But as soon as you'd gone, the good dwarfs arrived home
And with care and with caution they took out the comb,
And Snow White is alive and far lovelier than you.'

That made the queen stagger and clutch at the wall. The blood drained out of her face, leaving it a dirty white with patches of yellow and green. Then she drew herself up to her full height, and sparks flew out of her eyes.

'Snow White shall die!' she cried.

She went into her most private room and locked the door behind her. No one was allowed in there, not even the servants. Then, with the help of a book of spells and several little dark bottles, she set about making a poisoned apple. It was white on one side and rosy red on the other; anyone who saw it would want to take a bite; but if they did, even just the tiniest nibble, they would fall down dead at once.

Then the queen disguised herself a third time, put the apple in her pocket, and set off for the dwarfs' cottage.

She knocked on the door and Snow White looked out of the window.

'I can't let anyone in,' she said. 'I'm not allowed.'

'That's all right, my dear,' said the queen, who looked like an old peasant. 'I just wondered if you'd like an apple. I've had such a crop this year I don't know what to do with them all.'

'No, I'm not supposed to take anything,' said Snow White.

'Oh, what a pity,' said the old woman. 'They taste so good, too. Look, I'll take a bite in case you're worried.'

She had made the apple so cunningly that only the red half was poisoned. Of course she took a bite from the white half, and then held it out to Snow White.

It looked so delicious that the poor girl couldn't resist. She reached out through the window, took the apple, and bit deeply into the red part, and she'd hardly bitten off a piece when she fell to the floor, dead.

The wicked queen leaned in and saw her lying on the floor, and she laughed a loud laugh.

'White as snow, red as blood, black as ebony! And now dead as a doornail! Those little monkeys won't wake you up this time.'

When she got back to her boudoir she asked the mirror:

'Mirror, mirror on the wall,
Who in this land is the fairest of all?'

And the mirror answered:

'Your majesty, you are the fairest of all.'

She sighed a deep and happy sigh of satisfaction. If an envious heart can be at rest, hers was then.

When the dwarfs came home that evening, they found Snow White on the floor, stark and still. She wasn't breathing, her eyes were closed, she wasn't moving at all. She was dead. They looked around for whatever might have killed her, and found nothing; they unfastened her laces in case she couldn't breathe; they looked through her hair for a poisoned comb; they warmed her by the fire, they put a drop of brandy on her lips, they laid her on a bed and they sat her up in a chair, but nothing helped.

Then it struck home to them that she must be really dead, and they laid her out gently on a bier and sat beside her, weeping for three days. They had intended to bury her, but she still looked so fresh and beautiful, just as if she was only sleeping, that they couldn't bring themselves to put her under the black earth.

So they had a glass coffin made, and laid her inside. With

letters of gold they wrote 'PRINCESS SNOW WHITE' on it, and they carried it up to a mountain top. From then on one of the dwarfs stayed beside her all the time. They took it in turns to watch over her, and the birds came and mourned for her as well: first an owl, then a raven, and finally a dove.

And so things remained for a long, long time. The body of Snow White did not decay, for she still looked as white as snow, as red as blood and as black as ebony.

One day a prince happened to be hunting in the forest, and he came to the dwarfs' house and asked for shelter for the night. Next morning he saw the sunlight glitter on the mountain top and went to see what was there. He found the glass coffin, he read the golden inscription, and he saw the body of Snow White.

He said to the dwarfs, 'Let me take the coffin away with me. I'll pay you as much as you want.'

'We don't want money,' they said. 'We wouldn't sell that coffin for all the money in the world.'

'Then please give it to me,' he begged. 'I've fallen in love with Princess Snow White, and I can't live without being able to see her. I'll treat her with all the honour and respect I'd feel for a living princess.'

The dwarfs went away a little and spoke together quietly. Then they came back and said they'd taken pity on him, and they were sure he'd treat their dear Snow White properly, so he could take her back to his kingdom.

The prince thanked them and told his servants to pick up the coffin with great care and carry it along with him. But as they were going down the mountainside, one of the servants tripped and stumbled, and shook the coffin; and that dislodged the piece of apple from Snow White's throat, for she had never quite swallowed it.

And slowly she woke up, and then she pushed open the lid of the coffin and sat up, fully alive once more.

'Dear God, where am I?' she said.

The prince said joyfully, 'You're with me!' He told her everything that had happened, and then said, 'I love you more than anything else in the world. Come with me to my father's castle, and become my wife.'

Snow White loved him at once, and their wedding was arranged with great splendour and magnificence.

Among the guests invited to the ceremony was Snow White's wicked stepmother. After putting on the most beautiful of her dresses she stood in front of the magic mirror and said:

> *'Mirror, mirror on the wall,*
> *Who in this land is the fairest of all?'*

And the mirror answered:

> *'Your majesty, you are still lovely, it's true,*
> *But the young queen's a thousand times fairer than you.'*

The queen gasped with horror. She was so frightened, so terrified, that she didn't know what to do. She didn't want to go to the wedding and she didn't want to stay away, and yet she felt she had to go and see the young queen; so in the end she went. And when she saw Snow White she recognized her at once, and was struck with horror. She could only stand there trembling.

But a pair of iron shoes had already been placed in the fire. When they were red-hot they were brought out with tongs and placed on the floor. And the wicked queen was made to step into them, and dance till she fell down dead.

* * *

Tale type: ATU 709, 'Snow White'
Source: a story told to the Grimm brothers by the Hassenpflug family

Similar stories: Katharine M. Briggs: 'Snow-White' (*Folk Tales of Britain*); Italo Calvino: 'Bella Venezia', 'Giricoccola' (*Italian Folktales*)

The great gravitational attraction of Walt Disney's *Snow White and the Seven Dwarfs* will always pull at this tale, unless the storyteller simply decides to ignore it, which isn't actually very hard to do, if you take your lead from Grimm.

Disney was a great storyteller, though, and it's interesting to see how the artists in the Disney studio, working under his direction, focused not only on one aspect of the tale that is in Grimm (the wickedness of the stepmother/queen) but also on another that isn't (the comedy of the dwarfs, their individual names and personalities). 'Work to your strengths' is a good storytelling maxim. The Disney corporation was very good at visual gags and the easily read charm of little children, which are embodied in the forest animals (big eyes, simple trusting natures, round bodies) and in the dwarfs, who are toddlers with beards.

And I am all in favour stealing anything that works. What works in one medium won't necessarily work in another, though, and I don't think characterizing each separate dwarf works at all off the screen. They don't function like that in Grimm: here they are a band of little earth-spirits, benevolent and anonymous. They are perfectly capable of looking after themselves, unlike the bearded babies of Disney, who have to be cooked for and cleaned up after by Snow White the all-American mom.

In both Disney and Grimm they can mourn Snow White but they can't bring her back to life. Only a happy accident, engineered by a prince, can do that.

In the Grimms' first edition, of 1812, the wicked queen was Snow White's mother. She didn't become a stepmother until the second edition of 1819, when Snow White's mother died in childbirth. What happened to her father? Dim, faint and sketchy, like many of the males in Grimm, he was simply obliterated by the power of the monstrous queen.

TWENTY-SEVEN

RUMPELSTILTSKIN

There was once a poor miller who had a beautiful daughter. One day he happened to fall into conversation with the king, and in order to impress him he said, 'You know, your majesty, I have a daughter who can spin straw into gold.'

The king said to the miller, 'I like the sound of that. If your daughter is as clever as you say, bring her to the castle tomorrow, and we'll see what she can do.'

When the girl was brought to him, he took her to a room that was filled with straw right up to the ceiling. He gave her a spinning wheel and several spools and said, 'There you are. Work all day and all night, and if you haven't spun all this straw into gold by tomorrow morning, you'll be put to death.'

Then he himself locked the door, and she was left there all alone.

The poor girl sat there with no idea what to do. Of course she couldn't spin straw into gold, and the longer she sat there the more frightened she became, and finally she began to cry.

Then suddenly the door opened, and in came a little man.

'Good day, Miss Miller, and what are you blubbering for?'

'I'm supposed to spin this straw into gold, and I don't know how to do it, and if I don't they're going to kill me!'

'Oh. Well, what will you give me if I do it for you?'

'My necklace!'

'Let's have a look at it.'

He peered at the necklace and nodded, and put it in his pocket, and then he sat down at the spinning wheel. He set to work so fast she could hardly see his hands. *Whir! whir! whir!* went the wheel, and the first spool was full. He put another one on, and *whir! whir! whir!* and that one was full too. It went on like that till morning, and then all the straw was spun, and all the spools were filled with gold. Then the little man left without another word.

At sunrise the king came and unlocked the door. He was pleased to see all that gold, and a bit surprised, too, that the miller's daughter had managed to do it. But it wasn't enough for him, so he took her to another room, even larger, that was filled with straw like the first one.

'Spin all this in one night, or lose your life!' he said, and locked the door.

Once again the poor girl began to cry, and once again the door opened, and there was the little man.

'What will you give me if I spin all this into gold for you?'

'The ring from my finger!'

'Let's have a look at it.'

He squinted at it, and put it in his pocket. Then he began to spin. The wheel went *whir! whir! whir!* all night long, and by morning all the straw was turned into gold.

The king was even more delighted, but he still hadn't got enough gold. He took the miller's daughter to an even larger room filled with straw like the others, and said, 'Spin this into gold, and I'll make you my wife.' He was thinking: 'She's only a miller's daughter, but I'll never find a richer wife in all the world.'

When the girl was alone, the little man opened the door a third time.

'What will you give me?'

'I've got nothing left!'

'Then you've got to promise me that when you're queen you'll give me your first child.'

'Well, who can tell what'll happen in the future?' she thought, and she promised the little man what he asked for.

He set to work, and by the morning all the straw had been spun into gold. When the king saw it he kept his promise, and the miller's lovely daughter became the queen.

A year later she brought a beautiful child into the world. She'd put the little man out of her mind, but all of sudden there he was.

'Now you must give me what you promised!' he said.

'Oh, no, no, please, anything but that! I'll give you all the wealth in the kingdom.'

'What would I want that for, when I can spin gold from straw? I want a living baby, that's what I want.'

The queen began to cry and weep so much that the little man felt sorry for her.

'All right, I'll give you three days,' he said. 'You find out what my name is in three days, and you can keep your child.'

The queen sat up all night trying to remember every name she'd ever heard. She sent a messenger into the town to ask for any unusual names, and wrote down everything he came back with. When the little man returned, she began:

'Is it Caspar?'

'No, that's not my name.'

'Is it Melchior?'

'No, that's not my name.'

'Is it Balthazar?'

'No, that's not my name.'

She went on through all the names the messenger brought back, and each time the little man said, 'No, that's not my name.'

The second day she sent the messenger out into the country. There must be some strange names out there, she thought, and there were. When the little man came back she tried them out.

'Is it Pickleburster?'

'No, that's not my name.'

'Is it Hankydank?'

'No, that's not my name.'

'Is it McMustardplaster?'

But he always answered, 'No, that's not my name.'

She was getting desperate. On the third day, though, the messenger came back with a strange tale.

'I haven't heard any more names of the sort I found yesterday, your majesty, but when I was near the top of the mountain in the thickest part of the forest, I saw a little house. There was a fire burning in front of it, and a little man – you should have seen him, he looked absurd – was dancing about in front of it, hopping on one leg and singing out:

'One more day and then she'll see
The royal child belongs to me!
Water, earth, and air, and flame –
Rumpelstiltskin is my name!'

Well, you can imagine how pleased the queen was to hear that.

When the little man came in he was rubbing his hands together and hopping with glee and saying, 'Now, milady, what's my name? Eh? Eh?'

'Is it Tom?'

'No, that's not my name.'

'Is it Dick?'

'No, that's not my name.'

'Is it – let me see – Harry?'

'No, that's not my name.'

'Well, I wonder if it could be . . . Rumpelstiltskin?'

'The Devil told you that! The Devil told you that!' the little man yelled, and in his fury he stamped his right foot so hard that he drove it into the ground right up to his waist. Then he took hold of his left foot with both hands and tore himself in two.

Tale type: ATU 500, 'The Name of the Supernatural Helper'
Source: a story told to the Grimm brothers by Dortchen Wild
Similar stories: Katharine M. Briggs: 'Duffy and the Devil', 'Peerifool', 'Titty Tod', 'Tom Tit Tot', 'Whuppity Stoorie' (*Folk Tales of Britain*)

No selection from Grimm would be complete without 'Rumpelstiltskin'. The brothers revised the tale after the first edition, of 1812, mainly in the direction of greater elaboration: for example, in the first edition Rumpelstiltskin simply runs away angrily once his name is discovered, instead of bisecting himself in the ingenious manner described here, which comes from the edition of 1819. Stories with a repetitive structure can take a fair amount of elaboration.

Spinning was a household occupation of great economic importance before the Industrial Revolution put paid to that mode of subsistence. A wife who could spin well was a prize worth having, even (in a story anyway) for a king. We still talk about spinning a yarn when we mean telling a story, though the connection is long lost.

The English 'Tom Tit Tot' (from *Folk Tales of Britain*), with its greedy, slatternly, sexy heroine, is to my mind an even better version of this tale.

TWENTY-EIGHT

THE GOLDEN BIRD

In the old days there was a king who had a beautiful pleasure garden behind his palace, and in this garden there was a tree that bore golden apples. Every year, once the apples were ripe, the king had them counted and numbered, but one year, the very morning after the count was taken, one was found to be missing. The head gardener reported this to the king, and as a result the king ordered the tree to be guarded every night.

So important was this task that he sent his three sons to carry it out. On the first night he sent the eldest, but the prince couldn't stay awake, and at midnight he was fast asleep. In the morning another apple was missing.

Next night he sent the second son, but he didn't get on any better. When the clock struck twelve his eyes were closed, and in the morning one more apple was gone.

Then it was the third son's turn. The king didn't altogether trust him, and was reluctant to let him take guard, but the young man persuaded him, and finally the king agreed. Like his brothers, the third son lay under the tree and settled down for a long watch, determined to fight off sleep.

As the bells of midnight sounded from the palace, there was a rustling among the leaves above him, as a beautiful golden bird flew down and settled on a branch. It shone so brightly it was as if the whole garden was illuminated by a thousand lights. The young prince watched carefully, taking aim with his bow and arrow, and as the bird pecked off an apple he shot an arrow up into the tree. The bird flew away at once, but one of its golden feathers floated down to the grass.

In the morning the prince took the feather to the king and explained what had happened. The king called a meeting of the privy council and everyone examined the feather, and they decided that a feather like this was worth more than the kingdom itself.

'Well, if it's that precious,' said the king, 'I can't be expected to make do with just one feather. I want the whole bird, and I'll have it, see if I don't!'

So the eldest son set out to find the bird, convinced that he was clever enough to find it and bring it back. He had only gone a little way when he saw a fox sitting at the edge of the forest, watching him. The prince raised his gun and took aim, but the fox cried out: 'Don't shoot! I'll give you a piece of advice. You're looking for the golden bird, aren't you? Well, if you carry on this way you'll come to a village with two inns, one on each side of the road. One will be brightly lit, with the sound of songs and laughter, but don't go there whatever you do: go to the other one, even if you don't like the look of it.'

The prince thought, 'Call that good advice? How can a stupid animal like that give me any advice?' And he pulled the trigger. But the fox was too quick: in a moment he was away into the dark trees, his tail stretched out behind him.

The prince went on his way, and as evening fell he came to the village, which was just as the fox had described. Two inns stood there, one brightly lit and full of the sounds of merry-making, the other dismal and dark.

'Well, I'd be a fool if I stayed at that miserable hovel,' he thought, and he went into the cheerful place, had a high old time, and forgot all about the golden bird, his father, and all the good lessons he had learned.

After some time had gone past and the eldest son showed no signs of returning, the second son in his turn set out to look for the golden bird. Like his brother, he met the fox, listened to his advice, took no notice of it, and came to the two inns. And there was his brother calling out to him, and he couldn't resist: he went in and lived it up, forgetting everything but his pleasure.

More time went past, and then the youngest prince asked if he could go off and try his luck. But his father had other ideas. 'It's futile,' he said to the prime minister. 'He's got even less chance of finding the bird than his brothers did. And if he meets any danger, he won't know how to look after himself. Frankly, I don't think he's all there.'

However, the prince kept asking, and in the end the king gave way. The young man set off just as his brothers had done, and he found the fox sitting in the same place, and offering the same advice. The prince was a good-natured boy, and he said, 'Thank you, little fox. Don't worry, I won't harm you.'

'You won't regret it,' said the fox. 'Now if you just sit on my back, I'll take you to the village in a brace of shakes.'

The prince did as he said, and off set the fox, speeding up hill and down dale so fast that the wind whistled through the prince's hair. When they came to the village, the prince, following the fox's advice, stayed in the shabby inn, where he spent a quiet and comfortable night. Next morning he went out to the road, and found the fox there waiting for him.

'Since you were sensible enough to take my advice,' said the fox, 'I'll help you with the next part of the journey. We're going to a castle now, with a whole troop of soldiers outside it. Don't take any notice of them, because they'll all be lying on the ground fast asleep and snoring. Go right through the middle of them and into the castle itself. Go straight through all the rooms to the last one of all, and there you'll find the golden bird. It'll be in a wooden cage. Nearby there's a golden cage as well, but ignore that: it's just for decoration. Remember – whatever you do, don't try and take the bird out of the simple cage and put it in the fancy one. If you do, there'll be trouble.'

When he'd said that, the fox stretched out his tail again, the young prince sat on his back, and off they went as fast as before. When they reached the palace, the fox remained outside and the prince went in, where he found everything just as the fox had said. He went through all the rooms and found the golden bird in its wooden cage with the golden cage beside it. The three golden apples were there too, lying on the floor. The wooden cage looked so ugly and the golden one so beautiful that the prince felt he had to put things right, despite what the fox had said, and he took the bird out of the wooden cage and put it in the golden one.

As soon as he did that the bird uttered such a piercing cry that the soldiers outside all woke up at once, and they rushed in, took the young man prisoner and carried him off to the dungeons.

Next morning he was brought before the court. He admitted everything, and the judge sentenced him to death. However, the king of that country liked the look of the young prince, and said he'd spare his life on one condition: the prince had to bring him the golden horse that ran faster than the wind. If he did, the sentence would be annulled and he would receive the golden bird as a reward.

The prince set off, but without much hope. In fact he had no idea where to find the horse or how to start looking, and he felt pretty sorry for himself. However, as he stepped out along the road, he saw his friend the fox again.

'What did I tell you?' said the fox. 'All this trouble came about because you didn't listen to me. Well, never mind, I'm here now, and I'll tell you how to find the golden horse. Come with me, and I'll take you to a castle where the horse is in the stable. There are several grooms there, but they're all fast asleep outside, so you'll be able to lead the horse out without any problems. But mind you put the plain old leather saddle on him, and not the golden one you'll find there. Otherwise – trouble.'

The fox stretched out his tail, the prince sat on his back, and off they set, so fast that the wind whistled in the prince's hair. They reached the castle, where everything was as the fox had said. The prince entered the stable and found the golden horse, so beautiful that he had to shade his eyes; and as he looked around for the saddle, he thought it would be ridiculous to put the old battered leather one on, when there was such a beautiful golden one just waiting to be used.

So he put the golden one on, the horse neighed loudly, the grooms woke up, they seized the prince, he was sentenced to death. And the king of that castle spared his life too. The condition this time was that he had to bring back the golden princess from the golden castle.

And off set the prince with a heavy heart once more, and once more he met the faithful fox.

'You're a difficult man to help,' said the fox. 'I should really leave you to get on by yourself, but I feel sorry for you. The path we're on leads directly to the golden castle. We'll get there in the evening, and when it's dark and everything's quiet, the golden princess will go to the bathhouse to bathe. What you must do is run up as soon as you see her, and kiss her. Once you've done that she'll follow you, and you can take her anywhere. But you mustn't allow her to say goodbye to her parents. If you do that, it'll all go wrong.'

The fox stretched out his tail, the prince sat on his back, and off they went, the wind whistling through the prince's hair. They soon arrived at the golden castle, where everything was as the fox said it would be. The prince hid until midnight, and when everyone else was asleep, the princess went to the bathhouse. The prince ran up and kissed her, and she said she'd gladly go anywhere in the world with him, but first she must bid farewell to her mother and father. She begged him – she implored him – she wept – and although he resisted her pleas at first, she was so beautiful and in such distress that he finally gave in.

Naturally, as soon as she approached the royal bed, the king woke up. So did everyone else in the palace. The prince was seized and thrown into prison, and next morning he was brought before the king.

'Your life is worth nothing, young man,' said the king. 'I'd have you put to death at once, but there's a task that needs doing, and if you can do it I'll spare your life. Out of my window there's a mountain that blocks the view. Take that away within seven days and the princess is yours. Otherwise, you'll lose your head.'

They gave the prince a shovel and he set to work at once, but when six days had gone by and he stood back and looked at what he'd done, his heart sank. He'd hardly made any difference at all.

However, he kept on shovelling all through the seventh day until the evening. At that point the fox appeared again.

'I don't know why I bother,' he said. 'You don't deserve any help, but I've got a soft spot for you. Go to bed, and I'll move the mountain.'

Next morning, when the prince woke up and looked out of the window, he saw that the mountain had vanished. Full of joy, he rushed to the king.

'Your majesty, I've done it! The mountain's gone!'

The king looked out of the window, and he couldn't deny it: the mountain had vanished. 'Very well,' he said. 'Whether I like it or not, I shall keep my word. You may take my daughter.'

So the young prince and the golden princess set off together, and soon the faithful fox had joined them.

'You've got the best of all prizes right here,' said the fox, 'but the golden princess needs the golden horse.'

'How can I get that?' said the prince.

'I'll tell you, and listen to me this time,' said the fox. 'First you must take the princess to the king who sent you to fetch her. There will be great celebrations, and they'll gladly let you have the golden horse. When they bring it out, you must mount it straight away and then shake hands with everyone and say good-bye. Make sure you shake hands with the golden princess last of all, and when you've got her hand in yours, swing her up behind you and gallop away at once. No one can possibly catch you, because the horse goes faster than the wind.'

Everything went as the fox had said, the celebrations, the gift of the horse, the hand-shaking, the escape. The fox went with them, and when they slowed down at last, he said, 'You did as I told you – good. Now I'll help you get the golden bird. When you get near the castle where the bird is kept, let the princess down from the horse. I'll look after her while you do the rest. You must ride the horse into the courtyard, and everyone will rejoice when they see it, and they'll bring out the golden bird for you. As soon as you have the cage in your hand, set off like the wind and come back for the princess.'

That plan worked as well. Now that the prince had all the treasures he wanted, he got ready to set off for home, but the fox said, 'Before you go, I'd like a reward for all the help I've given you.'

'Of course!' said the prince. 'What would you like?'

'When we come to the forest, I'd like you to shoot me dead and cut off my head and my paws.'

'That would be a strange form of gratitude,' said the prince. 'I couldn't possibly do that.'

'Well, if you won't do it, I'll have to leave you. But I'll give you a last piece of advice: there are two things you have to beware of. Don't buy any gallows meat, and don't sit on the edge of a well.'

When he'd said that, the fox ran off into the forest.

The prince thought: 'What a strange animal, to have such ideas! Who'd buy gallows meat? And I've never wanted to sit on the edge of a well.'

He went on his way with the beautiful princess, and before long they came to the village where his two brothers had stayed behind. There he found a crowd gathering with a lot of noise and commotion, and when he asked what was going on, he was told that two men were about to be hanged. He pushed his way through, and found that the two men were his own brothers. They had run through all their money and got up to all kinds of wickedness.

The young prince asked if there was any way they could be pardoned.

'Well, you can buy their freedom,' he was told, 'but why spend good money on saving such wretches?'

He didn't hesitate. He paid over the money and bought their freedom, and his brothers were unshackled, with strict warnings not to visit that village ever again. Then they set off, and after a brisk morning's travelling they came to the forest where they had first met the fox. The sun was hot, and since it was pleasantly cool under the trees, the brothers said, 'Let's rest here a little. Look, we can get some water from the well.'

The young prince agreed. He forgot the fox's warning and sat down on the rim of the well, suspecting nothing. In a moment the two brothers pushed him into the well, and made off with the princess, the horse and the bird, and took them to their father.

'See, father!' they said. 'Not only the bird, but the golden horse and the princess from the golden castle as well! Not bad, eh?'

The king ordered a great celebration, but observant courtiers noticed that the horse refused to eat, the bird wouldn't sing, and the princess could do nothing but sit and weep.

Meanwhile, what of the youngest brother? He didn't drown, because the well was dry; and he didn't break any bones, because it was full of moss. He sat at the bottom puzzling how to get out, and he was at his wits' end when the faithful fox appeared once more. He jumped down the well and scolded the prince.

'What did I tell you?' he said. 'Well, I suppose I should have expected it. Never mind, I won't leave you down here. Get hold of my tail, and hang on tight.'

The prince did, and a minute later he clambered out after the fox and brushed himself down.

'Now you're not out of danger yet,' said the fox. 'Your brothers weren't sure that you died in the well, so they've stationed guards all around the forest with orders to shoot you on sight.'

They set off, and presently the prince came across a poor man and exchanged clothes with him. In that way he managed to get to the court without being recognized. As soon as he came in, the bird started singing, the horse began to eat, and the beautiful princess stopped crying.

The king was amazed. 'What does this mean?' he said.

'I don't know,' said the princess. 'I was sad, and now I'm joyful. I feel as happy as if my bridegroom had come.'

She told the king everything that had happened, defying the brothers, who had threatened to kill her if she revealed the truth. The king ordered the whole court to gather, and the young prince was there too, in the rags he'd got from the poor man. The princess recognized him at once, and ran to embrace him, and the wicked brothers were seized and put to death. The young prince was married to the princess, and appointed heir to the king.

But what about the poor fox? One day, a long time afterwards, the prince happened to be walking in the forest when he came across his old friend, who said: 'You've got everything you want now, but I've had nothing but bad luck for years; and you refused to set me free, even though I asked you to.'

And once again the fox begged the prince to shoot him and cut off his head and his paws. This time the prince did it, and as soon as it was done, the fox changed into none other than the brother of the princess, released at last from a spell that had been cast over him.

And from then on nothing was missing from their happiness as long as they lived.

* * *

Tale type: ATU 550, 'Bird, Horse and Princess'
Source: a story told to the Grimm brothers by Gretchen Wild
Similar stories: Alexander Afanasyev: 'Prince Ivan, the Firebird, and the Grey Wolf' (*Russian Fairy Tales*); Katharine M. Briggs: 'The King of the Herrings' (*Folk Tales of Britain*); Andrew Lang: 'The Bird Grip' (*Pink Fairy Book*)

Gretchen Wild and the Grimms made an exceptionally neat job of this tale, which can easily ramble. In doing so they turned it into something closely resembling an occult or esoteric narrative of quest and salvation, not unlike the third-century gnostic 'Hymn of the Pearl' or *The Chymical Wedding of Christian Rosenkreutz* of 1616. It would be easy to construct an interpretation on such lines: the young prince would be the questing individual, the golden princess his female other half, or in Jung's terms his *anima*, who has to be won from the unseeing powers of the world: unseeing because of the mountain blocking the king's view, of course. When the mountain is removed, that king becomes wise enough to see, and lets the young bride go to her true destination. The golden horse is the prince's own strength, which must not be saddled with the gaudy trappings of flattery and conceit, but only with the dignity of true and honest toil. The golden bird is the prince's soul: only he can see it in the king's garden, only he can follow it and win it at last. The two brothers are the prince's lower selves, overcome in the end by his innocent goodness; and he is aided by the fox, who of course is wisdom. Wisdom is closely related to the questing individual's own self (he is the princess's brother) but can't be seen for what it is till it's sacrificed. The golden apples in the king's garden are fragments of truth, which ought to be given away freely with a generous hand, but which the king, blinded by a narrow understanding, treats as possessions that must be counted and numbered, thus failing to . . .

And so on. I don't believe this interpretation for a moment, any more than I believe in most sub-Jungian twaddle, but it's possible. Such a reading could be sustained. What does that show? That the meaning preceded the story, which was composed to illustrate it like an allegory, or that the story fell accidentally into an interpretable shape?

Obviously the latter. Much ingenious interpretation of story is little more than seeing pleasing patterns in the sparks of a fire, but it does no harm.

TWENTY-NINE

FARMERKIN

There was once a village where every single farmer was rich except for one, whom they called Farmerkin. He didn't even have the money to buy a cow, though he and his wife longed to have one.

One day he said to her, 'Listen, I've got a good idea. You know your cousin the carpenter – let's get him to make us a calf out of wood, and paint it the proper colour, so it looks real. It's bound to grow up eventually, and then we'll have a cow. What d'you reckon?'

'That's a good idea,' said his wife.

So they went to the carpenter and explained what they wanted, and he got some good pieces of pine and sketched it out and then sawed and planed and carved and nailed it all together, and then he took some brown paint and painted it till you could hardly tell it wasn't real. He'd made it with its head down as if it were grazing, and given it some long black eyelashes too.

When the village cows were driven out to the pasture next morning, Farmerkin called the cowherd and said, 'I've got a young calf here, but she's too small to walk yet. She needs to be carried.'

'Fair enough,' said the cowherd, and he picked up the calf, carried it to the pasture, and set it down on the grass. The cowherd said to himself, 'She'll be running around soon. Look at her tuck into that grass!'

When it was time to drive the cows home that evening, the cowherd couldn't make the calf move. 'Damn it,' he said, 'you've been guzzling away all day long, I reckon you're strong enough now to walk home on your own four legs. I ain't going to carry you both ways.'

Farmerkin was standing outside his front door waiting for the calf to come back. Along came the herd of cows, and behind them was the cowherd, but there was no sign of the calf.

'Hey!' said Farmerkin. 'Where's my calf, then?'

'She's still out there grazing. I called her, but she didn't move. I can't wait all day – these cows want milking.'

The cowherd got the cows settled in the milking parlour, and then went back to the pasture with Farmerkin, but by the time they got there, someone had stolen the calf.

'That's your fault,' said Farmerkin.

'No, it ain't! She must have wandered off.'

'Well, you should have fetched her back,' said Farmerkin.

And he took the cowherd to the mayor, who was shocked at the cowherd's negligence and ordered him to give Farmerkin a cow to make up for his loss.

So now Farmerkin and his wife had the cow they'd been longing for. They were happy about it, but they had no feed and they couldn't afford to buy any, so they had to have her slaughtered. They salted the meat and tanned the hide, and it was a nice hide too, so Farmerkin set off for town with it, intending to sell it and buy a calf.

On the way he went past a mill, and there sitting on the ground was a raven with both wings broken. Farmerkin felt sorry for the bird, so he picked it up carefully and wrapped the hide around it. Dark clouds were gathering in the sky and the wind was getting brisker, and no sooner had he got the raven wrapped up than the rain started pouring down. There was nowhere else to shelter, so Farmerkin knocked on the door of the mill.

The miller's wife, who was alone there, opened the door to him.

'What d'you want?' she said.

'Sorry to trouble you, missis, but could I take shelter here?'

'Oh, I suppose it is coming down a bit . . . All right, come in. You can lie down in the straw over there.'

She pointed to a big heap in the corner, and when Farmerkin was comfortable she brought him some bread and cheese.

'Very good of you, missis!'

'Well, it looks as if it's set in for the night,' she said.

Farmerkin ate the bread and cheese and then lay down and closed his eyes, with the hide beside him. The woman, who was keeping an eye on him, thought he must have been tired, and as Farmerkin didn't stir, she was sure he'd gone to sleep.

Soon afterwards there came a soft knock on the door, and the woman answered it with her finger to her lips. Farmerkin opened his eyes wide enough to see the priest come in.

'My husband's out,' he heard her say, 'so we can have a feast!'

Farmerkin thought: 'A feast, eh? Then why did she fob me off with bread and cheese?'

He watched through half-closed eyes as the miller's wife sat the priest down at the table, fluttering her eyelashes and talking sweetly, and proceeded to serve him a joint of roast pork, a big dish of salad, a fruit cake just out of the oven, and a bottle of wine.

But the priest was just tucking in the napkin over his clerical collar when there was a noise outside.

'Oh, good grief!' the woman cried. 'It's my husband! In the cupboard, quick!'

The priest scuttled into the cupboard as quick as a cockroach, and the woman shoved the meat into the oven, the wine under the pillow, the salad under the bedclothes, and the cake on the floor under the bed.

Then she ran to the front door.

'Oh, thank God you're back!' she said. 'I was getting frightened. What a storm! You'd think it was the end of the world!'

The miller came in shaking the water off his clothes, and straight away he saw Farmerkin lying in the straw.

'What's he doing here?' he said.

'Oh, poor fellow,' said his wife, 'he knocked on the door just as the rain was beginning to come down. He asked for shelter, so I gave him some bread and cheese and let him lie down there.'

'Well, I don't mind,' said the miller. 'But I tell you what, I'm bloody starving. Get me something to eat, will you?'

'There's only bread and cheese, honey-bunch.'

'Whatever you've got in the larder will do me fine,' said the miller, and then he looked at Farmerkin and called: 'Hey, mate, get up and have another bite with me.'

Farmerkin didn't have to be asked twice. He jumped up, introduced himself, sat down at the table with the miller and tucked in.

After a minute or so, the miller saw the hide with the raven in it still lying on the straw.

'What you got over there?' he said.

'Ah, now that's something special, that is,' said Farmerkin. 'I've got a fortune-teller in there.'

'Really?' said the miller. 'Could he predict my future?'

'Certainly,' said Farmerkin. 'But he only predicts four things, and the fifth he keeps to himself.'

'Go on then, get him to predict something.'

Farmerkin picked up the hide very carefully and put it on his lap. Then he squeezed the raven's head gently till the bird croaked: '*Krr, krr*.'

'What's that mean?'

'Well,' said Farmerkin, 'he says there's a bottle of wine under the pillow.'

'Get away!' said the miller, but he got up to look, and found the wine. 'That's amazing! What else can he predict?'

Farmerkin squeezed the raven's head again: '*Krr, krr.*'

'What's he say now?'

'In the second place,' said Farmerkin, 'he says there's a joint of roast pork in the oven.'

'Roast pork? I don't believe it . . . Well, I'm damned! There is and all! Lovely bit of meat, look at that! What else does he say?'

Farmerkin made the raven prophesy again. 'This time,' he said, 'he predicts that there'll be a salad under the bedclothes.'

The miller found that too. 'This is incredible,' he said. 'I never seen anything like this in all me life.'

'*Krr, krr,*' said the raven for the fourth time, and Farmerkin interpreted: 'There's a cake under the bed.'

The miller brought it out. 'Well, I'm flabbergasted!' he said. 'And all we was going to eat was bread and cheese. Wife, what you doing over there? Come and sit down with us!'

'No,' she said, 'I've got a bit of a headache. I think I'll go to bed.'

Of course, really she was terrified. She got in the bed and tucked the bedclothes right over her, and made sure she had the keys to the cupboard.

The miller carved the joint of pork and poured some wine for himself and Farmerkin, and they began to eat.

'So this fortune-teller,' said the miller, 'he keeps the fifth thing to himself, does he?'

'That's right, yeah,' said Farmerkin.

'What sort of thing might it be, usually?'

'Could be anything really. But let's eat first, because I got a feeling that the fifth thing is something bad.'

So they ate their fill, and then the miller said, 'This fifth prediction . . . How bad might it be?'

'Well, the thing about the fifth prediction,' said Farmerkin, 'is that it's very valuable. He never gives it free.'

'Oh. What sort of price does he ask, then?'

'Four hundred talers.'

'Good God!'

'Well, like I told you, it's very valuable. But since you been a generous host, I reckon I can persuade him to let you have it for three hundred.'

'Three hundred, eh?'

'That's right.'

'He won't go lower than that?'

'Well, you seen how accurate he's been already. You can't fault what he's told you so far.'

'That's true. I can't deny that. Three hundred talers, eh?'

'Three hundred.'

The miller went and fetched his purse, and counted out the money. Then he sat down again and said, 'Let's have it, then, let's hear what he's got to say.'

Farmerkin squeezed the raven's head. '*Krr, krr,*' said the raven.

'Well?' said the miller.

'Oh, dear,' said Farmerkin. 'He says the Devil's got into your cupboard.'

'*What?*' said the miller. 'I'm not having that.'

And he hurried to unbolt the front door and wedge it open, and then said, 'Where's the key to the cupboard? Where's it gone?'

'I got it,' said his wife, muffled under the blankets.

'Well, give it here quick!'

He snatched the key, unlocked the cupboard, and the priest shot out as fast as he could and vanished through the front door.

The miller gaped, his hair standing on end. Then he hastened to bolt the front door again.

'He was bloody right, your fortune-teller!' he said. 'That was the Devil, and no mistake! I seen the bastard with me own eyes!'

And he had to drink the rest of the wine to settle his nerves.

Farmerkin went to bed on the straw, and slipped away early in the morning with his three hundred talers.

Once back in his village, Farmerkin began spending his money. He bought some land and built himself a fine house, and soon the villagers were saying, 'He must have been where the golden snow falls. You can bring home money by the shovelful from there.'

What they meant was, they didn't believe he'd got it honestly. Farmerkin was summoned to stand before the mayor and explain himself.

'It's quite easy,' he said. 'I took the hide of my cow and sold it in town. There's a big demand for leather now. Prices have gone way up.'

As soon as they heard that, people all over the village began slaughtering their cows and tanning the hides, and got ready to go to town and sell them at this amazing price.

'Me first,' said the mayor.

He sent his maid off with the first hide. She got three talers for it, and the rest of the villagers didn't even get offered that much.

'Well, what d'you expect me to do with all them hides?' said the leather merchant. 'There's no demand these days.'

Naturally, the villagers were furious with Farmerkin. They denounced him to the mayor as a swindler, and it didn't take long for the village council to decide his fate.

'You'll have to die,' said the mayor, 'by means of being nailed into a leaky barrel and rolled into the pond.'

A priest was summoned to say a mass for his soul, and the villagers left the two of them alone while that was being done. Luckily, Farmerkin recognized the priest.

'I got you out of that cupboard,' he said, 'now you get me out of this barrel.'

'Well, I wish I could—'

'Just back me up, that's all,' said Farmerkin.

He'd seen a shepherd coming along the road with his flock of sheep. He happened to know that that shepherd wanted one thing more than anything else, and that was to be mayor.

So Farmerkin shouted at the top of his voice: 'No, I won't do it! The whole world can ask me to, but I won't! I refuse!'

The shepherd stopped and said, 'What's going on? What won't you do?'

'They want me to be mayor,' said Farmerkin, 'and they said all I got to do is get in the barrel, but I won't do it. I just won't.'

'Serious?' said the shepherd. 'The only thing you got to do to be mayor is get in the barrel?'

Farmerkin nudged the priest, who said, 'Yes, that's right.'

'Oh, well, if that's all it takes,' said the shepherd, and he clambered in. Farmerkin put the lid on, and then took the shepherd's crook and drove the flock of sheep away.

The priest went to the village council and told them that the mass had been said, and the barrel was ready. The mayor led them out, and they all came hurrying along and rolled the barrel towards the pond.

As it bumped along the road, the shepherd shouted out, 'I'll be glad to be mayor!'

They thought it was Farmerkin shouting, of course, and called back, 'Course you will! But first you can have a look round down there!'

Then they rolled the barrel into the water, and set off for home. While the priest stayed behind, pulled up his cassock and tried to drag the barrel out so the shepherd wouldn't drown, the villagers had the surprise of their lives, because as they came into the village square, there was Farmerkin with a flock of sheep.

'Farmerkin! What the devil are you doing here? How'd you escape from the barrel?'

'Nothing to it,' he said. 'The barrel sank deeper and deeper till it got to the bottom, and then I kicked the end open and crawled out. And you've never seen such beautiful meadows as they've got down there! Rich green grass, warm sunshine and so many lambs you couldn't count. So I rounded up a handful and brought them back up with me.'

'Are there any left?'

'Oh, plenty. More than enough for everyone.'

So they all turned around and hurried back to the pond, each of them determined to bring back a flock of his own. Just then the sky happened to be full of those fleecy little white clouds that people call lambkins, and the villagers were so excited seeing the reflection of the clouds in the pond that they didn't notice the soaking wet shepherd on the other side belabouring the priest. All they could do was exclaim in delight at the clouds and jostle for position on the bank.

'Me first,' said the mayor, and plunged in with a splash.

There came a gurgle from the water as he went down, and thinking that he was calling for them all to join him, they jumped in after him.

After that there was no one left in the village, so Farmerkin found himself in charge of everything. He gave the shepherd his sheep back, declared himself mayor and became a rich man.

* * *

Tale type: AT 1535, 'The Rich Peasant and the Poor Peasant', including an episode of type 1737, 'Trading Places with the Trickster in a Sack'

Source: stories told to the Grimm brothers by the Hassenpflug family and Dorothea Viehmann

Similar stories: Alexander Afanasyev: 'The Precious Hide' (*Russian Fairy Tales*); Katharine M. Briggs: 'Jack and the Giants', 'Sheep for the Asking' (*Folk Tales of Britain*)

Farmerkin is a classic trickster. Quick wits and impudence are what you need to play that part, but a plentiful supply of dupes is also necessary. There was clearly no shortage of them in his village.

But how severely should dupes be punished for being dim-witted? It seems fair enough for the villagers who wanted Farmerkin dead to be drowned themselves, because it comes about as a direct result of their greed, but it's a bit rough on the shepherd, who has never wished Farmerkin any harm. In the original the shepherd is drowned, and what's more the priest gets away scot-free, which also doesn't feel right. In this version I have the priest rescue the shepherd and then get belaboured for his pains, which seems a bit more just all round.

Priests don't turn up very often in Grimm, but when they do, their function as often as not seems to be to get up to mischief with another man's wife. In the tale 'Old Hildebrand', for instance, there is a priest who tricks a peasant into going to Italy so that he and the peasant's wife can have a fine time together. He's caught out and walloped in the end, and quite right too.

THIRTY

THOUSANDFURS

Once there was a king whose golden-haired wife was so lovely that her equal couldn't be found anywhere in the world.

It so happened that she fell ill, and feeling that she was about to die, she said to the king, 'If you marry again when I'm dead, you mustn't marry anyone less beautiful than me, or with hair less golden than mine. You must promise me.'

The king gave his promise, and soon afterwards she closed her eyes and died.

For a long time the king was inconsolable, and couldn't even think about taking a second wife. But eventually his councillors said, 'Your majesty, there's no getting away from it: the country needs a queen. You must marry again.'

So messengers were sent out far and wide to look for a bride as beautiful as the queen had been. However, they had no success, no matter how far they looked. Besides, even if they had found someone as beautiful, she might not have had golden hair. The messengers came home empty-handed.

Now the king had a daughter whose hair was as golden as her mother's had been, and who gave every promise of being as beautiful. During her childhood the king hadn't noticed it, but one day soon after she came of age he happened to see her as the sun shone through the window on her golden hair. Suddenly he saw that she was as beautiful as her mother had been, and he fell passionately in love with her on the spot.

He summoned the privy council and announced, 'I have found a bride at last. There is no one in the nation as beautiful as my daughter, so I have determined to marry her.'

The councillors were appalled.

'Your majesty, this is impossible! The Lord God has forbidden any such thing! It is one of the very worst sins. No good could ever come of it, and the nation would fall into ruin!'

As for the girl, she was horrified. Hoping to gain a little time, she said, 'Dear father, before I marry you, I'll need three dresses: one as gold as the sun, one as silver as the moon and one that glitters like the stars. And what's more I must have a cloak made of a thousand different kinds of fur – one for every different kind of animal in the kingdom.'

She thought that would be impossible, and it would keep him from carrying out his wicked plan. But the king was so mad with love that nothing would stop him. He engaged the most skilful weavers in the land to weave three kinds of cloth, and the finest designers to cut it and sew it into three magnificent dresses. Meanwhile he set his huntsmen to work in the forest, and day after day they came home with their trophies of fur and skin. The best workers in leather and fur cut a thousand different pieces and sewed them together, and before long it was clear to the girl that her father was going to supply everything she'd asked for.

Then came a day when he said, 'My darling, everything is nearly ready. Tomorrow we shall be married!'

She saw there was no hope, and the only way out was to run away. When everyone in the palace was asleep, she gathered together three little things from her treasures: a gold ring, a tiny golden spinning wheel and a little golden bobbin. She folded the three dresses so small that they fitted into a nutshell, put on her thousand-fur cloak, and blackened her face and hands with soot.

Then, commending herself to God, she left the palace and set out on the high road.

She walked and walked till she came to a mighty forest. By that time the night was coming to an end, and the first birds were beginning to sing; and the princess was so tired that she found a hollow tree, curled up inside it, and was asleep in a moment.

The sun rose, and she was still asleep. Broad daylight came, and still she slept on. Now it happened that the king who owned that forest was out hunting that very morning. His hounds caught the scent of something strange, and they ran up to the tree and circled it, barking and barking.

'There's an animal hiding in there,' the king said to his huntsmen. 'Go and see what it is.'

They did as he said, and came back to say, 'It's a strange beast, your majesty, like nothing we've ever seen in these woods. Its skin seems to be made of a thousand kinds of fur, and it's just lying there asleep.'

'See if you can catch it alive,' said the king. 'We'll tie it to the cart and take it back to the castle.'

Taking care in case she was dangerous, the huntsmen reached into the hollow tree and seized the princess.

She woke up to find herself being dragged out of her hiding place, and full of fear she cried out, 'Don't hurt me! I'm a poor girl, that's all! My mother and father abandoned me and I was lost!'

'Well, Thousandfurs, you're not lost now,' they said. 'You're a trophy, you are. You belong to us. We'll take you to the kitchen and you can wash the dishes.'

Seeing that she wasn't a rare beast, the king himself lost interest. The huntsmen set her up on the cart and off they went, bumping over the ruts all the way back to the castle, where the domestic servants took her in and showed her a little cubbyhole under the stairs, dark and dusty.

'You can live in there, you furry creature,' they told her.

They made her work in the kitchen. She carried wood and kept the fire going, she drew water from the well, she plucked chickens, she washed and peeled the vegetables, she washed the greasy dishes – all the dirty work was given to Thousandfurs. And there she lived as a skivvy for a long time. Ah, my lovely princess, what's to become of you!

Well, one day it was announced that the king was to hold a grand ball in the castle. Thousandfurs was curious to see, and she said to the cook, 'Could I go upstairs and have a look? I'll stay outside the door.'

'Go on then,' said the cook. 'But make sure you're back here in half an hour. Those ashes won't clear themselves.'

Thousandfurs took a lamp and a bowl of water and went into her cubbyhole. There she took off her cloak and washed her hands and face, so that her beauty was clear to see. Then she opened the nutshell and took out the dress that was as gold as the sun, and put that on, and then she went upstairs to the ballroom. All the servants bowed to her, and the guests smiled politely, because everyone thought she must be a princess.

When the king saw her he felt as if a thunderbolt had struck his heart. He'd never seen such beauty in all his life. He danced with her, half dazed, and when the dance was over, she curtseyed and vanished so quickly that he didn't see where she went. He made enquiries of every guard and every sentry: had she left the castle? Had anyone seen where she'd gone?

But no one had, because she'd slipped away very quickly and gone back to her cubbyhole. She folded the dress away, put on her fur cloak, dirtied her face and hands, and once again she was Thousandfurs the kitchen maid.

She began to clear the ashes away, but the cook said, 'Leave that till tomorrow. I've got another job for you: make some soup for the king while I go and have a look upstairs. But mind you don't let a hair fall into it, or there'll be no food for you from now on.'

The cook went upstairs, and Thousandfurs set about making some bread soup, as well as she knew how. When it was ready she got her gold ring and placed it in the king's bowl.

After the ball was over the king called for his soup, and it tasted so good that he thought he'd never tasted better. And when he reached the bottom of the bowl . . .

'What's this? A gold ring? How in the world did that get in there? Send for the cook!'

The cook was terrified. As he hurried out of the kitchen he said to Thousandfurs, 'You must have let a hair fall in the soup. Didn't I warn you about that? Just you wait till I get back. You'll be black and blue, my girl.'

The cook came before the king, trembling and twisting his apron in his hands.

'Did you make this soup?' said the king. 'Stop fiddling. Stand up straight.'

'Yes, your majesty,' said the cook faintly.

'You're not telling the truth. This is different from what you normally send up, and it's much better. Who made it, eh?'

'I'm sorry, your majesty, yes, you're right, sire, it wasn't me; it was that little furry skivvy.'

'Send her up here.'

When Thousandfurs arrived the king said, 'Who are you?'

'I'm a poor child who has no mother or father.'

'How did you come to work in my castle?'

'I was found in a tree, sire.'

'H'mm. And where did you get this ring?'

'I don't know anything about a ring, your majesty.'

The king thought she must be simple, and dismissed her.

Some time later there was another ball, and as before Thousandfurs asked the cook for permission to go upstairs and have a look.

'Well, all right,' he said. 'Half an hour, that's all. And then come back here and make that bread soup the king likes so much.'

Thousandfurs ran to her cubbyhole, washed herself quickly, and put on the dress that was as silver as the moon. She went up into the ballroom, and the king saw her at once through all the crowd of dancers, for she was even more beautiful than before. They danced together, and it only seemed like a moment to him, for as soon as the dance was over she disappeared at once.

She ran down to her cubbyhole, put the dress away, and became Thousandfurs again before hurrying into the kitchen to make some bread soup. While the cook was upstairs watching the dancing, she put the little golden spinning wheel into the bowl and poured the soup over it.

And as before the king found it and sent for the cook, and the cook admitted that it was again Thousandfurs who'd made it, so the king sent for her.

'I have to say I'm puzzled by you,' he said to her. 'Tell me again where you came from.'

'From a hollow tree, your majesty.'

No, he thought, the poor girl must have lost her wits. Such a shame – she might be pretty under all that dirt. But she plainly knew nothing about the little golden spinning wheel, so he sent her away.

When the king gave a third ball, everything happened as before. The cook was getting suspicious, though, and he said, 'I think you must be a witch, you furry creature. You always put something in the soup that makes the king like it more than mine.' But he was good-natured enough, and he let her go up and look at the lords and ladies as she'd done before.

She put on the dress that glittered like the stars and hurried to the ballroom. The king had never seen anyone as lovely, and he ordered the orchestra to play a very long dance so that he might have the chance to talk to her. She was as light in his arms as the starlight itself, but she said very little; however, he did manage to slip a ring on her finger without her noticing it.

When the dance was over her half hour was up, so she tried to slip away. They had a little struggle, because he wanted to hold on to her, but she was too quick for him and ran out before he could stop her.

When she got back to her cubbyhole, she didn't have time to take the dress off, so she put her fur cloak on over it and then dirtied herself, but in her haste she missed one finger, which remained clean. Then she hurried to make the soup, and while the cook was upstairs she put her golden bobbin into it just as before.

When the king found the bobbin he didn't waste time calling the cook, but sent for Thousandfurs directly. As soon as she came, he saw her one white finger, and the ring he'd put on it while they were dancing. He seized her hand and held it fast, and as she struggled the fur cloak came open a little and revealed the glitter of the starry dress. The king pushed back the hood of her cloak, and her gold hair fell down; and then he pulled the cloak off altogether, and revealed the lovely princess he'd been dancing with not half an hour before. When her face and hands were washed, no one could deny that she was more beautiful than anyone who had ever lived.

'You shall be my dearest bride,' said the king. 'And we shall never part.'

Their wedding was celebrated soon afterwards, and they lived happily for the rest of their lives.

* * *

Tale type: ATU 510B, 'Peau d'Asne'

Source: a story told to the Grimm brothers by Dortchen Wild

Similar stories: Giambattista Basile: 'The Bear' (*The Great Fairy Tale Tradition*, ed. Jack Zipes); Italo Calvino: 'Wooden Maria' (*Italian Folktales*); Charles Perrault: 'Donkey-Skin'

(*Perrault's Complete Fairy Tales*); Giovanni Francesco Straparola: 'Tebaldo' (*The Great Fairy Tale Tradition*, ed. Jack Zipes)

This tale begins very well: the king promising his wife to marry no one less beautiful than she is after she dies, and then falling in love with his own daughter . . . But halfway through, when the princess runs away, we see no more of the obsessed father; the story changes altogether and becomes a variant of 'Cinderella' (p. 116). What happened to the incest theme? It seems to me that running away is no way for a story to deal with something so dramatic. It deserves a better resolution than that.

Straparola's version realizes that, and makes the king, Tebaldo, pursue his daughter relentlessly. Taking a hint from that, I would continue the tale the Grimms have given us by letting the good king and his new bride live happily and have two children. One day a merchant would arrive at the palace with a case full of pretty toys. He would give a toy to the boy and another to the girl, and say, 'Remember me to your mother.' They would run to show her a golden spinning wheel, a golden bobbin. Troubled, she would order this merchant to be brought to her, but he would have vanished.

Next day would be Sunday, and she would see him in the crowd as the royal family goes to the cathedral. He would look at her and smile, and there would be no doubt: her father. For the first time, she would confess to her husband the horror that led her to flee her home and become Thousandfurs. He would be appalled, and order that this merchant be sought out and arrested.

That evening, the queen would go to confession, afraid that she is somehow to blame for her father's abominable lust. The priest would assure her that she is innocent, but that she is misjudging her father, whose love for her is pure and holy. Furthermore, love between fathers and daughters is sanctified by holy scripture, as in the case of . . .

At that point she would recognize his voice and run, calling for help, only to find herself locked inside the church with her father. Her screams would arouse the guard, and they would break down the door to find the false priest on the point of ravishing her.

At the orders of the king, the villain would be taken away and hanged. After his death his arms and legs would be cut off and buried separately in unconsecrated ground.

That night the queen would wake from troubled dreams to find earthy fingers probing her lips: her father's right arm. Mad with terror, she would scream for her husband, only to find him in the bed next to her on the point of death by strangulation: her father's left arm. No one can help but herself. She would tear the arm away from her face and thrust it into the fire, and then do the same with the other from her husband's throat, and pile on more wood till they blazed up and finally crumbled into ashes.

I think that would work quite well.

THIRTY-ONE

JORINDA AND JORINGEL

Once upon a time there was an ancient castle in the middle of a deep forest, where an old woman lived all by herself. She was a powerful witch. Every day she turned herself into a cat or an owl, and every evening she turned herself back into her human form. She knew how to capture birds and other game, which she would slaughter and then roast and eat. If any man came within a hundred steps of the castle, she would cast a spell over him, making him unable to move until she freed him. If an innocent girl came that close, however, the old woman would change her into a bird and force her into a wicker basket. Then she would carry the basket up to a room in the castle, where she kept more than seven thousand other birds of this kind.

Now at that time there was a girl called Jorinda, who people said was the most beautiful girl in the whole kingdom. She was betrothed to a handsome boy called Joringel. It wasn't long before their marriage, and they loved nothing more than to be in each other's company.

One afternoon they wanted to be alone, so they went for a walk in the forest. 'We must be careful not to go too close to the castle,' Joringel said.

It was a lovely evening; the sun shone warmly on the tree trunks against the dark green of the deep woods, and turtle-doves cooed mournfully in the old beech trees. From time to time

Jorinda wept, though she didn't know why. She sat down in the sunlight and sighed, and Joringel sighed too. They felt as sad as if they were close to death. In the intensity of their emotions they lost track of where they were, and couldn't find the way home.

When the sun had not quite set, when it was half below and half above the mountains, Joringel, searching for the right path, parted the leaves of a bush and saw the wall of the castle only a few yards away. It was such a shock that he nearly fainted. In the same moment he heard Jorinda beginning to sing:

'My little bird with the red, red ring,
Sorrow, sorrow, sorrow sing;
My sweet bird with the ring so red,
The lovely turtledove is—'

But she couldn't complete the verse. Instead Joringel heard a nightingale pouring out its song, and he saw to his horror that there was indeed a nightingale perching on a branch just where Jorinda had been standing. Not only that, but a night owl with glowing eyes was flying around her. It flew around three times, crying: '*To-whoo! To-whoo! To-whoo!*'

And Joringel himself had been turned to stone. He couldn't move, couldn't cry out, couldn't even blink. It was almost dark by then. The owl flew into a bush and he lost sight of it, but then the leaves rustled and out came a bent old woman, haggard and yellow, with blood-red eyes and a crooked nose whose tip almost touched her chin. Mumbling to herself, she snatched the nightingale from the branch and carried it away.

And Joringel couldn't cry out, couldn't move a muscle. The nightingale was gone.

Before long the old woman came back empty-handed. In a cracked old voice she said, 'When the moon shines into the basket, Zachiel, set him free.'

And at that moment Joringel felt his limbs loosen, and he was able to move again. He flung himself to his knees before the old woman and cried, 'Oh, please give me back my Jorinda!'

'Never!' said the witch. 'You'll never get her back.'

He pleaded, he cried aloud, he wept, but nothing would change her mind. She didn't stop to listen, but left him crying, 'Oh, what's to become of me?'

He left the castle, and made his way to a village where he wasn't known. There he found work as a shepherd, which kept him there for a long time. He often went back to gaze at the castle, but never went close.

One night he had a strange dream: he dreamed he had found a beautiful red flower with a pearl nestling in its petals. In the dream he plucked the flower and took it to the castle, where he could open every door and every wicker bird cage just by touching it with the flower, and he managed to free his Jorinda.

When he woke up next morning, he set off at once to find the flower from his dream. He searched for eight days, and on the ninth he found a flower as red as blood, with a dewdrop among its petals as large as the finest pearl.

He plucked the flower with the greatest care and set off for the castle. As he passed within the magic circle, he felt nothing stopping him: he was able to move without hindrance as far as the gate. Encouraged by that, Joringel touched the flower to the gate, which immediately sprang open.

He went in and stood in the dismal courtyard listening for the sound of the birds. It wasn't hard to hear. He followed the sound of their singing and soon found himself in the great room where they were all kept in their seven thousand baskets.

The witch was feeding them at that moment, and when Joringel came in she stopped and turned to him, spitting and screaming with anger. Her curses were appalling, and she spat gall and venom from her wrinkled lips, but nothing touched him, and she couldn't get close enough to scratch him with her claw-like nails.

He took no notice, but went on freeing the birds one after another, wondering how in the world he would find his Jorinda among so many. But then he noticed that the old woman had taken one basket down and was making for the door.

He leaped across the room and touched the basket with the flower, and it flew open; and he touched the witch with the flower as well, and all her powers fell away. And there was Jorinda, as beautiful as ever, and she threw her arms around his neck and hugged him tight.

He released all the other birds, and then Joringel and his Jorinda went home, where they were soon married, and they lived together happily for many years.

* * *

Tale type: ATU 405, 'Jorinda and Joringel'
Source: Johann Heinrich Jung-Stilling's *Heinrich Stillings Jugend* (*Heinrich Stilling's Youth*; 1777)

This is an oddity, in that it isn't like a folk tale at all. For one thing, it is the only tale in Grimm in which a description of nature ('It was a lovely evening; the sun shone warmly . . .') is there simply for the sake of describing it; for another, the behaviour of the lovers seems to exhibit such an excess of sensibility that it can only belong to literary romanticism. It simply doesn't feel like a folk tale.

The Grimms' source for this tale is part of the autobiography of Johann Heinrich Jung (1740–1817), a physician and friend of Goethe and best known by his assumed name, Heinrich Stilling. The motif of the quest for the flower seen in a dream recalls the archetypal work of German Romanticism, Novalis's *Heinrich von Ofterdingen*

(1802). This sort of thing was very much in the air at the time. 'Jorinda and Joringel' could be worked up at greater length, but that would take it even further from the realm of the folk tale and firmly into that of the fantasy novel. Whatever you did with it, though, you'd never rid it of the literary flavour it was born with.

The red, red ring in the verse refers to the eye of the turtledove, whose iris does appear like a red ring.

THIRTY-TWO

SIX WHO MADE THEIR WAY IN THE WORLD

There was once a man who could turn his hand to anything. He had fought in the war and conducted himself bravely, but when the war came to an end, he was sent on his way with three pennies, and nothing more.

'Hold on,' he said. 'What sort of pay is this? If I find the right lads to help me, I'll make the king empty his treasury, you wait and see.'

Furious, he marched off into the forest. He hadn't gone far before he saw a man pulling up six trees as if they'd been stalks of corn. The soldier said to him, 'Will you be my servant and go with me?'

'Certainly,' said the man, 'but first I must take this bundle of twigs home to my mother.'

And he took one of the trees and tied it round the rest, and then slung the whole bunch up on his shoulder and carried it away. A little later he came back and went off together with his master, who said, 'We two will certainly make our way in the world.'

They had gone a little way when they saw a hunter who was down on one knee, taking aim at something they couldn't see.

The soldier said, 'Hunter, what are you shooting at?'

'Two miles from here,' said the hunter, 'there's a fly sitting on the branch of an oak tree. I'm going to shoot out its left eye.'

'Oh, come with me,' said the soldier. 'If we three go together, we'll certainly make our way in the world.'

The hunter was willing, so off they went. They soon came to seven windmills whose sails were busily turning round and round, even though there wasn't a breath of wind and not a leaf was stirring on the trees.

'Well, would you look at that!' said the soldier. 'I've never seen the like. What can be turning those sails?'

On he went with his two servants, and two miles further on they came to a man sitting in a tree holding one nostril closed and blowing through the other.

'What are you doing up there?' said the soldier.

'Two miles back along the road there are seven windmills. I'm blowing the sails round. I'm surprised you didn't see them.'

'Oh, come with me,' said the soldier. 'We saw them all right. With a talent like yours, we four will certainly make our way in the world.'

The blower agreed. They walked on, and after a while they came to a man who was standing on one leg, with his other one unhitched on the ground beside him.

'You look as if you've made yourself comfortable,' said the soldier. 'Having a rest, are you?'

'Well, you see, I'm a runner. I go fast – I can't help it. With both legs on I go faster than a bird can fly.'

'Oh, come with me,' said the soldier. 'That's a rare talent. Join forces with us, and we'll certainly make our way in the world.'

The runner joined in with them, and presently they came to a man who was wearing his cap on one side, with the flap over one of his ears.

'Why are you wearing your hat like that?' said the soldier. 'You look half-witted.'

'Ah, there's a reason for it,' said the man. 'If I put it straight, such a deep frost will fall, all of a sudden, that birds will drop dead out of the air.'

'Well, we can't let a gift like that go begging,' said the soldier. 'Join the rest of us, and we'll make our way in the world, all right.'

So he strode along with the rest, and soon they came to a city where the king had just made a proclamation. Whoever ran a race against his daughter and won would marry her and inherit the kingdom. If he lost the race, however, he'd lose his head as well.

The soldier thought this was worth risking, so he went to the king and said, 'I'll take on the race, your majesty, on condition that one of my servants can run instead of me.'

'As you wish,' said the king, 'but on the same condition. If he loses, you'll both go to the scaffold.'

They agreed on the terms: each runner was to be given a jug in which to bring some water from a spring that was a long way off, and the first one back would win. When everything was ready, the soldier buckled on his servant's leg for him and said, 'Don't hang about. It's your head too, remember.'

The runner and the king's daughter took their jugs and set off. After less than a minute, when the king's daughter had only gone a little way, the runner was already out of sight. In no time at all he reached the spring, filled his jug and turned around. Halfway back, though, he felt like taking a nap, so he lay down and closed his eyes, using for a pillow a horse's skull he found lying on the ground, so he wouldn't feel too comfortable; he didn't want to sleep too long and lose the race.

Meanwhile, the king's daughter, who was much better at running than common people, had reached the spring. She filled her jug and set off at once on the return lap, and soon she came across her opponent lying fast asleep.

'The enemy's been delivered into my hands!' she thought, and emptied his jug before running on.

And everything would have been lost, if the hunter hadn't happened to be standing on the castle walls, watching it all with his sharp eyes.

'The king's daughter shan't beat us!' he cried, and he loaded his gun, took aim and shot the horse's skull out from under the runner's head, waking him up with a jolt.

The runner sat up and blinked, and saw at once that his jug was empty and that the king's daughter had overtaken him. Not a bit worried, he raced back to the spring, filled his jug again and sped back to the town, managing to beat the king's daughter by ten minutes.

'I was just beginning to stretch my legs,' he said. 'It could hardly be called running, what I was doing in the first lap.'

The king wasn't at all pleased to lose his daughter to a common soldier, and as for the daughter, she liked it even less; so they put their heads together to think of a way of getting rid of both him and his companions. Finally the king said, 'Ah! I've got it. Don't you worry, we'll make sure they never see their homes again.'

He went to the six and said, 'I want to make sure you fellows have a good time. Eat, drink and be merry!'

He led them to a room that had an iron floor, and the doors were made of iron too, and the windows had heavy iron bars. In the middle of the room was a table spread with a splendid feast, and the king said, 'In you go, and enjoy yourselves!'

As soon as they were all inside, he had the door locked and bolted. Then he sent for the cook and told him to light a fire in the room below, and build it up and keep feeding it till the iron glowed red-hot. The cook did so, and before long the six companions sitting round the table began to feel warm. At first they thought that was because of the food they were eating, but when it got hotter and hotter and they tried to leave the room, they found the door locked and the windows barred. Then they realized what the king was up to: he was intending to burn them alive.

'Well, let him try,' said the man with the cap on sideways. 'I'll bring a frost that'll have this fire crawling away in shame.'

So he put his hat on straight, and such a frost set in that the heat faded at once and the food on the table began to freeze. After a couple of hours had gone by the king thought they must all have burned to death, so he had the door opened to see; but he found them all in the best of health. In fact they said they'd like to come outside and warm up a bit, because it was so cold in there that the food had frozen to the plates.

The king was furious, and went downstairs to scold the cook.

'I thought I told you to make the fire hotter and hotter!'

'And so I did, your majesty – here it is, look, blazing away!'

When the king saw the raging fire he realized that he hadn't got the better of the six companions yet, and he'd have to try something cleverer next time.

So he cudgelled his brains and finally thought he had found a way of getting rid of them. He said to the soldier, 'Look, you're a man of the world, let's be straight with each other. If I give you some gold, will you give up the princess and clear off?'

'Fair enough,' said the soldier. 'What about letting me take as much as one of my servants can carry? Then I'll say cheerio to the princess and we'll be off.'

'Just one servant?'

'Just the one. Give us a couple of weeks and then we'll come to collect it.'

The king agreed. The soldier went off and summoned all the tailors in the kingdom, and gave them the job of sewing one gigantic sack. It took them two weeks, and when it was ready the strong man, the one who pulled up trees, slung it over his shoulder and went with his master to the king.

The king saw them coming, and said, 'Who's that extraordinary fellow carrying that huge bundle of canvas over his shoulder? Good Lord, it's as big as a hou—'

Suddenly he realized who the man was. 'Oh no!' he thought. 'That's the servant who's going to carry the gold – and that's the sack he's going to carry it in! I don't believe it!'

The king ordered his treasurers to bring a ton of gold, thinking that surely that would be enough. It took sixteen mighty bombardiers to carry it all out, but the strong man tossed it into his bag with one hand and said, 'This hardly covers the bottom. Get a move on and bring some more – we want to leave today.'

Little by little all the king's treasury was brought out, and the strong man tossed it all into the sack.

'Still not half full!' he said. 'You've brought nothing but crumbs so far. Keep going!'

So they had to send for seven thousand wagons filled with gold from all over the kingdom, and the strong man tossed them all into the sack together with the oxen that pulled them.

'Well, it's not quite full, but that'll have to do,' he said. 'No point in being greedy about it.'

And he swung the sack up over his shoulder and went off with his companions.

The king watched all this, and when he saw all the wealth of his kingdom disappearing on the back of one man, he lost his temper.

'Send the cavalry after them!' he ordered. 'I won't stand for this. Bring back that gold!'

The two finest regiments soon caught up with the soldier and his servants, and their commander called out: 'Hands up! Put down that sack of gold and stand back, or we'll cut you to ribbons!'

'What's that he's trying to say?' said the blower. 'Hands up? Cut to ribbons? Let's see how you like dancing around in the air.'

He closed one nostril and blew through the other, and in moments every horse and every rider was whirled into the air as if a hurricane was tossing them about, here, there and everywhere. Some went high, some were scattered among the bushes, and one sergeant called out, 'Mercy! Mercy!'

He was a valiant fellow, who'd been wounded nine times in the king's service, so the blower and his companions didn't want to humiliate him, and they let him down gently.

'Now go back and tell the king to send as many regiments as he wants,' said the blower, 'and I'll make them all dance in the clouds like yours.'

When the king got the message, he said, 'Oh, let the fellows go. I've had enough.'

So the six made their way home, divided up their fortune, and lived happily for the rest of their days.

* * *

Tale type: ATU 513A, 'Six Go Through the Whole World'
Source: a story told to the Grimm brothers by Dorothea Viehmann
Similar stories: Alexander Afanasyev: 'The Seven Semyons' (*Russian Fairy Tales*); Italo Calvino: 'The Five Scapegraces' (*Italian Folktales*); Jacob and Wilhelm Grimm: 'The Six Servants' (*Children's and Household Tales*)

The story of the gifted companions lends itself to many variations. The version in Calvino is particularly lively.

The story also works very well in the cinema, where plots involving the recruiting of a team of specialists for some impossible task have often been popular. *Ocean's Eleven* (Steven Soderbergh, 2001) was one successful version. So, in a different way, was *The Dirty Dozen* (Robert Aldrich, 1967). The French film *Micmacs* (Jean-Pierre Jeunet, 2009) is more inventive and charming than either.

THIRTY-THREE

GAMBLING HANS

Once there was a man called Hans, who was crazy about gambling, so much so that everyone who knew him called him Gambling Hans. He just couldn't stop playing at cards or dice, and in the end he lost all his possessions, his pots and pans and tables and chairs, his bed and all the rest of his furniture, and finally his house itself.

On the evening before his creditors were going to take possession of the house, the Lord and St Peter turned up at the door and asked him to put them up for the night.

'You're welcome,' said Gambling Hans, 'but you'll have to sleep on the floor. I haven't got a bed left.'

The Lord said they didn't mind that, and they'd provide their own food, what's more. St Peter gave Hans three groschen and asked him to go to the baker's and buy a loaf of bread. He set off willingly, but on the way he had to pass the house where he used to gamble with the bunch of scoundrels who'd won most of his possessions, and when they saw him passing they called out, 'Hey! Hans! We're playing! Want to come and join in?'

'I can't,' he said. 'I've got nothing left. And these three groschen aren't mine.'

'Doesn't matter. They're as good as anyone else's. Come on!'

Of course he couldn't resist. All that time the Lord and St Peter had been waiting, and when Hans didn't come back they went to look for him. The money was gone by that time, and when he saw them coming he pretended to be looking for the coins in a puddle, and stood there bending over and poking at the water with a stick. It was no good, though: the Lord knew he'd lost it at the gaming table.

St Peter gave him another three groschen, and since he knew they were watching, he didn't gamble it this time but bought the bread as they'd told him. Then they went back to his house and sat on the floor to eat their dry bread supper.

'Hans, do you happen to have any wine in the house?' said the Lord.

'No, Lord, I'm sorry to say. That was one of the first things I gambled away. The barrels in my cellar are bone dry.'

'Well, go and have a look,' said the Lord. 'I think you'll find some wine down there.'

'No, honest, many a time I've tipped those barrels on end, and believe me, there isn't a drop.'

'I think it would be worth looking,' said the Lord.

Out of politeness, Hans went down and did as the Lord said, and he was flabbergasted to find that not only was there some wine left, it was wine of the highest quality. He looked around for something to carry it up in, flushed the cobwebs out of an old enamel jug, and filled it to the top. The three of them sat there passing the jug around and talking till they felt sleepy, and then they went to bed on the bare floorboards.

In the morning the Lord said, 'Now, Hans, I'd like to give you three gifts as a reward for your hospitality. What would you like?'

The Lord had been thinking that Hans would ask for a guaranteed place in heaven, but he soon found out he was wrong about that.

'Well, that's very handsome of you, Lord. I'd like a pack of cards that'll always win, I'd like a pair of dice that'll always win, and I'd like a . . . a . . . a . . . let me see: I'd like a tree that grows all kinds of fruit, right, and one other thing about this tree: if anybody climbs it, they can't get down till I give them permission.'

'Oh, very well,' said the Lord, and produced the cards and the dice with a flick of his fingers.

'And the tree?' said Hans.

'It's outside in a pot.'

So the Lord and St Peter went on their way.

After that, Hans began to gamble as he'd never gambled before. He won every bet he made, and before long he owned half the world. St Peter was keeping an eye on him, and he said to the Lord: 'Lord, we can't have this. Any day now he'll own the whole world. We've got to send Death to fetch him.'

So they did. When Death turned up, Hans was at the gaming table as usual.

'Hans,' said Death, 'it's time to stop gambling. In fact time's up for you altogether. Come along.'

Hans just happened to have a royal flush in his hand, and when he felt bony fingers grasping his shoulder and looked up and saw Death, he said, 'Oh, it's you. I'll be along in a minute. Do us a favour, would you? There's a tree outside with some nice fruit on it. Climb up and pick a bit of that, and we can eat it on the way.'

So Death climbed the tree, and of course he couldn't get down. Hans just left him there for seven years and in all that time nobody died.

Finally St Peter said to the Lord, 'Lord, this has gone on for long enough. We'll have to do something about it.'

The Lord agreed, and he told Hans to let Death down from the tree. Hans had to do that, of course, and Death went up to him at once and strangled him.

So off they went into the other world. When they got there, Hans went straight up to the gate of heaven and knocked.

'Who's there?' said St Peter.

'It's me, Gambling Hans.'

'Well, go on, clear off. You needn't think you're coming in here.'

Next he went to the gate of Purgatory and knocked there.

'Who is it?'

'Gambling Hans.'

'Go away. We've got enough misery here – we don't want gambling as well to make it worse.'

So Hans had nowhere to go but hell, and when he knocked on the gate there, they let him in at once. There was no one at home but the Devil himself and all the ugly devils, because the handsome devils had gone to earth on business. The second Hans got there he sat down to play. The Devil had nothing to stake but his ugly devils, and soon they all belonged to Hans, because he was playing with the cards that couldn't lose.

Once he'd won the ugly devils he took them all off to Hohenfurt, where they grow hops. They pulled out all the hop poles and climbed up to heaven, and then they began to lever up the walls.

The stonework was beginning to give way, so St Peter said, 'Lord, we'll have to let him in. We haven't got a choice.'

So they let him in. But as soon as he was inside, Hans set about gambling again, and very soon there was such a noise of shouting and arguing among the citizens that the angels couldn't hear themselves think.

St Peter went to the Lord once more.

'Lord, I've had enough,' he said. 'We've got to chuck him out. He's driving everyone mad.'

So they got hold of him and hurled him out of the gate and all the way down to earth. His soul was smashed to pieces, and the little splinters went everywhere; in fact there's one of them in the soul of every gambler who's alive today.

Tale type: ATU 330A, 'The Smith's Three Wishes'
Source: a story written and sent to the Grimms by Simon Sechter

Simon Sechter, who originally recorded this tale, was a composer and teacher of music from Weitra in Lower Austria, and the Grimms transmitted it in the dialect version in which it came from him:

> Is is emohl e Mon gewön, der hot ninx us g'spielt, und do hobend'n d'Leut nur in 'Spielhansl' g'hoaßen, und wal er gor nit afg'hört zen spielen, se hot e san Haus und ullss vespielt.

One of the Grimms' first impulses towards collecting folk tales was, of course, due to their philological interest in the varieties of the German language. It's debatable whether we should present this tale, and perhaps 'The Fisherman and His Wife' (p. 93) and 'The Juniper Tree' (p. 187), in some dialectal variety of English to try and imitate what they are like in German. My feeling is that if anyone is really interested in that aspect of language, they would probably rather look at the original than at some laborious attempt to replicate its effect, and that most readers who want an English version would prefer to read one that presents as few obstacles as possible.

The other thing to say about this tale is that it's lively, swift and ludicrous.

THIRTY-FOUR

THE SINGING, SPRINGING LARK

Once upon a time there was a man who was about to set off on a long journey. Before he left he asked his three daughters what they'd like him to bring back for them. The oldest daughter wanted pearls, the second asked for diamonds, and the youngest said, 'Dear father, I'd like a singing, springing lark.'

The father said, 'If I can find one, you shall have it.'

Then he kissed all three and set off. In the course of his journey he bought pearls and diamonds for the two eldest daughters, but he searched everywhere without success for a singing, springing lark. He was unhappy about that, because the youngest daughter was his favourite.

As it happened, his road led him through a forest, in the middle of which stood a magnificent castle. Near the castle was a tree, and right at the top of the tree there was a lark, singing and springing.

'You're just what I wanted,' he said, and he told his servant to climb the tree and catch the little bird.

But as the servant approached the tree, a lion leaped out from under it, shook himself, and roared till every leaf on the tree trembled.

'If anyone tries to steal my singing, springing lark,' cried the lion, 'I'll eat them up.'

'My apologies,' said the man. 'I didn't know the bird belonged to you. Let me make it up to you. I'll give you gold if you spare our lives.'

'Gold is no good to me,' said the lion. 'I want whatever first comes to meet you when you arrive home. Promise me that, and you can have your life, and your daughter can have the lark as well.'

At first the man refused. 'The first to meet me could be my youngest daughter,' he said. 'She loves me the most, and she always runs out to greet me when I get home.'

'But it might not be her!' said his servant, who was frightened. 'It might be a dog or a cat!'

The man let himself be persuaded. He took the singing, springing lark, and promised to give the lion whatever came to meet him first when he arrived home.

And when he got home and entered his house, the first to come and greet him was none other than his youngest, dearest daughter. She came running, kissed and hugged him, and when she saw that he'd brought a singing, springing lark for her, she was beside herself with joy.

Her father couldn't be glad, though, and he began to weep.

'My dearest child,' he said, 'this little bird cost me dear. To get it I had to promise to give you to a wild lion, and when he gets you, he'll tear you to pieces and eat you.'

He told her everything that had happened, and begged her not to go to the lion, come what may.

But she consoled him and said, 'Dearest father, we must keep your promise. I'll go there and pacify the lion, and come back safe and sound.'

Next morning her father showed her the way, and she set off confidently into the forest.

Now in fact the lion was an enchanted prince. During the day he and all his courtiers had the form of lions, but at night they turned back into human beings. When the girl reached the castle it was nightfall, and they welcomed her courteously. The prince was a handsome man, and soon their wedding was celebrated with great splendour and rejoicing. Because of the enchantment he was under, they slept all through the day, and stayed happily awake at night.

One day her husband said to her, 'Tomorrow your elder sister is getting married, and there's going to be a feast at your father's house. If you like, my lions will take you there.'

She said that she'd be glad to see her father again, so she set off, accompanied by the lions. There was great joy when she arrived, because they all thought that she'd been torn to pieces and was long dead, but she told them all about her handsome husband and the life they spent together. She stayed until the wedding celebrations were over, and then she went back to the forest.

When the second daughter got married she was invited again, and she said to the lion, 'I don't want to go on my own this time. I'd like you to come with me.'

The lion said that it would be very dangerous. If a ray of light fell on him, even the light of a single candle, he would be changed into a dove, and he would have to fly away with the doves for seven years.

'Oh, please come!' she said. 'I'll protect you. I'll keep every ray of light from you, I promise.'

He was persuaded, and off they went, taking their small child with them. At her father's house she had a special room built, with thick walls and no windows at all. When the wedding lights were lit he was to stay in the room for safety, but the builders had made the door out of unseasoned wood, and after it was hung it split and developed a tiny crack, which no one noticed.

The wedding was celebrated with great joy, and the procession set out from the church to the bride's father's house. Torches flared and lanterns shone, and as they went past the prince's room, a single ray of light no wider than a hair shone through and touched him. And when his wife came in looking for him, she didn't see him: all she found was a white dove.

The dove said, 'I must fly about the world for seven years. But every seven steps, I'll drop a white feather and a drop of blood to show you where I've gone. If you follow the trail you'll be able to save me.'

The dove flew out of the door, and she followed him at once. As he'd said, every seven steps a white feather and a drop of blood fell to show her the way.

She followed him further and further away, out into the wide world far from home. Thinking of nothing else but following him, she didn't look aside, and didn't rest until the seven years were nearly up. All that time she hoped that she would soon save him, but she was wrong: because one day as she was walking on, no feather fell, and no drop of blood either. She looked up, but the dove had vanished.

'Well, no human being can help me now,' she said, and so saying, she climbed right up to the sun.

'Sun,' she said, 'you shine over every mountain, and into every crack and cranny. Have you seen my little white dove flying past?'

'No,' said the sun, 'I haven't seen your dove, but I'll give you this casket. Open it when you're in great need.'

She thanked the sun and went on her way till night came and the moon was shining. She said to the moon, 'Moon, you shine all night on the fields and the forests. Have you seen my little white dove flying past?'

'No,' said the moon, 'I haven't seen your dove, but I'll give you this egg. Break it open when you're in great need.'

She thanked the moon and walked on. The night wind rose and blew against her, and she said to it, 'Night wind, you blow through all the trees in the world. Have you seen my little white dove flying past?'

'No,' said the night wind, 'I haven't seen him myself, but I'll ask the other winds. They might have seen him.'

He asked the east wind and the west wind, and they came blowing and told her that they'd seen no dove; but the south wind came and said, 'Yes, I saw the little white dove. He was flying to the Red Sea. He's become a lion again, because the seven years are over, and he's fighting a serpent. Be careful, though, because the serpent is an enchanted princess.'

The night wind said to her, 'Look, I'll give you some advice. Go to the Red Sea. On the right bank you'll see a bed of tall reeds. Count them carefully and cut the eleventh one, and hit the serpent with it. Then the lion will be able to beat it, and they'll both become human again. Nearby you'll see the griffin that lives by the Red Sea. Climb on his back with your beloved, and he will carry you home across the sea. And take this nut. When you're flying over the middle of the sea, drop it down and a tall nut tree will sprout at once for the griffin to rest on. If he doesn't have any rest, he won't be able to carry you home. Don't lose this nut whatever you do, or you'll all fall in the sea and drown.'

So she went to the Red Sea and found everything just as the night wind had said. She counted the reeds, plucked the eleventh one, and struck the serpent with it. Immediately the lion forced back the serpent and subdued it, and the moment the serpent surrendered, both of them became human again.

But before the lion's wife could move, the princess who had been the serpent seized the prince's hand and tugged him up on to the back of the griffin, and they flew away.

So there the poor wanderer stood, alone and forsaken once more. She had to sit down and cry. Eventually, though, she took heart and said, 'I'll keep going as far as the wind blows and as long as the cock crows, until I find him again.'

And she set off. She travelled a long, long way, until she came at last to a castle where the lion-prince and the serpent-princess were living together. There she heard that their wedding was to be celebrated very soon.

She said, 'God will help me yet,' and opened the little casket that the sun had given her. Inside was a golden dress that shone as brightly as the sun itself. She put it on and went into the castle, and everyone, including the bride, was struck with wonder. In fact the bride liked it so much she wanted it for her wedding dress, and she asked if it was for sale.

'Not for gold or for good,' said the girl, 'but for flesh and blood.'

'And what does that mean?' said the princess.

The girl asked to spend one night in the room where the bridegroom slept. The bride didn't like the sound of that, but she wanted the dress so much that she agreed. However, she told the prince's servant to give him a sleeping draught.

That night, after the prince was already asleep, the girl was taken to his room. When they closed the door, she sat on the bed and whispered to him: 'I've followed you for seven years. I went to the sun and the moon and the four winds to ask after you, and I helped you conquer the serpent. Are you going to forget me completely?'

But the prince was sleeping so soundly that he thought her whispers were merely the wind sighing in the fir trees.

When morning broke she was led out of his room, and she had to give up the golden dress. Seeing that her trick hadn't helped, she grew very sad and went out to a meadow, where she sat and wept. But then she remembered the egg that the moon had given her. She was certainly in great need now, so she broke it open.

Out came a mother hen and twelve little chicks, all made of gold. The chicks ran about cheeping and then ran back to their mother and sheltered under her wings. There was no prettier sight in the world.

The girl stood up and drove them ahead of her around the

meadow, until the castle window opened and the bride looked out. She liked them so much that, as before, she asked if they were for sale.

'Not for gold or good, but for flesh and blood; let me sleep one more night in the bridegroom's bedchamber.'

The bride agreed, and planned to trick her as she'd done the previous night.

However, this time the prince asked his servant about the murmuring and rustling in the night. The servant confessed that the bride had ordered him to give the prince a sleeping draught, because a poor girl wanted to sleep in his room.

The prince said, 'Well, tonight you can pour the drink out of the window.'

That night the girl was led in again, and this time when she began to whisper her story the prince recognized his dear wife's voice at once and embraced her.

'Now I'm free!' he said. 'I feel as if I'd been in a dream. I think the princess bewitched me and made me forget you. But God lifted the spell in time!'

They both tiptoed out and left the castle secretly, because they were afraid of the bride's father, who was a powerful sorcerer.

They found the griffin and climbed on his back, and he set off at once to fly them home. Halfway across the Red Sea the wife remembered to drop the nut. At once a tall nut tree grew up high, and the griffin rested in its branches before flying on to their home. There they found their child, who had grown tall and handsome; and from then on they lived happily until they died.

* * *

Tale type: ATU 425C, 'Beauty and the Beast'
Source: a story told to the Grimm brothers by Dortchen Wild

(Somewhat) Similar stories: Katharine M. Briggs: 'The Three Feathers' (*Folk Tales of Britain*); Italo Calvino: 'Bellinda and the Monster' (*Italian Folktales*)

As with a number of the Grimm tales, there's a question here. What is the meaning of the singing, springing lark? Why does it vanish from the story as soon as the youngest daughter receives it? What's happened to it? And is there a connection between the lion (*Löwe*) and the dialect word the characters use for the lark (*Löweneckerchen*, not *Lerche*)?

If we were going to give the lark more to do in the story (which wouldn't be too difficult: he could share the wife's wanderings, he could fly to the sun and the moon for her, he could prompt the serpent-princess to look out of the window and see the golden hen and her chicks, for example), we'd have to have clear in our minds the relationship between the wife, the lion and the lark. There are few clues in the tale as it is.

THIRTY-FIVE

THE GOOSE GIRL

There once lived an old queen whose husband had been dead for many years. She had a beautiful daughter, and when the daughter grew up she was betrothed to a prince who lived a long way away. Soon the time for the marriage arrived, and the daughter had to leave for the foreign land where the prince lived. The old queen packed all manner of costly things, gold and silver, fine goblets and rare jewels of every kind, everything that was suitable for a royal dowry, for she loved her daughter with all her heart.

She also gave her a maidservant who was to ride with her and make sure she arrived safely at the bridegroom's palace. Each of them had a horse for the journey. The princess's horse was called Falada, and he could speak. When it was time to leave, the old queen went into her bedchamber, took a knife and cut her finger. She let three drops of blood fall on to a white handkerchief, gave it to her daughter and said, 'My dear child, take good care of this. You will need it on your journey.'

Then they said a sad farewell. The princess put the handkerchief into her bodice, and they set off on the journey to her bridegroom.

When they had ridden for an hour the princess felt a burning thirst and said to her maidservant, 'Could you get down and bring me some water from the brook in the golden goblet you're carrying? I'm so thirsty I must have something to drink.'

The maid said, 'Get it yourself. If you're thirsty you can just lie over the stream and lap it up. I'm not going to wait on you.'

The princess was so thirsty that she did just that. The maid wouldn't even let her use the goblet.

'Dear Lord!' thought the princess, and the three drops of blood replied: 'If your mother knew of this, it would break her heart.'

But the princess was humble. She said nothing and remounted her horse. They rode on for a few more miles, but the day was warm, the sun was scorching and soon she grew thirsty again. When they came to another stream she said to the maidservant, 'Could you bring me some water in the golden goblet?'

She had forgotten the maidservant's harsh words. But the maid said even more haughtily: 'I've told you, I'm not waiting on you. If you're thirsty, get down and drink for yourself.'

The princess got down again and drank from the stream. She wept a little, and again she thought, 'Dear Lord!'

Again the three drops of blood responded silently: 'Oh, if your mother knew, her heart would break in two!'

And as the princess leaned over the stream and sipped the water, the handkerchief fell out of her bodice and floated away. She didn't even notice it in her distress, but the maidservant had seen it, and she gloated. She knew that the princess was weak and powerless now.

So when the princess wanted to remount Falada, the maid said, 'What d'you think you're doing? That's not your horse. I'm having him now. And in fact you can take off all your fancy clothes and give them to me. You can wear these dingy rags of mine. Go on, hurry up.'

The princess had to do as she said, and then the maidservant made her swear under the open heavens not to say one word about it in the royal court. If she hadn't taken that oath, the maidservant would have killed her on the spot.

But Falada saw all of this, and took good note of it.

So with the chambermaid riding Falada and the true princess riding the nag, they went on their way till they came to the royal palace. There was great rejoicing when they arrived, and the king's son ran ahead to meet them. Naturally he thought that the chambermaid was his bride, and he lifted her down from her horse and led her upstairs, while the real princess was left standing below.

The old king looked out of the window and noticed her waiting in the courtyard, and thought how beautiful she was, how fine and delicate her features; so he went at once to the royal apartments and asked the bride about the girl she had with her, the one who was standing below in the courtyard.

'I picked her up on the way to keep me company,' said the false bride. 'Give her some work to do; she'll only laze around otherwise.'

But the old king had no work to give her. 'I suppose she could help the goose boy,' he said.

So the true bride had to tend the geese along with the little goose boy, whose name was Conrad.

A little while later the false bride said to the king's son, 'Husband dearest, I'd like you to do something for me.'

'Of course!' he said. 'I'll do it gladly.'

'Then send for the knacker, and have him cut off the head of the horse I rode here,' she said. 'The brute gave me a lot of trouble on the way.'

In fact, of course, she was afraid that Falada might tell the truth about how she had behaved with the princess. The longer he stayed alive, the greater the risk that the truth would come out.

So it was arranged, and the faithful Falada had to die. The real princess heard about it, and she secretly promised the knacker a gold coin if he would do her a small favour. In the city wall there was a large dark gateway through which she had to drive the geese every morning. She asked the knacker if he'd hang Falada's head in there, where she could see it when she passed through.

The knacker agreed, and nailed the head up on the wall by the gate.

Early next morning, when she and Conrad drove the flock of geese out through the gateway, she said as she passed:

'Oh, poor Falada, hanging there!'

And the head answered:

'Oh, princess with the golden hair,
If your dear mother knew,
Her heart would break in two.'

The princess said no more, and she and Conrad drove the geese out into the fields. When they came to the right spot, she sat down and loosened her hair, which was the purest gold. Conrad loved to watch her do this, and he reached up and tried to pull out a strand or two.

So she said:

'Wind, strong wind, take Conrad's hat,
And blow it here and there,
Let him chase it all around
Until I've done my hair.'

And such a strong wind started blowing that it snatched Conrad's hat and blew it right across the meadow, and then led him a chase up and down, this way and that, until he managed to catch up with it. By that time the princess had combed and braided her hair and tied it up in a bun, and there were no loose strands for Conrad to tug; so he sulked, and didn't say another word that day. When evening came they drove their flock home again.

Next morning as they went through the gateway in the city wall, the girl said:

'Oh, poor Falada, hanging there!'

And the head answered:

'Oh, princess with the golden hair,
If your dear mother knew,
Her heart would break in two.'

When they reached the meadow, once again the princess sat down to braid her hair, and once again Conrad tried to pluck a strand of it, and once again she said:

'Wind, strong wind, take Conrad's hat,
And blow it here and there,
Let him chase it all around
Until I've done my hair.'

The wind blew up suddenly and snatched little Conrad's hat again, and gave him such a chase up and down the meadow that by the time he'd caught the hat, the princess had done up her hair, and again there were no strands to pluck at. And so they tended their geese until the evening.

When they returned to the palace, Conrad went to the old king and said, 'I don't want to tend the geese with that girl any more.'

'Why not?' said the old king.

'Oh, she annoys me all day long!'

'Well, what does she do?'

'In the morning, when we go through the gate in the city wall, she talks to the head of the old nag that's nailed up there. She says, "Oh, poor Falada, hanging there!" And the head says, "Oh, princess with the golden hair, if your dear mother knew, her heart would break in two."'

Then Conrad went on to tell the king what happened in the goose meadow, and how she made the wind blow his hat about.

'Well, you just go out with her tomorrow as normal,' said the old king. 'And I'll be watching.'

So in the morning the old king wrapped himself in a cloak and sat inside the gateway and heard the princess talking to Falada's head. Then he followed them discreetly out to the meadow and hid himself among the bushes to watch what happened. Just as Conrad had told him, the goose girl summoned the wind, and it blew Conrad's hat all over the meadow, and she unpinned her beautiful long golden hair and braided it up again.

The king saw it all, and then he went back to the palace. When the goose girl came back in the evening, he called her to him, and asked why she did those things.

'I'm not allowed to tell you,' she said. 'It's a secret. I can't tell anyone. I had to swear under the open heavens that I wouldn't say a word about it. If I hadn't sworn, I'd have been killed.'

The old king tried to persuade her, but she wouldn't be moved. Nothing would make her break her vow.

But finally he said, 'I tell you what. Don't tell your troubles to me; tell them to the iron stove in the corner. That way you'll be keeping your vow, and you can still unburden yourself.'

So she crept into the old iron stove, and there she began to cry, and soon she had poured out her whole heart.

'Here I sit, all alone and forsaken by the whole world, and all the time I'm the daughter of a king. A false maidservant forced me to change clothes with her, and she took my place as the bride. And now I have to work in the meadow looking after the geese. If my mother knew about this, it would break her heart in two.'

The old king was standing outside by the chimney, and he heard everything she said. He came back inside and told her to come out of the stove. He had her dressed in royal clothes, and it was a wonder to see how beautiful she was.

Then the old king summoned his son and explained that his bride had married him by deceit, and that she was no princess, but only a maidservant. His true bride was right there, the one who had been a goose girl. When the king's son saw how lovely the true bride was, and learned how virtuously she had behaved, he was full of joy.

They ordered a great feast to which all the court and every good friend they had were invited. At the head of the table sat the bridegroom, and on one side sat the false bride, and on the other the true one. The maidservant was completely taken in, because she didn't recognize the princess in her beautiful dress.

After they had eaten and drunk, and were all in good spirits, the old king put a riddle to the false bride: what punishment would someone deserve if they had treated their mistress in this way? And he told the whole story, asking again when he'd finished, 'What sentence does such a person deserve?'

The false bride said, 'She deserves nothing better than to be stripped naked and put in a barrel studded on the inside with sharp nails. Then two white horses should be harnessed to it, and drag her up and down the streets until she's dead.'

'That is you,' said the old king. 'You have pronounced your own sentence. Everything you described shall be done to you.'

And when the sentence had been carried out, the king's son married his true bride, and they reigned over their kingdom in peace and happiness.

* * *

Tale type: ATU 533, 'The Speaking Horsehead'
Source: a story told to the Grimm brothers by Dorothea Viehmann
Similar stories: Giambattista Basile: 'The Two Cakes' (*The Great Fairy Tale Tradition*, ed. Jack Zipes); Katharine M. Briggs: 'Roswal and Lilian' (*Folk Tales of Britain*)

Poor Falada! He deserved a better fate. We might think he deserved a bigger part in the story, too. Perhaps if he'd spoken up sooner, his mistress wouldn't have had such a bad time.

And good and beautiful though she undoubtedly is, the princess/goose girl has to give second place, as far as enterprise and vigour are concerned, to the wicked maidservant, who deserves a longer story. It's hard for a storyteller to make an attractive character out of a meek and docile victim who doesn't argue or fight back once; but then, this isn't a novel.

The name Falada, with an extra 'L', was used by the German novelist Rudolf Ditzen (1893–1947), author of *Jeder stirbt für sich allein* (*Every Man Dies Alone*; 1947) in his nom de plume Hans Fallada.

THIRTY-SIX

BEARSKIN

Once there was a young fellow who enlisted as a soldier, fought bravely, and was always at the front when red-hot bullets were raining down. As long as the war lasted everything went well, but when peace was signed, he was discharged. The captain said he could go wherever he liked. His parents were dead and he no longer had a home, so he went to his brothers and asked if he could live with them until there was another war.

But his brothers were hard-hearted and said, 'What have your problems got to do with us? We don't need you here. Clear off and shift for yourself.'

All the soldier had left was his musket, so he put it on his shoulder and went out into the world. Soon he came to a great heath where there was nothing to be seen but a circle of trees. He sat under them thinking about his fate, and feeling pretty sorry for himself.

'I've got no money and no prospects,' he thought. 'All I can do is make war, but if all they want is peace, I'm useless. I'll probably starve to death.'

Suddenly he heard a rustling, and when he looked round to see what it was, he saw a strange man standing there. He wore a smart green jacket and looked perfectly respectable, except for the hideous great horse's foot he had at the end of one leg.

'I know what you want,' he said to the soldier, 'and you can have all of it, as much gold and property as you like, but first you must show me how brave you are. I'm not going to give my money to someone who runs away at the first sign of danger.'

'Well, I'm a soldier, and it's my profession to be afraid of nothing. And you can test me if you like.'

'All right,' said the man, 'look behind you.'

The soldier turned around and saw a huge bear running towards him, growling furiously.

'Oh ho,' said the soldier, 'I'll tickle your snout for you, you ugly brute. See how you feel like growling after this.'

He levelled his musket at the bear and fired a shot. It hit the bear in the muzzle, and it fell down at once.

'I can see you don't lack for courage,' said the stranger, 'but I haven't finished yet. There's one more condition.'

'As long as it doesn't spoil my chances of going to heaven,' said the soldier, who knew quite well who the stranger was. 'If that's at risk, I'll have nothing to do with it.'

'Well, we'll see about that,' said the stranger. 'Here's what you've got to do: for the next seven years, you mustn't wash yourself, or comb your hair, or cut your nails, or say the Lord's Prayer. I'll give you a jacket and a cloak to wear all that time. Now if you die during those seven years, you're mine, you understand? If you stay alive, you're free, and rich as well, don't forget, for the rest of your life.'

The soldier thought about it. He'd faced death so often on the battlefield that he was used to danger, but poverty was another matter. He decided to take up the Devil's offer.

The Devil took off his green jacket and handed it to the soldier, saying, 'If you put your hand in the pocket when you've got this jacket on, you'll always find a handful of money.'

Then the Devil skinned the bear and said, 'You must use this bearskin as your cloak, and you must sleep in it too, and you mustn't lie in any other bed. And you must go by the name of Bearskin.'

With those words the Devil disappeared.

The soldier put the jacket on and reached into the pocket, and found that the Devil had been telling the truth. He put the bearskin on like a cloak, and started his wanderings. He went wherever he liked, did whatever he pleased, and spent as much as he found in his pocket.

For the first year he looked all right, but during the second he began to look like a monster. His face was almost entirely covered with his long coarse beard, his hair was matted and tangled, his fingers ended in claws, and he was so dirty that if you sowed cress on his face, it would have sprouted. Everyone who saw him shuddered or ran away. However, he always gave money to the poor to pray that he'd stay alive for seven years, and because he always paid in full and at once for anything he wanted, he could always find shelter.

In his fourth year of wandering, he arrived at an inn. The landlord wouldn't let him in, and even refused him a place in the stable in case he frightened the horses. But when Bearskin put his hand in his pocket and pulled out a handful of cash, the landlord relented a little and let him stay in a lean-to in the yard, on condition that he didn't show his face to anyone.

One night he was sitting alone in there, heartily wishing that his seven years were up, when he heard someone sobbing with misery in a nearby room. Bearskin was a kind-hearted man, and wanting to help, he opened the door and saw an old man weeping bitterly and striking his fists together. As soon as the old man saw Bearskin he struggled up and tried to run away, but on hearing a human voice he stopped and let the monster talk to him.

Bearskin spoke kindly and got the old fellow to sit down again and tell him his troubles. It seemed that little by little he'd lost what money he had, and now he and his daughters were on the brink of starvation. He couldn't pay his bill to the landlord, and he was sure to be sent to prison.

'If money's your only problem,' said Bearskin, 'I've got enough to help you.'

He called for the landlord and paid the bill, and then he put a bag of gold into the old man's pocket. When the old man saw that all his troubles were over, he didn't know how to thank his strange helper.

'Come home with me,' he said. 'Come and meet my daughters. They are all wonderfully beautiful, and you must choose one of them to be your wife. When they hear what you've done for me, they won't refuse you. You do look a bit, well, eccentric, but whichever one you choose will soon have you looking neat and tidy.'

Bearskin liked the sound of the daughters, so he went home with the old man. However, when the eldest daughter saw him, she screamed and ran away. The second daughter looked him up and down and said, 'You expect me to marry a thing like that? He doesn't even look like a man. I'd sooner marry that bear who came here once, you remember; they'd shaved all his fur off and he was wearing a hussar's uniform and white gloves. I could have got used to *him*.'

The youngest daughter, however, said, 'Father dear, he must be a good man if he helped you like that. And if you promised him a bride, I'm ready to keep your word.'

It was a shame that Bearskin's face was covered in hair and dirt, because otherwise father and daughter would have seen how joyfully his heart leaped at those words. He took a ring from his finger, broke it in two and gave her one half, keeping the other for himself. He wrote her name in his half, and his name in hers, and asked her to take good care of it.

'I've got to be off now,' he said. 'I've got three more years' wandering to get through. If I don't come back after then, you're free, because I shall be dead. But I hope you'll pray to God and ask him to keep me alive.'

The poor bride dressed herself all in black, and when she thought about her future bridegroom, tears came to her eyes. From her sisters all she had for the next three years was scorn and ridicule.

'Better be careful,' said the elder sister. 'If you give him your hand, he'll crush it in his paw.'

'Watch out,' said the second sister, 'bears like sweet things. If he takes a fancy to you, you'll be down his gullet in a moment.'

'And you better do as he tells you. I wouldn't care to be you if he starts to growl.'

'But the wedding will be fun. Bears always dance well.'

The bride-to-be said nothing and didn't let them upset her. As for Bearskin, he wandered all over the world, doing good wherever he could and giving generously to the poor so that they'd pray for him.

Finally, at dawn on the very last day of the seven years, he went once more to the heath and sat down under the circle of trees. Quite soon the wind began to howl, and there was the Devil again, scowling at him.

'Here's your jacket,' he said, throwing Bearskin's old jacket to him. 'Now give me back my green one.'

'Not so fast,' said Bearskin. 'First of all you're going to clean me up. I want four tubs of water, from very hot to lukewarm, and four kinds of soap, from that yellow stuff they scrub the floors with to the finest Parisian *savon de luxe*. As for shampoo, I want several kinds of that, from the sort they use on horses to the most delicate stuff scented with lavender. Then I want a gallon of eau de cologne.'

And whether the Devil wanted to or not, he had to bring water and soap and several kinds of cosmetic product and wash

Bearskin from head to foot, cut his hair, comb it neatly, shave his beard and trim his nails. After that, Bearskin looked like a dashing soldier once more; in fact, he looked more handsome than ever.

When the Devil had vanished, complaining bitterly, Bearskin felt joyful. He strode into the town, bought a splendid velvet jacket, hired a carriage drawn by four white horses, and drove to the house of his bride. Of course, no one recognized him. The father assumed he was a distinguished officer, a colonel at least, and led him into the dining room where his daughters were sitting.

He took a seat between the two eldest. They made a real fuss of him. They poured wine for him, they chose the finest morsels to put on his plate, they flirted and simpered and thought they'd never seen a more handsome man. But the youngest daughter sat across the table from him, not raising her eyes, not saying a word.

Finally Bearskin asked the father if he'd let him choose one of the daughters for a wife. At that the two eldest daughters leaped up from the table and raced to their bedrooms to put on their finest dresses. Each one thought she was the one Bearskin wanted.

As soon as he was alone with his bride-to-be, the visitor brought out his half of the broken ring and dropped it into a glass of wine, which he handed to her across the table. She took the wine and drank it, and when she found the half-ring in the bottom of the glass, her heart beat faster; and she took the other half which she wore on a ribbon around her neck, and put them together. And the two halves matched perfectly.

The stranger said, 'I'm your bridegroom, whom you knew as Bearskin. By the grace of God, I've found my clean human form again.'

He embraced her and kissed her warmly. And at that moment the two sisters came in wearing all their finery, and when they saw Bearskin and their sister together, and realized who he was and what had happened, they went mad with fury. They ran outside, and one of them drowned herself in the well, and the other hanged herself from a tree.

That evening there was a knock at the door. Bearskin opened it, and there was the Devil in his green jacket.

'What do you want?' said Bearskin.

'I've just come to thank you. I've now got two souls to play with, instead of your one.'

* * *

Tale type: ATU 361, 'Bear-Skin'
Source: a story told to the Grimm brothers by the von Haxthausen family and a tale by Hans Jakob Christoffel von Grimmelshausen, 'Vom Ursprung des Namens Bärnhäuter' ('The Origin of the Name Bearskin'; 1670)
Similar stories: Katharine M. Briggs: 'The Coat' (*Folk Tales of Britain*); Italo Calvino: 'The Devil's Breeches' (*Italian Folktales*)

This seems a curious bargain for the Devil to make. Surely there should be easier and less expensive ways of getting the soldier's soul. Still, the soldier is a pious and charitable fellow, and might not be easy to seduce in the usual diabolical manner. The damnation of the two sisters seems harsh, but after all, there are those long years of mockery to be taken account of.

Calvino's version is full and inventive. I borrowed from him the suggestion that water alone wouldn't be enough to get rid of seven years' worth of dirt.

THIRTY-SEVEN

THE TWO TRAVELLING COMPANIONS

The mountain and the valley never meet, but the children of men, both good and bad, meet one another all the time. So it was that a shoemaker and a tailor once met up on their travels. The tailor was a good-looking little fellow, always cheerful and full of merriment. He saw the shoemaker coming towards him on the other side of the road, and, seeing from the shape of his knapsack what trade he followed, began to sing a teasing little song:

'Sew the seam and pull the thread,
Whack the nail right on the head—'

But the shoemaker wasn't the type to take a joke. He scowled and shook his fist. The tailor laughed and handed over his bottle of schnapps.

'Here, take a swig of this,' he said. 'No harm intended. Have a drink and swallow your anger.'

The shoemaker knocked back half the bottle, and the storm in his eyes began to clear. He gave the bottle back and said, 'Nice drop. They go on about heavy drinking, but they don't say much about great thirst. Shall we travel together for a while?'

'Suits me,' said the tailor, 'as long as you don't mind making for the big towns, where there's plenty of work.'

'Just what I had in mind. There's nothing to be earned in these small towns, and the country people prefer to go barefoot anyway.'

So on they went together, putting one foot in front of the other like weasels in the snow. They had plenty of time, but little to eat. Whenever they reached a town they looked for work, and because the tailor was an engaging little fellow with rosy red cheeks, he found work easily enough, and if he was lucky he got a kiss from the master's daughter when he left, to wish him good cheer on the way.

Whenever he met up with the shoemaker again, it was always the tailor who had the most in his pocket. The shoemaker, an ill-tempered so-and-so, used to make a sour face and say, 'The bigger the rascal, the better the luck.'

But the tailor only laughed and sang all the more, and shared what he had with his companion. Whenever he had a couple of coins in his pocket, he'd order something good to eat and thump the table till the glasses danced. 'Easy come, easy go' was his principle.

After they'd been travelling for some time, they came to a great forest. There were two paths that led through it to the capital, but one of them took two days' walking and the other took seven, and they didn't know which was which. They sat down beneath an oak tree and talked about it. Should they carry seven days' food, or only two?

'Always prepare for the worst,' said the shoemaker. 'I'm going to carry enough bread for a week.'

'What?' said the tailor. 'Lug all that bread about like a beast of burden, and not be able to enjoy the scenery? Not me. I shall trust in God as I always do. My money's as good in summer as in winter, but bread isn't – in the hot weather it dries out and goes mouldy all the quicker. Why shouldn't we find the right way? A one-in-two chance is pretty good, when you think about it. No, I'll take bread for two days, that's quite enough.'

So they each bought the bread they wanted to carry, and set off into the forest. It was as quiet as a church under the trees. There was no breeze, no murmuring brook, no birdsong, and not a single sunbeam found its way through the dense leaves. The shoemaker didn't say a word. He just trudged on with the bread weighing heavier and heavier on his back, and the sweat streaming down his sour and gloomy face.

The tailor, however, couldn't have been happier. He laughed and sang and walked ahead with a spring in his step, whistling on a blade of grass. He thought, 'God up there must be pleased to see me so happy.'

And so they went on for two days. On the third day, though, they were still deep in the forest, and the tailor had eaten all his bread. He was a bit less cheerful now, but he didn't lose courage; he relied on God and on his luck. On the evening of the third day he lay down hungry, and rose even hungrier the following morning. The fourth day passed in the same way, and in the evening the tailor had to sit and watch as the shoemaker made a fine meal out of his supplies.

The tailor asked for a slice of bread, and the shoemaker just laughed at him, saying, 'You were always too fond of singing and playing the fool. Now you can see where that gets you. Birds that sing too early in the morning get caught by the hawk before nightfall.'

In fact, he was merciless. On the fifth morning the poor tailor could hardly stand up and his voice was just a croak. All the red in his cheeks had gone; they were as white as chalk now, and it was his eyes that were red.

And then the shoemaker said, 'Well, you're in trouble, and it was all of your own making. I tell you what – I'll give you a piece of bread. But in return, I'll put out your right eye.'

The poor tailor had to live, so he had to agree. He wept with both eyes while he still had them, and then held up his head so the stony-hearted shoemaker could put out his right eye with the breadknife. The tailor remembered what his mother had said when she found him gobbling up a pie in the pantry: 'Eat all you can, and suffer what you must.'

He ate the thin slice of bread the shoemaker gave him, and felt a little better, and was able to stand up; and he walked on thinking that he could still see well enough with his left eye, after all.

But on the sixth day the hunger had him in its grip again, and even more fiercely than before. That evening he simply fell down and lay where he fell, and on the seventh morning he was too weak to get up at all. His death was not far away.

The shoemaker said, 'I'll be merciful. I can see the state you're in, and I'll give you another slice of bread. But you're not getting it for nothing. You've got one eye left, and I'll have that one like the first.'

The poor tailor felt as if he'd wasted all his life. What had he done wrong, that he should come to this? He must have offended God in some way, so he prayed for forgiveness, and said to the shoemaker, 'Go on then. Put it out. But remember, God sees everything you do, and the time will come when he'll punish you for this evil deed. When times were good, didn't I share what I had with you? One stitch follows another, and I used to see them clear and easy, but if I haven't got my eyes and I can't sew any more, I'll have to go begging. At least don't leave me here alone when I'm blind, or I'll die of hunger.'

The shoemaker cared nothing for this talk of God; he'd driven God out of his heart a long time ago. He took his knife and put out the tailor's other eye, and then gave him a small piece of bread, held out his stick for the tailor to hold on to, and led him along.

At sunset they came out of the forest. The tailor could feel the warmth of the sun on his face, but of course he couldn't see a thing, and he didn't realize that the shoemaker was leading him towards a gallows that stood at the edge of a field. The shoemaker left him there alone and walked on. The poor tailor, overcome by weariness, pain and hunger, simply fell down where he was and fell asleep.

He woke up at dawn, shivering with cold. There were two poor sinners hanging on the gallows above him, with a crow sitting on the head of each one.

One of the hanged men spoke to the other, saying, 'Brother? Are you awake?'

'Yes, I'm awake,' said the second.

'Well, I'll tell you something worth knowing. The dew that settles on us at night and drips off on to the grass below has a special property. If a blind person washes their eyes in it, they get their sight back. If the blind knew that, how many d'you think there'd be crowding around our gallows every morning?'

The tailor could hardly believe his ears. But he took his handkerchief, pressed it down on the grass till it was as wet as it could be, and washed out his eye sockets. Immediately what the hanged man had said came true: a healthy new eye grew at once and filled each one. The sun was about to rise, and the tailor watched with wonder as the light came over the mountains and filled the whole valley and plain in front of him. There lay a great city with magnificent gates and a hundred towers, and the sun caught the golden balls and crosses on the tops of the church spires and made them sparkle in the clear morning. He could see every leaf on the trees, every bird flying past, and even every gnat that danced in the air. But here was the greatest test: he took a needle from his needle-case, snapped off a bit of thread, and threaded it as quickly and easily as he'd ever done. His heart leaped for joy.

He threw himself to his knees and thanked God for his mercy. Then he said his morning prayer, and he didn't forget to pray for the two poor sinners who were swinging in the breeze like pendulums. The tailor hoisted his bundle on to his back and went on his way, singing and whistling as if he'd never endured any sorrow at all.

The first thing he came to was a fine brown foal running wherever it pleased in the meadow. The tailor caught hold of its mane and tried to mount it and ride it into town. But the foal begged for his freedom, saying, 'Look, I'm only young, and even a skinny little tailor like you is too much for me. You'd snap my spine in half if you tried to ride me. Let me grow bigger and stronger, and perhaps I'll be able to repay you one day.'

'Oh, go on then, off you go,' said the tailor. 'I can see you're a frisky devil like me.' He gave the foal a pat on the rump, and the young creature kicked his heels for joy and galloped away, leaping hedges and ditches and galloping off into the distance.

The little tailor hadn't eaten anything since the meagre lump of bread the shoemaker had given him the day before. 'The sunlight fills my eyes,' he said, 'but I've got nothing to fill my belly with. The next thing I see that's even half edible . . . Ah! What's that?'

It was a stork, and it stepped daintily over the meadow towards him. The tailor leaped on it at once and seized it by one leg.

'I don't know what you'll taste like,' he said, 'but I'm going to find out. Now stand still while I cut your head off, and then I'll roast you.'

'No, please don't do that,' said the stork. 'It really isn't a good idea. You see, I'm sacred. I'm a friend to everyone, and no one harms me. If you spare my life, I'll certainly be able to do you some good in a different way.'

'Oh, off you go then, longlegs,' said the tailor, and let go. The great bird rose gracefully up on his long wings, letting his legs hang down, and flew away.

'Where's this all going to end?' said the tailor to himself. 'My hunger gets bigger and bigger, and my belly emptier and emptier. Well, whatever I see next is doomed.'

At that moment he was passing a pond where a couple of young ducks were taking their morning swim. One of them came a bit too close, and the tailor seized it at once.

'Just in time!' he said, and he was about to wring its neck when there was a terrible squawking from across the pond, and an old mother duck flapped out from among the reeds and half swam, half flew across towards him.

'Spare my child!' she cried. 'Can you imagine how your own poor mother would feel if someone wanted to eat you?'

'Oh, calm down,' said the good-natured tailor. 'You can keep your child.'

And he set the duckling back on the water.

When he turned away ready to set off again, he found he was standing in front of an old hollow tree where dozens of wild bees were flying in and out.

'Honey!' he thought at once. 'Thank goodness! That's my reward for sparing the duckling.'

But he'd hardly moved a step towards the tree when the queen bee came flying out.

'If you touch my people and destroy our nest,' she said, 'you'll be sorry for it. You'll feel ten thousand red-hot needles piercing your skin. But leave us alone and go on your way, and one day we'll do you a favour in return.'

The tailor couldn't win that one. 'Three empty dishes and nothing in the fourth,' he said to himself, 'makes a miserable dinner.'

So he dragged himself and his ravening stomach into the town, and since all the clocks were striking twelve, there was food already cooked in the first inn he came to. He sat down and devoured an enormous meal.

When he was finally satisfied, he said to himself, 'Well, it's time to find some work.'

He set off around the town to find a tailor's shop, and soon found himself a job. He was a master of his trade, so it wasn't long before he was well known, and every fashionable person was eager to have a new coat or jacket made by the little tailor. And day by day his reputation grew.

'I can't get any cleverer,' he said, 'so all I can do is get more successful.'

The summit of his success came when the king appointed him Tailor Royal to the court.

But strange things happen in this world. On the very same day of his royal appointment, his former companion the shoemaker was appointed Cobbler Royal. When the shoemaker caught sight of the tailor and saw that he had two healthy eyes, he was astonished and alarmed, and his conscience pricked him. 'Before he takes revenge on me,' he thought, 'I'll dig a pit for him.'

But whoever digs a pit for someone else falls into it himself. One evening when it was getting dark, the shoemaker went to the king and said humbly, 'Your majesty, I don't like to speak ill of anyone, but that tailor fellow has been saying that he can find the golden crown that was lost all that time ago.'

'Oh, he has, has he?' said the king.

Next morning he had the tailor summoned.

'I hear you've been boasting you can find my golden crown,' he said. 'Well, you'd better make good your boast, or leave the city and not come back.'

'Oh ho,' thought the tailor, 'I can see the way the wind's blowing. There's no point in hanging about if he wants me to do the impossible; I'll go straight away.'

He tied up his bundle and made his way to the city gate. Once he was outside, however, he couldn't help regretting the need to leave this city where he'd been doing so well. He was walking along thinking about it when he came to the pond where he'd made the acquaintance of the ducks. At that moment, the old mother duck whose young one he'd spared was sitting on the grass preening herself, and she recognized him at once.

'Morning,' she said. 'What's the trouble? Why are you down in the dumps?'

'Oh, duck,' he said, 'you won't be surprised once I tell you all about it.' And he told the duck everything that had happened.

'Well, if that's all,' said the duck, 'you can forget your troubles. The crown is down below at the bottom of the pond. We'll bring it up for you. Spread your handkerchief out on the grass and enjoy the sunshine.'

She called her twelve children, and they all dived down and vanished. A couple of minutes later she came up with the crown balanced on her wings.

'Careful now,' she said to the ducklings. 'Some of you this side, some of you that . . .'

They all swam round her supporting the heavy crown with their beaks, and in less than a minute the crown was resting on the tailor's handkerchief. What a magnificent sight! The sun sparkled on the gold so it shone like a hundred thousand carbuncles.

The tailor thanked the ducks, tied the four corners of his handkerchief together, and carried the crown to the king. The king was so delighted that he hung a gold chain around the tailor's neck.

When the shoemaker saw that his first plan had failed, he thought of another. He went to the king and said, 'Your majesty, I'm sorry to say that the tailor's boasting again. His latest claim is that he can make a wax model of the royal palace, every room and every detail, furniture and all, inside and out.'

The king sent for the tailor and ordered him to make a model like that, every detail, furniture and all.

'And if you fail to include so much as a single nail on a wall, I'll have you imprisoned underground for the rest of your life,' said the king.

The tailor thought, 'This gets worse and worse. Who could put up with this sort of thing?'

He slung his knapsack over his back and set off again. He got as far as the hollow tree, and he was so depressed that he just slumped down and hung his head. The bees flying in and out must have told the queen he was there, because very soon she came out and sat on a twig beside him.

'Got a stiff neck?' she said.

'Oh, hello. No, I'm just hanging my head in despair.'

And he told her what the king had ordered him to do. The queen bee flew up and had a buzzing conversation with several others, and then she came back down again.

'Just go back to the city now,' she said, 'but come back here tomorrow morning and bring a large cloth with you. Don't worry. It'll all come right in the end.'

So he turned back and kept out of the way. Meanwhile, the bees flew to the palace and in through the windows, and buzzed around looking at every single detail. Then they all flew out again and went back to their hive, where they started modelling the palace in wax. They worked so quickly that anyone watching would have sworn it was just growing by itself. By the evening it was all ready. When the tailor came back the next morning, he could hardly believe what he saw. The whole building was there, from the tiles on the roof to the cobbles in the courtyard, and not one single detail was missing, not even a single nail on a wall. What's more, it was as white and delicate as a snowflake, and it smelled like honey.

'Oh, bees, I don't know how to thank you!' said the tailor.

He placed it in the large cloth, wrapped it as carefully as he possibly could, and carried it all the way to the throne room, taking the greatest care in the world not to drop it or fall over. He got there safely, and unfolded the cloth and showed it to the king, who walked all round staring in at the windows, peering at the sentry-boxes, admiring the details of the ironwork on the balconies.

He couldn't admire it enough. He had it set up in the largest hall, and rewarded the tailor with a handsome stone house.

The shoemaker was beaten once more, but he didn't give up. He went to the king and said, 'I'm truly sorry to tell you this, your majesty, but that tailor has been boasting again. He's heard that there's no water under the castle courtyard, but he says that's nothing to a man like him. If he wanted to he could cause a fountain to spring up there as tall as a man, flowing with crystal-clear water.'

The king sent for the tailor.

'I've heard this claim of yours about making a fountain spring up in the courtyard. If you don't do it I shall look like a fool, and I won't have that. So you put a fountain of crystal-clear water there as you've promised, or else there'll be a fountain of your blood when the Executioner Royal cuts your head off.'

The poor tailor hurried out of the city gate as fast as he could. This time his life was at stake, and he couldn't stop the tears rolling down his face.

He wandered out into the country, with no idea how he could possibly fulfil this latest command. As he passed a wide green meadow, the foal he'd given his liberty to some time before came galloping up. He had now become a beautiful chestnut horse.

'The time has come,' he said to the tailor, 'for me to repay your kindness. No need to tell me what you want – I know already, and I can make it happen. Just climb on my back. I'm strong enough now to take a brace of tailors.'

The tailor's courage came back all at once. With one bound he leaped on the horse's back, and clung on to his mane as the horse galloped at full speed towards the city. Pedestrians scattered as he charged through the gate and made straight for the castle. Ignoring the sentries, they galloped right up the steps and into the courtyard, where the horse raced round and round faster and faster, the tailor clinging on with all his might, and then crash!

The horse fell down right in the middle. At the same moment there was an almighty clap of thunder, a great clump of earth and cobblestones flew straight up into the air and way over the castle roof, and then a spring of water shot into the air as high as a man on horseback. The water was so clear that the sunbeams sparkled on it, making rainbows.

The king was standing in the doorway, watching in amazement. As the horse got to his feet again and the tailor staggered up, shaking and trembling, the king ran to him and embraced him in the sight of all the court.

So the tailor was in the king's good books again, but it didn't last long. This time the wicked shoemaker took a calculating look at the royal family. The king had plenty of daughters, each one more beautiful than all the others, but no son, and it was known that his majesty was eager for a prince to succeed him on the throne. The shoemaker went to him and said, 'Your majesty, I'm afraid you won't like what I'm going to tell you now, but it can't be hidden. That insolent tailor has boasted that if he wanted to, he could have a son brought to your majesty through the air.'

That was too much for the king. He summoned the tailor again.

'I hear you've been making claims about the succession. I hear that you've said you could bring me a son. Well, you've got nine days. Bring me a son in that time, and you can marry the eldest princess.'

The tailor thought, 'She'd be a prize worth winning. I'd do a lot to marry her, but those cherries are growing too high for me. If I tried to climb that high, the branch would break. What am I going to do now?'

He went to his workshop, sat himself cross-legged on the bench, and wondered what on earth he could do. Finally he gave up.

'It's no good!' he cried. 'It can't be done, and I'm going to have to go away for good this time. I can't live here in peace.'

He tied up his bundle and set off once again. When he got to the meadow he saw his friend the stork walking slowly up and down, looking just like a philosopher. Every so often he'd stop, look closely at a frog, then pick it up and swallow it.

Seeing the tailor, the stork strolled over to greet him.

'I see you're carrying your possessions with you. Are you leaving the city, then?'

The tailor told him what the trouble was. 'He keeps asking me to do these impossible things, and with the help of some good friends I've managed the other tasks, but this one's completely beyond me,' he said.

'Well, don't let it turn your hair grey,' said the stork. 'We storks have a certain expertise in this field. It won't take me long to fish a little prince out of the well where they grow. Go home, my dear tailor, and put your feet up. Nine days, was it? Go to the palace in nine days' time, and I'll meet you there.'

The little tailor went home feeling much more cheerful, and on the appointed day he went to the palace. Just as he arrived, there was a tapping at the window, and there was the stork. The tailor opened the window and the stork came in, carrying a bundle in his beak. He walked very carefully over the smooth marble floor, and laid the bundle in the lap of the queen, who opened it to find the most beautiful baby boy reaching up his arms for her. She picked him up and caressed him and kissed him, transported with delight.

Before he flew away, the stork took another bundle off his back and handed it to the king. In it there were combs, mirrors, ribbons and what not, presents for all the princesses except the eldest, because her present was the tailor for a husband.

'It seems to me that I've got the best prize of the lot,' said the tailor. 'My old mother was right after all. She always used to say that whoever trusts in God can't fail, as long as his luck holds, that is.'

The shoemaker had to make the shoes in which the tailor danced at his wedding. After that, though, he was ordered to leave the city for ever. He left in a foul mood and slouched along the road towards the forest, which led him past the gallows. By that time he was worn out; tired, hot, angry and bitter, he threw himself down and was about to fall asleep when the two crows who'd been sitting on the heads of the hanged men flew down and pecked his eyes out. At that point he went mad, and he ran off into the forest, where he must have died of hunger, for he was never seen again.

* * *

Tale type: ATU 613, 'The Two Travellers', continuing as ATU 554, 'The Grateful Animals'
Source: a story told to the Grimm brothers by a student named Mein from Kiel
Similar stories: Alexander Afanasyev: 'Right and Wrong' (*Russian Fairy Tales*); Katharine M. Briggs: 'The King of the Herrings' (*Folk Tales of Britain*); Italo Calvino: 'The Two Muleteers' (*Italian Folktales*); Jacob and Wilhelm Grimm: 'The Queen Bee', 'The Sea-Hare', 'The White Snake' (*Children's and Household Tales*)

This tale didn't appear in the Grimms' collection until their fifth edition, in 1843. It's one of the most delightfully vigorous of all the stories; it moves forward without a pause or a hitch, and the two tale types are sewn together so neatly that you can't see the join. The little tailor himself would be proud of this workmanship. So should the student called Mein, who was the Grimms' source.

Like many folk-tale tailors, this one is small, cheerful and lucky. He has a great deal in common with other Grimm protagonists, who, as Jack Zipes points out, 'come largely from the peasant, artisan, or mercantile class. By the end of many of the tales, these protagonists, whether male or female, experience a rise in fortune that enables them to win a wife or husband, amass a fortune and power . . . The succession to power of lower-class figures is legitimized by their essential qualities of industriousness, cleverness, opportunism, and frankness' (*The Brothers Grimm*, pp. 114–15).

That certainly describes the little tailor, though luck plays a big part in his good fortune as well. As for the shoemaker, he is a villain from the start. Bad luck to him.

THIRTY-EIGHT

HANS-MY-HEDGEHOG

Once there was a farmer who had all the money and land he wanted, but despite his wealth there was one thing missing from his life. He and his wife had never had any children. When he met other farmers in town or at the market, they would often make fun of him and ask why he and his wife had never managed to do what their cattle did regularly. Didn't they know how to do it? In the end he lost his temper, and when he got back home, he swore and said, 'I will have a child, even if it's a hedgehog.'

Not long afterwards his wife did have a child, a boy, as they could see from his bottom half. The top half, though, was a hedgehog. When she saw him, she was horrified.

'See what you've done!' she cried. 'This is all your fault.'

'It can't be helped,' said the farmer. 'We're stuck with him. He'll have to be baptized like a normal boy, but I don't know who we can ask to be godfather.'

'And the only name we can give him,' she said, 'is Hans-my-Hedgehog.'

When he was baptized, the priest said, 'I don't know what you'll do for a bed. He can't sleep on a normal mattress, he'd jab holes all over it.'

The farmer and his wife saw the truth of that, and put some straw down behind the stove and laid him there. His mother couldn't suckle him; she tried, but it was too painful altogether.

The little creature lay behind the stove for eight years, and his father grew sick to death of him. 'I wish he'd kick the bucket,' he thought, but Hans-my-Hedgehog didn't die; he just lay there.

One day there happened to be a fair in the town, and the farmer wanted to go. He asked his wife what she'd like him to bring back for her.

'A bit of steak and a half a dozen rolls,' she said.

Then he asked the maidservant, and she asked for a pair of slippers and some fancy stockings. Finally he said to his son, 'Well, what would you like?'

'Papa,' said Hans-my-Hedgehog, 'I'd like some bagpipes.'

When the farmer came back, he gave his wife the steak and the rolls, he gave the maid the slippers and stockings, and finally he went behind the stove and gave Hans-my-Hedgehog his bagpipes.

Then Hans-my-Hedgehog said, 'Papa, go to the blacksmith's and have him make some shoes for the cockerel. Once you've done that, I'll ride away and never come back.'

The farmer was happy to get rid of him, so he took the cockerel to the blacksmith's and had him shod. Once that was done, Hans-my-Hedgehog jumped on the cockerel's back and rode away, taking some pigs with him to tend in the forest.

When they were in the forest he spurred the cockerel up, and it flew high into a tree with him. There he sat keeping an eye on his pigs and learning how to play the bagpipes. Years went by, and his father had no idea where he was; but the herd grew bigger and bigger and he played more and more skilfully. In fact the music he made was quite beautiful.

One day a king came riding past. He had lost his way in the forest, and he was amazed to hear such lovely music, so he stopped to listen to it. He had no idea where it was coming from, so he sent a servant to find the musician. The servant looked around and finally came back to the king.

'There's a strange little animal sitting up in that tree, your majesty,' he said. 'It looks like a cockerel with a hedgehog sitting on it. And the hedgehog's playing the bagpipes.'

'Well, go and ask it the way!' said the king.

The servant went and called up into the tree, and Hans-my-Hedgehog stopped playing and climbed down to the ground. He bowed to the king and said, 'What can I do for you, your majesty?'

'You can tell me the way to my kingdom. I'm lost.'

'With pleasure, your majesty. I'll tell you the way if you promise in writing to give me the first thing that greets you when you arrive home.'

The king looked at him, and thought, 'That's easy enough to promise. This monster won't be able to read, so I can write anything.'

So he took pen and ink and wrote a few words on a piece of paper. Hans-my-Hedgehog took it and showed him the way, and the king set off and was soon home again.

Now the king had a daughter, and when she saw him coming back, she was overjoyed and ran down to greet him and kiss him. She was the first person he met on the way in, and of course the king thought about Hans-my-Hedgehog, and told his daughter how he had nearly had to promise her to a strange animal that sat on a cockerel and played the bagpipes.

'But don't you worry, my dear,' he said. 'I wrote something quite different. That hedgehog creature won't be able to read.'

'That's a good thing, because I wouldn't have gone with him anyway,' said the princess.

Meanwhile, Hans-my-Hedgehog stayed in the forest enjoying himself, tending his pigs and playing his bagpipes. The forest happened to be very large, and not long afterwards another king came by, with all his servants and messengers, and he too was lost. Like the first king, he heard the beautiful music and sent a messenger to find out where it was coming from.

The messenger saw Hans-my-Hedgehog up in the tree playing the bagpipes, and called up to ask what he was doing.

'I'm keeping an eye on my pigs,' Hans-my-Hedgehog called down. 'What do you want?'

The messenger explained, and Hans-my-Hedgehog came down and told the old king that he'd tell him the way in exchange for a promise, and it was the same promise as before: the king must give him the first creature that greeted him when he got home. The king agreed, and signed a paper saying so.

Once that was done, Hans-my-Hedgehog rode ahead on the cockerel to show them the way to the edge of the forest, where he said goodbye to the king and went back to his pigs; and so the king came home safely, to the joy of all his courtiers. This king too had an only daughter, who was very beautiful, and she was the first to run out and welcome her beloved father.

She threw her arms around him and kissed him, and asked him where he'd been and why he'd taken so long.

'We lost our way, my love,' he said. 'But in the depths of the forest we came upon the strangest thing: a half-hedgehog, half-boy sitting on a cockerel and playing the bagpipes. Playing them remarkably well, too. He showed us the way, you see, and . . . Well, my dear, I had to promise to give him whoever came out to greet me first. Oh, my darling, I'm so terribly sorry.'

But the princess loved her father, and said that she wouldn't make him break his promise; she would go with Hans-my-Hedgehog whenever he came for her.

Meanwhile, back in the forest, Hans-my-Hedgehog looked after his pigs. And those pigs had more pigs, and then *those* pigs had more pigs, until there were so many that the forest was full of pigs from one end to the other. At that point Hans-my-Hedgehog decided that he'd spent all the time he wanted to in the forest. He sent a message to his father, saying that they should empty all the pigsties in the village, because he was coming with such a large herd of pigs that anyone who wanted some pork or bacon could join in and help themselves.

His father was a bit put out to hear this. He thought Hans-my-Hedgehog was dead and gone. But then along came his son driving all those pigs in front of him, and the village had such a slaughter that they could hear the noise two miles away.

When it was all over Hans-my-Hedgehog said, 'Papa, my cockerel needs new shoes. If you take him to the blacksmith and have him shod again, I'll ride away and never come back as long as I live.'

So the farmer did that, and was relieved to think that he'd seen the back of Hans-my-Hedgehog at last.

When the cockerel was ready, Hans-my-Hedgehog jumped on his back and rode away. He rode and rode till he came to the kingdom of the first king, the king of the broken promise. The king had given strict orders that if anyone approached the palace playing the bagpipes and riding on a cockerel, they should be shot, stabbed, bombed, knocked down, blown up, strangled, anything to prevent them from entering.

So when Hans-my-Hedgehog appeared, the brigade of guards was ordered out to charge at him with their bayonets. But he was too quick for them. He spurred the cockerel up into the air and flew right over the top of the soldiers, over the palace wall and up to the king's window.

He perched there on the sill and shouted out that he'd come for what he'd been promised, and that if the king tried to weasel out of it he'd pay for it with his life, and so would the princess.

The king told his daughter that she'd better do what Hans-my-Hedgehog wanted. She put on a white dress, and the king hastily ordered a carriage with six fine horses to be made ready, and piled gold and silver and the deeds to several fine farms and forests into it, and ordered two dozen of his best servants to go with it.

The horses were harnessed, the servants were all lined up, the princess climbed in, and then Hans-my-Hedgehog took his place beside her with the cockerel on his knee and the bagpipes on his lap. They said goodbye and off they went. The king thought he'd never see his daughter again.

He was wrong about that, though. As soon as they were out of the city, Hans-my-Hedgehog ordered the princess out of the carriage, and told the servants to take several paces backwards and look the other way. Then he tore the princess's white dress into shreds and stuck her all over with his prickles until she was covered in blood.

'That's what you get for trying to deceive me,' he said. 'Now clear off. Go home. You're no good to me, and I don't want you.'

And she went home with the servants and the gold and the carriage and all, disgraced. So much for her.

As for Hans-my-Hedgehog, he took his bagpipes and jumped on the cockerel and rode away to the second kingdom, whose king had behaved very differently from the first one. He had given orders that if anyone arrived in the kingdom looking like a hedgehog and riding a cockerel, he should be saluted, given a cavalry escort, greeted with crowds cheering and waving flags, and brought with honour to the royal palace.

The king had told his daughter what Hans-my-Hedgehog looked like, of course, but when she saw him she was shocked all the same. However, there was nothing to be done about it; her father had given his word, and she had given hers. She bade Hans-my-Hedgehog welcome, with all her heart, and they were married at once, and sat next to each other at the banquet.

And then it was time to go to bed. He could see she was afraid of his prickles.

'You mustn't be frightened,' he said. 'I'd do anything rather than hurt you.'

He told the old king to have a large fire made in the fireplace on the landing, and to have four men ready outside the bedroom door.

'I'm going to take off my hedgehog skin as soon as I go into the bedroom,' he explained. 'The men must seize it at once and throw it on the fire, and stay there till it's all burnt to ash.'

When the clock struck eleven, Hans-my-Hedgehog went into the bedroom, took off his skin, and laid it down by the bed. Immediately the four men rushed in, seized the prickly skin, flung it on the fire and stood around watching till it had all burned up, and the moment the last prickle was consumed by the last flame, Hans was free.

He lay down on the bed like a human being at last. However, he was scorched and charred all over, as if he himself had been in the fire. The king sent at once for the royal physician, who cleaned him up and tended to his skin with special balms and ointments, and soon he looked like an ordinary young man, though more handsome than most. The princess was overjoyed.

Next morning they both rose from the royal bed full of happiness, and when they had eaten breakfast they celebrated their wedding again; and in time Hans-my-Hedgehog succeeded the old king, and inherited the kingdom.

Some years later he took his wife all the way back to see his father. Of course the old farmer had no idea who he was.

'I'm your son,' said Hans-my-Hedgehog.

'Oh, no, no, that can't be right,' said the farmer. 'I did have a son, but he was like a hedgehog, all covered in prickles, and he went off to see the world a long time ago.'

But Hans said that he was the one, and told so many details about his life that the farmer was finally convinced; and the old man wept for joy, and returned with his son to his kingdom.

Tale type: ATU 441, 'Hans My Hedgehog'
Source: a story told to the Grimm brothers by Dorothea Viehmann
Similar stories: Italo Calvino: 'King Crin' (*Italian Folktales*); Giovanni Francesco Straparola: 'The Pig Prince' (*The Great Fairy Tale Tradition*, ed. Jack Zipes)

This tale is a very distant descendant of the ancient story of Cupid and Psyche, as the two Italian variants make plain. This version, though, has acquired a lot of intriguing details on the way to the Grimms' collection. It has Dorothea Viehmann's characteristic swiftness and economy of movement (see the note to 'The Riddle', p. 132), and a wonderfully absurd hero whose gallantry, patience and charm, not to mention musical talent, make him one of the most memorable characters in the whole collection.

THIRTY-NINE

THE LITTLE SHROUD

There was once a little boy, seven years old, so sweet and beautiful that no one could look at him without loving him, and as for his mother, she loved him more than anything else in the world. One day without any warning he fell ill and died; nothing could console his mother, and she wept day and night.

Soon afterwards, not long after he was buried, the child began to appear every night in the places where he used to sit and play when he was alive. If his mother cried, he cried as well, and when morning came, he disappeared.

But his mother would not stop crying, and one night the child appeared in the white shroud in which he'd been buried, and with the little wreath on his head that had been placed in the coffin with him.

He sat on her bed and said, 'Oh, mother, please stop crying, or else I won't be able to fall asleep! My shroud's all wet from the tears you keep dropping on it.'

That startled the mother, and she stopped crying.

Next night the child came to her bed again, holding a little light in his hand. He said, 'See, my shroud's nearly dry now. I'll be able to rest in my grave.'

His mother offered her grief to God and bore it patiently and quietly; and the child never came again, but slept in his little bed under the earth.

Tale type: unclassified
Source: a story from Bavaria, told to the Grimm brothers by an unknown informant

See my note to the following story.

FORTY

THE STOLEN PENNIES

Once a father and his wife and their children were sitting around the table for their midday meal, and a good friend of the family, who had come to visit, was sitting with them. While they were sitting there the clock struck twelve, and just then the visitor saw the door open and a deathly-pale child, dressed in snow-white clothes, come into the room. He didn't look around or say a word, but went straight into the next room. A few moments later he came out, still saying nothing, and went out of the door again.

Next day, and the next, the child came back in the same way. Finally the visitor asked the father who this beautiful child was who came in and went into the next room at noon every day.

'I didn't see him,' said the father. 'I've got no idea who he can be.'

Next day, when the child came again, the visitor pointed him out, but neither father nor mother nor the other children could see a thing. The visitor got up and went to the door of the next room, and opened it a little way. There he saw the child sitting on the floor, probing the cracks between the floorboards with his fingers; but as soon as he saw the visitor, he disappeared.

The visitor told the family what he'd seen and described the child exactly. The mother recognized him at once, and said, 'Oh, it's my dear son, who died four weeks ago.'

They lifted the floorboards and found two pennies that the mother had given the child to give to a poor man. However, the child had thought, 'I can buy myself a cake with that,' and hidden the pennies under the floor.

That was why he had had no peace in his grave, and came every day at noon to look for them. The parents gave the money to a poor man, and after that the child was never seen again.

* * *

Tale type: ATU 769, 'The Child's Grave'
Source: a story told to the Grimm brothers by Gretchen Wild

I've put the notes to this and 'The Little Shroud' (p. 319) together because of their obvious similarity. 'The Little Shroud' is unclassified in the Aarne-Thompson-Uther index, and the only tale listed there to exemplify this type is this tale itself, under the title of 'The Child's Grave'.

Each of these tales is straightforward and pious. They are pure ghost stories, but their intention is not to make us shiver so much as to point a simple moral. The belief system they come from is almost pre-Christian: the dead deserve their rest, and the living can help them find it; excessive grief is self-indulgent; sin must be atoned for. Once the human action has been taken, the supernatural withdraws.

The effect is to give them the character of ghost stories of the traditional 'true' type, such as those gathered in the well-known *Lord Halifax's Ghost Book* (1934), or more recently in Peter Ackroyd's *The English Ghost* (2010). All that would be needed to make them identical to that sort of story is names for the characters concerned and for the places where the events took place. To complete the illusion, a source cunningly disguised by means of an initial and a dash could be invented, thus: 'Herr A—, a highly respected official of the town of D—, was travelling in the Duchy of H— when he heard the following story . . .'

FORTY-ONE

THE DONKEY CABBAGE

There was once a young hunter who went out to his hide in the forest. He was happy and light-hearted, and he whistled on a blade of grass as he went along.

All at once he came across a poor old woman. She said, 'Good morning, my fine young hunter. I can see you're in a good mood, but I'm hungry and thirsty. Can you spare me any change?'

The hunter felt sorry for the old woman, so he put his hand in his pocket and gave her the few coins he had. He was about to go on his way when the old woman clutched his arm.

'Listen, my good hunter,' she said. 'You've been kind to me, so I'm going to give you a gift. Carry straight on, and in a little while you'll come to a tree with nine birds sitting in it. They'll have a cloak in their claws, and they'll be fighting over it. Take your gun and shoot right into the middle of them. They'll drop the cloak all right, and one of the birds will fall dead at your feet. Take the cloak with you, because it's a wishing cloak. Once you throw it round your shoulders, all you've got to do is wish yourself somewhere, and you'll be there in a flash. And you should take the heart from the dead bird, too. Cut it out and then swallow it whole. If you do that, you'll find a gold coin under your pillow every morning of your life.'

The hunter thanked the wise woman and thought to himself:

'These are certainly fine gifts she's giving me; I hope she's telling the truth.'

He'd gone no further than a hundred yards when he heard a great squawking and flapping in the branches above him. He looked up and saw a flock of birds all tearing at a piece of cloth with their claws and beaks, as if each one wanted it for itself.

'Well,' said the hunter, 'this is odd. It's happening just as the old girl said it would.'

He took his gun and fired a shot right into the middle of the birds. Most of them shrieked and flew away at once, but one fell to the ground dead, and the cloak fell too. The hunter did just as the old woman had advised. He cut the bird open with his knife, took out the heart and swallowed it, and went home with the cloak.

When he woke up next morning, the first thing he thought of was the old woman's promise. He felt under his pillow, and sure enough, there was a gleaming gold coin. Next day he found another one, and then another, and so it went on each time he woke up. Quite soon he had a fine heap of gold, and then he thought, 'It's all very well collecting this, but what use is it to me here? I think I'll go out and see the world.'

He said goodbye to his parents, slung his gun and his knapsack over his shoulders, and set off. After walking for a few days, he was just coming out of a dense forest when he saw a beautiful castle standing in the open country beyond the trees. He went closer, and saw two people standing at one of the windows, looking down at him.

One of them was an old woman, and she was a witch. She said to the other, who was her daughter, 'That man who's just coming out of the forest has got a great treasure inside him. We must get it for ourselves, my honey, because we can make much better use of it than he's doing. You see, he swallowed the heart of a particular bird, and as a result he finds a gold coin under his pillow every morning.' She went on to tell her daughter the whole story of the hunter and the wise woman, and she finished by saying, 'And if you don't do exactly as I tell you, my dear, you'll be sorry.'

As the hunter came closer to the castle he saw them more clearly, and thought, 'I've been wandering about for quite a while now, and I've got plenty of money. Maybe I'll stop at this castle for a day or two and have a rest.'

Of course, the real reason was that the girl was very beautiful.

He went into the castle, where they welcomed him and looked after him generously. Before long he was in love with the witch's daughter, so much so that he could think of nothing else; he had eyes only for her, and whatever she wanted him to do, he did. In fact he was besotted.

Seeing this, the old woman said to the girl, 'This is the time to act. We've got to get that bird's heart. He won't even notice it's gone.'

She prepared a potion, and poured it into a cup for the girl to hand to the young man.

'My dearest one,' she said to him, 'won't you drink to my health?'

He drank it all down in one, and almost immediately he was so sick that he vomited up the bird's heart. The girl helped him to lie down, with many soft words of concern, and then went straight back, found the heart, rinsed it in clean water and swallowed it herself.

From then on the hunter found no more gold coins under his pillow. He had no idea that they were appearing under the girl's, and that the witch collected them every morning and hid them away. He was so infatuated that all he wanted to do was spend time with her daughter.

The witch said, 'We've got the heart, but that isn't enough. We must have the wishing cloak too.'

'Can't we leave him that?' said the daughter. 'After all, the poor man's lost his fortune.'

'Don't you be so soft!' said the witch. 'A cloak like that is worth millions. There aren't many of them about, I can tell you. I must have it, and I will have it.'

She told her daughter what to do and said that if she didn't obey, she'd regret it. So the girl did as the witch said: she stood at the window gazing out as if she were very sad.

The hunter said, 'Why are you standing there looking so sad?'

'Ah, my treasure,' said the girl, 'out there lies Mount Garnet, where the most precious jewels grow. When I think of them I want them so much that I can't help feeling sad . . . But who can go there and gather them? Only the birds, who can fly. I'm sure a human being could never get there.'

'If that's all that's troubling you,' said the hunter, 'leave it to me. I'll soon cheer you up.'

He took his cloak and swung it around his shoulders, and over her as well, so it enfolded both of them. Then he wished to be on Mount Garnet. The blink of an eye later, they were sitting near the top of it. Precious stones of every kind sparkled brilliantly all around them; they had never seen anything so lovely.

However, the witch had cast a spell to make the hunter sleepy, and he said to the girl, 'Let's sit down and rest a while. I'm so tired my legs can't keep me up.'

They sat down, he laid his head in her lap, and a moment later his eyes began to close. As soon as he was fast asleep, she took the cloak from around his shoulders and wrapped it around herself, before gathering as many garnets and other jewels as she could carry and wishing herself back home.

When the hunter awoke and found himself alone on the wild mountain, and that his cloak had gone too, he realized that his beloved had deceived him.

'Oh,' he sighed, 'I didn't know the world was so full of treachery!'

He sat there too distressed to move. He couldn't think what to do.

Now the mountain happened to belong to some ferocious giants, great thundering brutes, and it wasn't long before the hunter heard three of them coming. He lay down quickly and pretended to be fast asleep.

The first giant prodded him with his toe and said, 'What's this earthworm doing here?'

'Squash him,' said the second. 'I would.'

But the third one said, 'Don't bother. There's nothing here for him to live on, so he'll be dead soon in any case. Besides, if he climbs to the top, the clouds will carry him away.'

They left him alone and carried on talking as they walked off. The hunter had heard everything they'd said, and as soon as they were out of sight, he got to his feet and clambered up the mountain to the peak, which was surrounded by clouds.

He sat down on the jewelled pinnacle, while clouds came and bumped into him, and finally one of them grabbed him and tossed him on board. It floated around the sky for some time, and very comfortable it was too, and the hunter saw many interesting things as he peered over the side; but eventually it began to sink towards the ground, and soon enough he was deposited in someone's kitchen garden, which had high walls around it.

The cloud floated up again and left him standing between the cabbages and the onions.

'Pity there's no fruit,' he said to himself. 'I wouldn't mind a nice apple or a pear, and I'm so hungry. Still, I can always have a mouthful of cabbage. It doesn't taste wonderful, but it'll keep me going.'

There were two kinds of cabbages growing in the garden, pointed ones and round ones, and to begin with the hunter pulled a few leaves off a pointed one and started to chew. It tasted good enough, but when he'd only had a few bites, he felt the strangest sensation: his skin tickled all over as long hairs sprouted out of it, his spine bent forward and his arms lengthened and turned into hairy legs with hooves on the ends of them, his neck thickened and grew longer, his face lengthened and two long ears shot up from the sides of his head, and before he knew what was happening, he was a donkey.

Needless to say, that made the cabbage taste much better. He went on eating it with relish, and then moved on to a round cabbage. He'd only had a couple of bites when he found it all happening again, but in reverse, and in less time than it takes to tell it, he was a human being again.

'Well,' he said to himself, 'how about that? Now I can get back what belongs to me.'

So he picked a head of the pointed cabbage and a head of the round one, put them safely in his knapsack, and climbed the wall and got away. He soon discovered where he was, and set off back to the castle where the witch lived. After some days' walking he found it again, and kept out of sight while he dyed his face so brown that even his own mother wouldn't have recognized him.

Then he knocked at the door. The witch herself opened it.

'Can you give me shelter for the night?' the young man said. 'I'm worn out, and I can't go any further.'

'Who are you, my dear?' said the witch. 'What brings you out this way?'

'I'm a royal messenger, and the king sent me specially to look for the most delicious cabbage in the world. I was lucky enough to find it, and it really is delicious, but the weather's been so hot that it's beginning to wilt. I don't think I'll get it back in time.'

When the witch heard about this delicious cabbage, she couldn't wait to try it herself.

'Have you got a little bit my daughter and I could taste?' she said.

'I brought two heads of it. I don't see why you shouldn't have one of them, since you're being kind enough to let me stay the night.'

He opened his knapsack and gave her the donkey cabbage. She took it eagerly and hurried to the kitchen, her mouth already watering. She put some water on to boil and chopped the cabbage up daintily, and boiled it for just a few minutes with some salt and a little butter. It smelt so good that she couldn't resist, and before she brought it to the table she nibbled at one of the leaves, and then another, and of course as soon as she swallowed them she started to change. In a matter of seconds she was an old donkey, and she ran out into the courtyard to kick up her heels.

Next the serving girl came in, and smelling the buttery cabbage she couldn't help having a bite herself. This was an old habit of hers, and sure enough, the same thing happened to her. She couldn't hold the bowl with her new hooves, so she dropped it where it was and ran outside.

Meanwhile the witch's daughter was sitting talking to the messenger.

'I don't know what's keeping them,' she said. 'It does smell good.'

The hunter thought that the magic must have happened by this time.

'Leave it to me,' he said. 'I'll go and get it.'

When he got to the kitchen he saw the two donkeys running around the courtyard, and thought, 'Good! Just as I planned it, and serve them right.'

He scooped up the cabbage that had fallen to the floor, put it in the bowl and brought it to the girl. She had some at once, and she too became a donkey and ran outside.

The hunter washed his face so that they could recognize him, and went out to the courtyard with a length of rope.

'Yes,' he said, 'it was me. I've got you good and proper, and now you're going to pay for your treachery.'

He tied all three to the rope, and drove them ahead of him out of the castle and along the road till then came to a mill. He knocked on the door.

'What d'you want?' said the miller.

'I've got three ugly bad-tempered beasts here, and as they're no good to me I want to get rid of them. If you take them and treat them as I tell you, I'll pay whatever you ask.'

That wasn't the sort of offer the miller got every day, so he agreed at once.

'How d'you want me to treat them, then?' he said.

'Beat the old one three times a day, and feed her once' (that was the witch). 'The middle one can have three feeds a day and one beating' (that was the servant), 'and the young one's not too bad. Feed her three times and don't beat her at all.' He couldn't bring himself to have the girl beaten.

He went back to the castle and put his feet up. After a couple of days the miller came to see him.

'That old donkey,' he said, 'she wasn't much good. She's dead now. But the other two are looking really down in the mouth. I don't know what to do with them.'

'Oh, all right,' said the hunter. 'I think they've probably been punished enough.'

He told the miller to drive the other two donkeys back to the castle, where he spread some of the round cabbage leaves on the ground and let them eat, so they became human beings again.

The witch's beautiful daughter fell on her knees and said, 'Oh, my dearest, forgive me for all the evil I did you! My mother forced me to do it. I never wanted to betray you, because I love you with all my heart. The wishing cloak is in the hall cupboard, and as for the bird's heart, I'll drink something to make me bring it up again.'

'No need for that,' he said, because he'd found himself in love with her all over again. 'You can keep it. It won't make any difference who has it, because I want to marry you.'

Their wedding was celebrated soon afterwards, and they lived together very happily until they died.

Tale type: ATU 567, 'The Magic Bird-Heart', continuing as ATU 566, 'The Three Magic Objects and the Wonderful Fruits'
Source: a story from Bohemia, told to the Grimm brothers by an unknown informant
Similar stories: Alexander Afanasyev: 'Horns' (*Russian Fairy Tales*); Katharine M. Briggs: 'Fortunatus' (*Folk Tales of Britain*); Italo Calvino: 'The Crab with the Golden Eggs' (*Italian Folktales*)

As quite often in Grimm, we have two separate story types sewn together here. Once the hunter has the bird's heart and the wishing cloak, he could in theory go on to any kind of adventure. The story of the cabbage (sometimes translated as 'lettuce') which turns whoever eats it into a donkey has no logical connection with the first part of the story, but they fit together very well.

In Afanasyev's Russian version of the story, the food (two kinds of apple, in this case) causes horns to grow on or to vanish from the eater's head. Less inconvenient than turning into a donkey, no doubt, but still not easy to explain.

What I especially like about this tale is the young hunter's cheerful good nature. It's remarkable how few details of behaviour we need to evoke a personality.

Cippenham Library
Elmshott Lane,
Cippenham, Slough, SL1 5RB
Tel: (01628) 661745
www.slough.gov.uk/libraries

Borrowed Items 02/06/2018 11:18
XXXXXXXXXX9933

Item Title	Due Date
* The drowned world	23/06/2018
Grimm tales : for young and old	20/06/2018
Trigger warning : short fictions disturbances	20/06/2018
The Mistletoe murder and other stories	20/06/2018

* borrowed today
Thank you for using Cippenham's Self Service Unit

Renew or reserve books online with your membership card and pin number
http://slough.spydus.co.uk
Follow us on Facebook and Twitter
@SloughLibraries

FORTY-TWO

ONE EYE, TWO EYES AND THREE EYES

There was once a woman who had three daughters. She called the eldest One Eye, because she had one eye in the middle of her forehead. The second was called Two Eyes, because she had two eyes just like other people, and the youngest Three Eyes, because she had three eyes, the third one in the middle of her forehead like her eldest sister's.

Because Two Eyes looked no different from everyone else, however, her mother and her sisters couldn't stop criticizing her.

'You two-eyed monster,' they said, 'who d'you think you are? There's nothing special about you, my girl. You don't belong with us.'

They gave her the shabbiest clothes to wear and nothing but leftover scraps from the table to eat. Between them, they made her life a misery.

One day Two Eyes had to go out and look after the goat. She was hungry, as usual, because there had been nothing but the dirty saucepan they'd cooked the porridge in to lick out for breakfast, and it was burnt, what's more. She sat down on the grassy slope and began to cry. When the first sobbing had died away, she was surprised to see a kindly-looking wise woman standing nearby.

'Why are you crying, Two Eyes?' she said.

'Because I've got two eyes like other people,' replied Two Eyes. 'Like you, for instance. My mother and my sisters hate me, and they push me around and give me nothing but worn-out old clothes to wear and make me eat the scraps they leave on the table. Today I only had the porridge saucepan to lick out, and it was burnt, too.'

'Well, Two Eyes, you can stop crying now,' said the wise woman. 'I'll tell you a secret, and you won't be hungry any more. Just say to the goat:

"Little goat, bleat,
Bring me good things to eat,"

and a beautiful table with all sorts of good food will appear in front of you, and you can eat as much as you like. When you've had enough, just say:

"Little goat, bleat,
I've had all I can eat,"

and it'll disappear.'

No sooner had she said that than the wise woman herself disappeared. Two Eyes thought she'd better try it straight away before she forgot it, and besides, she was too hungry to wait.

So she said:

'Little goat, bleat,
Bring me good things to eat,'

and as soon as she'd said the words, there in front of her stood a table covered in a snowy white cloth. There was a plate with a silver knife and fork and spoon, and a snowy linen napkin as well, and of course a chair to sit on; but the food! There were hot dishes and cold dishes, casseroles and roast meat, vegetables of all kinds, and a great big apple pie, all freshly cooked and steaming hot.

Two Eyes could hardly wait. She said the shortest grace she knew: 'Lord, be our guest now and for ever, Amen.' Then she sat down and ate all she wanted. It was all so delicious that she had a little bit of everything, and when she was full up she said:

'Little goat, bleat,
I've had all I can eat,'

and the table vanished in the blink of an eye.

'Well, I like that sort of housekeeping,' thought Two Eyes, and she was happier than she'd been for years.

When she got home with the goat that evening, she found an old clay pot with a bit of cold greasy stew in the bottom that her sisters had left for her, but she didn't touch it. And in the morning all there was for her were the crumbs from the toast they'd made, but she didn't eat those either. The first couple of times that happened her sisters didn't see, because they usually ignored whatever she did, but when it happened the next day, and the next, they couldn't help noticing.

'What's up with Two Eyes? She's not eating.'

'I bet she's up to something.'

'Probably got someone to bring her a picnic. Greedy cow.'

'Typical!'

They thought they'd better try and find out what was going on, so next time Two Eyes took the goat out to pasture, One Eye said to her, 'I think I'll come with you. I'm not sure you're looking after the goat properly.'

Two Eyes guessed what One Eye was up to. She took the goat out to the usual meadow, where there was plenty for it to eat, and then she said, 'Come and sit down, One Eye. I'll sing you a song.'

One Eye was tired, because she'd had more exercise walking out to the meadow than she'd had for weeks, and besides, the warm sun was making her drowsy. So she slumped down in the shade and Two Eyes began to sing:

'One Eye, are you awake?
One Eye, are you asleep?'

One Eye's single eyelid drooped and sank lower and lower and finally she started snoring. Once Two Eyes was sure her sister was fast asleep, she said:

'Little goat, bleat,
Bring me good things to eat.'

And at once the magic table appeared, and on it there was leek soup, roast chicken and strawberries and cream. Two Eyes ate as much as she wanted and then said:

'Little goat, bleat,
I've had all I can eat,'

and the table vanished.

Two Eyes woke One Eye and said, 'Didn't you say you wanted to help me look after the goat? You've been asleep all day! She could have run away and fallen in the river. Lucky I was here. Come on, let's go home.'

They went home, and once again Two Eyes left her scraps of food untouched. This time it was a few crusty bits of burnt pastry. Three Eyes and their mother couldn't wait to hear what had happened out in the meadow, but all One Eye could say was, 'I dunno. I fell asleep. Well, it was hot.'

'Useless!' said their mother. 'Tomorrow, you go, Three Eyes. There must be *something* going on.'

So next morning Three Eyes said to Two Eyes, 'I'm coming with you today, and I'm going to keep a close eye on what you're up to.'

Off they went with the little goat. Two Eyes could see at once that Three Eyes was up to the same trick as One Eye had been, so as soon as they were safely in the meadow and Three Eyes had slumped down by the hedge, she began to sing:

'Three Eyes, are you awake?'

But then instead of singing, as she meant to,

'Three Eyes, are you asleep?'

she sang:

'Two Eyes, are you asleep?'

And she kept singing:

'Three Eyes, are you awake?
Two Eyes, are you asleep?'

Gradually two of Three Eyes's eyes closed as they became drowsy, but the third one didn't close because Two Eyes hadn't sung it to sleep. Three Eyes let the eyelid droop and seem to close, but she was only pretending. That eye could see perfectly.

When Two Eyes thought Three Eyes was asleep, she sang:

'Little goat, bleat,
Bring me good things to eat.'

The table appeared at once. This time there was beetroot soup, a big meat pie and a delicious cake. Two Eyes ate and drank happily till she was full, and then sang:

'Little goat, bleat,
I've had all I can eat,'

and the table disappeared.

Three Eyes was watching everything, but she closed her third eye quickly when Two Eyes came over to wake her up.

'Come on, Three Eyes!' said Two Eyes. 'You've been asleep all day. It's a good thing I was here to look after the goat. Come on, let's go home.'

When they got back to the house, Two Eyes again refused the food they gave her. It was the water some cabbage had been boiled in.

The mother took Three Eyes aside and said, 'Well? What happened? Did you see?'

'Yes, I did. She tried to send me to sleep, but my third eye stayed awake. What she does is sing to the goat like this:

"Little goat, bleat,
Bring me good things to eat,"

and a table all covered with lovely food just comes out of nowhere and she eats as much as she wants. Then she sings:

"Little goat, bleat,
I've had all I can eat,"

and it disappears. Honest! It's true! I saw it. She put two of my eyes to sleep, but the third one stayed awake.'

Well, the mother was furious when she heard that. She yelled, 'Two Eyes! Come here at once! What makes you think you're better than us, eh? Playing magic tricks with the goat! How dare you! I'll make you sorry, just you watch.'

And she took the biggest knife in the kitchen and stabbed the little goat in the heart, so that it fell dead on the floor.

Two Eyes ran outside at once and ran all the way to the meadow, and burst into tears. She sobbed and sobbed for the poor little goat, which had never done anything wrong, and for herself, too.

Then she realized that the wise woman was standing there.

'Why are you crying, Two Eyes?' she said.

'I can't help it,' said Two Eyes. 'My mother stabbed the poor little goat in the heart and killed it, and now it's dead and I'll never be able to ask it for a table of food again.'

'Let me give you some good advice,' said the wise woman. 'Ask your sisters to give you the entrails of the goat, and bury them in the garden near the front door. That will bring you luck.'

Then she disappeared. Two Eyes went slowly home and said to her sisters, 'I'd like to have something to remember the goat by. Can I just have the entrails?'

'Well, if that's all you want,' said One Eye, and Three Eyes said, 'Oh, let her have them. She might stop snivelling then.'

Two Eyes put the entrails of the goat in the washing-up bowl and carried them out to the front garden, where she buried them in a little patch of grass.

Next morning there was a beautiful tree standing there. Its leaves were made of silver, and among them there were dozens of fruits the size of apples, made of solid gold. No one had ever seen a lovelier tree, and of course no one had any idea about how it had grown in the night; only Two Eyes knew, because it was growing in the spot where she'd buried the entrails of the goat.

As soon as the mother saw it, she said, 'Up you go, One Eye, climb up and get some of that golden fruit.'

One Eye climbed up, huffing and puffing, and tried, but each time she reached for a golden apple, the branch pulled itself up out of her reach. She grabbed for this one and that one, but she couldn't so much as touch one, no matter what she did.

'Useless,' said the mother. 'She can't see what she's doing. Three Eyes, you get up there. You can probably see better than she can.'

One Eye came down and Three Eyes clambered up, but in spite of her better eyesight, she got on no better than her sister. Every time she reached for an apple, the branch moved just enough to take it out of reach, and finally she had to give up.

'Can I try?' said Two Eyes. 'Maybe I'll have more luck.'

'You, you freak?'

'Yes, monster, what makes you think you can do any better than us?'

Two Eyes climbed the tree, and instead of pulling themselves out of her reach the apples positively dropped into her hands. She gathered more and more until she had a whole apron full. When she climbed down, her mother took them away, and instead of treating her better because she was the only one who could reach the fruit, One Eye and Three Eyes grew envious and spiteful, and treated her even worse than before.

Now one day when they were all in the garden, a young knight happened to ride by.

The sisters saw him coming and said, 'Quick, Two Eyes! Under the barrel! If he sees you, he'll think we're all horrible to look at!'

And they shoved her under a barrel that stood near the tree, together with the golden apples she'd already picked. Then they stood by the tree, preening themselves and simpering. As the knight came closer, they could see how handsome he was and what fine armour he was wearing.

'Well, good morning, ladies,' he said, getting off his horse. 'That's a splendid tree you have there. Gold and silver! If I could have a branch of it, you could have anything you wanted in exchange.'

'Oh, yes, the tree belongs to us,' said One Eye.

'It's completely ours,' said Three Eyes. 'I'll break off a branch for you.'

But when she tried, there was the same result as before, and One Eye had no success either. However quickly they reached for a branch, it would always snatch itself out of their reach.

'That's odd,' said the knight. 'You say the tree is yours, but it won't let you pick anything from it.'

'Oh, it's ours all right,' said One Eye.

'It's just shy,' said Three Eyes. 'Probably because you're looking.'

'Let me have another go,' said One Eye.

But as they were speaking, Two Eyes lifted the barrel a little, and rolled out some of the golden apples towards the knight's feet. The knight saw them, and stepped back in astonishment.

'I say! Where did they come from?' he said.

'Well, we've got another sister, but she—'

'She looks a bit odd, you see, because she's got two eyes, and—'

'Well, we keep her out of sight. We don't want to shame the family.'

'I'd like to see her,' said the knight. 'Two Eyes, wherever you are, come out!'

Two Eyes managed to lift the barrel off and stood up. The knight was amazed at how lovely she was.

'And can you break off a branch for me, Two Eyes?' he said.

'Yes, I can,' said Two Eyes, 'because the tree belongs to me.'

And with the greatest of ease she climbed the tree and broke off a branch with beautiful silver leaves and gold fruit, and gave it to the knight.

'And what would you like in return, Two Eyes?' he said.

'Ah,' said Two Eyes, 'I have nothing but hunger and thirst, sorrow and distress from early morning till late at night. If you could take me away from all that, I'd be grateful.'

The knight lifted her on to his horse and took her to his father's castle. He gave her some beautiful clothes and enough to eat and drink to her heart's content, and because he'd fallen in love with her, he married her; and the wedding was celebrated joyfully all through the kingdom.

After Two Eyes had been taken away by the handsome knight, her two sisters were consumed with envy. But at least the beautiful tree is still ours, they thought, and even if we can't pick the gold apples, people will stop to admire it, and who knows what good luck may flower from that?

But next morning they were aghast to see that the tree had disappeared, and all their hopes had gone with it. Meanwhile, Two Eyes was looking out of her bedroom window to see the tree standing happily in the castle courtyard, for in the middle of the night it had pulled its roots out of the ground and tiptoed all the way there to find her.

Two Eyes lived happily for a long time. One day many years later, two poor women came knocking at the castle gate to beg for something to eat, because they had been stricken with poverty and had to wander the world begging for bread from door to door. Two Eyes welcomed them and treated them so kindly that they were sorry for all the wrong they'd done to her; and the strange thing was that although so many years had passed, Two Eyes recognized One Eye and Three Eyes at once.

***

Tale type: ATU 511, 'One Eye, Two Eyes, Three Eyes'
Source: a story by Theodor Peschek, published in the journal *Wöchentliche Nachrichten für Freunde der Geschichte, Kunst und Gelahrtheit des Mittelalters* (*Weekly News for Friends of the History, Art and Learning of the Middle Ages*), vol. 2 (1816)
Similar stories: Alexander Afanasyev: 'Burenushka, the Little Red Cow' (*Russian Fairy Tales*); Jacob and Wilhelm Grimm: 'Cinderella' (*Children's and Household Tales*)

This is 'Cinderella' (p. 116), of course, with added absurdity. The presence of the wise woman, the goat, the entrails and the tree confirms it beyond any doubt: they are all aspects of the necessary but absent good mother, who turns up in every 'Cinderella' variant in one form or another.

In Afanasyev's Russian version, Two Eyes invites her nosy sisters to put their heads in her lap and let her delouse them. That nice hygienic detail turns up in 'The Devil with the Three Golden Hairs' (p. 152), too.

FORTY-THREE

THE SHOES THAT WERE DANCED TO PIECES

There was once a king who had twelve daughters, each one more beautiful than all the rest. They slept together in one room, their beds all in a row, and every evening, when they were all tucked up, the king himself locked the door and bolted it. However, when he opened the room every morning, he discovered that their shoes had been danced to shreds, and no one knew how that could possibly have happened. The princesses would say nothing about the matter.

The king announced that anyone who could discover where his daughters went to dance in the night could choose one of them for his wife, and in time become king himself. On the other hand, if he failed to find out the truth after three nights, he would lose his own life.

Soon a prince from another country arrived and offered to take on the task. He was made welcome, and taken to a room next to the princesses' bedroom, where he was to keep watch and see where they went to dance. A bed was made up for him, and to make the task even easier, the door to the princesses' bedroom was left open.

But unfortunately the prince's eyes felt heavier and heavier as the night wore on, and he fell asleep. And when he woke up in the morning, the princesses' shoes were nearly worn to pieces. The same thing happened the second night, and the third, and so the prince lost his head. Many others came to try their luck at this dangerous task, but they all failed as he had done.

Now it so happened that a poor soldier, who had been wounded and could no longer serve in the army, was making his way to that very city. On the way he met an old woman begging for alms, and feeling sorry for her he sat down and shared his last bit of bread and cheese with her.

'Where are you going, dear?' she said.

'I'm not too sure, to be honest,' he replied, but then went on, 'Tell you what, though, I'd like to discover where those princesses go to dance their shoes to pieces. I could marry one of 'em then, and be king myself.'

'That's not difficult,' said the old woman. 'They'll bring you a glass of wine when you go to bed, but don't drink it whatever you do.'

Then she unfolded a cloak from her bundle, and said, 'And when you put this on you'll become invisible, and you can follow them and find out where they go.'

The soldier thanked her and went on his way, thinking: 'This is getting serious now.'

At the palace they received him generously, showed him to his room, and gave him a splendid new suit of clothes to wear. And at bedtime, the oldest princess brought him a goblet of wine.

He'd made plans for that, and tied a sponge under his chin. He let the wine run into that, and didn't let a single drop pass his lips. Presently he lay down and closed his eyes and snored a little to make them think he was asleep.

The twelve princesses heard him, and laughed, saying, 'There's one more who's going to lose his life.'

They got up and opened their wardrobes and drawers and closets, trying on this dress and that one, putting up their hair, making themselves as beautiful as possible, and all the time skipping and hopping with excitement at the thought of the dancing to come. Only the youngest wasn't sure. 'You can laugh and joke,' she said, 'but I've got a feeling something bad is going to happen.'

'You're a silly goose,' said the oldest princess. 'You're afraid of everything! Think of all those princes who've tried to watch us, and all for nothing. I bet I didn't even need to give this soldier a sleeping draught. He'd have fallen asleep all by himself.'

When they were ready, the oldest princess looked at the soldier again, but he seemed to be fast asleep, so they thought it was safe. Then the oldest princess went to her bed and knocked on it. At once it sank down through the floor, and one by one the princesses climbed down into the opening. The soldier was watching secretly, and as soon as they'd all gone down, he put on the cloak and followed them. So as not to lose them, he walked so close behind them that he trod on the dress of the youngest one, and she felt it and called out, 'Who's that? Who's pulling my dress?'

'Oh, don't be silly,' said the oldest. 'It just caught on a nail or something.'

They went on down the staircase till they came to a beautiful avenue between rows of trees. The leaves on the trees shone and gleamed like moonlight, because they were made of silver, and the soldier thought, 'I'd better take something back as proof,' and he snapped off a branch.

It made such a loud crack that the youngest princess was frightened again.

'Didn't you hear that? Something's wrong . . .'

'You're cuckoo,' said the oldest. 'They're just firing a salute to welcome us.'

The silver avenue changed into one where the trees were all made of gold, and finally to one where they were made of diamonds. The soldier broke off a branch from each of them, and they made such a noise that the youngest princess was frightened again each time, and each time the oldest one said it was the sound of a salute.

On they went till they came to a large body of water, where twelve boats were waiting, each with a prince at the oars. As the princesses arrived, the princes stood up and helped them into the boats, one each; but the soldier joined the youngest princess and her prince in theirs without their knowing.

The prince said, 'I don't know why the boat's so heavy today. I can hardly make it move.'

'I expect it's the heat,' said the princess. 'I'm suffocating.'

On the other side of the water there stood a beautiful castle that was brilliantly lit by a thousand lanterns. The joyful music of trumpets and kettledrums sounded clearly through the air, and the princes brought their boats to rest at the bank and helped their princesses out, and then they began to dance. The soldier danced along with them, and whenever a princess lifted a glass of wine to her lips, the soldier drank it before she could. The older ones were merely puzzled by this, but the youngest was frightened, and the oldest one had to calm her down yet again.

They stayed there until three o'clock, by which time their shoes were all danced to pieces and they had to leave. The princes rowed them back across the water, and this time the soldier sat in the boat next to the oldest princess. He got out first and ran ahead, and by the time the tired princesses reached their beds again, he was already snoring in his.

'We're safe,' they said, and took off their lovely dresses, placed their worn-out shoes under their beds, and went to sleep.

Next morning the soldier said nothing. He wanted to see that beautiful castle and the avenues of precious trees again. He went along with them the second night and then the third, and saw it all happen just as before, and each time their shoes were danced to pieces; and on the third night he brought back a goblet as more evidence.

On the final morning he had to give his answer, so he took the three branches and the goblet and went to the king. The princesses stood behind the door to listen.

The king said, 'Well, you've had your three nights. Where did my daughters dance their shoes to pieces?'

And the soldier replied, 'In a castle under the ground, your majesty. They met twelve princes who rowed them across a lake.'

He told the whole story, and showed the king the branches from the silver tree, the golden tree and the diamond tree, and also the goblet he'd brought from the castle. The king called his daughters before him.

'I expect you've heard what this man told me,' he said. 'Now then: was he telling the truth?'

The princesses had no choice: they had to admit everything.

'So you've done it,' said the king to the soldier. 'Now, which of these daughters of mine would you like for a wife?'

'Well, I'm not as young as I used to be,' said the soldier, 'so I reckon the oldest would do me best.'

'You shall have her,' said the king, and their wedding was celebrated the very same day.

The king promised that the soldier would succeed him to the throne, and as for the princes under the ground, they were placed under a spell for as many nights as they had danced with the twelve princesses.

* * *

Tale type: ATU 306, 'The Danced-out Shoes'
Source: a story told to the Grimm brothers by Jenny von Droste-Hülshoff
Similar stories: Alexander Afanasyev: 'The Secret Ball' (*Russian Fairy Tales*)

Sometimes known as 'The Twelve Dancing Princesses', this tale has the charm that belongs to any account of the marvels that lie under the ground, especially those that include little boats, pretty lights, trees with precious foliage, music and dancing. It lends itself, of course, to beautiful illustration. I have done little to the story except make the old woman's gifts (of advice, and of the cloak) a reward for the soldier's charity.

FORTY-FOUR

IRON HANS

There was once a king who had a great forest near his castle, where there lived all kinds of wild animals. One day he sent out his senior huntsman to shoot a deer, but the huntsman didn't come back.

'Perhaps he's had an accident,' said the king, and next day he sent two more huntsmen after the first, but they didn't come back either.

On the third day he called all his huntsmen together and said, 'Search through the whole forest, and don't give up till you've found all three.'

But none of those huntsmen came back, and nor did any of the hounds from the pack they took with them. From that day on, no one dared to go into the forest, and it lay in deep silence and solitude, and the only life that was seen was an occasional eagle or hawk flying above the trees.

For many years things remained like that, until one day a huntsman no one knew, a stranger, presented himself to the king saying he was looking for a job, and volunteered to go into the dangerous woods. However, the king didn't allow him to go.

'There's something uncanny in there,' he said. 'The place is probably under a spell. I don't see how you can do any better than the others; I'm afraid you'd get lost like them.'

But the huntsman said, 'I'm willing to risk it, your majesty. I know nothing of fear.'

So the huntsman set off with his hound into the forest. It wasn't long before the hound picked up a scent and started to follow it, but he hadn't run more than a few steps when he came to the edge of a deep pool and could go no further.

Then a naked arm reached up out of the water, seized the hound and dragged him below the surface.

When the huntsman saw that, he went back and got three men to go with him and bring buckets to empty the pool. They did so, and when it was nearly empty they found a wild man lying on the bottom. His skin was brown like rusty iron, and his hair hung down over his face and fell right to his knees. They bound him tightly with ropes and led him away to the castle.

Everyone was amazed to see the wild man. The king ordered him to be put into an iron cage in the courtyard, and forbade anyone to unlock the door of the cage, on pain of death; and he gave the key into the care of the queen herself. From that time on, people could go safely into the forest again.

Now the king had a son who was eight years old. One day he was playing in the courtyard when his golden ball bounced through the bars and into the wild man's cage.

The boy ran over to it and said, 'Give me my ball.'

'Not until you open the door for me,' said the wild man.

'No, I can't do that,' said the boy. 'Papa's forbidden it.'

And he ran away. Next day he came back and asked for his ball, but the wild man only said, 'Open my door.' Again the boy refused.

On the third day, when the king had gone out hunting, the boy came to the cage and said, 'Even if I wanted to, I couldn't open your cage. I haven't got the key.'

The wild man said, 'It's under your mother's pillow. You could easily get it.'

The boy desperately wanted his ball back, so he threw caution to the winds and got the key. The lock was hard to turn, and the boy pinched his finger; but when the door was open the wild man came out, gave the boy his ball, and hurried away.

The boy was frightened. He cried out, 'Oh, wild man, don't run away, or they'll beat me!'

The wild man turned back, picked the boy up and set him on his shoulders, and strode off quickly towards the forest.

When the king came home he noticed the empty cage and asked the queen at once what had happened. She didn't know anything about it, so she looked for the key, and found it gone. Then they realized the boy was missing, and called him, but no one answered. The king and the queen sent servants to look in the royal park around the castle, and in the fields and meadows beyond, but they didn't find the boy; and then his parents guessed what had happened, and the court fell into deep mourning.

Once the wild man had reached the dark forest he set the boy down and said, 'You'll never see your father and mother again. But I'll look after you, because you set me free, and I feel sorry for you. Do as I tell you, and everything will be all right. I've got plenty of treasure and gold, more than anyone else in the world, in fact.'

He gathered some moss and made a bed for the boy, who soon fell asleep. Next morning the wild man led him to a spring and said, 'See this? This is my golden spring. It's clear and bright, and I want it to stay like that. You sit here and guard it, and make sure nothing falls in that shouldn't, because I don't want it polluted by anything at all, you understand? I'll come back every evening to see if you've done as I tell you.'

The boy sat down at the side of the spring, and watched the water. Sometimes he saw a golden fish or a golden snake deep down under the surface, and he took care to let nothing fall in. But as he sat there, the finger that he'd pinched in the cage door began to hurt so badly that he couldn't help dipping it into the water. He pulled it out again at once, but he saw that it had turned to gold, and no matter how hard he tried to wipe it off his skin, it was gold all through.

That evening when Iron Hans came home, he looked at the boy and said, 'What's happened to the spring?'

'Nothing, nothing,' said the boy, holding the finger behind his back so Iron Hans couldn't see it.

But the man said, 'You've dipped your finger in the water. Well, I'll let it go this time, but be very careful you don't let anything else fall in.'

Early in the morning the boy got ready and went to the spring to keep watch. His finger hurt again, and this time he rubbed it across his head; but as he did so a hair unluckily fell out into the water. He snatched it out as quickly as he could, but it was already covered in gold.

By the time he came home, Iron Hans already knew what had happened. 'You let a hair fall into the spring,' he said. 'That's the second time. I'll overlook it just once more, but if it happens again the spring will be polluted, and you won't be able to stay here any more.'

On the third day the boy sat there carefully and didn't move his finger, no matter how much it hurt. But the time went by very slowly, and for want of anything else to do, he bent over and looked at his reflection in the water. He bent his head lower and lower, trying to see his eyes, and then his long hair fell forwards from behind his head and down into the water. He jerked his head back at once, but it was too late: all his hair had turned gold, and it shone like the sun. You can imagine how frightened the poor boy felt. The only thing he could think of was to wrap his handkerchief around his head so that Iron Hans wouldn't see it.

But of course as soon as he came home, that was the thing he noticed first of all.

'Untie that handkerchief,' he said.

The boy had to. All his golden hair fell down around his shoulders, and he couldn't even think of an excuse.

'You've failed the test,' said Iron Hans. 'You can't stay here any longer. You'll have to go out into the world, and there you'll learn what it feels like to be poor. But you're not a bad boy, and I wish you well, so I'll grant you one favour: if you're ever in real need, go into the forest and call out "Iron Hans", and I'll come and help you. I've got great powers, much more than you think, and more than enough gold and silver.'

So the prince left the forest and wandered along wild paths and well-trodden ones until at last he came to a great city. There he looked for work, but he couldn't find any, because he'd never learned a trade to earn his living with. Finally he went to the palace and asked if they'd give him a job.

The palace officials didn't know how they could make use of him, but he was a likeable boy, and they took him in. In the end the cook said he could find things for him to do, and set him to carrying wood and water, and raking out the ashes of the fire.

One day when the other waiters were busy, the cook told the boy to carry a dish to the royal table. The boy didn't want anyone to see his golden hair, so he kept his cap on. Naturally the king was astonished at this, and said, 'Boy, when you come to the royal table, you must always take your cap off.'

'I better not, your majesty,' said the boy, 'because my scalp's all covered in dandruff.'

The king summoned the cook and told him off for letting a boy with a condition like that serve at the royal table. He was to dismiss him at once. However, the cook felt sorry for the boy, and let him change places with the gardener's assistant.

Now it was his job to plant and water, to prune and hoe, and put up with the wind and the rain. One summer's day when he was working alone in the garden, it happened to be so hot that he took off his hat to let the breeze cool him down. As the sun shone on his golden hair, it sparkled and gleamed so much that the reflections shone into the princess's bedroom.

She jumped up to see what it was, and saw the boy and called out: 'Boy! Bring me a bouquet of flowers.'

He quickly put his cap back on, picked some wildflowers, and tied them together. As he was climbing the steps out of the garden the head gardener saw him, and said, 'What d'you think you're doing, taking the princess a bunch of common flowers like those? Throw them away, quick, and get her some of the rare ones. That pink rose has just come out – take her a bunch of those.'

'Oh, no,' said the boy, 'that rose has got no scent. But these wild ones are so fragrant – I'm sure she'll like them better.'

When he entered the princess's room, she said, 'Take your cap off. It's not polite to leave it on in my presence.'

'I can't do that, your royal highness,' he said. 'My head's all covered in scurf.'

At that the princess grabbed his cap and pulled it off. At once his golden hair fell down to his shoulders, and a beautiful sight it was. He wanted to run out, but she held his arm; and then she gave him a handful of ducats, and let him go. He took the ducats away, but he didn't want them, so he gave them to the gardener.

'Something for your children to play with,' he said.

Next day the princess called for him again, demanding another bouquet of wildflowers. When he took it in, she grabbed at his cap at once, trying to take it away, but he held on tightly. Again she gave him some ducats, and again he gave them to the gardener for his children. It all happened once more on the third day: she couldn't get his cap; he didn't want the gold.

Not long after that, the country found itself at war. The king called his councillors together, but they couldn't decide whether to fight or to give in, because the enemy had a large and powerful army.

The gardener's boy said, 'I'm grown up now. Just give me a horse, and I'll go to war and fight for the country.'

The other young men laughed and said, 'Don't you worry, you can have a horse after we've left. We'll leave one in the stable for you.'

So he waited till they'd gone and then looked in the stable for his horse. He found it had a lame foot, and it could only walk *hobbledy-clop, hobbledy-clop*.

All the same, he mounted it and rode off towards the thick forest. When he came to the edge of the trees, he stopped and called out 'Iron Hans!' three times, so loudly that it echoed all around.

The wild man appeared at once and said, 'What do you need?'

'I'm going to war,' said the boy, 'and I need a good horse.'

'Then you shall have it, and much more besides.'

The wild man went back into the woods, and very soon afterwards a stable-boy came out of the trees, leading a magnificent horse that snorted and stamped and could hardly be controlled. What was more, behind him came a regiment of knights in iron armour, their swords flashing in the sun.

The boy left his lame horse with the stable-boy, mounted the other horse, and set off at the head of the knights. When they reached the battlefield they found that many of the king's men had already fallen, and that the rest would soon have to give way as well. So the young man galloped up with his iron regiment and fell on the enemy like a storm, striking down every man in their path. The enemy fell back in confusion, but the young man was merciless, and didn't stop until they were all either dead or in flight.

When the battle was over, he didn't return to the king. Instead he led his iron army by a roundabout way into the forest, and once again called for Iron Hans.

'What do you need?' said the wild man.

'Take back your horse and your knights, and give me my lame old hack.'

Iron Hans did just as he asked, and the young man rode home on the hobbledy-clop horse.

As for the king, when he arrived back at the palace his daughter ran out to meet him, and congratulated him on the great victory.

'I had little to do with it,' he said. 'We were saved by a strange knight who rode to our rescue with his regiment of iron-clad knights.'

The princess was keen to know who the mysterious knight was, but the king couldn't tell her.

'All I know,' he said, 'is that he put the enemy to flight, and then he rode away.'

She went to the gardener and asked where his boy was, and the gardener laughed.

'He's just come back on his three-legged horse,' he said. 'The others are all making fun of him. "Look, here's old hobbledy-clop!" they says. And they asks, "What hedge have you been sleeping under, then?" and he says, "I did better'n any of you. If it wasn't for me, you'd have lost the battle," he says. And then they split their sides.'

The king said to his daughter, 'I'm going to announce a great tournament. It's going to last for three days, and you can throw a golden apple for the knights to catch. Perhaps the unknown knight will turn up. You never know.'

When he heard about the tournament, the young man went out into the forest and called Iron Hans.

'What do you need?'

'To catch the princess's golden apple.'

'It's as good as done,' said Iron Hans. 'And what's more, you shall wear a suit of red armour, and ride a proud chestnut horse.'

When the tournament opened, the young man galloped up and

took his place among the knights, and no one recognized him. Then the princess came and threw a golden apple among the knights, and he was the one who caught it, and as soon as he had it safe, he galloped away.

Next day Iron Hans gave him white armour and a snow-white horse. Once more he caught the apple, and once more he rode away at once.

But now the king lost his temper. 'If that knight rides away again without leaving his name,' he announced, 'everyone else must chase after him, and if he doesn't comc back willingly, they can use their spears and swords. I won't have that sort of behaviour.'

On the third day, Iron Hans gave him black armour and a horse as black as night, and again he caught the apple. This time, though, the other knights chased after him, and one of them got close enough to stab him in the leg. He must have stabbed the horse as well, for it leaped so high that in trying to control it the young man lost his helmet. It fell to the ground, and they all saw that he had hair like gold. But that was all they saw, for he managed to make his escape; and they rode back and reported it to the king.

Next day the princess asked the gardener about his boy.

'He's pruning the roses, your royal highness. He's a strange fellow. He's been at the tournament, and all. He come home yesterday evening, and he showed my children three golden apples. He said he'd won 'em, but I don't know.'

The king had him summoned, and he came before the court still wearing his cap. The princess went up to him and took it off, and his golden hair fell down on to his shoulders; and he was so handsome that everyone was astonished.

'Young man, are you the knight who came to the tournament each day in different-coloured armour, and who caught the three golden apples?'

'Yes,' said the young man, 'and here they are.' He took the three apples out of his pocket and gave them back to the king. 'If you need more proof,' he went on, 'you can see the wound the other knights gave me when they chased me yesterday. But I'm also the knight who helped your army to victory over the enemy.'

'If you can do that sort of thing, you're no gardener's boy,' said the king. 'Tell me, who is your father?'

'He's a powerful king, and I have as much gold as I need.'

'H'mm. I see. Well, clearly I owe you some thanks,' said the king. 'Is there anything I can do for you?'

'Indeed there is,' said the young man. 'You can give me your daughter for my wife.'

The princess laughed and said, 'He doesn't beat about the bush! But I knew as soon as I saw him that he wasn't a gardener's boy.'

And then she went to him and kissed him.

His father and mother came to the wedding, and were filled with joy. They had given up all hope of ever seeing their dear son again.

At the height of the wedding feast, the music suddenly stopped. The doors flew open, and a proud king came in with a great retinue. He strode up to the young man, embraced him, and said, 'I am Iron Hans, and I was turned into a wild man by a spell, but you have set me free. All the treasures I have shall be yours.'

* * *

Tale type: ATU 502, 'The Wild Man'
Source: a story told to the Grimm brothers by the Hassenpflug family and 'Eiserne Hans' ('Iron Hans'), a tale in Friedmund von Arnim's *Hundert neue Mährchen im Gebirge gesammelt* (*Hundred New Tales from the Mountains*; 1844)

Similar stories: Alexander Afanasyev: 'Prince Ivan and Princess Martha' (*Russian Fairy Tales*); Katharine M. Briggs: 'Three-for-a-pot' (*Folk Tales of Britain*); Andrew Lang: 'The Hairy Man' (*Crimson Fairy Book*)

This story acquired a good deal of fame in the early 1990s, as a result of Robert Bly's *Iron John: A Book About Men* (1990), a central text of the men's movement section of the Mind, Body and Spirit shelves in bookshops. Bly maintained that modern men had become feminized and exiled by contemporary ways of life from authentic patterns of psychic development, and needed a model of masculinity that involved initiation into true manhood by those who were themselves true men. Apparently this story, and the wild man at its centre, is such a model.

There may be something in it, but my guess is that if such things work at all, they work a great deal better when you don't know they're doing it. Nothing is more likely to drive listeners away than a ponderous interpretation of what they've just marvelled at. It's a very good story, whatever it means.

As for the sound of the poor old lame horse's hooves, in English versions we have a choice of 'higgledy-hop' (D. L. Ashliman, *A Guide to Folktales in the English Language*), 'clippety clop' (Ralph Mannheim, *The Penguin Complete Grimms' Tales for Young and Old*), 'hobblety jig' (Margaret Hunt, *The Complete Grimm's Fairy Tales*), 'hippety-hop' (Jack Zipes, *Brothers Grimm: The Complete Fairy Tales*) and 'hobbledy-clop' (David Luke, *Brothers Grimm: Selected Tales*). Luke's version was a clear winner, so I stole that.

I think it worth noting that the German for it is *hunkepuus*.

FORTY-FIVE

MOUNT SIMELI

There were once two brothers, one rich, the other poor. The first brother, rich as he was, gave no help to the poor one, who barely scraped a living as a corn merchant. Things went badly for him, and quite often he had hardly a crust of bread to feed his wife and children with.

One day the poor brother was pushing his cart through the forest when he noticed a high rocky mountain to one side of the path. Since he'd never seen it before, he stood looking at it with some surprise, and while he was standing there, he saw a dozen rough-looking men approaching. They hadn't yet seen him, and thinking they might be robbers, he shoved his cart into the bushes and climbed a tree to be out of the way.

The men went to the foot of the mountain, which wasn't far away, and called out: 'Mount Semsi, Mount Semsi, open up!'

At once, with a rumble of rock, a cave opened in the middle of the mountain. The twelve men walked into it, and as soon as they were inside, it shut again.

The corn merchant sat in his tree wondering what to do next. But he hadn't been there for long when there was another rumble and the cave opened once more, and the men came out carrying heavy sacks on their backs.

Once they were all out in the daylight they called out, 'Mount Semsi, Mount Semsi, close up!'

The entrance to the cave closed up so tight that it couldn't be seen at all, and the twelve robbers went back the way they'd come.

When they were all completely out of sight, the poor man climbed down from his tree. He was curious to see what was inside the cave, so he went to the foot of the mountain and called, 'Mount Semsi, Mount Semsi, open up!'

The mountain opened straight away, and in he went. The whole interior of the mountain was full of silver and gold coins, of great heaps of pearls, rubies, emeralds and diamonds, piled up higher than any heap of grain the poor corn merchant had ever seen. He stood there wondering what he should do, and whether he should take any of this treasure for himself. In the end he couldn't resist, and he stuffed his pockets full of gold coins. He left the jewels where they were, though.

Once he'd done that he looked out cautiously, tiptoed outside and called out, 'Mount Semsi, Mount Semsi, close up!'

The mountain closed obediently, and the corn merchant went home with his empty cart.

For some time after that he was happy, because he had enough gold to buy bread for his family, and meat and wine as well. What's more, he could give money to the poor, and so he did; he lived happily and honestly and did a lot of good. When he ran out of money he borrowed a bushel measure from his brother and went back to Mount Semsi, where he filled it with gold coins. As before, he left the jewels alone.

When he wanted to get a third helping of gold coins, he asked his brother once more for the bushel. His brother was very curious by this time; he couldn't imagine where the corn merchant had got the money to furnish his house so richly and to live so well, so he set a trap. He covered the bottom of the bushel with pitch. And when he got it back, there was a gold coin sticking to it.

He went to see his brother straight away.

'What did you want to measure in my bushel?' he said.

'Wheat and barley, as usual,' said the corn merchant.

Then his brother showed him the gold coin.

'Which is this then, wheat or barley? Come on, I want the truth! And if you don't tell me exactly what you're up to, I'll have the law on you!'

The corn merchant had to tell his brother everything. And as soon as he heard about the treasure inside Mount Semsi, the rich man hitched the donkey to his wagon and drove there, intending to take far more gold than his brother had, and to bring home a large quantity of those jewels, too.

When he came to the mountain he called out, 'Mount Semsi, Mount Semsi, open up!'

The mountain opened and in he went. He stood for a long time gaping at all the treasure in front of him; he didn't know what to plunge his hands into first. Finally he went for the jewels, and thrust handful after handful into his pockets, intending to take them out to the wagon; but since his heart and soul were so bound up with the treasure, he'd forgotten the most important thing, and when he wanted to open the mountain to go out, he called, 'Mount Simeli, Mount Simeli, open up!'

And of course that was the wrong name. The mountain didn't move an inch. The rich brother began to get frightened, and tried one name after another: 'Mount Sipsack! Mount Sepsick! Mount Spittelboom! Mount Spotnik! Mount Sizwiz!'

Of course none of them worked. The more confused he got, the more frightened he became, and the more frightened he was, the more confused he became.

And time went past, and he broke all his fingernails scrabbling at the rocks trying to find the place where the mountain opened up. He kept on trying to find the right name: 'Mount Snipfish! Mount Saucehorse! Mount Snakepaste! Mount Sagsausage! Mount Siccapillydircus!'

All the treasure in his pockets was no use to him; his counting house, his real estate, his bank accounts, his stocks and shares – none of them could help him one bit.

Then to his horror he heard a voice outside calling: 'Mount Semsi! Mount Semsi! Open up!'

Of course! *That* was the name! How could he have forgotten it?

And then the mountain was opening, and twelve fierce robbers were looking at him.

'There you are,' said the largest and fiercest. 'Got you at last. Did you think we hadn't noticed that you'd been here twice already?'

'It wasn't me! It was my brother! Honest! He stole these jewels! I came here to put them back! I swear it!'

But whatever he said, and however much he begged and pleaded, it was no use. That morning, he had gone into the mountain in one piece. That evening he came out in several.

* * *

Tale type: ATU 676, 'The Forty Thieves'
Source: a story told to the Grimm brothers by Ludowine von Haxthausen
Similar stories: 'The Story of Ali Baba and the Forty Thieves Killed by a Slave Girl' (*The Arabian Nights*); Italo Calvino: 'The Thirteen Bandits' (*Italian Folktales*)

Quite clearly, this is the first half of the well-known tale from *The Arabian Nights*. At least, it comes from the French translation of the original tales by Antoine Galland (1646–1715), which isn't quite the same thing, because, in the absence of Arabic manuscripts of 'Ali Baba' and 'Aladdin' that predate Galland's translation, scholars suspect that Galland made them up himself. Calvino's Italian version is similar to this tale.

But where is the second half? I miss the body of the chopped-up brother being sewn together and the thieves hiding in the oil-jars and the faithful slave boiling them to death. Either Ludowine von Haxthausen didn't know it (but then Calvino's source didn't know it either) or someone, possibly the Grimms, decided it was better without it. It isn't, though. And it wouldn't be hard to Germanize the exotic elements of Galland's marvellous tale, and round it all off properly.

FORTY-SIX

LAZY HEINZ

Heinz was bone idle. Though he had nothing to do but drive the goat out to pasture every day, he complained every evening when he came home.

'Honestly,' he said, 'it's a devil of a job driving this goat to the meadow day in day out all year round. It's not like some jobs, where you can shut your eyes for a nap occasionally. No, no. It's a heavy responsibility. I've got to watch every second to see it doesn't nibble the young trees, or shove its way through the hedge into someone's garden, or even run away for good. How on earth can I get a bit of rest, put my feet up, enjoy life?'

He sat down and collected his thoughts. They were quite easy to collect, because there weren't very many of them, and they all concerned the same subject – what a burden his life was. For a long time he sat there staring at nothing, and then suddenly he sat up and clapped his hands.

'I know what I'll do!' he said. 'I'll marry Big Trina. She's got a goat as well, and she can drive mine out with hers, and save me the trouble. Brilliant idea!'

So he heaved himself up out of the chair and trudged all the way across the street to the house where Big Trina's parents lived, and asked for the hand of their virtuous and hard-working daughter. They didn't have to think about it very hard, because they'd been wondering how to get rid of her for years.

'Birds of a feather flock together,' they thought, and gave their consent.

So Big Trina became Heinz's wife, and every day she drove out both goats to pasture. Heinz had a fine time, with nothing whatever to do. He did go out with her occasionally, but only so he'd enjoy it even more when he had the following day off.

'I'd lose all feeling for it otherwise,' he said. 'Variety is the spice of life.'

However, Big Trina was just as lazy as he was.

'Heinz, darling,' she said one day, 'I've been thinking.'

Thinking was just as much of an effort for her as it was for him, so he knew what she'd gone through, and he listened with close attention.

'What about?' he said.

'Them goats,' she said. 'They wake us up ever so early with their bleating.'

'You never said a truer word,' he said.

'So I thought maybe we could ask the neighbour to swap them for his beehive. We could put it in that sunny corner in the back garden and then forget about it. You don't have to drive bees out to pasture, do you? They fly out and find their way to the flowers and then come home again all by theirselves. And they collect honey all the time and we don't have to do nothing.'

'Did you think of that all by yourself?' said Heinz.

'Yeah,' she said modestly.

'Well, I think it's bloody brilliant. I really do. We'll do it right away. Well, maybe leave it till tomorrow. And I tell you something else,' he said, almost enthusiastically, 'honey tastes a lot nicer than what goats' milk does.'

'And it keeps longer too,' she added.

'Oh, Trina, darling! If you come over here I'll kiss you.'

'Maybe later,' she said.

'Yeah, all right.'

Next morning they suggested this idea to the neighbour, and he agreed at once. He took the goats and carried the beehive over to Heinz and Trina's back garden, and put it in the sunny corner; and from then on the bees did their work tirelessly, flying in and out from early morning till late in the evening, gathering nectar and filling the hive with fine sweet honey. And late in the year, Heinz was able to take out a whole jugful.

He and Trina put the jug on the shelf over their bed. Trina was worried in case thieves got in and stole it, or mice got into it and made a mess, so she found a stout hazel stick and kept it under her side of the bed. That way she could reach it and drive away the mice or the burglars without having to get up.

Heinz thought that was another good idea. He was full of admiration for his wife's power of foresight; thinking about things that hadn't happened yet made him tired, and he never used to get up before noon anyway. 'Early rising is a waste of the bed,' he said.

One morning as the two of them lay there eating breakfast, a thought occurred to him, for a change.

'You know,' he said, putting his piece of toast down on the bedspread, 'you're like most women, you've got a sweet tooth, you have. If you keep on dipping into that honey, there won't be any left. What I reckon is, we ought to swap it for a goose and a gosling before you eat it all up.'

'A goose and a gosling?' said Trina. 'But we haven't got a child yet!'

'What's that got to do with it?'

'He's got to look after the goose, of course! I'm not going to do it. When have I got time to chase around after geese?'

'Oh,' said Heinz. 'Yeah. I hadn't thought about that. But d'you think he'll do what he's told anyway? Kids don't, these days. No respect at all for their parents. You see it all the time.'

'I'll show you what he'll get if he doesn't,' Trina said, and seized the stick from under the bed. 'I'll take this stick and I'll wallop him. I'll tan his hide, you see if I don't. Like this!'

And she whacked the bed again and again with such hearty blows that dust and feathers and breadcrumbs flew high into the air. Unfortunately, as she raised her stick for the last time, she hit the jug of honey on the shelf above. It broke into several pieces, and honey dripped down the wall and on to the floor.

'Well, there goes the goose,' said Heinz. 'And the gosling. And I don't suppose they'd've needed much looking after anyway. Hey, it's a good job the jug didn't fall on my head. Where's that toast gone?'

He found it on the floor, butter side down, and used it to mop up some of the honey running down the wall.

'Here you are, darling,' he said. 'You have this last bit.'

'Thank you, sweetie,' she said. 'I gave myself a fright there.'

'We need a rest, that's what it is. Doesn't matter if we get up a bit later than usual.'

'Yes,' she said with her mouth full of toast, 'there's plenty of time. Like the snail that was invited to the wedding, and he set off nice and early, and arrived just in time for the first child's baptism. "More haste, less speed," he said as he fell off the fence.'

* * *

Tale type: AT 1430, 'Air Castles'
Source: a story in Eucharius Eyering's *Proverbiorum Copia* (*Plenty of Proverbs*; 1601)
Similar stories: Aesop: 'The Milkmaid and her Pail' (*The Complete Fables*); Alexander Afanasyev: 'The Daydreamer' (*Russian Fairy Tales*); Katharine M. Briggs: 'Buttermilk Jack' (*Folk Tales of Britain*)

There are many variations on the old idea of the daydreamer who speculates on what she'll do with the milk she's taking to market, and imagines the fine dress she'll buy, and tosses her head to show how elegant she'll look, and in doing so spills the pail she's carrying on her head and loses all the milk. It could have any setting and be spun out any number of ways; but here I liked the mutual fondness of this bone-idle pair and the deep contentment they feel in their slovenly ways.

FORTY-SEVEN

STRONG HANS

A man and his wife lived in a remote valley, all alone except for their little son. One day the wife went into the woods to gather some pine branches for the fire, and she took little Hans, who was only two years old. It was springtime, and since the little boy loved the bright colours of the flowers, she wandered with him further and further into the forest.

Suddenly two robbers sprang out of the bushes, seized the mother and child, and made off with them deep into the darkest part of the forest, where no innocent human being went from one year's end to the next. The poor woman begged the robbers to set her and the child free, but she might as well have said nothing: they were deaf to her sobs and pleas, and drove her on without mercy through the briars and the brambles for two hours, until they came to a large rock with a door in it.

The robbers knocked, and the door opened. They made their way along a dark passage that led into a large cave, where a fire was burning on the hearth. On the walls hung swords and sabres and other deadly weapons, their blades glittering in the firelight, and in the middle of the cave there stood a black table where four other robbers sat playing dice. The chief robber sat at the head of the table, and when he saw the woman and her child, he stood up and spoke to her.

'Stop crying,' he said. 'You've got nothing to fear as long as you do the housekeeping for us. You sweep the floor and keep everything neat and tidy, and we'll treat you well enough.'

When he'd said this, he gave them some bread and meat, and showed her a bed where she and the child could sleep.

They stayed with the robbers for some years, and Hans grew big and strong. His mother told him stories and taught him to read with the help of an old book about knights and chivalry that she'd found in the cave.

When Hans was nine years old, he made himself a heavy club out of a pine branch that he'd stolen from the robbers' woodpile. He hid it behind his bed, and then went to his mother and said, 'Mama, I need to know, and you must tell me: who is my father?'

The woman said nothing. She didn't want to tell him anything about their life before the cave, because he might become homesick, and she knew the robbers would never let him leave; but it broke her heart to think that Hans would never see his father.

That night, when the robbers returned from one of their criminal raids, Hans took out his club, went to the chief, and said, 'Now I want to know who my father is. My mother won't tell me, so I'm asking you, and if you don't tell me, I'll knock you down.'

The chief laughed, and gave Hans such a clout that he fell over and rolled under the table. He didn't cry or make a sound; he just thought, 'Let some time go by, and when I'm bigger, he'd better watch out.'

After a year had come and gone Hans took out his club, blew the dust off it, swung it this way and that, and thought, 'Yes, it's a good strong club.'

When the robbers came back early next morning, they were in a drinking mood. They drained so many jugs of wine that their heads began to droop. Hans was waiting for that, and he took his club and stood in front of the chief and asked him again: 'Who's my father?'

As he'd done before, the chief gave him a clout on the head, and once again Hans fell down. This time, though, he bounced up at once, took a tight grip of his club, and gave the chief and all the robbers a beating that left them so dazed and battered that they couldn't move. His mother was watching from the corner of the cave, and she was amazed at his strength and his courage.

When he'd finished he turned to her and said, 'You see, I'm serious about this. I want to know who my father is.'

'Well, my brave Hans,' said his mother, 'let's go and look for him.'

While she looked through the keys hanging from the chief's belt, Hans filled a large flour sack with as much gold and silver and jewellery as it would hold. Then he swung it up on his back and followed his mother out of the cave.

And when he stepped out of the dark into the light of day and saw the trees, the flowers, the birds, the sun in the bright sky, Hans was amazed, and stood gaping around at everything as if he'd lost his wits. Meanwhile his mother was looking around to find the way home, and soon they set off; and after walking for a few hours they came back to their little house in the valley.

Hans's father was sitting in the doorway, and when he learned that this woman was his wife and this strapping boy was his son he wept for joy, because he'd given them up for dead a long time before.

Young as he was, Hans was a head taller than his father, and much stronger by far. When they went into the house, Hans put the sack down on the bench by the fire, and at once there was the sound of cracking and breaking, and first the bench collapsed and then the floor gave way, and the sack plunged down into the cellar.

'Good grief, boy, what have you done?' said the father. 'Are you going to demolish the whole house?'

'You needn't worry, father,' said Hans. 'There's more than

enough gold and treasure in that sack to build a whole new house.'

Sure enough, Hans and his father soon began to build a fine new house. What's more, they bought some land around it, and some cattle, and set up a farm. When Hans walked behind the plough and pushed the blade deep into the soil, the oxen hardly needed to pull.

Next spring Hans said, 'Father, I want to go and see the world. You keep all the money and have the blacksmith make me a walking staff that weighs a hundred pounds. Once I've got that I'll set off.'

When his staff was ready, Hans left home. He set off briskly and soon arrived in a deep valley, where he heard an odd sound and stopped to listen. It was a tearing, crunching sort of noise, and when he looked around he saw a pine tree that was being twisted like a rope from top to bottom. Doing the twisting was a huge fellow who had the tree in both hands and was twisting it as easily as if it had been a bundle of rushes.

'Hello there!' Hans called up. 'What are you up to?'

'I cut some logs yesterday,' the big man replied, 'and I need a rope to carry them with.'

'Well, this is my sort of fellow,' thought Hans. 'He's no weakling.' And he called up: 'Leave your logs and come with me, and we'll have a good time!'

The big man climbed down, and he turned out to be taller than Hans by a whole head, and Hans wasn't small, either.

'I'm going to call you Pine Twister,' Hans told him. 'Glad to meet you.'

They went on their way, and presently they heard a hammering and a pounding that made the very earth shake beneath their feet. When they turned a corner they saw the cause of it: a giant was standing in front of a cliff face, smashing great boulders off it with his fists.

'Good day to you, mate,' said Hans. 'What are you doing that for?'

'Well, I can't sleep,' said the giant. 'I lie down and close my eyes, and five minutes later the bears and the wolves and the foxes come sniffing and prowling around, and I can't get any rest. So I'm going to build a house, you see, so I can get a bit of peace and quiet.'

'Oh, right,' said Hans. 'Well, I've got a better idea. Forget the house and come along with me and Pine Twister.'

'Where are you going?'

'I don't know. We're looking for adventures.'

'Good idea,' said the giant.

'And I'll call you Rock Smasher,' Hans added.

The giant agreed, and the three of them set off through the forest, terrifying all the animals wherever they went. In the evening they came to a deserted castle, where they lay down to sleep.

Next morning Hans got up and went to look at the garden, which was wild and overgrown with brambles. As he was looking around, a wild boar charged out of a bush and made straight for him, but Hans struck him a blow on the head with his staff, and the beast fell dead on the spot. Hans hoisted it up on his shoulders and carried it into the castle, where the companions put it on a spit and roasted it over the fire, and had a fine breakfast. They agreed that they would take turns hunting and cooking, two of them going out each day to hunt and the other staying home and cooking. They reckoned they could get by with nine pounds of meat per day for each of them.

On the first day it was Hans's and Rock Smasher's turn to hunt, while Pine Twister stayed in the castle to cook. He was busy making a sauce when a little shrivelled-up old man came into the kitchen.

'Give us a bit of meat,' he said.

'Clear off, you old scrounger,' said Pine Twister. 'You don't need any meat.'

At that the scrawny little man leaped at Pine Twister and gave him such a walloping that he couldn't defend himself, and he fell down dazed. The little man didn't stop thumping him, either, but kept on punching and kicking till he'd worked off all his anger. Pine Twister had never known anything like it.

By the time the other two came home from hunting, Pine Twister had recovered a bit, and he decided to say nothing about the little old man; after all, he himself hadn't come out of the experience with much credit. Let's see how *they* get on with the little monster, he thought.

Next day it was Rock Smasher's turn to cook. The same thing happened to him: he refused to give the little man any meat, and he got a horrible drubbing in return. When the others got back Pine Twister looked closely at Rock Smasher's face, and saw that he'd been through the same experience. But both of them kept quiet, because they were keen to see how Hans would get on.

On the following day the other two went off to hunt, and Hans stayed behind to cook. He was standing by the fire skimming off the fat from a big pot of stock when the little man came in and asked for a piece of meat.

'He's a poor little devil,' thought Hans; 'I'll give him a bit of my share, so the other two won't have to do without.' He sliced off a decent piece of meat, which the little man gobbled up at once. As soon as that piece had gone, the little man demanded some more, and Hans in his good-natured way cut off another slice and said, 'That's a good helping. That ought to be enough for you.'

The little man devoured that too, and then said, 'More! More!'

'Now you're getting cheeky,' said Hans. 'You've had enough.'

The little man sprang at him, but he'd picked the wrong man this time. Without exerting himself Hans gave him a back-hander that knocked him flat, and followed it up with a kick to the backside that sent the little man flying down the steps and into the hall. Hans chased after him, but tripped and fell, and by the time he'd picked himself up the little man was way ahead of him and scuttling off into the forest. Hans ran after him as fast as he could, and saw him squeeze himself into a hole in a big rock. Hans made a note of the spot, and then went back to skimming the stock.

When the others came back to the castle, they were surprised to find Hans in such good spirits. He told them what had happened, and they told their stories in return. Hans laughed heartily.

'It serves you right for being so stingy,' he said. 'And you ought to be ashamed, big fellows like you, to let yourselves be beaten by a little monkey like him. Never mind, we'll teach him a lesson.'

They found a basket and a rope and went to the rock in the forest where the little man had slipped away. The hole went a long way down. They tied the rope to the basket and let Hans and his hundred-pound staff down first.

At the bottom Hans found a door, and when he opened it the first thing that met his eyes was a maiden so lovely she seemed like a picture come alive. She was chained to the wall, and her expression was full of disgust and despair, because standing on a chair right next to her was the little man, leering and stroking her hair and her cheeks with his horny little fingers.

As soon as he saw Hans, he gave a shriek and bounded away like a monkey. Hans slammed the door so he couldn't get away, and then tried to catch him, but the little man bounced off the walls and leaped this way and that, howling and gibbering, and Hans couldn't touch him. It was like trying to hit a fly with a pencil. Finally Hans got him cornered, and whirled his staff over his head and dealt the little devil a blow that squashed him flat.

The moment the little man fell dead, the chains dropped away from the maiden, and she was free. Hans could hardly believe his eyes; he'd never seen anything or anyone so lovely. She was the daughter of a king, she told him.

'I'm not surprised,' said Hans. 'I could tell you were a princess. But how did you come to be chained up down here?'

'A savage nobleman wanted to marry me, and he wouldn't take no for an answer,' she said. 'I think it drove him mad. He kidnapped me and locked me down here with this creature to guard me. But the little man was getting more and more demanding himself. You saw how he was treating me. If you hadn't come along . . .'

'Yes, well, never mind that,' said Hans. 'We've still got to get you out of this cavern. I've got a basket out here, and two fellows on top to haul you up. In you get.'

He helped her into the basket and gave the rope a tug. Straight away the other two began to pull her up, and presently the basket came down again empty.

But Hans wasn't sure he could trust his two companions. 'They didn't tell me about the little man beating them up,' he thought; 'I don't know what they might be planning now.' So instead of getting in the basket himself, he put his iron staff in and tugged the rope once more. Up it went, but when it was no more than halfway up, the other two let it fall with a crash to the bottom. If Hans had been sitting in it, he'd have been killed at once.

'Well, I was right about those two,' he thought, 'but what am I going to do now?'

He walked round and round the little space at the bottom of the shaft, getting more and more desperate. He couldn't think of any way to escape. 'It'd be a miserable end to perish down this wretched hole,' he thought. 'I wasn't born to end like this.'

Then he noticed that the little man had a ring on his finger that sparkled and glittered. 'I wonder if that's magic,' he thought. 'You never know.'

So he took the ring off the dead man's finger and put it on his own. And at once he heard something whizzing and buzzing and whirling about in the air just above his head. He looked up, and saw a thousand or more little air-spirits hovering there. When they saw him looking at them they all bowed, and the biggest one said: 'Master, here we are at your command. What would you like us to do?'

Hans was flabbergasted, but he collected his wits and said, 'You can take me up to the top of this ruddy hole, that's what you can do.'

'Immediately, master!'

Each of the air-spirits seized one of the hairs on his head, and then they began to fly upwards. It seemed to him as if he was floating up all by himself. After only about ten seconds he was standing on the forest floor looking all around. There was no sign of Rock Smasher or Pine Twister, or of the maiden either.

'Where have those scoundrels gone?' he said.

The air-spirits all shot into the sky, and after a minute or so they all came diving back down, to hover in front of him like a cloud of friendly midges.

'They've taken ship, master,' said the chief spirit.

'Already? And is the maiden with them?'

'Yes, master, she is, and they've got her tied up in case she throws herself overboard.'

'Oh, that poor girl! What she's gone through! Well, I'll soon deal with those wretches. Which way is the sea?'

'Over there, master.'

Hans set off, running as fast as he could, and before long he reached the seashore. Standing on tiptoe on the top of a sand-dune and shading his eyes against the setting sun, Hans could just make out the dark shape of a little ship.

'Is that them?'

'That's right, master.'

'Grrr! I'll teach them to betray their friend!'

And full of righteous indignation, Hans charged at the water, meaning to swim out and overtake the ship. He might have managed it, too, but his hundred-pound staff weighed him down. In fact it dragged him right to the bottom of the sea, causing a great stir among the starfishes and the octopuses.

'*Bubbllbubblldebub!*' yelled Hans, but nothing happened till he remembered the ring. He twiddled it with his other hand, and at once a shower of bubbles shot down to find him as the air-spirits obeyed his call. They hoisted him to the surface and then pulled him through the water so quickly that he sent sheets of spray flying out to left and right.

Only a few seconds later he was standing on the deck of the ship, and Rock Smasher and Pine Twister were scrambling to get away. Pine Twister shot up the mainmast like a squirrel, and Rock Smasher tried to hide among the cargo in the hold; but Hans hauled him out and whacked him senseless with the staff, and then shook the mainmast till Pine Twister fell down and landed on a sharp corner of the wheelhouse. Hans threw them overboard, and that was the end of them.

Then he set the beautiful maiden free.

'Which way's your father's kingdom?' he said.

'South-west,' she told him, and Hans told the air-spirits to blow on the sails. With the fine fair wind they provided, the ship soon reached the harbour, where Hans restored the princess to her father and mother.

She explained all about Hans's bravery, and of course there was nothing else to be done but for him to marry her. The king and queen were delighted with their son-in-law, and they all lived happily ever after.

Tale type: ATU 301, 'The Three Stolen Princesses'
Source: a story told to the Grimm brothers by Wilhelm Wackernagel
Similar stories: Katharine M. Briggs: 'The Little Red Hairy Man', 'Tom and the Giant Blunderbuss', 'Tom Hickathrift' (*Folk Tales of Britain*); Italo Calvino: 'The Golden Ball' (*Italian Folktales*); Jacob and Wilhelm Grimm: 'The Gnome' (*Children's and Household Tales*)

This is a story made up of bits and pieces, not very tidily strung together. The robbers in their cave exist only to be escaped from; Pine Twister and Rock Smasher, the gifted companions, never have a chance to use their particular gifts; and as for the savage nobleman who kidnapped the princess, he appears in this tale only as the agent who puts the princess in the cave, and is never heard of again. Did he forget about her? Was he killed while on some other savage business? Couldn't he reappear, so that Hans could win a tremendous fight and become even more of a hero?

Alternatively, why doesn't the story make the evil little man her captor instead of just her guard? That would have been the simplest way to clear up the matter.

And then there is the ring that summons the air-spirits. Finding something like that in a cave from which there's no means of escape sounds remarkably like 'Aladdin'. And why doesn't the evil little man use it to help defeat Hans?

And so on. Once you start 'improving' a tale like this, it can easily come apart in your hands.

FORTY-EIGHT

THE MOON

A very long time ago there was a country where the night was always dark. After sunset the sky covered the world like a black cloth, because the moon never rose, and not one star twinkled in the darkness. A long time before, when the world was created, everything used to glow gently and give enough light to see by, but later that faded.

One day four young men from that country set out on a journey and came to another kingdom just as the sun was setting behind the mountains. When the sun had gone completely, they stood still in amazement, because a gleaming ball appeared at the top of an oak tree and cast a soft light all around. It wasn't as bright as the sun, but it gave enough light to see by and to tell one thing from another. The four travellers had never seen anything like it, so they stopped a farmer who happened to be driving past in his wagon, and asked him what it was.

'Oh, that's the moon, that is,' he told them. 'Our mayor bought it. He paid three talers for it. He's got to pour oil into it every day and keep it clean so it always shines nice and bright, and we pay him a taler a week for his trouble.'

When the farmer had driven away one of the young men said, 'You know what, we could use this moon thing at home. My dad's got an oak tree about as big as this in his front garden. I bet he'd let us hang it there. Wouldn't it be good not to have to blunder about in the dark any more?'

'That's a good idea,' said the second. 'Let's get hold of a wagon and a horse and carry this moon away. They can always buy another.'

'I'm a good climber,' said the third. 'I'll go up and get it.'

The fourth one fetched a wagon and horses, and the third one climbed the tree, drilled a hole in the moon, passed a rope through it and hauled it down. When they had the glowing ball safely in the wagon, they covered it with a tarpaulin so no one could see what they'd done, and then they set off homewards.

Back in their own country they hung the moon on a tall oak tree. Everyone was delighted when this new lamp cast its light over all the fields and shone through every window. Even the dwarfs came out of their mountain caves to have a look at it, and the little elves in their red jackets came out to the meadows and danced in the moonlight.

The four friends looked after the moon; they kept it clean, they trimmed the wick and made sure it was always full of oil. They were paid a taler a week by public subscription.

And so it went on till they grew old. One day one of them felt his death was near, so he sent for the lawyer and changed his will, saying that as a quarter of the moon was his, it should go into the grave with him. Accordingly, when he died, the mayor of the town climbed the tree and cut off a quarter of the moon with his secateurs, and it was placed in the coffin. The light from the rest of the moon was a little bit dimmer, but people could still see their way around.

When the second one died, another quarter of the moon was buried with him, and the light grew dimmer still. The same thing happened with the third, and after the fourth died and was buried, there was no light at all, and when people went out without a lantern they bumped into things just as they'd done in the old days.

When the four parts of the moon were together in the underworld, where it had always been dark, the dead became restless and woke up from their sleep. They were astonished at being able to see again; the moonlight was quite bright enough for them, because their eyes had been closed for so long that the sun would have been too bright. They cheered up no end, got out of their graves, and began to have a high old time. They played cards, they danced, they went to the taverns and got drunk, they quarrelled and fought and raised their sticks and walloped one another, and the row they made got louder and louder until it reached all the way to heaven.

St Peter, who guards the gate up there, thought a revolution was breaking out, and he called all the heavenly host together to repel the Devil and his infernal crew. However, when the devils didn't turn up, he got on his holy horse and rode down to the underworld to see what was going on.

'Lie down, you brutes!' he roared. 'Back in your graves, every one of you! You're dead, and don't you forget it.'

Then he saw what the problem was: the moon had reassembled itself, and no one could sleep. So he unhooked it, took it up to heaven, and hung it up where no one could reach. Since then it shines over every country no matter where it is, and St Peter takes a bit away at a time till there's hardly any left and puts them back again over the course of a month to remind people who's boss.

He doesn't take the cut-off bits down to the underworld, though. He's got a special cupboard to put them in. It's just as dark down among the dead as it ever was.

Tale type: unclassified
Source: a story in Heinrich Pröhle's *Märchen für die Jugend* (*Tales for the Young*; 1854)

Wilhelm Grimm included this in the seventh and last edition of *Die Kinder- und Hausmärchen* (*Children's and Household Tales*), of 1857, and it is a little different in kind from most of the other tales, being a kind of creation-myth that soon turns into a tale of the ridiculous. It has an irresistible zest, though it ends rather abruptly, with St Peter just hanging the moon up in the sky. I thought that could do with a little elaboration.

FORTY-NINE

THE GOOSE GIRL AT THE SPRING

Once upon a time there was a very old woman who lived with her flock of geese in a lonely place among the mountains, where her little house lay surrounded by a deep forest. Every morning she took her crutch and hobbled off into the woods, where she kept herself busy gathering grass for her geese and picking any wild fruit she could reach. She put it all on her back and carried it home. If she met anyone on the path, she would always greet them in a friendly way, saying, 'Good day, neighbour! Nice weather! Yes, it's grass I've got here, as much as I can carry; we poor people all have to bear our burdens.'

But for some reason people didn't like meeting her. When they saw her coming, they'd often take a different path, and if a father and his little boy came across her, the father would whisper, 'Beware of that old woman. She's a crafty one. It wouldn't surprise me if she was a witch.'

One morning a good-looking young man happened to be walking through the forest. The sun was shining, the birds were singing, a fresh breeze stirred the leaves, and he was feeling happy and cheerful. He hadn't seen anyone else that morning, but suddenly he came across the old witch kneeling on the ground cutting grass with a sickle. There was already a big load of grass neatly cut, and beside it two baskets filled with wild apples and pears.

'Good grief, my dear old woman,' he said, 'you can't be intending to carry all that!'

'Oh, yes, I must, sir,' she said. 'Rich people don't have to do that sort of thing, but we poor folk have a saying: "Don't look back, you'll only see how bent you are." Would you be able to help me, I wonder, sir? You've got a fine straight back and a strong pair of legs. I'm sure you could manage it easily. It's not far to go, my little house, just out of sight over that way.'

The young man felt sorry for her, and said, 'Well, I'm one of those rich people, I have to confess – my father's a nobleman – but I'm happy to show you that farmers aren't the only people who can carry things. Yes, I'll take the bundle to your house for you.'

'That's very good of you, sir,' she said. 'It might take an hour's walking, but I'm sure you won't mind that. You could carry the apples and pears for me too.'

The young count began to have second thoughts when she mentioned an hour's walk, but she was so quick to take up his offer that he couldn't back out of it. She wrapped the grass up in a cloth and tied it on to his back and then put the baskets into his hands.

'You see,' she said, 'not much really.'

'But it's actually quite heavy,' said the young man. 'This grass – is it grass? It feels like bricks! And the fruit might as well be blocks of stone. I can hardly breathe!'

He would have liked to put it all down, but he didn't want to face the old woman's mockery. She was already teasing him cruelly.

'Look at the fine young gentleman,' she said, 'making such a fuss about what a poor old woman has to carry every day! You're good with words, aren't you? "Farmers aren't the only people who can carry things!" But when it comes to deeds, you fall at the first hurdle. Come on! What are you standing around for? Get a move on! Nobody's going to do it for you.'

While he walked on level ground he could just about bear the weight, but as soon as the path began to slope upwards his feet rolled on the stones, which slipped out as if they were alive, and he could barely move. Beads of sweat appeared on his face and trickled hot and cold down his back.

'I can't go any further,' he gasped. 'I've got to stop and rest.'

'Oh, no, you don't,' said the old woman. 'You can stop and rest when we've got there, but till then you keep walking. You never know – it might bring you luck.'

'Oh, this is too much,' said the count. 'This is outrageous!'

He tried to throw off the bundle, but he just couldn't dislodge it. It clung to his back as if it were growing there. He squirmed and twisted this way and that, and the old woman laughed at him and jumped up and down with her crutch.

'No point in losing your temper, young sir,' she said. 'You're as red in the face as a turkey cock. Carry your burden patiently, and when we get home, I might give you a tip.'

What could he do? He had to stumble on after the old woman as well as he could. The odd thing was that while his load seemed to be getting heavier and heavier, she seemed to getting more and more nimble.

Then all of a sudden she gave a skip and landed right on top of the pack on his back and stayed there. She was as thin as a stick, but she weighed more than the stoutest peasant girl. The young man's legs wobbled, all his muscles trembled with effort and blazed with pain, and whenever he tried to stop for a moment, the old woman lashed him with a bunch of stinging nettles. He groaned, he sobbed, he struggled on, and when he was sure he was going to collapse, they turned a corner in the path and there was the old woman's house.

When the geese saw her, they stretched out their necks and their wings and ran towards her, cackling. After them came another old woman, carrying a stick. This one wasn't as old as the first one, but she was big and strong with a heavy, dull, ugly face.

'Where've you been, mother?' she said to the old woman. 'You've been gone so long I thought something must have happened to you.'

'Oh, no, my pretty one,' said the old woman. 'I met this kind gentleman and he offered to carry my bundle for me. And look, he even offered to take me on his back when I got tired. We had such a nice conversation that the journey passed in no time.'

Finally the old woman slid off the young count's back and took the bundle and the baskets.

'There we are, sir,' she said, 'you sit yourself down and have a breather. You've earned your little reward, and you shall have it. As for you, my beautiful treasure,' she said to the other woman, 'you better go inside. It wouldn't be proper for you to stay alone with a lusty young fellow like this. I know what young men are like. He might fall in love with you.'

The count didn't know whether to laugh or to cry; even if she were thirty years younger, he thought, this treasure would never prompt a flicker in his heart.

The old woman fussed over her geese as if they were children before going inside after her daughter. The young man stretched himself out on a bench under an apple tree. It was a beautiful morning; the sun shone warmly, the air was mild, and all around him stretched a green meadow covered with cowslips and wild thyme and a thousand other flowers. A clear stream twinkled in the sunlight as it ran through the middle of the meadow, and the white geese waddled here and there or paddled in the stream.

'What a lovely place,' the young man thought. 'But I'm so tired I can't keep my eyes open. I think I'll take a nap for a few minutes. I just hope the wind doesn't blow my legs away; they're as weak as tinder.'

The next thing he knew, the old woman was shaking his arm.

'Wakey wakey,' she said, 'you can't stay here. I admit I gave you a hard time, but you're still alive, and here's your reward. I said I'd give you something, didn't I? You don't need money or land, so here's something else. Look after it well and it'll bring you luck.'

What she gave him was a little box carved out of a single emerald. The count jumped up, feeling refreshed by his sleep, and thanked her for the gift. Then he set out on his way without once looking back for the beautiful treasure. For a long way down the path he could still hear the happy noise of the geese.

He wandered in the forest for at least three days before he found his way out. Eventually he came to a large city, where the custom was that every stranger had to be brought before the king and queen; so he was taken to the palace, where the king and queen were sitting on their thrones.

The young count knelt politely, and since he had nothing else to offer, he took the emerald box from his pocket, opened it and set it down before the queen. She beckoned to him to bring the box closer so that she could look inside it, but no sooner had she seen what was there than she fell into a dead faint. The bodyguards seized the young man at once and were about to drag him off to prison when the queen opened her eyes.

'Release him!' she cried. 'Everyone must leave the throne room. I want to speak to this young man in private.'

When they were alone, the queen began to cry bitterly.

'What use is all the splendour of this palace?' she said. 'Every morning when I wake up, sorrow rushes in on me like a flood. I once had three daughters, and the third was so beautiful that everyone thought she was a miracle. She was as white as snow and as pink as apple blossoms, and her hair shone like the beams of the sun. When she wept, it wasn't tears that flowed down her cheeks but pearls and precious stones.

'On her fifteenth birthday, the king called all three daughters to his throne. You can't imagine how everyone blinked when the third daughter came in – it was just as if the sun had come out.

'The king said, "My daughters, since I don't know when my last day will arrive, I'm going to decide today what each of you shall receive after my death. You all love me, but whoever loves me most shall have the largest part of the kingdom."

'Each of the girls said she loved him most of all, but he wanted more than that.

'"Tell me exactly how much you love me," he said. "Then I'll know just what you mean."

'The oldest daughter said, "I love you as much as the sweetest sugar." The second daughter said, "I love you as much as I love my prettiest dress."

'But the third daughter didn't say a word. So her father said, "And you, darling, how much do you love me?"

'And she said, "I don't know. I can't compare my love with anything."

'But he kept on and on demanding an answer until she found something to compare her love to, and she said, "No matter how good the food, it won't taste of anything without salt. So I love my father as much as I love salt."

'When the king heard this, he became furious and said, "If that's how you love me, then that's how your love will be rewarded."

'And he divided his kingdom between the two eldest daughters, and he ordered the youngest to have a sack of salt bound to her back, and then two servants were to lead her out into the depths of the forest. We all begged and pleaded for mercy, but he wouldn't change his mind. Oh, how she wept when she was forced to leave! The path she'd trodden was covered with pearls. Not long afterwards, the king regretted what he'd done, and had the forest searched from end to end; but she was never found.

'When I think that wild animals may have eaten her, I can hardly bear the pain. Sometimes I comfort myself by thinking that she's found shelter in a cave, or she's being looked after by kind people, but . . .

'So you can imagine the shock when I opened the emerald box and saw a pearl just like the ones my daughter wept. And you can imagine how my heart was stirred. And now you must tell me: where did you get this? How does it come to be in your possession?'

The young count told her how it had been given to him by the old woman in the forest, who he believed must be a witch, because everything about her had made him feel uneasy. However, he said, this was the first he had heard about the queen's daughter. Accordingly, the king and queen decided to set out at once to find the old woman, in the hope that she might be able to give them some news about their child.

That evening the old woman was sitting in her little house, spinning with her spinning wheel. Night was falling, and the only light came from a pine log burning on the hearth. Suddenly there were loud cries from outside, as the geese came home from their pasture, and a moment later the daughter entered the house, but the old woman merely nodded and didn't say a word.

Her daughter sat down beside her and took up her own spinning, twisting the thread as deftly as any young girl. The two of them sat together for two hours without exchanging a word.

Finally there came a rustling from the window, and they looked up to see two fiery red eyes glaring in at them. It was an old owl, who cried out, '*Tu-whoo, tu-whoo,*' three times.

The old woman said, 'Well, my little daughter, it's time for you to go outside and do your work.'

The daughter stood up. Where did she go? Out across the meadow, and down towards the valley, until she came to three old oak trees next to a spring. The moon was full, and had just risen over the mountain; it was so bright that you could have found a pin on the ground.

The daughter unfastened the skin at her neck, and pulled her face right over her head before kneeling down at the spring and washing herself. When she'd done that, she dipped the skin of her false face in the water, wrung it out, and laid it to dry and bleach on the grass. But what a change had come over her! You wouldn't believe it! After the dull heavy face and the grey wig had come off, her hair flowed down like liquid sunlight. Her eyes sparkled like stars, and her cheeks were as pink as the freshest apple blossom.

But this girl, so beautiful, was sad. She sat down by the spring and cried bitterly. Tear after tear rolled down her long hair and fell into the grass. There she sat, and she would have stayed there for a long time if she hadn't heard a rustling among the branches of a tree nearby. Like a deer startled by the sound of a hunter's rifle, she jumped up at once. At the same time a dark cloud passed over the face of the moon, and in the sudden darkness the maiden slipped into the old skin and vanished like a candle flame blown out by the wind.

Shivering like an aspen leaf, she ran back to the little house, where the old woman was standing by the door.

'Oh, mother, I—'

'Hush, dear,' said the old woman gently, 'I know, I know.'

She led the girl into the room and put another log on the fire. But she didn't go back to the spinning wheel; she took a broom and began to sweep the floor.

'We must make everything neat and clean,' she said.

'But, mother, what are you doing it now for? It's late! What's happening?'

'Don't you know what time it is?'

'It's not past midnight,' said the girl, 'but it must be past eleven.'

'And don't you remember that it was three years ago today

when you came to me? Time's up, my dear. We can't stay together any longer.'

The girl was frightened. 'Oh, mother dear,' she said, 'you're not really going to throw me out, are you? Where shall I go? I've got no friends, I've got no home to go to. I've done everything you've asked of me, you've always been satisfied with my work – please don't send me away!'

But the old woman wouldn't give her an answer. 'My own time here is up,' she said. 'But before I leave, the house must be spick and span. So don't get in my way, and don't worry too much either. You'll find a roof to shelter you, and you'll be quite satisfied with the wages I'm going to give you.'

'But please tell me, what's happening?'

'I've told you once, and I'm telling you again: don't interrupt my work. Go to your room, take the skin off your face, and put on the silk dress you were wearing when you first came here. Then wait there till I call you.'

Meanwhile, the king and queen were continuing their search for the old woman who had given the count the emerald box. He had gone with them, but he'd become separated from them in the thick forest, and he'd had to go on alone. He thought he'd found the right path, but then as the daylight waned he thought he'd better not go any further in case he got really lost; so he climbed a tree, meaning to spend the night safely up among the branches.

But when the moon came out he saw something moving down the meadow, and in its brilliant light he realized it was the goose girl he'd seen before at the old woman's house. She was coming towards the trees, and he thought, 'Aha! If I catch one of these witches, I'll soon have my hands on the other.'

But then she stopped at the spring, and removed her skin, and the count nearly fell out of the tree with astonishment; and when her golden hair fell down around her shoulders, and he saw her clearly in the moonlight, he knew that she was more beautiful than anyone he had ever seen. He hardly dared to breathe. But he couldn't resist leaning forward to get a little closer, and in doing so he leaned too heavily on a dry branch, and it was the sound of it cracking that startled her. She leaped up at once and put on the other skin, and then the cloud passed in front of the moon; and in the sudden darkness she slipped away.

The count climbed down from the tree at once and ran after her. He hadn't gone very far up the meadow when he saw two figures making for the house. It was the king and queen, who'd seen the firelight in the window, and when the count caught up with them and told them about the miracle he'd seen at the spring, they were sure the girl must be their daughter.

Full of joy and hope, they hurried on and soon arrived at the little house. The geese were all asleep with their heads tucked under their wings, and not one of them moved. The three searchers looked in at the window, and saw the old woman quietly sitting and spinning, nodding her head as she turned the wheel. Everything in the room was as clean as if the little fog men lived there, who carry no dust on their feet; but there was no sign of the princess.

For a minute or two the king and queen just looked in, but then they plucked up their courage and knocked at the window.

The old woman seemed to be expecting them. She stood up and called out in a friendly voice, 'Come in. I know who you are.'

When they were all inside the house, the old woman said, 'You could have spared yourself this sorrow and this journey, you know, if you hadn't banished your daughter so unjustly three years ago. But she hasn't come to harm. She's tended the geese for three years, and made a good job of it. She's learned nothing evil and she's kept a pure heart. But I think you've been punished enough by the unhappiness you've suffered.'

Then she went to the door and said, 'Come out, my little daughter.'

The door opened, and the princess came into the room, wearing her silken dress, with her golden hair shining and her bright eyes sparkling. It was as if an angel had come down from heaven.

The princess went straight to her mother and father and embraced them both, and kissed them. Both of them wept for joy; they couldn't help it. The young count was standing nearby, and when she caught sight of him her cheeks became as red as a moss rose, and she herself didn't know why.

The king said, 'My dear child, I gave my kingdom away. What can I give you?'

'She needs nothing,' said the old woman. 'I shall give her the tears she shed because of you. Each one is a pearl more precious than any they find in the sea, and they're worth more than your whole kingdom. And as a reward for looking after the geese, I shall give her my house.'

And just as the old woman said that, she vanished. The walls of the house rumbled and shook, and when the king and queen and the princess and the count looked around, they saw that it had been changed into a beautiful palace. A table had been set with a feast fit for an emperor, and there were servants bustling everywhere to do their bidding.

The story doesn't end there. The trouble is that my grandmother, who told it to me, is losing her memory, and she's forgotten the rest.

But I think that the beautiful princess married the count, and they remained together and lived in happiness. As for the snow-white geese, some say that they were really girls that the old woman had taken into her care, and it's likely that they regained their human form and stayed there to serve the young queen. I wouldn't be surprised.

As for the old woman, she can't have been a witch, as people thought, but a wise woman who meant well. Why did she treat the young count like that when he first came across her? Well, who knows? She might have seen into his character and found a seed or two of arrogance there. If so, she knew how to deal with it.

Finally, it's almost certain that she was present at the birth of the princess, and gave her the gift of weeping pearls instead of tears. That doesn't happen much any more. If it did, poor people would soon become rich.

* * *

Tale type: ATU 923, 'Love Like Salt'
Source: 'D'Ganshiadarin', an Austrian dialect story by Andreas Schumacher (1833)
Similar stories: Katharine M. Briggs: 'Cap o' Rushes', 'Sugar and Salt' (*Folk Tales of Britain*); Italo Calvino: 'Dear as Salt', 'The Old Woman's Hide' (*Italian Folktales*); William Shakespeare: *King Lear*

This is one of the most sophisticated of all the tales. At the heart of it is the old story of the princess who told her father she loved him as much as salt, and was punished for her honesty. There are many variations on this tale, including *King Lear*.

But look what this very literary telling does. Instead of beginning with the unfortunate honest princess, it hides her until much later in the story, and begins with another figure altogether, the witch or wise woman; and not with a single event, either, but with a sketch of what she usually did, what her habitual way of life led her to do, and the reaction that aroused in others. But is she a witch, or isn't she? Fairy tales usually tell us directly; this one instead shows us what other people thought of her, and allows the question to remain equivocal, undetermined. The story-sprite here is flirting with modernism already, in which there is no voice with absolute authority, and we can have no view except one that passes through a particular pair of eyes (the father and his little son); but all human views are partial. The father might be right, or he might not.

Then we meet the count, and the events of the story begin. The old woman treats the young man with what seems like high-handed and meaningless harshness; he meets another woman younger than the first, but ugly, dull; the old woman gives him the present of a box containing something which, when the queen opens the box in the next city he visits, causes her to faint. The storyteller has given us a tale full of mystery and suspense, and still we haven't got to the heart of it.

But now, in the words of the queen (the story-sprite again, making sure that we can only know something that someone in the story knows) comes the kernel of the tale, the story of the girl who told the truth about loving her father as much as salt. She wept tears that were pearls, says the queen, and in the box there is one of those very pearls. *Now* we can see the connections that the storyteller has established between these mysterious events, and from here the tale moves swiftly on towards the climax. The goose girl takes off her skin in the moonlight (and again, we can only see this because the count is observing it) and reveals her hidden beauty; the old woman, treating her with great tenderness, tells her to put on her silk dress; the participants come together, and the truth is revealed.

And then there's another reminder of the partiality of knowledge: the storyteller says that the story doesn't end there, but the old woman who originally told it is losing her memory and has forgotten the rest. Nevertheless, it *might* happen that . . . and so on. This marvellous tale shows how complex a structure can be built on the simplest of bases, and still remain immediately comprehensible.

FIFTY

THE NIXIE OF THE MILLPOND

There were once a miller and his wife who lived happily with enough money and a bit of land, comfortably getting a little richer every year. But misfortune comes even to people such as them, and they had one piece of bad luck after another, so that the wealth they had grew smaller and smaller until they barely owned the mill they lived in. The miller was in great distress; he couldn't sleep, and all night long he tossed and turned while his anxieties grew and grew.

One morning, after a night of ceaseless worry, he got up very early and went outside, hoping the fresh air would lift his heart a little. As he was walking across the mill dam the first rays of the sun touched his eyes, and at the same moment he heard something disturbing the water.

He turned around to look, and saw a beautiful woman rising up out of the millpond. Her delicate hands were holding her hair away from her shoulders, but it was so long that it flowed down around her pale body like silk. He knew at once that she was the nixie of the pond. He was so frightened that he didn't know whether to run away or to stay where he was, but then she spoke, and in a soft voice she called him by his name and asked him why he was so sad.

At first the miller couldn't find his voice, but when he heard her speaking so sweetly, he took heart and told her how he'd once been rich, but that his fortune had diminished little by little and now he was so poor he didn't know what to do.

'Don't worry,' said the nixie. 'I'll make you happier and richer than you've ever been. All you have to do is promise me that you'll give me what has just been born in your house.'

That can only be a puppy or a kitten, thought the miller, and he promised to do what she asked.

The nixie slipped back under the water, and the miller, feeling much better, hurried back to the mill; but he hadn't even reached the door before the maid came out, smiling broadly, and said, 'Congratulations! Your wife's just given birth to a baby boy.'

The miller stood there as if he'd been struck by lightning. He realized at once that the nixie had tricked him. With his head low and his heart heavy he went to his wife's bed. She said, 'Why are you looking so sad? Isn't he beautiful, our little boy?'

He told her what had happened, and how the nixie had deceived him.

'I should have guessed!' he said. 'No good comes of trusting creatures like that. And what good is money, after all? What's the use of gold and treasure, if we have to lose our child? But what can we do?'

Even the relatives who came to celebrate the birth didn't know what advice to give him.

However, at exactly that time, the miller's luck began to change. Every enterprise he undertook was successful; harvests were good, so there was plenty of grain to mill, and prices held up too; it seemed as if he could do nothing wrong, and his money-box filled up almost by itself, and his safe was full to bursting. Before long he was richer than he'd ever been.

But he couldn't enjoy it. His bargain with the nixie tormented him; he didn't like walking by the millpond in case she came to the surface and reminded him of his debt. And of course he never let his little son go anywhere near the water.

'If you find yourself close to the edge,' he told him, 'be careful, and come away at once. There's a bad spirit in there. You only have to touch the water and she'll grab hold and pull you under.'

But the years passed, and there was no sign of the nixie, and little by little the miller began to relax.

When the boy was old enough, he was apprenticed to a huntsman. He learned quickly and did well, and the lord of the village took him into his service. In the village there happened to live a beautiful, honest and kindly girl who had won the young huntsman's heart, and when the lord realized this, he gave the young couple a small house as a wedding present. There they lived in peace and happiness, loving each other with all their hearts.

One day the young huntsman was chasing a deer when it turned aside and ran out of the forest and into a meadow. As soon as he had a clear view, the huntsman fired and dropped it with one shot. Exhilarated by that success, he didn't at first realize where he was, and as soon as he'd skinned and gutted the animal, he went to wash his hands in the pool of water nearby.

But it was his father's millpond. And the moment he dipped his hands in the water, the nixie rose up laughing, embraced him with her dripping wet arms, and dragged him down so quickly that the waves all surged together overhead.

When evening came, and the huntsman hadn't returned home, his wife became anxious. She went out to look for him, and remembering how often he'd told her that he had to beware of the millpond, she guessed what had happened. She hurried there, and as soon as she found his game-bag lying on the grassy bank, she no longer had any doubt. She cried aloud and wrung her hands, she sobbed, she called his name again and again, but it was all in vain. She ran round to the other side of the millpond and called again from there, she cursed the nixie with all the passion in her heart, but there was no response. The surface of the water was as flat as a mirror in the twilight, and all she could see in it was the reflection of the half-moon.

The poor woman didn't leave the pond. She walked round and round the edge, sometimes quickly when she thought she saw something stirring on the other side, and sometimes going slowly and carefully to look down deep into the water right at her feet, but she never stopped for a moment. Some of the time she cried her husband's name aloud, some of the time she whimpered; and when a good part of the night had gone and she was at the end of her strength, she sank down to the grass and fell asleep in a moment.

And at once she found herself in a dream. She was climbing up the face of a rocky mountain, terrified. Thorns and brambles tore at her feet, rain hit her face like hail, and the wild wind lashed her hair to and fro. As soon as she reached the summit, though, everything changed. The sky was blue and the air was warm, and the ground sloped gently down towards a green meadow scattered with flowers, where there stood a neat little hut. She walked down to the hut and opened the door, and found a white-haired old woman who smiled at her in a friendly way – and at that point the poor young wife woke up.

The day had already dawned. Since there was nothing to keep her at home, she decided to follow the dream. She knew where the mountain was, and so she set off at once; and as she made her way there the weather changed and became just as she'd experienced it in the dream, the wind wild, the rain as hard as hail. Nevertheless she struggled up, and found everything just as she'd seen it: the blue sky, the flower-covered meadow, the neat little hut, the white-haired old woman.

'Come in, my dear,' the old woman said, 'and sit down beside me. I can see you've had an unhappy time; you must have done, to seek out my lonely hut.'

Hearing her kindly words the young wife began to sob, but soon she gathered herself and told the whole story.

'There now, don't you worry,' said the old woman. 'I can help you. Take this golden comb. Wait till the next full moon, and then go to the millpond, sit down on the bank, and comb your long black hair with this comb. When you've done that, lie down right there, and see what happens.'

The young wife went home, and the next few days were very slow in passing. Finally the full moon rose above the trees, and she went to the millpond, sat on the grassy bank, and began to comb her hair with the golden comb. When she'd finished she laid the comb at the water's edge and lay down; and almost at once there was a stirring in the water, and a wave rose up and rushed to the bank, and when the water subsided, it took the comb with it. And at that very moment the surface of the water parted, and the huntsman's head rose above the surface and gazed in anguish at his wife, but she only saw him for a second, because another wave came along at once and took him under again. When the water was finally still there was nothing to be seen except the reflection of the full moon.

The young wife went home heartsick. But that night she had the dream again, so once more she set off to find the hut in the flowery meadow. This time the old woman gave her a golden flute.

'Wait till the next full moon,' she said, 'and take the flute to the water. Sit on the bank and play a beautiful tune, and when you've done that, lay it down on the grass and see what happens.'

The huntsman's wife did just as the old woman told her. She played a tune, and as soon as she'd set the flute down on the grass, the water surged towards the bank and took it down into the depths; and a moment later, there was a disturbance in the middle of the pond, and the water parted to let the huntsman's head and the upper part of his body appear above the surface. He reached out towards her desperately, as she reached to him, but just as their hands were almost touching, the waves pulled him under, and yet again she was left alone on the bank.

'Oh, this will break my heart!' she thought. 'To see my dear one twice, only to lose him again – it's too much to bear!'

But when she slept, she had the dream again. So she set off for the mountain for the third time, and the old woman comforted her.

'Don't be too distressed, my dear. It's not all over yet. You must wait for another full moon, and take this golden spinning wheel to the millpond. Sit on the bank and spin, and when the spindle is full, leave the spinning wheel and see what happens.'

The young wife did exactly what she was told. When the moon was full, she spun a full spindle of flax at the water's edge, and then left the golden wheel and stepped aside. The water swirled and bubbled and then rushed at the bank with more violence than ever, and a great wave swept the spinning wheel down into the pool. And at the same moment another wave surged up, and brought with it first the huntsman's head and arms, and then his whole body, and he leaped for the bank and seized his wife's hand, and they ran for their lives.

But behind them a great convulsion was sweeping the water up and out of the millpond altogether. It rushed up the bank and across the meadow after the fleeing couple with terrible force, smashing down trees and bushes, so that they feared for their lives. In her terror the wife called out to the old woman, and at once wife and husband were transformed into a toad and a frog. When the water overwhelmed them it couldn't drown them, but it tore them apart from each other and carried them a long way away.

After the flood had subsided, and the two little animals were left on dry land, they regained their human forms again; but neither knew where the other was, and they were each among strangers in strange lands. Many high mountains and deep valleys lay between them. To earn a living, they each found work herding sheep, and for some years they tended their flocks among the fields and the forests; and wherever they wandered, each of them felt a constant sadness and yearning.

One day, when spring had come again and the air was fresh and warm, they both set out with their sheep. As chance would have it, they began moving towards the same place. The huntsman saw a flock of sheep on a distant mountain slope, and drove his own in that direction, and in the valley that lay between them the two flocks and the two shepherds came together. They didn't recognize each other, but they were glad to have each other's company in that lonely place, and from then on they drove their flocks together, not speaking much, but each taking comfort from the other's presence.

One night, when the moon was full in the sky and the sheep were safely gathered in, the huntsman took a flute from his pocket and played a sad and beautiful little tune. When he put the flute down, he saw that the shepherdess was weeping.

'Why are you crying?' he said.

'Oh,' she said, 'the moon was full just like this when I played that same tune on a flute, and the head of my darling rose out of the water . . .'

He looked at her, and it was as if a veil had fallen from his eyes, for he recognized his dear wife. And when she looked at his face in the moonlight, she knew him as well. They fell into each other's arms and kissed and hugged and kissed again, and no one need ask whether they were happy; indeed, they lived in bliss for the rest of their lives.

* * *

Tale type: ATU 316, 'The Nix of the Mill-Pond'
Source: a story by Moritz Haupt, published in *Zeitschrift für Deutsches Alterthum* (*Magazine of German Antiquity*), vol. 2 (1842)

Nixies, selkies, mermaids, *rusalki*, whatever they're called they're trouble. This one is no exception to the rule, but she's beaten in the end: the faithful wife outloves her. The depiction of the mutual discovery of husband and wife at the end is very touching, and the pattern of lunar imagery set up earlier requires that the discovery be made at the full moon, which thus makes artistic as well as ocular sense. On any other night they wouldn't have been able to see each other so clearly.

I'd like to know the tune that was played on the flute. Dvořák's 'Song to the Moon', from his opera *Rusalka* of 1901, would do very well.

FIFTY-ONE

THE TWELVE HUNTSMEN

Once there was a prince who was betrothed to a princess whom he loved dearly. One day, as they were sitting together happily, a message came to say that his father was very ill, and wanted to see him before he died.

The prince said to his beloved, 'My dear, I'll have to go and leave you for a while. Keep this ring to remember me by, and when I'm king I'll come back and take you home with me.'

Then he rode away, and when he reached his father's palace, he found the king mortally ill: at the point of death in fact.

The king said to him, 'My dearest boy, I wanted to see you one more time before I die. And I want you to make a promise.'

'Anything, father!'

'Promise me to marry the princess I choose.' And he named the daughter of a different king.

The prince was so grief-stricken that he didn't think, but said, 'Of course, father, I'll do whatever you want.'

Satisfied, the king closed his eyes and died.

His son was proclaimed king, and when the period of mourning was over, he was crowned; and then he remembered the promise he'd given his father. He sent ambassadors to the court of the other king and asked for the princess's hand in marriage, and after a short negotiation they became betrothed.

Naturally, news of this spread far and wide, and it wasn't long before his first fiancée heard about it. She was shocked by his infidelity, so much so that she nearly pined away.

'My darling, what's troubling you?' her father said. 'Is there anything I can get to make you happier? Just name it, and you shall have it.'

So she thought, and then said, 'Father, what I want most is eleven girls as much like me as possible.'

The king said, 'I'll get it done at once.'

So he sent messengers to every corner of his kingdom to look for girls who resembled her. Many were found and brought to the palace, and the princess chose those who looked most like her, though there were few who were very like. Having chosen eleven of them, she ordered eleven huntsmen's costumes to be made for them, and one more for her.

Once all twelve girls were ready, the princess said farewell to her father, and they rode away to the court of her faithless fiancé, whom she still loved even so. There she asked if he needed any huntsmen.

'My companions and I are skilled at that kind of work,' she said. 'You couldn't do better than take all twelve of us.'

The king looked at the princess without recognizing her. The twelve of them were all so good-looking in their hunting dress, though, that he said he'd take them on; so they were all engaged in his service, and were known as the King's Huntsmen.

Now the king happened to have a marvellous lion, far more intelligent than any lion at the court of any other king; and cleverer than many humans, in fact, for he knew all kinds of secret things that were hidden from common knowledge. One day the lion spoke to the king and said, 'Those twelve huntsmen of yours . . .'

'Splendid-looking fellows, aren't they?' said the king.

'So they may be. But they're not huntsmen. In fact they're not men at all. They're girls.'

'No! I don't believe it.'

'I'm afraid it's true.'

'Prove it!'

'Very well,' said the lion. 'Get some dried peas and scatter them over the floor of your antechamber. If they're men, they'll walk over them with a firm step; but if they're girls, they'll go on tiptoe and skitter and shuffle them out of the way. You watch – see if I'm wrong.'

'That's a good idea,' said the king, and did exactly as the lion advised.

However, one of the king's servants had conceived a great liking for the twelve huntsmen, and hearing that they were going to be tested in that way, he went and told them.

'Thank you!' said the princess, then told her eleven companions: 'Now remember, when we go into the antechamber we must walk straight over the peas as if they weren't there.'

And next morning, when the king summoned the huntsmen, they walked right over the peas like the manliest of men and not a pea rolled out of place.

After they'd been dismissed, the king called the lion.

'Fine adviser you are!' he said. 'They walked exactly like men, every one of them.'

'They must have known they were going to be tested,' said the lion. 'I've got a better idea, though. This time, have twelve spinning wheels put in the antechamber. The thing about girls and women is that they can disguise their way of walking, but they can't conceal what they really feel, and they all love spinning wheels. When they see these, they'll go up and admire them and try them out. Mark my words, they won't be able to resist.'

'Ah,' said the king, 'I like that. Yes, that's very ingenious. Well done, lion.'

He had the spinning wheels set up in the antechamber, and

once again the servant who liked the huntsmen told them what the lion had advised.

'Hear that, huntsmen?' said the princess to her companions. 'When you see the spinning wheels, just ignore them. A cursory glance, and no more.'

And next morning the huntsmen strode through the antechamber without so much as a peep at the spinning wheels. The king was baffled, and sent for the lion.

'I'm fed up with your advice,' he said. 'It's not worth listening to.'

'But they must have known!' said the lion. 'Someone gave the plan away.'

'Oh, rubbish,' said the king. 'Get back to the zoo.'

Having discarded the lion's advice, the king continued to hunt with his twelve huntsmen, and the longer they spent together, the more fond he became of them. Now one day when they were out hunting, a messenger came galloping up to the king to say that his intended bride was on her way. The true fiancée heard this, and her heart convulsed in her breast and she fell to the ground in a faint.

Thinking that his favourite servant had had an accident, the king rushed over and pulled off the fellow's glove in order to feel his pulse; and there was the ring he'd given his beloved to remember him by. He looked at the huntsman's face with astonishment, and recognized it at once.

Helplessly he kissed the princess, and when she opened her eyes he said, 'You are mine and I am yours. Nothing and no one can change that.'

He sent the messenger back to tell the other princess to return to her kingdom, for, as he said, he already had a bride, and having found an old key, he didn't need a new one.

So their wedding was celebrated with great joy, and the lion was restored to favour, because after all he'd been right about the huntsmen, even if his advice had not succeeded in revealing their secret.

* * *

Tale type: AT 884, 'The Forsaken Fiancée'
Source: a story told to the Grimm brothers by Jeanette Hassenpflug
Similar stories: Italo Calvino: 'The King of Portugal's Son' (*Italian Folktales*); Jacob and Wilhelm Grimm, 'The True Bride' (*Children's and Household Tales*)

This is not the only prince in Grimm who seems surprisingly forgetful about the beautiful girl he's promised to marry. Whether this was a common problem among princes is not easy to say. He's lucky to have a lion as his adviser, or he would be if the lion's advice weren't so idiotic. This is one of those stories in which the individual elements (the twelve pretty huntsmen, the talking lion) are more memorable than the course of the story, and in which the happy ending comes about by sheer accident. Now, if the lion had only managed to give some good advice instead of the bumbling fatuity of an elderly club bore, the prince might have found his true bride much sooner.

FIFTY-TWO

THE BUFFALO-HIDE BOOTS

No danger can discourage a brave soldier, but the fire of the enemy is not everything a soldier has to face. Once there were two brothers, the sons of a peasant. The older joined the army, fought well, and had the good fortune to find his period of service coinciding with several victories in battle. He soon became a general.

His younger brother, however, who joined up a year or two later, was no less brave, but not so lucky. The wars were over and there was nothing for an honest trooper to do but carry out his sentry duty and march up and down looking smart; but as smart as he looked, there was no chance of promotion for him.

One day the soldier was detailed to stand guard outside the general's quarters while the general was giving a banquet. One of the guests going in was so struck by the disconsolate expression on the soldier's face that he stopped and said, 'What's the matter, young fellow?'

'It's my brother,' said the soldier. 'He's the general, but he takes no notice of me at all. It's as if he's forgotten I even exist.'

The guest went inside and told the general.

'Don't believe the wretch!' the general said. 'He's lying, and I'll have him lashed.'

The soldier was given a hundred lashes. But there was an old sergeant who felt sorry for him, and when he'd recovered from the lashing the sergeant said to him, 'Look here, I'm going to teach you a trick. It's a good 'un, and I haven't told it to anyone else. You never know, you might need it some day.'

So he taught the young man his trick, and soon afterwards, seeing that this was the only benefit his army service was ever going to bring him, the soldier took his discharge papers and went his way. He had nothing but a woollen cloak and a pair of buffalo-hide boots, and as he'd never learned a trade, he found it hard going.

One day as he was wandering through the forest he came upon a man dressed in a smart green hunting costume and a pair of glossy boots. The hunter was sitting on a felled tree looking perplexed.

'Fine pair of boots,' said the soldier. 'Must have taken you a fair time to shine 'em up as glossy as that. These old buffalo-hide boots of mine could never take a polish, but they've seen me through thick and thin, and there's years of wear in 'em yet. Where are you off to, mate?'

'I have to admit I'm lost,' said the hunter. 'D'you know where this road leads?'

'Every road leads to a town in the end,' said the soldier. 'That's all I know. What d'you say to joining up and going along together?'

'I don't mind if we do,' said the hunter, and off they went together.

They hadn't walked far before night began to fall.

'Well, we're still in the woods,' said the soldier, 'but look, there's a light shining over there. Let's go and see if they'll give us a bite to eat.'

They came to a crumbling old stone house and knocked on the door. An elderly woman opened it and said, 'What do you want?'

'Here's two honest men,' said the soldier, 'and we're tired and we're hungry. Can you give us something to eat and somewhere to lie down for the night?'

'Oh, no,' she said, 'not here I can't. This house belongs to a band of robbers, and if you know what's good for you, you'll scarper before they get home. If they find you here they'll do you in.'

'Frankly,' said the soldier, 'it's all the same to me whether I die of hunger in the forest or from a robber's dagger in the heart. I've gone two days without food already and my stomach can't wait a moment longer. You're a kind-looking lady – have mercy on an old soldier and his mate.'

'Oh, well, I suppose . . .' she said.

The hunter wasn't keen on going in, but the soldier pulled his sleeve. 'Come on,' he said, 'we'll have time to swallow something before they finish us off.'

'I can hear 'em coming,' said the old woman. 'Quick! Get behind the stove. I'll slip you any leftovers.'

The soldier and the hunter had only just crawled behind the stove when twelve robbers came in. They were big fierce-looking men, bristling with weapons, and they sat down at once and banged the table for their supper. The old woman carried in a huge joint of roast beef, and the chief robber carved it up with his sword and handed it round, and they all fell to eating at once. It smelled so good that the soldier couldn't wait.

'I can't stand it,' he whispered to the hunter. 'I'm going to join them at the table.'

'You'll get us both killed!'

'No, you leave it to me.'

And he clambered out from behind the stove and said, 'Evening, all.'

The robbers were astounded.

'What are you doing here?' roared the chief.

'He's spying on us!' cried another.

'Hang him up and cut bits off him,' suggested a third.

'Mind your manners,' said the soldier. 'Don't you know you should never kill a hungry man? Move up there and let me sit down.'

The robbers had never seen anything like it. The chief was impressed by the soldier's coolness, though, and said, 'All right, you come and sit down. You can have some roast beef. When you've had your supper, though, that's it. We'll make you wish you'd kept away and stayed hungry.'

'All in good time,' said the soldier, and helped himself to a large slice of meat. 'Hey, Shiny Boots!' he called. 'Come and join us. You must be as hungry as I am, and I don't care where you come from, you won't find a better roast than this.'

The hunter came out from behind the stove, and the robbers cried, 'There's another one!'

'Make yourself at home, why don't you?' said the robber chief. 'Come and sit down. Join your pal. All the more fun for us later on.'

'No, I'm not hungry, thank you,' said the hunter.

The robbers watched the soldier sharing their food, and their amazement grew as he sat there so calmly finishing his slice of beef and helping himself to another.

'Food's good,' he said with his mouth full, 'but I could do with a drink. Pass the bottle. Oh, look at that, it's empty. What a shame.'

The robber captain was enjoying the spectacle. He said to the old woman, 'Go down to the cellar, and fetch up a bottle of the best.'

When the wine arrived, the soldier pulled the cork with a loud *pop* and said quietly to the hunter, 'Now watch. I bet you've never seen this before.'

He stood up and held the bottle high, took a deep swig, and then waved it over the robbers' heads and said, 'Here's to your health! Raise your right hands and open your mouths, all at once, *now*.'

To the hunter's amazement, all the robbers did exactly that. They raised their right hands and opened their mouths, and then they stuck fast just like that. They couldn't move an inch. They were just like stone statues.

'Good God!' said the hunter. 'How did that happen?'

'Animal magnetism,' the soldier explained. 'It's a little trick I learned in the army.'

'That's astounding,' said the hunter. 'But look, hadn't we better make our escape?'

'Not while there's still food on the table. I haven't seen such a feast as this for months. Come on, sit down, eat your fill. These little birds won't move till I tell 'em to.'

The old woman brought them another bottle of the best, and a fine apple tart, what's more, and a jug of cream. The soldier didn't get up till he'd eaten enough for three.

Finally he sighed and pushed his chair back and said, 'Time to strike tents. It's not far to town – the old woman'll show us the way.'

When they got to the town, the soldier sought out the barracks at once and told the officer in charge about the robbers.

'Come back with me,' he said to the hunter. 'I want to see their faces when they wake up.'

The soldiers surrounded the robbers, who were still sitting animal-magnetized at the table.

'I'll need another bottle,' the soldier said to the old woman. 'One of the best.'

As soon as he'd drawn the cork and taken a swig, he waved it over the robbers' heads and called out, 'Good health to you!'

Instantly the robbers woke up and began to move, but before they could draw their weapons, the soldiers had overpowered them. They tied them hand and foot and threw them into a cart.

'To prison with the lot of 'em,' said the soldier.

While he put the cork back in the bottle and stowed it in his knapsack, the hunter took one of the soldiers aside and spoke to him quietly. The man galloped ahead of the others back to town.

'Well, Shiny Boots,' said the soldier, 'that was a good day's work, eh? We've beaten the enemy and had a fine meal. Now let's bring up the rear as these gallows-birds trundle into town.'

When they reached the town gate, they found a big crowd all cheering and waving flags, and then the royal bodyguard rode up, saluting and presenting arms.

'What's going on?' said the soldier, amazed.

'The king's been away,' said the hunter, 'and he's returning to his palace. It's only right for him to have a welcome like this.'

'Where's the king?' said the soldier, looking all around. 'I can't see him.'

'Here I am,' said the hunter, and opened his hunting coat to show the royal insignia on his waistcoat. 'I sent word ahead that I was coming.'

The soldier fell to his knees.

'Oh, blimey, your majesty,' he said, 'forgive me! I shouldn't have called you Shiny Boots. In fact I should have treated you a lot more proper than what I did.'

But the king gave him his hand and said, 'You're a good soldier, and you saved my life. I'm going to make sure you have the best of treatment from now on.'

And when he heard about how the soldier's brother had had him lashed, he ordered the general demoted to private and offered to make the soldier a general in his place.

'That's very kind of you, your majesty,' the soldier said, 'but I don't think I'm cut out to be a general. A life of leisure would suit me best.'

'Then that is what you shall have,' said the king. 'And if you ever want a meal, just come to the door of the royal kitchen and there'll always be a slice of beef for you. But if you want to drink anyone's health, you'll have to ask my permission first.'

* * *

Tale type: AT 952, 'The King and the Soldier'
Source: a story in Friedmund von Arnim's *Hundert Märchen im Gebirge gesammelt* (*Hundred Tales from the Mountains*; 1844)
Similar stories: Alexander Afanasyev: 'The Soldier and the King' (*Russian Fairy Tales*)

Here the 'magic' is brought about by hypnotism or, as it would probably have been called in those days, mesmerism, after the German physician Franz Mesmer (1734–1815). Grimm (or their source, Friedmund von Arnim) provides no explanation for how the soldier acquired this mesmeric skill, so I put one in. No doubt hypnotism, as a fashionable and intriguing phenomenon, was familiar to the Grimms' readers, just as the feats of Derren Brown are to a television audience today; and anyway, it's funny.

Hypnotism turns up in another Grimm tale, 'The Chicken Beam', in which a magician tricks a crowd into thinking that a chicken is carrying a heavy beam when all it has in its beak is a straw. The comic-book character Mandrake the Magician, who began his crime-busting career in 1934, persuaded criminals, mad scientists and other undesirables that they had been turned to stone by 'gesturing hypnotically'. I tried it when I was a small boy, and it doesn't work.

The idea of the brother who became a general comes from Afanasyev's story, which is a tight and well-shaped narrative, but it has no hypnotism. Instead, the soldier cuts the robbers' heads off one by one, and wallops the king for falling asleep on guard.

FIFTY-THREE

THE GOLDEN KEY

One winter's day, when the snow lay deep on the ground, a poor boy was sent to the forest to bring back firewood. He gathered some fallen branches and loaded them on his sled, but after doing that, he was so cold that he thought he'd make himself a fire right away and warm himself up a bit before going home.

He cleared a space to build the fire, and as he brushed the snow away he found a little golden key.

'Where there's a key,' he said to himself, 'there must be a lock nearby.'

So he dug into the ground, and a little way under the surface he found an iron box. He dug all around it and with a struggle he pulled it up out of the frozen earth, thinking, 'There must be some treasure in here. I hope the key fits!'

At first he couldn't find the keyhole, but it was a very small key, after all. Finally he found the hole, so small he could hardly see it. He took the key in his frozen fingers, and he could hardly hold it. He put the key in the hole and started to turn – and now we'll have to wait till he turns it all the way and opens the lid. Then we'll know what marvellous things the box contains.

* * *

Tale type: AT 2260, 'The Golden Key'
Source: a story told to the Grimm brothers by Marie Hassenpflug

This is one of a number of formula stories that are never quite finished. Many of them concern a shepherd who has to get his very large flock of sheep across a very small bridge one at a time: 'So he took the first one across, and then he took the second one across, and then he took the third one across . . .' Or it might be an ant filling a barn with corn: 'He carried the first grain in, and then . . .'

Another way of setting up such a story is with the famous opening sentence: 'It was a dark and stormy night'. In this variation, someone is telling a story in which someone is telling a story in which – and so on.

'The Golden Key' depends not on repetition but on terminating before the terminus, so to speak. This is the pattern followed by a number of annoying novels or films or plays in which, for instance, the outcome depends on a letter saying whether X has got a university place or not, or the result of a pregnancy test, or the verdict of a jury. The postman arrives at the door; the heroine begins to open her hand to disclose the colour of the test result; the jury returns to the courtroom – and then: THE END.

Which raises the suspicion that the author just doesn't know how to end the story. It's cheating.

In this case, though, the set-up is a little more interesting. From the Grimms' second edition of 1819 onwards, this tale was always placed last, suggesting perhaps that there are more marvellous tales yet to be discovered. Given the treasures they have already disclosed in their great collection, I'm willing to take that on trust.

'The Golden Key' is also the name of a literary fairy tale from a collection published in 1867 by George MacDonald (1824–1905), which is much better than most specimens of that genre. It, too, ends without ending. Mossy and Tangle are searching for the land whence the shadows fall: 'And by this time I think they must have got there.'